Praise for

MURDER IS A GIRL'S BEST FRIEND

"December 1954 in Manhattan is a trip down memory lane and Amanda Matetsky captures the ambience of the era to perfection. The heroine's friend Abby makes a perfect crime-solving partner and some of their adventures are funny. Readers will thoroughly enjoy *Murder is a Girl's Best Friend* because of Paige, Abby, and 1950s New York." —*Midwest Book Reviews*

"This book is a great example of fun fiction that uses much of the style of film noir. . . . Paige is a clever, interesting heroine who's well-balanced by her Bohemian artist neighbor, Abby. This is an excellent book to read in any venue because it immediately transports the reader to New York in 1954." —*The Best Reviews*

Praise for

MURDERERS PREFER BLONDES

"A beautifully realized evocation of time and place; 1950s New York City comes alive for those of us who were there and even those who weren't. Amanda Matetsky has created a very funny and interesting female protagonist, Paige Turner, and put her in the repressed and male-dominated year of 1954, which works like a charm. This is more than a murder mystery; this is great writing by a fresh talent." —Nelson DeMille

continued . . .

"Paige Turner is the liveliest, most charming detective to emerge in crime fiction in a long time. She is the product of her time and place—New York in the fifties—with a little Betty Boop and a little Brenda Starr in her makeup, but she is also her own woman, funny, smart, energetic, brave, hard-working, and determined to get to the bottom of the mystery. She is irresistible, a force of nature."

—Ann Waldron, author of *The Princeton Murders*

"Matetsky adeptly captures the atmosphere of the 1950s, and her characters—especially Paige and her friend Abby—are a delight. This journey back to a time that now seems innocent is refreshing." —*Romantic Times*

"A fun new mystery series . . . a real page-turner . . . a delightful historical amateur sleuth tale." —*BookBrowser*

"A fast-paced, smart debut with a feisty heroine that entertains and keeps readers eagerly turning Paiges."

—*The Mystery Reader*

How to Marry a Murderer

Amanda Matetsky

BERKLEY PRIME CRIME, NEW YORK

THE BERKLEY PUBLISHING GROUP
Published by the Penguin Group
Penguin Group (USA) Inc.
375 Hudson Street, New York, New York 10014, USA
Penguin Group (Canada), 10 Alcorn Avenue, Toronto, Ontario M4V 3B2, Canada
(a division of Pearson Penguin Canada Inc.)
Penguin Books Ltd., 80 Strand, London WC2R 0RL, England
Penguin Group Ireland, 25 St. Stephen's Green, Dublin 2, Ireland (a division of Penguin Books Ltd.)
Penguin Group (Australia), 250 Camberwell Road, Camberwell, Victoria 3124, Australia
(a division of Pearson Australia Group Pty. Ltd.)
Penguin Books India Pvt. Ltd., 11 Community Centre, Panchsheel Park, New Delhi—110 017, India
Penguin Group (NZ), Cnr. Airborne and Rosedale Roads, Albany, Auckland 1310, New Zealand
(a division of Pearson New Zealand Ltd.)
Penguin Books (South Africa) (Pty.) Ltd., 24 Sturdee Avenue, Rosebank, Johannesburg 2196,
South Africa

Penguin Books Ltd., Registered Offices: 80 Strand, London WC2R 0RL, England

This is a work of fiction. Names, characters, places, and incidents either are the product of the author's imagination or are used fictitiously, and any resemblance to actual persons, living or dead, business establishments, events, or locales is entirely coincidental.

HOW TO MARRY A MURDERER

A Berkley Prime Crime Book / published by arrangement with the author

PRINTING HISTORY
Berkley Prime Crime mass-market edition / July 2005

Copyright © 2005 by Amanda Matetsky.
Cover design by Rita Frangie.
Cover art by Kim Johnson.
Interior text design by Kristin del Rosario.

ISBN: 0-425-20400-6

BERKLEY® PRIME CRIME
Berkley Prime Crime Books are published by The Berkley Publishing Group,
a division of Penguin Group (USA) Inc.,
375 Hudson Street, New York, New York 10014.
The name BERKLEY PRIME CRIME and the BERKLEY PRIME CRIME design are trademarks belonging to Penguin Group (USA) Inc.

PRINTED IN THE UNITED STATES OF AMERICA

10 9 8 7 6 5 4 3 2 1

For Ira and Liza—
more, most, most of all

ACKNOWLEDGMENTS

I rely heavily (okay, *totally*) on the interest and support of family and friends—especially Harry Matetsky*, Molly Murrah, Liza, Tim, Tara and Kate Clancy, Ira Matetsky, Matthew Greitzer, Rae and Joel Frank, Sylvia Cohen, Mary Lou and Dick Clancy, Ann Waldron, Nelson DeMille, Dianne Francis, Art Scott, Betsy Thornton, Santa and Tom De Haven, Nikki and Bert Miller, Herta Puleo, Marte Cameron, Mirella Rongo, Cameron Joy, Sandra Thompson and Chris Sherman, Donna and Michael Steinhorn, Kathy and Mark Voger, Gayle Rawlings and Debbie Marshall, Regina Grassia, Joan Unice, Judy Capriglione, Martha Cevasco, Betty Fitzsimmons, Nancy Francese, Jane Gudapati, Carleen Kierce, April Margolin, Margaret Ray, Doris Schweitzer, Carol Smith, Roberta Waugh and her pal Joey.

My dear friends at Literacy Volunteers of America–Nassau County, Inc. are a constant source of encouragement and goodwill, as are my fellow mystery writers and readers at Sisters in Crime–Central Jersey. And my coagents, Annelise Robey and Meg Ruley of the Jane Rotrosen Agency, and my editor at Penguin Group (USA), Martha Bushko, are the most talented (not to mention most *tolerant*) advocates a writer could have. How did I get to be so lucky?

*Another nod to my husband, Harry, for writing the hip (okay, *harebrained*) poems of Jimmy Birmingham. Nobody could have done it better!

"Most women use more brains
picking a horse in the third
at Belmont than they do
picking a husband."

—as spoken by Schatze Page
(Lauren Bacall) to Pola Debevoise
(Marilyn Monroe) and Loco
Dempsey (Betty Grable) in
How to Marry a Millionaire,
20th Century Fox, 1953

Prologue

SOME PEOPLE SEEK THE TRUTH; OTHERS just go looking for trouble. But in my experience the two are inseparable. They stick together like Adam and Eve. Like Sodom and Gomorrah. Like Dean Martin and Jerry Lewis. And no matter how honorable your initial motives may be, if you dig down too deep for the truth, you're sure to shovel up a whole pile of trouble.

At least that's the way things always happen to me. No exaggeration. Whenever I set out on a simple search for the facts, I wind up trapped in a dragnet of death and deception. My boyfriend Dan says it's my own fault—that I cause the calamities myself, that I'm a born troublemaker. But I don't agree with him. In fact, I hold the exact opposite opinion. I think of myself as a healer, a fixer—a born trouble*shooter*.

Don't get me wrong, though. I totally understand why Dan feels the way he does. He is, after all, one of the most highly respected homicide detectives in all of Manhattan, while I'm a writer for a sleazy true crime magazine called *Daring Detective*. And it must be kind of hard on him to have a girlfriend who's always lurking around the city, sticking her nose into one murder case after another, getting herself (and sometimes other people) almost killed (and sometimes *really* killed) in the process.

But it's hard on me, too. Does Dan think I *like* being the way I am? Can he possibly believe that I enjoy tripping over dead bodies, having my apartment broken into and trashed, being almost raped and strangled, and getting shot in the leg and shoulder? Does he imagine that I'm having fun? Or does he understand, somewhere down deep in that stern but lovable soul of his, that I simply can't help myself? That my fierce curiosity controls me, instead of the other way around.

I've tried to change; I really have. Last Christmas, when I was laid up in the hospital from my leg and shoulder wounds, I had a lot of time to think about my life—how precious it was to me and how stupid I'd been to risk it—just because I was pursuing another murder story. (Okay, okay! so I was pursuing the *murderer,* too, but that's a different story.) So while I was lying there in that hospital bed, staring up at the flat white ceiling, then gazing over at Dan's handsome, deeply concerned face, I promised myself—and Dan—that I'd never, ever, ever get involved in an unsolved homicide case again.

And I didn't. Not for four whole months! I was so good I was golden. I didn't quit my job or anything like that (I couldn't go *that* far), but I didn't start any secret investigations, or go chasing after a single killer. Not even one! Of course the fact that I was on crutches for two of those four months may have had something to do with my restrained behavior, but—you can take it from me—I was still working my snoopy little tail off to keep my promise.

And it's a miracle I succeeded for as long as I did. Because, to tell you the truth, it's not just my extreme curiosity—or my desire to get a scoop story—that makes me do the things I do. It's also my conscience, my bred-in-the-bone sense of right and wrong. It's the moral code I inherited from my parents—the elemental system of ethics and justice by which I've lived my entire life. All twenty-nine years of it. And please answer this question for me, if you can: how in the name of all that's holy (well, at least semi-respectable) can I stop being who I am?

My best friend Abby Moscowitz, the beatnik artist and free-love enthusiast who lives next door, thinks I'm crazy to even try. She says a girl's gotta do what a girl's gotta do. So what if I break a few rules? Abby says rules are like bread crumbs—strictly for the birds. So what if I fly in the face of our country's bedrock social conventions? Abby says being conventional is a one-way ticket to Dopeyville.

I should be proud to be the first and only woman writer ever employed by a national detective magazine, Abby says. And I should be thrilled that I've been able to earn a little extra money by turning a couple of my exclusive, hard-won *Daring Detective* stories into "fictional" full-length dime store paperbacks. I'm just exercising every American's right to free enterprise, she insists, and I should be happy that I'm finally living up to my lawful, albeit ludicrous, name.

But only a cartoon character could be happy with a name like Paige Turner. Paige Turner! Did you ever hear anything so absurd in your life? I'm flushed with embarrassment every time I take a breath. It wouldn't be so bad if I had a normal job—if I were a secretary or a nurse or a teacher, like every other single (i.e., widowed or unmarried) working woman in the city. But no, I have to be a *writer.* Of sensational crime stories and mystery novels, no less! I might as well be a dancer named Hoochie Coochie.

Still, I wouldn't change my name for all the beans in Boston. I've been Paige since the day I was born. And I've been Paige Turner since the day I married a wonderful, laughing, brown-eyed man named Bob Turner—four years and two and a half months ago—on February 14, 1951.

Yep, Bob and I eloped and got married on Valentine's Day. Pretty corny, but we did it anyway, just a few days after we learned that Bob had been drafted into the Army. We left our homes and families in Kansas City and ran off to Brooklyn, where we lived together in wedded bliss for one whole delirious, unspeakably glorious month—until Bob was summoned to basic training at Fort Benning in Georgia, and then shipped

4444 Amanda Matetsky

off to fight in Korea, where he died eight and a half months later. Three bullets to the chest from a Russian-made machine gun. I think those bullets blasted through my chest, too, because my heart pretty much stopped working after that.

The rest of me, however, started working harder than ever. I threw myself into my job with a vengeance. And as the only woman on the *Daring Detective* staff of six, I always had plenty to do: all the typing, filing, editing, rewriting, proofreading, mail sorting, phone answering, dictation taking, record keeping, news clipping, and—natch!—coffee making. I went to work early and always left late, trying to kill as much time on the job as possible. I even moved into a modest women's hotel in the city, and then down to a cheap apartment in Greenwich Village so I could live closer to the office (and afford to pay the rent).

It wasn't enough, though. (The work, I mean, not the rent—which, at fifty-five dollars a month, was still too high.) After two and a half years of mournful drudgery, I realized that the big void in my life just couldn't be filled with menial tasks and secretarial chores. Katharine Gibbs be damned. I needed something *interesting* to do—something that would lift me out of the clerical quicksand before my brain was engulfed in mud.

Therefore—drawing on the fact that I'd wanted to be a crime and mystery writer since the age of fourteen, when I discovered I preferred Dashiell Hammett and Dorothy L. Sayers to Shakespeare—I decided it was time for me to break out and write a real, honest-to-gosh *Daring Detective* story. A story so exciting, so spectacular, so exclusive and so *true,* that my number one boss, Harvey Crockett, and my number two boss, Brandon Pomeroy, would have to swallow their "manly" pride, relinquish their chauvinistic ban against female writers (an unspoken ban in force throughout the industry), and publish my work in the magazine.

So that's what I set out to do. And—get this!—my efforts were successful. Against-all-odds successful. And that's how it all got started: the covert murder investigations, the secret fact-finding missions, the big fat lies and cover-ups, the dangerous forays into the dead of night armed with nothing but a pad and pencil (and the staunch but truly knuckleheaded conviction that right will always triumph over might).

That's how my relationship with Detective Sergeant Dan Street got started, too. Dan was in charge of the first homicide case I "interfered with" (his words, not mine), and he was really furious at me for getting involved, for risking my life to get the story, for even thinking I might be smart and courageous enough to track down a cold-blooded murderer. But after all was said and done (i.e., after I *had* flushed out the murderer and miraculously lived to tell the tale), I think he was a little impressed with me, too.

Which was lucky for me, since I was more than a little impressed with him. (Okay, okay! So the right word here is *attracted*. I was thoroughly, unequivocally, brazenly *attracted* to him. There, I've said it. Are you happy now?) I thought Dan was—next to my late husband Bob—the brightest, bravest, strongest, most appealing man I'd ever met. And I still feel the same way about him, even though he's always yelling his head off at me about one thing or another and telling me to keep my nosy snoot out of police business.

Too bad I can't comply. It would be much better for both of us if I could. But, as I told you before—and as my cartoon compatriot, Popeye, is so fond of saying—"I yam what I yam, and that's all I yam." And what *I* yam is a very inquisitive woman with a driving, incontrovertible desire to write an honest story and to see justice done.

Which compels me to dig for the truth.

And thereby shovel up a whole heap of trouble.

Chapter 1

WE ALL HAVE CERTAIN MOMENTS IN OUR
lives that, because of their profound shock value or deep emotional significance, are etched in our memory for all time. For
instance, I'll bet every American over the age of twenty-five
remembers exactly where they were and what they were
doing nine and a half years ago, on August 6, 1945, when they
first learned we'd dropped the A-bomb on Hiroshima. (I was
in a public park in Kansas City, sunbathing by the pool.) And
many of us, I'm sure, can recall the precise circumstances and
every soaring particular of our first solo bike ride, our first
dive off the high board, or our very first open-mouthed kiss.

My friend Abby's sharpest (and no-doubt happiest) memory is the day, about a zillion years ago, when she lost her vir-
ginity. Twice. In the same afternoon. (With Abby, anything's
possible.) And I will always remember that on the evening of
June 19, 1953, I was sitting cross-legged on my living room
floor in front of my rented Sylvania TV—wearing one of
Bob's old Army T-shirts and eating a bologna sandwich—
when I first got the news that Julius and Ethel Rosenberg had
been executed.

I haven't been able to eat bologna since.

I mention all this stuff not because I want to transport you back to the past, or make you think about something you'd rather forget, but because I want to convey—in as visceral a way as possible—how each of us, in his or her own fashion, stockpiles a string of vivid mental mementos to mark the explosive, electrifying (and sometimes horrifying) progress of our lives.

And because I want you to understand why I will always recall every single tiny detail of my first meeting with Ginger Allen.

The date is carved in marble in my mind: April 1, 1955. April Fools' Day. (This should have been a warning to me, I guess, but I was too foolish to take notice.) All six *DD* staffers were in the office that Friday afternoon, but, as usual, I was the only one working very hard. I was madly clipping the latest crime articles out of the newspapers, filing stacks of photos that had recently been returned from the printer, and proofreading a pile of galleys that were so full of typos I figured the typesetter had been hitting the bottle again. I wanted to clear my desk completely, get the entire mountain of clerical work finished so I could enjoy a carefree weekend and be ready to tackle a more serious project—i.e., a new story assignment—come Monday morning.

I was being wildly optimistic, you should know. Brandon Pomeroy, the pompous, patronizing, misogynistic editorial director of *Daring Detective*, hadn't given me a new story assignment in months. Pomeroy hated the fact that our editor in chief, Harvey Crockett, had promoted me to staff writer, and he did everything in his power to keep me buried so deep in paperwork (or, as he called it, "woman's work") that I wouldn't have time to put my own pen to paper. That way he could assign all the full-length stories to Mike Davidson—the other, "more accomplished" (i.e., male) writer on the staff—whose grammar and spelling skills equaled those of a duck-billed platypus.

And whose stories, as a result, always had to be rewritten by me.

Nevertheless, I remained hopeful, feeling sure I'd be given

a new *DD* tale to tell soon, if for no other reason than to meet an urgent copy deadline. And since our next major editorial deadline was Monday, I wanted to be prepared.

I had filed the last of the photos and begun correcting the galley proofs when Harvey Crockett burst out of his small private office in the rear and huffed his way up to the front of the large communal workroom where my desk was situated. "I'm goin' uptown," he said to me. "Got a meetin' with the brass. If Lois calls," he said, naming one of the two middle-aged "girlfriends" he'd been stringing along for years, "tell her I'm gonna be late. I was supposed to meet her at six, but I'm not gonna make it."

"Yes, sir," I said, glancing up at the big round clock on the wall. It was 4:15. With any luck, I could finish my work and flee the office promptly at 5:00, before Lois's phone call came in. Lois was *not* the agreeable, accepting type. "Should I tell her what time to expect you?"

"No!" Mr. Crockett growled, grabbing his fedora off the coat tree near the door and planting it firmly on his white-haired head. "Just tell her to wait." He pulled his trench coat on over his large bulge of a belly and, without so much as a "See you Monday" or "Have a nice weekend," disappeared through the office door into the hall.

I made a cross-eyed face at the ceiling, lit up another L&M filter tip, tucked my wavy brown hair behind my ears, and went on with my proofreading.

Within seconds of Mr. Crockett's departure, Brandon Pomeroy stood up from his desk directly across the aisle from mine, smoothed his dark brown mustache, and tapped his pipe clean in the ashtray. Nestling the empty Dunhill in the pocket of his expensive gray flannel jacket, he straightened his horn-rimmed glasses, scraped his palm over his neatly trimmed dark hair, and marched right past me to the coat rack. "Good evening," he mumbled, to nobody in particular—least of all to me—then he nabbed his hat and coat and made a beeline for the elevator (or, rather, for the bar around the corner, where he always went after work. Before work, too. Pomeroy was a big martini fan—and he liked 'em dry as the Sahara).

Two minutes after Pomeroy left, Mario Caruso made his move. As the art director of the magazine, Mario was the next cock in the pecking order. And as the least principled member of the remaining staff, he was the most likely to duck out before closing time. Passing my desk on his way to the coat rack, he reached out and gave my shoulder a squeeze. (Whenever Mario's fingers were anywhere close to my body, they always found something to squeeze. Or pinch, as was more often the case.)

"I'm knockin' off now, cupcake," he said, stretching a wide, lascivious grin across his wide, puffy face, from one scruffy black sideburn to the other. "And I hate to disappoint you," he added, in a voice loud enough for the two coworkers still sitting behind us to hear, "but I can't meet you later at the hotel like we planned. I've got to take my kid to the Dodgers game." Laughing like a lunatic, he gave my shoulder another stealthy squeeze.

"Oh, that's okay, loverboy," I retorted. "You'd just put me to sleep anyway." It was a pitifully weak comeback, but it was still stupid of me to say it. Mario didn't appreciate back talk, especially from me. And since he could easily get me fired, I was playing a dangerous game. But I couldn't help myself, you know? Abby's right. A girl's gotta do what a girl's gotta do. *Some* of the time, at least.

Mario's laughter snorted to a stop. He glowered at me for one ugly second, then propelled his short, stocky self over to the rack for his hat and coat. "C'mon, Mike," he called to the head writer, whose desk was next to mine. "Let's get outta here! The weekend is waiting." (Mario and Mike always stuck together. They arrived at the office together every morning, they went out to lunch together every day, and at the end of the workday, they always left at the same time. A regular Frick and Frack.)

"I can't go yet, Mar," Mike whined, angrily squashing his Lucky butt in the ashtray. "I got to write this stupid story. If it's not ready for the typesetter Monday morning, Pomeroy'll fry my ass in the oven."

I smiled to myself. Mike really knew how to turn a phrase.

He didn't, however, know much about proper cooking procedures.

"So give it to Paige to do," Mario said, aiming a nasty smirk in my direction. He looked like a greedy Roman emperor who'd just popped a peeled grape into his mouth. "She's always sniffin' around with her snotty, stuck-up nose," he jeered, "lookin' for new stories to write. She wasn't named Paige Turner for nothin'."

Uh oh . . . payback time.

Mike's skinny, freckled jaw dropped open like a trap door with a faulty hinge. "Hey, yeah! Why didn't I think of that? That's a good idea!" Yanking the sheet of paper from the roller of his Royal, he jumped up from his desk, hopped over to mine, and slapped the half-typed page down on top of the galley I was proofing. "Finish this up for me will ya, Paige?" he said with a wink. "That's a good girl. It's gotta be at least eight pages, and it has to be ready for the Monday morning pickup."

"But you've only done one paragraph!" I cried.

"Yeah, but it's a good one," he blithely replied.

I had serious doubts about that. Mike began most of his stories with the sentence, "It was a dark and stormy night," or a rough equivalent thereof.

"Here's the clips," Mike said, handing me a file of newspaper articles about the crime in question. "Some rich college guy killed his girlfriend. Shot her right between the knobs with a thirty-eight. You should play up the sex angle."

He didn't have to tell me that. At *Daring Detective,* we were supposed to play up the sex angle of *every* story—even when there wasn't one.

"I gave it a title already," Mike added, smiling proudly. "'BANG, BANG, SHE'S DEAD!' Pretty snappy, huh? It'll make a great cover line."

"Yeah, great."

If my sarcasm was showing, Mike didn't notice. He let out a satisfied giggle, gave Mario the high sign, then swept his hand over the perfectly level roof of his khaki-colored flattop.

"That's it then," he said to me. "Make sure it's done by Monday morning."

I was fuming, but I didn't protest. I knew it wouldn't change anything, except maybe for the worse. Mike was male and I was female, and we both knew what that meant: either I did whatever job he gave me to do, or I could be out of a job altogether. Either I sat there for another hour or two, researching and writing the rest of Mike's scarcely begun clip story—a story that would bear *his* byline, not mine—or I could kiss my weekly seventy-five-dollar paycheck goodbye. (And one peek at my pitiful bank balance would have shown you that was not an option.)

Mario was enjoying my submissive discomfort to the hilt. The whole time he was standing by the door waiting for Mike to get his hat and coat, he was grinning at me and also making the most lewd and annoying kissy-lip expressions. I tried to alleviate my anger by throwing an imaginary (and thoroughly rotten) tomato in his face, but the fantasy attack brought me little relief. Long after Mario and Mike were gone, I was still fuming.

"They're morons," Lenny said, finally getting up the nerve to approach me. "They always put their shoes on the wrong feet." Lenny Zimmerman was Mario's art assistant and my only real friend in the office. He was smart, shy, loyal, and sensitive, and he knew everything about my life. He had even saved it once.

After walking the length of the workroom—from his desk in the rear to mine in the front—Lenny leaned his slight, narrow-shouldered torso down over my typewriter and gave me a look of sheer pity. "How long do you think you'll have to stay?"

"A couple of hours. Maybe three. All he has is a lousy title and a boring opening paragraph. I'll have to start from scratch."

"I'm sorry," Lenny said. His thin, bespectacled face was blushing, as usual.

"Yeah, me too. I'm dying to get out of this place."

"I know what you mean," he said, smiling sadly. "But, listen, if you want me to stay here with you, I will. I could get a jumpstart on the cover pasteup."

Was Lenny a good guy, or what? "Oh, no!" I said, gratefully patting his arm. "There's no reason for you to suffer, too. You go on home. I'll bet your mother's making a good dinner." Lenny was twenty-three, unmarried, and still lived with his parents on the Lower East Side. "What's on the menu tonight?" I asked. "Broiled chicken?"

His gaze of sheer pity turned to one of pure delight. "Pot roast," he said, eyes gleaming, "and after that I'm going to a movie with my friend Berkie. 'East of Eden' with James Dean. It's playing in Cinemascope at the Astor."

"Go! Go!" I said, feeling sorry for myself but happy for Lenny. He lived for the movies. And pot roast didn't hurt, either.

"So you'll be okay?" His eyes begged me to say yes.

"You bet your boots, cowboy," I assured him, putting on a false show of optimism. "I'll finish this saga in no time."

Lenny breathed a thankful sigh and straightened his bent-over spine to its normally hunched position. "Well, if you're sure . . ."

"Go on, get out of here!" I urged. The sooner he left, the sooner I could get to work. And the sooner I could get my work *finished*.

"Okay, then," he said, sidling over to the coat rack and grabbing his cap and jacket. "I'll see you Monday. Have a nice weekend."

"You, too," I said, smiling and waving as he backed out through the door. Then I released a loud moan of self-pity, made another cross-eyed face at the ceiling, lit up another cigarette, and put my snotty, stuck-up nose to the grindstone.

LESS THAN TEN MINUTES LATER THE OFfice entry bell jingled, and a huge, beefy Negro wearing a navy blue slouch cap and a tailored navy blue suit pushed his way inside. The man was immense, and a complete stranger to me, and I was so startled by his sudden appearance I almost wet my pants.

"Can I help you, sir?" I spluttered, trying not to let my astonishment show.

"I didn't mean to frighten you, miss," he said, in a very gravelly but gentle voice. "I spoke to the custodian downstairs, and told him why I was here, and he gave me permission to come on up. Told me to use the service elevator."

"I see," I calmly replied. My curiosity had surpassed my surprise. "Well, then, what can I do for you, sir? Why are you here?"

"My boss told me to come," he said. "Told me to go on up to the *Daring Detective* office on the ninth floor and ask for a lady reporter named Paige Turner." He removed the navy blue cap from his enormous half-bald head and nodded politely. His mustache was thick and, like the fringe of fuzzy black hair curling around the back and sides of his head, flecked with gray.

"I'm Paige Turner," I said, gaping up at the man's dark, fleshy face, enthralled by what he was saying as well as his size. "How can I help you?"

"It's my boss that needs your help, miss. She wants you to come downstairs to her automobile so she can talk to you about something. Something important."

"She? Your boss is a woman?" This was getting interesting.

"That's right, miss."

"But why do I have to go downstairs to her car? If she wants to discuss something with me, why didn't she come up to the office herself?"

"She can't get out of the car, miss. Somebody might recognize her and cause a scene."

The plot was thickening. "A scene? What do you mean? What kind of scene?" I was panting for more information. Literally. My breath had begun whooshing in and out of my lungs in short, raspy gusts.

"See, all the businesses are letting out just about now," the gentle behemoth explained. "It's rush hour, and the sidewalks are right crowded. So if Miss Allen stepped out of the car she'd prob'ly be swamped by a flock of fans wanting her autograph. It happens all the time."

"Miss Allen?"

"Yes, Miss Allen. She's my boss, miss. She's the star of *The Ginger Allen Show* on TV. I'm her chauffeur," he said, pronouncing the word as if it rhymed with gopher (which, coming from Kansas City, was the way I pronounced it, too).

I was flabbergasted. "You mean Ginger Allen—*the* Ginger Allen—is waiting downstairs in her car, wanting to talk to *me?*"

"That's right, miss."

I wasn't panting anymore. Now I was hardly breathing at all. Next to Lucille Ball, Ginger Allen was the most popular female personality on TV. She was beautiful, smart, sexy, a talented actress and comedienne, happily married to a very rich and powerful man, and she could sing a sultry torch song better than anybody. Even Peggy Lee. What on earth could she possibly want with me?

"What's this all about?" I asked her driver, even though I knew he probably couldn't, or wouldn't, tell me.

He shuffled his schooner-sized feet and gave me a pleading look. "If you'll just come on downstairs with me, miss, and communicate with Miss Allen for a spell, she'll answer all your questions for you."

I was hooked like a fish on a line. Hurriedly gathering up all my stuff (including the clip file for Mike's story, which I figured I'd write at home over the weekend), I put on my beige jacket, red beret, and white cotton gloves, closed up the office, and accompanied the gigantic Negro chauffeur down to the navy blue limousine parked at the curb outside my building. Then the giant opened the car door for me, and Ginger Allen reeled me in.

Chapter 2

I WAS SHOCKED BY HER APPEARANCE. I
guess I was so accustomed to seeing her blurred black-and-
white image on my twenty-one-inch Sylvania screen that I
just wasn't prepared for her sharp, life-size, full-color reality.
On television her skin was gray; in reality it was peaches and
cream. (Yes, I know that's a hackneyed expression, but it de-
scribes her complexion perfectly.) On television the irises of
her eyes looked like tiny bits of charcoal; in real life they resembled ten-carat emeralds. (Okay, that's a cliché too, but it's
still an apt depiction.)

It was her hair, however, that was the most shocking and
colorful of all. It was long, thick, wavy, and the most brilliant,
fiery red I'd ever seen. There are no clichés to describe the effect that Ginger Allen's blazing, red-gold tresses must have
had on all who, like me, suddenly came into her presence. All
I can say is she glowed. She put Lucille Ball, Rita Hayworth,
and Brenda Starr to shame.

That said, I should also report she was so nervous and
jumpy her emerald green eyes were spinning like windmills in
a tornado.

"What took you so long?" she screeched, grabbing my

gloved hand the minute I slipped onto the plush leather back-seat beside her. "I thought you weren't coming!" She was wearing gloves, too, only they climbed halfway up her arm and were made of black satin instead of white cotton.

Since my hostess had dispensed with the introductions, I saw no reason to waste time being polite. "But as you see, I *did* come," I said. "And now I'm very curious to know *why.*" I wanted some answers, and I wanted them fast. Otherwise, I might start panting again, and I wasn't sure my overworked lungs could take it. "What do you want to talk to me about, Miss Allen?"

"Ginger," she said. "You can call me Ginger."

"Fine," I replied. "And you can call me Paige."

She adjusted the hem of her flouncy black satin skirt, crossed one long slender silk-sheathed leg over the other, leaned back against the cushy upholstery, and looked me over from head to toe. She didn't seem so hot and bothered now. All of a sudden she looked cucumber-cool.

"How'd you get a crazy name like Paige Turner?" she asked. "Were you ever in television?"

"No!" I said, laughing. "Turner is my married name. I'm a widow now, but—" I stopped myself from saying more. "Is that why you sent your chauffeur to bring me down here, Miss Allen? So you could ask me about my name?"

"Oh, please!" she said, fidgeting with the silver fox stole clasped (seemingly by the teeth in the unfortunate animal's perfectly preserved head) around her shoulders. "I told you to call me Ginger."

"Okay, Ginger, but—"

"And, no, I didn't bring you down here just to talk about your name." She took a cigarette out of the gold case in her purse, tapped it repeatedly on the side of the case, and then held it to her mouth between two gloved fingers. "Do you have a light? Woodrow usually lights my cigarettes for me, but I told him to wait outside till we finish talking."

So her driver's name was Woodrow. And he was more than a chauffeur. He was her personal servant as well. And in his absence, she expected *me* to take over his job.

Conditioned to servility by my own job, I snatched a book of matches out of my purse and fired her up. I lit myself up, too. "So, what do you want to talk to me about?" I asked, thinking that if she didn't tell me soon, I'd pop like a pricked balloon.

She expelled a stream of smoke through puckered coral lips and fastened her steady, inquisitive gaze on mine. "Can I trust you, Paige Turner? Can you keep a secret?"

More questions, when all I wanted were answers. "That depends," I warily replied, "on what the secret is. If you tell me you're an alcoholic or a nymphomaniac, my lips are sealed. But if you tell me you just murdered your husband, I'm going straight to the police."

She let out a raucous laugh and gave her hair a flippant pat. Her false eyelashes were fluttering like hummingbird wings. "Fair enough," she said, turning to face me more squarely, "because I haven't killed anybody. The problem is," she added with a crooked coral smile, "somebody is trying to kill *me*."

"What?" I wasn't sure I'd heard her right.

"I said somebody is trying to kill me." She didn't look like she was joking.

"Why? Who?" I stuttered, unable to form a full sentence. The idea that someone would try to kill Ginger Allen—the most beautiful and second-most beloved TV star in the whole country—was unspeakable.

"I don't *know* why," she exclaimed. "And I definitely don't know *who!* That's why I came to see you, Paige." She grabbed my hand again. "You've got to help me. You've got to find out who's trying to kill me before he *does* kill me." She was getting nervous again.

"He? If you don't know who it is, then how do you know it's a man?"

"I *don't* know, really, I just assumed . . ." She paused, ostensibly giving some thought to the question.

"And why did you come to me?" I barreled on. "What makes you think I can help you? I'm a writer, not a detective.

And I'm certainly not a bodyguard! Why didn't you go to the police?"

"I wasn't sure they'd believe me. And I couldn't take the chance they'd let the story out to the newspapers."

I wasn't sure I believed her either. And if she really didn't want the story released to the press, why tell it to me? I was, after all, a member of the press myself. (Well, sort of, anyway.) And how did she get my name in the first place? I never used my full name in the magazine. (*Paige Turner* was just too ridiculous. And too obviously female. I used P. Turner instead.)

As if reading my mind, Ginger said, "I read about you in the *Daily Mirror* a few months ago, around Christmastime, when you ran rings around the police and solved a couple of connected murder cases on your own. They put your picture in the paper and said you were as smart as Perry Mason— and," she added, with an unladylike snicker, "a damn sight smarter than the homicide detective in charge." (The detective in question was *not* my friend Dan Street, in case you're wondering. He was a lazy son of a gun named Hugo Sweeny, who, thankfully, was now retired from the force. Brass plaque, gold watch, and all.)

"When I read that article," Ginger went on, "It really knocked me flat. A snoopy woman writer tracking down an armed and dangerous murderer before the police even picked up the trail! What a kick that was! And your name was so amusing it stuck in my mind. So, when I started having my . . . uh . . . trouble, and then finally woke up to the fact that my life was in serious danger, you were the first person I thought of to help me. I knew you'd be—"

She was interrupted by several loud taps on the window. "Miss Allen, Miss Allen!" Woodrow called through the tinted glass. "We got to head on uptown now. You're supposed to be making a speech at that charity cocktail party in twenty minutes." Bending down till his face was level with the window, he gave us an apologetic smile and pointed anxiously at his watch.

Ginger rolled down the window and said, "Damn it to hell!

I forgot all about the stupid charity shindig. What time am I scheduled to speak?"

Woodrow pointed at his watch again. "At six-thirty, Miss Allen. Prompt and on the dot."

"Oh, crap!" she said, with a loud groan of annoyance. "I hate these mealymouthed do-gooder tea parties. But if I don't show up, they'll put a curse on my head. Better get in the damn car, Woodrow, and give it some gas." She turned and gave me a resolute gaze. "Stay right where you are, Paige Turner. You'll take the drive uptown with me. We can talk on the way." She didn't *ask* me to join her; she just *told* me what I was going to do. She took for granted I'd want to go along for the ride.

And she was right.

WOODROW PULLED THE DARK BLUE LIM-ousine away from the corner of 43rd, out into the steady stream of traffic heading uptown on Third. It was my favorite time of day in Manhattan. Twilight. The street lamps were gleaming, the headlights were beaming, the office and store windows were glimmering, and still it wasn't too dark to see the majestic outlines of the city's tallest towers against the purple sky.

I wasn't looking up, though. I was staring sideways at Ginger Allen's famous profile, wondering what insane thunderclap of fate had determined that I should be sitting here next to her in her car, taking a final drag on my L&M filter tip, and waiting (okay, *yearning*) to hear all the dirty details about how somebody was trying to murder her. *If* somebody was trying to murder her.

"You're the only person I'm going to tell about this," Ginger said, smashing her cigarette in the limousine ashtray and taking a fresh one out of the case in her purse. She held it out to me for a light, and, aching to speed things along, I gave it to her as fast as I could, from my own still-burning stub. "And you have to promise me you won't tell anyone else," she stressed. "If the newspapers get wind of this story, every reporter and photographer in the city will pitch a tent on my doorstep. They'll follow me around like rabid dogs. They'll turn my life into a goddamn circus!"

"Maybe that would be a good thing," I said. "It might scare away your would-be killer and keep you safe."

"Are you out of your mind?" From her choice of words and the way she was glowering at me, I could tell she was readjusting her estimation of my intelligence. "That would be the absolute worst thing that could happen!" she sputtered. "A big press hullabaloo would create so much craziness and confusion it would be *easier* for somebody to kill me. And to get away with it, too. Chaos is the world's best cover."

Good-bye, Perry Mason. Hello, Jughead. "You've got a point," I said, face growing warm with embarrassment. "But we're getting way ahead of ourselves." I was eager to change the subject before it bit me again. "You haven't given me any of the particulars. You still haven't told me *why* you think your life is in danger."

"Let's get one thing straight right now, pussycat. I don't *think* my life is in danger. I *know* it is." Ginger's temperament was as fiery as her hair.

"What makes you so certain?" I dared to ask. "Have you been threatened in some way?"

"I was nearly decapitated by a runaway microphone boom," she shrieked. "Is that threatening enough for you? If I hadn't dropped my script and stooped down to pick it up at the exact moment I did, *The Ginger Allen Show* would have been canceled forever. And a couple of days after that, during dress rehearsal, I barely escaped being flattened by a piece of heavy scenery. It was the façade of a church, for godsakes, and it came crashing down at the very moment I was supposed to be standing in front of it, singing 'In the Chapel in the Moonlight.' If I had followed the director's orders instead of dashing off to the little girls' room for a pee, I'd be singing in heaven now."

God works in mysterious ways, I thought, but what I said was, "Are you sure those incidents weren't just accidental? From what I've read, *all* TV studios are dangerous. Just last week two kids in the Peanut Gallery on *The Howdy Doody*

Show got hit in the face with splinters of glass from an exploding spotlight. One is okay, but the other may lose the sight in his left eye, poor thing."

"What a shame," she said, with an unmistakable tone of sarcasm in her voice. "Too bad Buffalo Bob wasn't the one who got struck. Struck off the show entirely, I mean! He's a boring blockhead. The show would be better without him."

I couldn't tell if she was kidding or not. Frankly, it seemed more like not. I took a look out the window and saw that we were on Park Avenue now, still heading uptown. The dark was falling fast.

Ginger heaved a dramatic sigh. "Anyway, the things that happened to me on the set were *not* accidents. They were planned attempts against my life. I know this for a fact, because there have also been other 'incidents,' as you so blithely describe them—treacherous, horrifying incidents—and it's a goddamn miracle I'm still alive!" She was on the verge of having a tantrum. Planned, or otherwise.

I was on the verge of throwing a fit myself. "What other incidents?" I begged. "What else happened?"

"Somebody pushed me in front of a bus."

"Oh, my God! Were you hurt? Where did this happen?"

"On Fifth Avenue and Fiftieth Street, right near the studio. My *driver* was supposed to be waiting there to pick me up, but he was *late,*" she said, speaking louder and stressing certain words so Woodrow could hear the condemnation in her tone. "It was the evening rush hour and the sidewalks were packed. I pulled my hat veil down over my face so nobody would recognize me, and pushed my way out to the curb. Then I leaned over and gazed up the street, looking for Woodrow.

"The next thing I knew," she went on, "I was flat on my face in the gutter and the Fifth Avenue bus was screeching to a stop just inches from my head. Two, three inches at the most!" she gasped, holding her cigarette-free hand to her heart as if reciting the Pledge of Allegiance. "My cheek, hands, elbows, and knees were scraped and bleeding and I was staring straight into the filthy treads of an enormous rubber tire. I've never been so terrified in my life. The smell of burning rubber will make me sick for the rest of my life. However long *that* is."

I let out a soft groan of sympathy. "When did this happen?"

"Two weeks ago," she snapped. "Three days after the falling church 'incident.'" She coated the last word of her sentence with a thick glob of disdain. "And don't tell me it could have been an accident, either, pussycat. Somebody shoved me in the back so hard I had a bruise the size of a baseball on my spine."

I was troubled by her tone. Could it be America's second-most beloved TV star was really a first-class shrew? Or was she just too scared to be civilized? Whatever the case, Ginger Allen was getting on my nerves. I felt like she was accusing me. And Woodrow, too. And I didn't like it one bit.

"If you want me to help you, Miss Allen," I said, straightening my backbone to its ultimate height (which I hoped was as tall as a palm tree, but was surely as short as a shrub), "then you're going to have to speak to me in a nicer, more polite manner. And you'll have to stop getting mad every time I question you. If I don't ask a lot of questions, I'll never get the right answers. And, trust me, the wrong answers won't be worth a dime. They could even put you in more danger."

She shot me a sidelong glance of annoyance, then turned as sweet as sugar. "I'm sorry, Paige. I've been so afraid and upset, I'm really not myself these days. Please forgive my impatience. And please call me Ginger! I want us to be good friends." Her false eyelashes were fluttering again.

I wasn't eager to be her friend, but I was dying to know if somebody was really trying to kill her. "Okay, Ginger," I said, softening my attitude considerably. "Then will you allow me to ask you a few more questions?"

"Fire away!" she said, hitting me between the eyes with a knockout smile.

"Have there been other suspicious or perilous incidents besides the three you've mentioned?" (I purposely used the word "incidents" again, figuring she might as well get used to it.)

"Yes, one."

"What happened?"

"Somebody poisoned my highball at a network publicity party."

"That's awful!" I said, eyes widening in astonishment. Ginger's aspiring killer was a busy little devil. "How many sips did you take? Did you get very sick?"

"What the hell are you talking about? Do you think I'm crazy? I didn't drink any of it! I went straight to the little girls' room and poured it down the sink."

"Then how do you know it was poisoned?"

"I could smell it!" she hissed, getting cranky again. "I had ordered straight vodka on the rocks, and that usually doesn't have any odor at all, but *this* drink smelled like camel piss. And it had a weird rusty color to it, too. I knew immediately something was wrong."

I wondered two things: 1) if she really knew what camel piss smelled like, and 2) if she might have been given another partygoer's drink by mistake—a Rusty Nail, say, or maybe a Moscow Mule. (I didn't ask her these questions, of course. She clearly wasn't in the mood.)

Woodrow pulled the limousine into the far right lane and then came to a stop in front of a tall sandstone building with an elegant green awning that stretched from the ornate wooden door to the curb. "We're here now, Miss Allen," he said, shooting an anxious glance over his shoulder. "You've got to get inside pretty quick."

"Let the goddamn goody-goodies wait!" she cried. "They won't start anything without me. I'm the whole blasted show. They should thank their lucky stars I'm here at all! Get out of the car now, Woodrow. I want some privacy. I'll be out in a minute."

"Are you sure you'll be okay?" I asked as soon as Woodrow was gone. "Do you think the person who wants you dead will be here tonight?"

"How the hell should I know?" she said, with a shudder. "He—or she—could be anywhere at any time. I'm scared every goddamn minute of the day. My husband Leo's going to meet me here, though, so I think I'll be all right. He doesn't know a thing about what's been happening to me, but he'll be protective just the same. He always sticks close and watches me like a hawk."

"Good," I said, deciding not to ask why she hadn't confided in her husband, and choosing not to mention that according to all recorded homicide statistics, most murdered women were "offed" by their own loving spouses. We didn't have much time, and Ginger was testy enough as it was.

"So you'll help me, right?" she demanded, snatching her black satin hat from the back ledge of the limousine, positioning it at a flirtatious angle on her fiery red head, and securing it with a pearl-studded hatpin. "I've given this a lot of thought, and you're the one I want." She pulled the black net hat veil down over her emerald eyes. "And after it's all over—after you identify the murderer, and he gets put in jail, and my life gets back to normal—I'll give you exclusive rights to the story. And, believe you me, pussycat, it'll be the biggest, hottest, most sensational story of your whole goddamn career. You'll be bigger than Eric Sevareid."

She was very sure of herself and of me, too. She took for granted I'd swallow the bait, and, once again, she was right.

"Okay," I said. "I'll do what I can. How and when do you want me to start?"

"Tomorrow," she said. "I'll call you when I know my schedule." Then, quick as a flash, she rolled down her window and screamed, "Woodrow! I'm ready!"

Woodrow appeared out of thin air and opened her door for her. She stepped out of the car and gave him instructions to take me home. "Then come back up here to get me and Leo," she said. "And you'd better put on some speed! I'm blowing this joint as fast I can, then we're off to El Morocco . . . Byebye, Paige Turner," she added, giving me a coy (and truly irritating) little wave. "I'll be in touch."

It felt more like a threat than a promise.

Chapter 3

"WHERE TO, MISS?" WOODROW ASKED AS soon as he was seated back behind the wheel.

"The West Village," I said. "Two sixty-five Bleecker, between Sixth and Seventh." Woodrow pulled away from the curb, up to the corner, and turned east on 92nd Street. At the end of the block he made a right and headed downtown on Lexington.

I felt kind of weird all of a sudden. Quite lightheaded, if you want to know the truth. Riding in a limousine was nothing like riding in a taxi. The driver was sitting so far away, for one thing, and instead of bumping and lurching along like a crate of potatoes in a delivery truck, I was gliding—quietly cruising homeward on a cloud. I might have put my head back, closed my eyes, and drifted off to sleep, if my head hadn't been spinning with unsettling thoughts and visions of red hair, green eyes, and murder.

I tried to keep my thoughts and visions to myself, but it was a losing battle. (I'm a woman of many talents, but caution and discretion are not at the top of the list.) "Woodrow," I called, leaning as far forward as I could without tumbling over, "did you hear any of the things Miss Allen was saying to me on the drive uptown?"

"Uh . . . no, miss," he said, keeping his eyes on the road ahead. "Not really. I was trying not to. Miss Allen doesn't like for me to listen."

"But you heard *some* of the conversation, didn't you? She was speaking pretty loud. You couldn't help but hear."

Woodrow turned his enormous head and glanced nervously over his shoulder. "Yes, I heard some parts, miss," he admitted, "but I wasn't trying to." He returned his gaze to the road. "And I'll never breathe a word to a soul. I swear it on the baby Jesus. So please don't tell Miss Allen, miss. It would just upset her."

"Oh, don't worry, Woodrow! I would never say anything to get you in trouble. I won't even tell her that we had this conversation. I have a feeling she wouldn't like *that,* either."

Woodrow nodded vigorously. "She sure wouldn't, miss."

"But you don't mind talking to me, do you?" I asked, scooching to the edge of my seat and leaning a drop closer. "As long as I don't tell Miss Allen about it, I mean."

He didn't know how to answer. I had put Woodrow in a very uncomfortable position. As a Negro male working in the white community, he was expected to follow the racial rules—i.e., do as he was told without expressing any opinions of his own. And he could never be disloyal to his boss. But he couldn't be disrespectful to me either. He was paralyzed in powerlessness between two white women. (As a female working in an all-male office, I knew exactly how he felt.)

"It's for Miss Allen's own good," I quickly went on, hoping to ease his discomfort. "You heard what she said about how scared she is—how she believes somebody's trying to kill her. And you know that she's asked me to try to find out who it is. And I'm determined to do that, Woodrow. I'm going to do my level best to figure out who the person is before he does anything to really hurt her. So I have to talk to everybody who's connected with Miss Allen, you see? I have to ask them a lot of questions and find out everything I possibly can about what's going on."

"Yes, miss," he said, nodding again. "I understand."

"And since you're the first person I've met who is in fact connected with Miss Allen, it makes sense for me to begin my investigation with you. I need to ask you a bunch of questions and find out everything you know about this . . . er . . . situation."

"But I don't know anything, miss! And, Miss Allen, she wouldn't like for me to—"

"I know, Woodrow. Believe me, I know. She'd have a royal fit if she knew you were talking with me behind her back. She'd probably send you to the butcher to have your tongue cut off."

He let out a soft, deep chuckle. "My tongue *and* my ears, miss."

I laughed. "Well, your tongue and ears are safe with me. But don't say you don't know anything, Woodrow, because you probably know more than anybody. You know Miss Allen's schedule, for one thing. You know when and where you picked her up and dropped her off, and you know when and where you'll be taking her next. You know who else has been in the car with her, and why they've been in the car with her, and I'm sure you've overheard some other conversations besides the one she had with me this evening."

Woodrow grunted but didn't say anything. He stroked his mustache with his sausage-sized fingers and just kept on driving. We were in Midtown now, cruising past the lit-up main entrance of the Chrysler Building.

"I know I'm asking a lot of you, Woodrow, but it's crucial that you talk to me. It looks like Miss Allen is in grave danger and really needs our help. There's so much I need to find out, and the clock is ticking, and, for all we know, you could have the one piece of information that could save your boss's life.

"And I'll never tell her that you spoke to me," I stressed. "I'll never tell anybody, I promise. I swear it on the baby Jesus."

Woodrow chuckled again. "Well, since you put it that way . . ."

Happy to learn that the man had a sense of humor, and even happier to learn that he was willing to confide in me, I heaved a big whoosh of relief and leaned even closer. One more inch and I'd've been down on my knees on the limo's carpeted floor. "So what do you think about this whole thing, Woodrow?" I probed. "Do you think Miss Allen is overdramatizing the incidents she told me about, or do you think somebody's really trying to kill her?"

"I don't know what to make of it, miss," he said, coming to a stop at the light on 31st Street. "I never heard tell about any microphone attacks, or falling churches, or poisoned drinks before tonight." He turned and gave me a worried look. "I *do* know she was almost run over by a bus, though, on account of I got there right after it happened. And I saw how crazy upset she was. Her face was scratched and she was crying and the front of her dress was all torn and dirty. And she was so mad at me she like to bust a gasket. Screaming and yelling, she was—calling me a moron in front of the bus driver and all those nice people who helped her get up off the ground. I thought she was going to fire me, but she didn't."

"Did she tell you that someone had *pushed* her in front of the bus?"

"No, miss. She didn't say a word about that. She just kept saying it was all my fault—that if I'd been there when I was supposed to be, nothing would have happened." The light turned green and he pulled ahead, continuing southward at a smooth and steady speed.

"Where did you take her after that?" I inquired. "Did she go to a doctor?"

"She went straight home, miss, and told me to wait outside till she came back."

"How long did you have to wait?"

"About two hours. Then she came downstairs all dressed up like a queen and told me to take her and her party to Delmonico's."

"Her party? She had other people with her?"

"Yes, miss. Her sister and brother-in-law, Mr. and Mrs. Burnett. They must've been waiting for her upstairs. They go out with her lots of nights." Woodrow turned right on 17th Street and squeezed into the traffic moving slowly across town.

"Was Ginger's husband there?"

"Uh, no, miss. He didn't come in the car. He met them later at the restaurant."

"How do you know?"

"'Cause he was there when I drove them home."

Moaning in discomfort, I flopped back against the cushioned car seat. I couldn't lean so far forward anymore. My back and my neck were killing me. I was longing to sit up front with Woodrow so we could hear each other more easily and I could watch his face for his reactions while he talked, but I knew that was out of the question. Ginger would go off her rocker if she ever found out about that! And total strangers on the street—people who just happened to catch sight of a Negro man and a white woman sitting next to each other alone in a car—wouldn't like it either. We might cause a commotion.

I propped my head on the backrest and gazed out the window. It was almost totally dark now, but the sidewalks were still streaming with people in a hurry. People dashing to get home, or to the train, or to the closest cocktail lounge. People rushing to start their weekends with their families, friends, and lovers. And there I sat, coasting like Cleopatra toward my lonely, empty apartment, planning to spend my entire weekend writing one murder story and beginning investigations on another.

Am I some kind of pervert? I asked myself. *Or am I just plain crazy in the head?* The only answer I could come up with was yes.

WOODROW HOOKED A LOUIE ON SEV-enth Avenue and headed south again. We were just twelve blocks away from Bleecker. There wasn't much time left.

I pulled myself up straight, then craned my torso as close

to the front seat as I could. "How long have you worked for Miss Allen, Woodrow?"

"Long time, miss. Going on five years now."

"Then you must know her pretty well. And you must know all the people closest to her—her relatives and friends and most familiar coworkers."

"Well, I don't really *know* them, miss. Nobody ever talks to me, 'cept to say, 'Evening, Woodrow' or 'Merry Christmas, Woodrow' or 'Did the Yankees win tonight?' I just know who they are due to me driving them places with Miss Allen."

"Yes, but you've formed your own impressions about some of them, right?"

"I guess so, miss, but I sure wouldn't want to—"

"And you think some of them are nice and some aren't so nice."

"Uh, yes, but—"

"Well, here's what I need you to do for me, Woodrow. I need you to tell me who Miss Allen's closest associates are, and then tell me what you think of them—who you like and who you don't like, and who you think might be capable of murder." I had a feeling he would be a great judge of character.

Woodrow shot me a frantic look over his shoulder. His eyes were as big as golf balls. "I can't do that, miss!" he cried. "I can't tell who the killer's going to be! What if I made a mistake? Oh, that would be awful, miss, plum awful. And what if Miss Allen found out I told you things about her family and friends? I'd probably lose my job!"

"If Miss Allen gets killed, you'll *definitely* lose your job." I took a deep breath and paused for a few seconds to let the impact of my words sink in.

Several drops of sweat broke out on the side of Woodrow's face, dribbling down his mammoth neck and rolling under the collar of his crisp white shirt. I really hated to put him on the spot this way, but I believed him to be a sensitive and honest man, and I thought he would be my best, most reliable, source of information. Much more reliable than Ginger Allen herself.

"Let's start with Miss Allen's husband," I hurried on. We were at Sheridan Square already, just a couple of blocks to go.

"His name is Leo Marx, right? I've read about him in the papers and I know he's a rich, important television producer. But what's *your* opinion of him? Is he a good guy or a bad guy?"

"Oh, I wouldn't know, miss. Mr. Marx doesn't talk much. He just sits and listens while Miss Allen does all the talking."

"Does he seem like a happy man? Is he cheerful? Does he like to laugh?"

"Well, now that you mention it, he hardly laughs at all. Always acts real serious. Like a tax collector . . . the kind that really likes his job."

I smiled. Woodrow was going to make a great "informer." The kind that dislikes the job, but is so naturally observant and sincere he can't help being good at it.

I had tons of questions for him, but I didn't have any more time. "How far up, miss?" he asked, making a left onto Bleecker and slowing the big car down to a sleepy snail's speed. Like many old streets in the Village, Bleecker was quite narrow—not very welcoming to yacht-sized limousines.

"It's just ahead on the left," I said, "between Jones and Cornelia. I live over the fish store."

(Yes, you heard me right. I had the dubious distinction—some would call it di*stink*tion—of living directly on top of Luigi's Fish Market. I was so used to the smell I hardly noticed it anymore—except when Luigi's refrigerators went on the blink—but I could tell by the platoon of stray cats always patrolling the building's rear courtyard that the fish fragrance was still wafting strong. Which was why I spent so much time in the laundromat. And took so many showers. And tended to use a tad too much perfume.)

"Just one more question before I go," I said, as Woodrow pulled to a stop in front of my door. "Do you think Miss Allen and Mr. Marx are happy together? Do they have a good marriage?"

"I don't have the least notion about that, miss," he said, mopping his brow with a clean white handkerchief. "I've never seen them have a fight . . . but I've never seen them spooning, either. Who knows what goes on between a man and a woman? Even the man and the woman don't usually know."

Wise words from a wise Woodrow. I gave him a quick pat on one very large shoulder. "Thank you for your help, Woodrow, and thanks for bringing me home. Will you give some thought to the things I asked you about—who Miss Allen's closest associates are, and which ones strike you as suspicious? I'm eager to hear your opinions, and I'm sure we'll get the chance for another private conference soon."

"I'll think on it, miss," he said with a nod. "I'd be proud as punch to help you save Miss Allen's life. But please don't 'spect me to come up with any glorifying revelations. I'm just a chauffeur, not a prophet."

"Time will tell," I said prophetically. Then I grabbed hold of my purse and the clip file for Mike's story, scooched over to the left side of the car, and reached for the handle to open the door.

But Woodrow was way ahead of me. He suddenly materialized at the side of the car, clicked the door open and pulled it wide, then offered his arm to help me disembark. As I placed my white-gloved hand on his navy blue sleeve and allowed him to assist me onto the sidewalk, he gave me a glorious smile. And I felt like a million bucks. Not because of the plush limousine, or the famous and wealthy TV star it belonged to, but because I believed an enormous Negro chauffeur named Woodrow had, by some incredibly odd but significant stroke of fate, become my friend.

Chapter 4

IT WAS VERY DARK NOW; ALL THE BLEECK-
er Street merchants had closed up shop and gone home. I was
able to unlock the street door to my building and slip inside
unseen. This was a lucky break, you should know, because if
I had arrived in my humble Italian neighborhood in a big fat
fancy limousine during daytime business hours, it would have
caused a communal convulsion.

Every shopper and shopkeeper on the block would have
hustled out to the sidewalk and crowded around for a closer
look. Luigi, the owner of the fish store under my apartment,
and Angelo, the owner of the fruit and vegetable store under
Abby's place, probably would have smeared the limousine's
glossy finish with fingerprints and taken turns kicking the
tires. And the "members" of the storefront "social club"
across the street might have scrambled for cover under their
card tables, thinking a rival Mafia boss had decided to pay
them a surprise visit.

Darting up the single flight of stairs in my building's dim,
narrow chute of a stairway, I came to a halt on the small landing between my apartment and Abby's—the only two apartments in the modest three-story structure—and started

banging like a madwoman on Abby's door. I couldn't wait to tell her about my meeting with Ginger Allen. I was really dying to get her reaction. (Okay, I was also dying to quaff down one or more of the wildly creative, and wildly potent, cocktails Abby whipped up almost every night around this time.)

But there was no answer. Abby was either out for the evening, or upstairs in bed with her new lover, too wrapped up in her own passionate pursuits to be bothered with mine.

Heart sinking like an anvil in the ocean, I turned to my own door and let myself in. I flipped on the overhead light and plopped my stuff down on the yellow Formica kitchen table. As I was unbuttoning my jacket and moving toward the coat closet to get a hanger, I saw it: a hand-scribbled note, written on a scrap of pink paper, lying smack in the middle of my black-and-white-checked linoleum floor.

My first thought was that the note had been slipped under my door by Abby. But when you're in my line of work, and your apartment has been broken into twice, and you've received more than one threatening message from a crazy, cold-blooded killer . . . well, let's just say you don't take notes on the floor for granted. I snatched it up in my hand and read it at once, with a bug-eyed intensity that would've made Imogene Coca look drowsy.

Big waste of energy. It *was* from Abby. *Why are you so late getting home?* the note said. *Jimmy and I are going to Chumley's. He's been invited to read his new poem there tonight. So be there or be square. You can spring for your own hamburger, but the beers are on us.*

Well, that was all I needed to hear. It was, after all, Friday night. A girl's entitled to a hamburger and a couple of beers on Friday night, right? She can't be expected to stay home and ghostwrite a lazy, imbecilic coworker's eight-page clip story on the first night of the weekend!

I knew Dan was planning to drop by later, but he wouldn't show up until after eleven. Probably *way* after eleven. Friday nights, as a rule, were even more eventful for Manhattan homicide dicks than they were for crazed and hungry crime writers.

I didn't bother to change out of my work clothes (a dark green shirtwaist dress with a white collar and cuffs, seamed stockings, and high-heeled pumps) or put on my Village play clothes (a black scoop neck sweater, black capris, and black ballet flats). I didn't even take off my jacket and beret. I just ran a comb through the ends of my shoulder-length hair and applied a fresh coat of lipstick. Then I snatched my clutch purse and keys off the kitchen table, dashed back down the stairs to the street, and took off like a greyhound (the dog, not the bus) for Chumley's.

I DIDN'T HAVE FAR TO GO. JUST A FEW blocks over to the corner of Bedford and Barrow. When Chumley's first opened as a speakeasy during Prohibition, the Bedford Street entrance of the secret establishment had no name on the door. And today, some thirty-or-so years later, the portal was still nameless. There was only a number: 86. I pulled the small arched wooden door open and scooted up the four wooden steps to the restaurant area of the legendary bar—a favorite hangout of many famous (and plenty not-so-famous) writers of the twenties, thirties, and forties.

The crowded dining room was thick with smoke—both from the swarms of burning cigarettes and the crackling, wood-burning fireplace on the far wall. The tiny yellow lamps positioned on every table gave so little light you could barely make out the titles and pictures on the faded book jackets edging all four walls of the room. The large, framed black-and-white photos of the authors hanging above the hallowed book covers were, however, much more visible.

Abby was more visible, too. She was sitting alone in our favorite booth—the one tucked tight in the far right corner and bordered with pictures of James Joyce, Scott and Zelda Fitzgerald, and Edna St. Vincent Millay—and she was waving both arms in the air like some sort of sports referee. "Paige!" she shrieked at the top of her everloving lungs. "Over here!"

I was glad she didn't have a whistle around her neck. My ears were ringing enough as it was.

"Hi!" I said, happily slipping into the booth across from her. "Thanks for leaving me the note. I was *not* in the mood to be alone tonight. Can I have a sip?" Without waiting for an answer, I grabbed her beer and downed about half of it.

"Hey!" she said, laughing. "What's tickin', chicken? Are you just dry, or are you aiming to get high?" Her gorgeous Ava Gardner face was glowing, one eyebrow raised in the arc of a question mark.

"Oh, Abby, you won't believe what happened to me today!" I gasped, leaning over the scarred wooden table, hot words pouring out of my mouth like lava. "Mr. Crockett left work early, so everybody else left early, too, except for me, because I had to stay late to work on stupid Mike's stupid story, so I was all alone by myself in the office when, out of the blue, this really big Negro chauffeur in a really big navy blue suit suddenly appears at my desk and tells me his boss wants to talk to me downstairs in the car about something really important, but he wouldn't tell me what it was, so I—"

"Down, girl!" Abby interrupted. "You're losing your cool . . . and you're losing me, too. Better take a deep breath and relax for a second, you dig? I don't feel like carting you over to St. Vincent's emergency room." She pulled her shiny, waist-length black hair away from her face, twisted it into a thick rope, and draped it, snakelike, over one shoulder. "Here. Finish my beer. And have a cigarette, why don't you? Then you can tell me your story again, starting from the top."

I took a deep breath and guzzled the rest of her brew—but relaxing was out of the question. I'd have found it easier to juggle eggs while riding a unicycle. "Where's Jimmy?" I croaked, snatching a Philip Morris from the open pack sitting on the table. "Practicing his poetic pout in front of the mirror in the men's room?"

Abby laughed. Her new boyfriend of the past three months, Jimmy Birmingham (a fellow I'd introduced her to during my last murder story investigation), was such a strikingly handsome young man, everybody was always staring at him. And, like other really good looking (and vain) people I've known, whenever Jimmy was near any kind of reflective surface—a mirror, a store window, a car bumper, a blank TV screen—he was always staring at himself.

"Lord Birmingham will be back in a minute," Abby said. "He and Otto went out for a walk." Otto was Jimmy's closest friend and constant companion—a miniature dachshund with the softest ears and sweetest nature in the world (once he got to know you).

I lit the cigarette and exhaled in a noisy swoosh. "How did Jimmy get this gig tonight? I didn't know Chumley's had po-etry readings."

"They don't usually, but some avant-garde poetry group is having a meeting in the back room later and they asked Jimmy to come. They said e. e. cummings was going to be here. Groovy, huh? Of course, I don't know if that's really true, but cummings *does* have an apartment nearby, on Patchin Place, so it's entirely possible. Jimmy's so excited he can't sit still. That's why he shlepped Otto out for another stroll."

A waiter appeared at our table and we ordered two more beers. I ordered a bowl of chili, too. With lots of crackers.

"Can I tell you my story now?" I urged, leaning over the table again, feeling even more anxious than I had before. If I couldn't grab Abby's full attention before Jimmy came back, I might not be able to grab it at all. Whenever a sexy, well-made young man was in our near vicinity, Abby was emo-tionally inclined (okay, physically compelled) to concentrate on *him*.

"Spill it out," she said, smiling. "But just one sentence at a time."

Trying to stifle my excitement, and working hard to keep my words to a minimum, I began recounting the details of my surprising evening. I told Abby about Woodrow's strange and abrupt appearance in my office, then related how he had con-vinced me to go downstairs for a chat in the car with his boss. "And you'll never guess who his famous boss turned out to be," I said, trying, but failing, to keep the astonishment out of my tone.

"Wanna bet?" Abby said. "From the totally daft and silly look on your face I can tell it was either Eddie Fisher or Fernando Lamas."

"Wrong!" I snapped, a little annoyed that she was making fun of me. Couldn't she see how serious I was?

"No? Then it must have been Peter Lawford."

"Arrrgh! For your information it was a woman. And she's in television, not the movies."

"Well, why didn't you say so? It was Betty Furness, right?"

I groaned. How did this ridiculous guessing game get started?

"Gayle Storm? Dinah Shore?"

"Oh, hush!" I sputtered. "I didn't mean for you to pick the name out of the hat! I was going to tell you who it was!"

"So, why didn't you then?"

"You didn't give me a chance!"

"Well, you said I'd *never* guess," she teased, "and I wanted to see if I could."

Abby was my very best friend in all the world, but sometimes she drove me right out of my gourd. "Oh, forget it!" I said, with an extra-loud sigh of annoyance. "I'll tell you later."

Exasperation wasn't the sole cause of my retreat. Not only had the waiter reappeared to deliver our beers, but I could see out of the corner of my eye (and from the way all the female patrons were turning their blushing faces and batting lashes toward the door) that Jimmy Birmingham had reentered the restaurant.

"HI, PAIGE," JIMMY SAID, SLIDING INTO our booth next to Abby. Otto was cradled, as usual, in the crook of his left arm. "Glad you could make it."

"Me, too," I said, really meaning it. As frustrated as I was that I hadn't been able to tell Abby about Ginger Allen, I was still longing for a little fun. A little food, a couple drinks, a few laughs, and—if absolutely necessary—a few lines of poetry. "What are you reading tonight? Something new?"

"Yeah," he said, sitting up straight and squaring his shoulders. His big brown bedroom eyes were beaming with pride. "It's a really cool poem about the tragedy of the human condition. Very deep."

"The deeper the better, I always say," Abby declared, giving Jimmy a *very* suggestive wink and curling her fingers through his dark brown Vandyke beard.

Grinning like a kid (which, at the tender age of twenty-two, he almost *was*), Jimmy lowered his bearded chin onto Abby's shoulder and started nibbling on her neck.

If we had been sitting, as usual, around the table in Abby's kitchen, this would have been my cue to cut out and leave the two lovebirds alone. But we were blocks away from Abby's kitchen. We were crammed in a corner booth at Chumley's, and I couldn't escape to my apartment across the hall. And I didn't have the slightest desire to go to the bathroom. All I could think to do to ease my embarrassment was avert my eyes from the neck-nibbling spectacle and focus my attentions on Otto.

"Hey, baby," I said, leaning down and around the side of the booth to fondle the little weinie dog's warm, floppy ears. "How are you doing tonight?"

Otto answered me by licking my fingers and burrowing his fuzzy snout into the palm of my hand. I felt a whole lot better after that. I liked being nuzzled as much as the next girl.

"Hey, Paige," Jimmy said, tearing his fuzzy snout away from Abby's neck. "Did Ab tell you e. e. cummings is gonna be here tonight?"

"You betchum, Red Ryder. I got the message. You must be very excited."

"Yeah. But I'm kinda nervous, too."

"Why? Are you scared he won't like your poem?"

"No way! He's gonna love it. It's solid as cement."

"Then what are you nervous about?"

"I'm afraid he might get jealous and try to wreck my career."

At first I thought Jimmy was joking, but when I took a closer look at his youthful, beautiful, and naïvely self-important face, I saw that he was serious. Luckily, I was spared the discomfort of trying to deliver an honest yet tactful reply by the arrival of my chili and crackers.

Chapter 5

I HAD JUST FINISHED EATING WHEN A short, stocky guy with dirty blond hair and a scruffy, sand-colored beard waltzed over to our booth. I knew at once he was with the poetry group. Beards and poets just seemed to cling together. I didn't know the reason for this symbiotic attachment, but I suspected it had something to do with Walt Whitman. (Old Walt was a real trendsetter.)

The stocky, scruffy fellow leaned over our table and began speaking to Jimmy in a hushed, conspiratorial tone. "The gang's all here, man, and we're ready to roll. Since you're the top guest, you'll be the first to read. You've drawn a big crowd and the back room's full. Not a seat left."

"Is e. e. here?" Jimmy asked.

"No, man. He couldn't make it. He's up at his farm in New Hampshire."

"Oh." Jimmy allowed his disappointment to show for one brief, unguarded second, but then pulled himself together like a pro—consoled, no doubt, by the thought that his burgeoning career would now be safe from destruction at the hand of his envious elder.

Jimmy stood up and slipped out of the booth, holding Otto

to his chest like a baby. "Hey, Jerry, can my friends come watch?" he asked, gesturing toward Abby and me with a twitch of his shoulder.

"Yeah, man," the sandy-bearded fellow replied. "There aren't any more chairs, though. They'll have to sit at the bar."

His words were poetry to my ears. The closer to the booze, the better.

Abby and I stood up and followed Jerry, Jimmy, and Otto out of the dining area and along the narrow, crowded bar toward the small, smoky barroom in the back. As our leaders worked their way into the center of the back room, Abby and I planted ourselves on two stools at the very end of the bar, close enough to see and hear the action. Then we ordered two more beers and lit up two more cigarettes.

"He's a crummy poet, but he sure is cute," Abby said, watching Jimmy arrange his lean, lanky body in a sexy sprawl on the tall wooden stool set against the far wall. When he stretched Otto out on his thigh and stroked the pup from head to tail, she giggled out loud. "Otto's cute, too. I think I'll keep them both."

For Abby, this was tantamount to a declaration of undying love. She was far more inclined to dump new paramours than to keep them. Not because she was promiscuous or hard-hearted, but because she was a woman of great beauty, talent, intelligence, and humor, with an inextinguishable lust for life few men (or boys) could match, let alone satisfy.

"Have you heard Jimmy's new poem before?" I asked.

"About eighty times," she said, laughing. "And the more you hear it, the sillier it gets."

"Good evening, everybody!" Jerry bellowed, standing in the middle of the back room and raising his hands for silence. "Welcome to the Downtown Poets Society's Fourth Annual Celebration of the Muse!" There was a smattering of applause as Jerry spun his stocky frame around in a circle, then froze like a statue with his arm stretched out toward Jimmy. "And please give a warm welcome to our guest of honor, Jimmy 'The Bard' Birmingham. He's the cat with the dog, the scribe of our tribe, a pen for all men. He's the poet laureate of the

Village Vanguard, and he's here to read his new opus to us tonight!"

Snapping their fingers and calling out phrases like "crazy, man," and "way out," and "large charge," the black-turtlenecked young men and women in the audience made up in exuberance for what they lacked in experience. They were real cool cats; they were hip to the tip; they were ready, willing, and eager to be impressed—or *de*pressed, which would be even better.

And Jimmy was happy as a clam at high tide. Who needs e. e. cummings when you've got an adoring, ready-made fan club? He pushed up the sleeves of his own black turtleneck, gave Otto's little brown body another sensual stroke, swept his big bedroom eyes over his flock, and—in the deepest, most delectable baritone you ever heard in your life—began to recite:

> Melted memories past another winter
> Springs tomorrow ahead.
> Perfidious forgiving and failing again.
> No reviling the ever-wailing
> Deadly moments at the Strand.
> Beneath my feet, vibes from the lowest depths,
> In an epileptic gesture.
> The sacred stench lurking beneath,
> Smoky whispers abound.
> More change for all!
> Lost souls rising
> Must prevail.

It took every ounce of self-control I had left in my wretched body to keep from laughing like a hyena. What the hell did those words mean? And why were all these black-clad bohemians jumping to their feet, clicking their fingers, and swaying back and forth in some kind of surging mutual entrancement? Was I missing something? Were Abby and I the only two people in the place who thought Jimmy's poem was just plain dopey?

Nope. The clean-shaven, muscle-bound bartender was in complete agreement. "What a load of crap!" he grumbled. "Who is that guy, anyway? Elmer Fudd?"

I started giggling, but Abby sprang like a snapping turtle to Jimmy's defense. "His name is Jimmy Birmingham," she seethed, black hair rippling in a fury down her back. "If you had bothered to pay attention, you would know that. And if you had one seed of sensitivity in that pathetic plot of soil you call a soul, you would know he's the most promising new poet of the brave new world. He's an artist, a wizard, a lyrical god! You dig?"

"Whatever you say, doll," the muscle-bound bartender mumbled, suddenly applying himself to the absorbing task of wiping down the countertop, hurriedly swabbing his way toward the other end of the bar.

As soon as he was out of earshot, I gave Abby a sardonic smile. "An artist or a wizard, maybe. But a lyrical god? Methinks you've gone too far."

Abby threw her head back and laughed out loud. "Poetic license," she said.

"What's so funny?" Jimmy wanted to know. He had exited the back room and come over to us, still glowing with the pride of his performance. Otto was in his usual passenger seat, with his rump tucked into the bend of Jimmy's elbow and his tiny tube of a body balanced along the length of Jimmy's forearm. I gave his little head an affectionate pat. (Otto's, I mean, not Jimmy's.) "What are you laughing at?" he asked. (Jimmy, I mean, not Otto.)

"Oh, nothing, really," Abby said. "Paige just came out with an amusing little bon mot."

"A little what?"

"Never mind, baby," she cooed, giving his Vandyke a playful tug. "Let's talk about you. You looked so good and read so well it was sinful. They really dug your poem. I'm so proud of you."

Jimmy was in heaven. His lids dropped lower, and his cheeks turned pinker, and he leaned over and started nibbling on Abby's neck again. One of her earlobes, too.

I had had enough. Enough beer, enough poetry, enough observational neck nibbling. (If the neck had been my own, and the nibbler had been Dan Street, I'd have been humming a different tune.)

I left a tip on the bar and hopped down from my stool. "Gotta go, kids," I said, giving Otto another pat on the head. "Dan's coming over when he gets off work. I'll catch you tomorrow morning, Ab, okay? I really need to talk to you about what happened today. It's important."

"That's cool," she said, not really paying attention. She was too busy collecting slobber on her earlobe.

"Later, Paige," Jimmy muttered between mouthfuls.

Otto whimpered and looked up at me with the sweetest and saddest little eyes you can imagine. At least *somebody* was sorry to see me go.

I HAD BARELY HUNG UP MY JACKET IN the coat closet when my buzzer rang. I lunged through my living room to the front window, pried a peephole between the closed shade and the window frame, and peered down at the sidewalk in front of my building. (When you've been stalked, strangled, and shot twice, as I have, you don't open your door to anybody till you've got a damn good idea who that body is.)

I had figured it would be Dan, of course, but my heart still jumped for joy when I saw the top of his gray fedora and the wide shelf of his tan trench-coated shoulders. I'd have recognized those shoulders anywhere. From any angle. Coat or no coat. Scrambling back to my door to buzz Dan in, I flung open the pearly gates to my apartment and watched him ascend.

And what a soul-stirring ascent it was!

Taking the steps two at a time, and arriving on the landing in a flash, Dan scooped me into his arms, crushed me to his chest in a hammerlock, and planted the mother of all kisses on my gasping, happy mouth.

Dan often greeted me this way. And I don't mind telling you it was a *very* welcome howdy-do. Sure beat a handshake. There was just one problem. Sometimes Dan's embrace was so ardent, and his hot lips so hungry, that he squeezed the air right out of my lungs and sucked the consciousness right out of my skull—i.e., turned me on so much I felt faint.

Which was exactly what happened tonight. I was even more overcome than usual, though, because I actually *did* faint! I kid you not. My knees went soft and my brain went black. For one brief, stunning moment, I didn't know my own name (which, considering the absurd and embarrassing name I'd been saddled with, was a delightful respite), and I didn't know where in the world I was. I had a vague, swirly notion that I was somewhere on the planet Earth, but I might as well have been on the moon. I was gone. Real gone.

"Are you okay?" Dan said, breaking off the kiss and looking down at me with concern. "You look like you're going to pass out."

I didn't tell him that I already had.

"What kind of drinks did Abby make tonight?" he teased. "Must have been Molotov cocktails." His black eyes were crackling with their usual combination of wisdom and wit.

I giggled. (At least I *think* that weird gurgling sound coming out of my mouth was a giggle. In my bleary, wanton, nymphomaniacal state it might have been more of a groan.) Finally pulling myself together enough to speak, I told him that I'd just gotten home from Chumley's and I'd only had three beers. "Don't worry, I'm not drunk."

"Then I guess I'll have to abandon my plan."

"What plan?"

"To whisk you inside and take advantage of you."

Oh, how I wished he would! I was longing to make love with Dan—and had been for all the ten months we'd been together—but I hadn't yet given in to those desires. Holding fast to our society's unyielding moral codes, I believed a couple should become husband and wife before they became lovers. That may sound prudish to you, since, as a widow, I was no virgin. And as a divorced father, Dan certainly wasn't either. But, prudish or not, I was still determined to live by the rules, and Dan respected my decision.

My self-enforced self-denial wasn't built on morality alone. Actually, morality had *nothing* to do with it. I was just

being practical. I wasn't willing to bring an illegitimate child
into the world—ever!—and I wouldn't have wanted to have
a child then, at that particular point in time, even if Dan and I
were married. I knew all about the latest, most modern
method of birth control (I had gone to the Margaret Sanger
Clinic to be fitted for a new diaphragm, even though I had no
plans to use it), but I also knew it wasn't infallible. Neither
were the new "fail-safe" condoms. (Only a fool would believe
those things were foolproof!) The only way I could make
dead certain I didn't get pregnant was to forgo sexual inter-
course altogether—or, as the Village bohemians would say,
not "go all the way."

Which is not to suggest that sexual pleasure was outlawed.
Quite the opposite, as a matter of fact. (There are *other* ways,
you know.) So let it be noted that, between Dan and me, a certain amount (okay, a *lot*) of petting was allowed (okay, *invited*), and—as you've probably already perceived—deep,
soul-sucking, mind-rocking kisses were fundamental to the
program.

I smiled at Dan and he smiled at me; then he helped me
back inside my apartment (my knees were still wobbly) and
closed the door.

"Coffee or Chianti?" I asked, breathing deeply to clear my
head.

"Anything," he said, "as long as it's red, comes in a bottle,
and is at least twelve percent alcohol."

Stepping into the living area, Dan took off his hat and coat
and put them down on the living room chair. Then he took off
his suit jacket and loosened his tie. Finally—and somewhat
reluctantly, I thought—he removed his leather shoulder holster and the 9mm gun it carried, and carefully set the appara-
tus down on top of his jacket.

I had watched Dan perform this same routine over a hundred times in the past ten months, but it never ceased to thrill
me. It was like watching him get undressed. Dan had once
told me he felt naked without his gun, and—until he decided
to get married again (and by that I mean married to *me*), or
until I decided to break the rules and become the slut I

yearned to be, or until we could go out to Coney Island together and spend the day lolling around on the beach in skimpy bathing suits—well, that was as naked as he was likely to be in my presence.

Turning his tall, lean, wide-shouldered body back toward the kitchen, Dan walked over to the table and sat down. "How was your day?" he asked, giving me a long, slow, deliberate once-over. "You seem anxious, preoccupied, out of sorts." He took a Camel out of the pack in his shirt pocket and lit it with the monogrammed silver lighter I'd given him for Christmas. "What's going on? Are you working on a new story?"

Jeez! Am I wearing a goddamn sign or something?

"No!" I snapped, too hastily, and haughtily, for my own good.

Alerted by my edgy response, Dan narrowed his pitch-black eyes, furrowed his noble brow, and began studying me as if I were a paramecium under a microscope. From the ultra-firm way his jaw was set, I could tell he was clenching his teeth . . . and doubting my honesty.

"Well, that's not exactly true," I hurried on, trying to recover my cool (which was impossible since I hadn't had any cool in the first place). I filled two jellyglasses with wine and took them over to the table. "I *am* working on a new story, but it's not *my* story. It's stupid Mike's story, and he only wrote one stupid paragraph. But it has to go to the typesetter first thing Monday morning, so he gave it to me to do. Can you believe it? I have to research the clip file and write the whole damn thing over the weekend. *That's* why I'm out of sorts!"

He bought it. Probably because it was true. (Well, it *was!* So what if I didn't tell him about Ginger Allen?! That didn't make me a liar. It just proved I could be discreet when I had to. I had promised Ginger I wouldn't reveal her murderous plight to anybody—least of all the police—and I intended to keep that promise. With Dan, I mean. Abby didn't count.)

"I won't be able to go to the movies with you on Sunday," I said, canceling our weekend plans to pave the way for my new investigation. I knew Saturday wouldn't be a problem. Dan *always* had to work on Saturday. "There's no way I can finish this story in one day." (Okay, I was lying now. An eight-page clip story usually took me three hours from start to finish, coffee breaks included.) I took a big gulp of wine and sat down at the table.

"Too bad," Dan said. "I thought we'd take a walk in Central Park, grab an early dinner at Schrafft's, then go see *Blackboard Jungle,* with Glenn Ford. It's supposed to be pretty good." He took a drag on his cigarette and exhaled in that slow, sexy way that made my nerve endings dance. With his tie hanging loose, his white shirt opened wide at the collar, and his disheveled dark brown hair curling low over his forehead, he looked so gorgeous I thought I might faint again.

Am I out of my everloving mind? Am I certifiably insane? Am I really going to turn down a stroll around the lake, a steak dinner and a hot fudge sundae, and a cuddle in the balcony with this incredibly luscious and attractive man, just because a snotty, overbearing TV star wants me to figure out who's trying to kill her?

Yes, to all of the above. (What can I say? I'm a sucker for a mystery. My screws are so loose they're dangling.)

"I'm sorry, Dan," I said. "I really hate to miss our Sunday together, but it can't be helped. If I don't get this story done, Mike will make my life unbearable." I took another sip of wine, peering at Dan over the rim of my jellyglass. "Maybe you could spend the day with Katy," I said, knowing this suggestion would please him. Katy was the light of his life, his adored and adorable fourteen-year-old daughter—the daughter he'd still be living with if his unfaithful ex-wife, Veronica, had been content being loved by just one man.

Dan gave me one of his characteristically crooked smiles. "That's a good idea. I can take her to see *Seven Brides for Seven Brothers* again. Katy loves that movie so much, she claims she won't be happy till she's seen it seven times." His black eyes sparkled with mirth. For a big, rugged, manly thirty-seven-year-old cop, he sure looked like a boy sometimes.

"I'll miss seeing you, though," he added.

"Me, too, you," I said.

"Maybe I should put Mike under house arrest and make him write his own lousy story."

I laughed. "It would be lousy all right."

"Or maybe you could come on over here and sit on my lap and let *me* tell *you* a story."

I didn't waste any time. In the blink of an eye I was sitting on Dan's muscular thighs, wrapping my arms around his sturdy neck. (I wanted to wrap my legs around his waist as well, but I didn't think that would be very ladylike.) "What story are you going to tell me?" I murmured into his ear. "The one about Goldilocks and the three bears? Or the one about Little Red Riding Hood and the big, bad homicide detective?"

"Shut up," he said.

And then he made sure that I did.

Chapter 6

I WAS STANDING ON THE EDGE OF A
rocky cliff about to dive into a lake full of snakes when the
telephone rang. Leaping halfway out of my dream and all the
way out of my bed, I stumbled down the stairs to answer it.
The voice on the other end was female and slithery.

"Good morning, Paige Turner," the voice said, writhing its
way into my sleepy brain. "Have you figured out who's trying
to kill me yet?"

In my dreamlike state, I thought I was talking to a snake.
Then I realized it was Ginger Allen. "What time is it?" I
croaked. (Some pair we made: a squirming serpent and a
comatose frog.)

"Half past nine."

No wonder I was having so much trouble waking up. I
hadn't gone to bed until after three—after Dan had strapped
on his holster and headed for home—and then I'd been too
wound-up (okay, sexed-up) to fall asleep right away.

"You sound like crap," Ginger said. "Late night last
night?"

"Mmm hmm," I mumbled, "and a tad too much Chianti."

"Well, you'd better sober up and pull yourself together,

pussycat, because you're in for another late and boozy night tonight."

"Oh, really?" I was annoyed by her bossy attitude, wondering what demands she had in store for the evening. "I take it you've made some plans for me."

"Sure have, pussycat," she said, apparently oblivious to my sardonic tone. "My darling hubby Leo is giving a little dinner party at the Stork Club tonight and you're going to be there."

Well, that didn't sound too bad. "And who *else* is going to be there?" I asked, hoping the guest list would include Ginger's nearest and dearest (i.e., those most likely to want her dead).

"Leo and I will be there, of course, plus five of our closest friends and enemies." She placed a snide emphasis on the last word of her sentence. "My younger sister, Claire, and her husband, Rusty Burnett, are coming, and Tex and Toni Taylor have also been invited."

I recognized the last two names immediately. The famous husband-and-wife duo hosted, from their own luxurious Manhattan dining room, the country's most popular morning radio show, *Breakfast with Tex and Toni.*

"Thelonius Kidd will be there, too," Ginger added. "He's the hotheaded, pain-in-the-ass director of my TV show, and he's a confirmed bachelor. He doesn't know it yet, but you're going to be his date tonight." I wondered how the hotheaded Thelonius would feel about that.

"And how are you going to introduce me?" I asked. "As your private secretary or your personal maid?"

Still oblivious to my insolent inflection, she said, "I told Leo we went to college together, that you were my roommate at Ohio State, and that you're in town—without your husband—to see a few shows and do some shopping. Think you can handle that?"

"Uh, yes, that sounds all right. But I hope you didn't give him my real name."

"Of course not!" she spat, making her own insolence obvious. "I told Leo your name was Patty. Patty Turner. It was the first name that came to mind, and it seemed easy to remember."

Ugh. I *hated* the name Patty. It made me think of hamburger patties and sausage patties and, worse, cow patties. It seemed that every irksome, overly peppy high school cheerleader in the U.S.A. was named Patty. But it was too late now. Ginger had dubbed me Patty, and Patty I would have to be. I was doomed to spend the next few days, or weeks, or—God forbid!—*months* of my life in the flattened yet perky world of Pattydom.

"All right," I said, with a heavy sigh, "Patty it is. But we'd better make up some other stuff, too—flesh out our stories and get them synchronized. For instance, were we good friends? Did we have a lot of boyfriends? What did we major in?"

"Oh, we got along okay," Ginger said, suddenly sounding bored with the conversation. "I was more popular than you were, of course, but you were a better student. I majored in drama and you majored in English."

"Fair enough." At least she'd given me the more intelligent part to play. I rubbed the sleep out of my eyes and asked the all-important question. "Do you think the person who's trying to kill you will be there tonight?"

"Stop asking me that! How the hell am I supposed to know?" she screeched. "That's for *you* to find out!" Her patience was as thin as paper. She paused for a second, then adopted a sickeningly sugary tone. "Do you have a nice dress to wear, sweetie? Some decent jewelry? If not, you'd better go pick something up at Bergdorf's. You can charge it to me. We can't have you sticking out like a sore thumb now, can we?"

"Don't worry," I said with a haughty sniff. "I won't embarrass you." I figured Abby could fix me up and make me presentable. As a freelance magazine illustrator with a roomful of colorful props and costumes—including fancy dresses and furs—Abby had everything a snazzy Stork Club patron (or a sneaky undercover agent) might need. "What time do you want me to be there?"

"Woodrow will pick you up at seven."

"Okay, but not at my apartment. I don't want to shake up

the neighborhood or attract any undue attention. Tell
Woodrow I'll be waiting on the northeast corner of Sixth Avenue and West Third."

"What a stealthy little detective you are," she mocked,
making me feel small and stupid with her derisive manner of
speaking. I didn't know if she meant to belittle me specifically, or if that was just the way she talked to everybody. "So,
pussycat, you will meet Woodrow this evening, promptly at
seven, at the corner of Sixth and Third. He'll deliver you to
the Stork. And prepare yourself for a full day tomorrow.
You're coming to brunch at my place at eleven, and we're
dining later at the Copa. "

"Fine," I said, surrendering, without a further shred of sarcasm, to Ginger's relentless and discourteous control. There
was no point in resisting. The rules were unspoken but clear
as crystal: if I was going to identify Ginger's potential killer
and then write her exclusive story, I was going to have to do
it her way—i.e., follow her orders to the letter.

Luckily, I was well-trained in the art of taking dictation.

AS SOON AS I HUNG UP THE PHONE, I
dashed back upstairs to the bathroom and washed my face.
Then I grabbed my aqua chenille bathrobe off the hook on the
back of the door and pulled it on over the large khaki T-shirt
I'd slept in—one of the four worn, U.S. Army T-shirts that
had arrived in the box of personal effects I received after Bob
was killed in Korea. (I sleep in one of these shirts almost
every night. For some ironic, animal reason I'll probably
never understand, they make me feel more secure.)

After cleaning my teeth and tugging a brush through my
thick, unruly hair, I ran barefoot down the stairs and out into
the hall. "Abby?" I called, knocking softly on her door. "Are
you up yet?"

To my great relief, she was. "Greetings, Garbo!" she said,
pulling the door wide open and gesturing for me to enter. "I
was wondering when you'd show your face. I've been up for
hours, working on a new illustration."

She didn't have to tell me that. The streaks of green paint

on her cheeks and chin were a sure tip-off. The fact that she was wearing her paint-smeared white smock and brandishing her paintbrush in the air like a conductor's baton was also a clue. Likewise, the John Coltrane music blaring on the hi-fi. Abby claimed she couldn't create "diddlydreck" without Coltrane.

"So, you got a new assignment," I said, stepping inside and walking over to the large wooden easel standing in the middle of the living room (or, rather, the room that used to be a living room until Abby turned it into her art studio). The painting propped on the easel pictured a busty, blindfolded blonde, clad in a skimpy, leopard-skin bikini, roped—with her legs apart and her arms behind her back—to a tree. The shirtless man kneeling on the ground in front of her was carrying a pistol in one hand and a whip in the other. There were three bleeding gashes on his hairy chest.

"What magazine is this one for?" I asked.

"A pulpy rag called *Men in Danger*," she scoffed. "Real classy."

"Looks like the *woman's* in more danger than the man."

"Yep. Ain't that always the way? The art director who gave me the job told me to make her look real sexy, helpless, and scared, like she was about to get raped by a grizzly."

"Why the blindfold?"

"Oh, that was my own idea," Abby admitted. "I figured if the poor thing was going to get raped by a bear, the least I could do was keep her in the dark about it. That way, when the attack starts, she can imagine she's being mauled by Clark Gable, or Victor Mature, or some other bristly stud."

I laughed. "Speaking of bristly studs," I said, "where is the bearded Birmingham?"

"Upstairs," she said. "Still sleeping."

"And the affable Otto?"

"Curled up next to him, I'm sure." She leaned over and dabbed another dollop of green onto her painting's woodsy background. "They'll probably sleep till noon. Jimmy was so jazzed up after last night's reading, he stayed up a whole twenty minutes later than usual, writing another poem. And then he stayed up another whole hour after that, reciting the poem, over and over again, to Otto and me." She stuck her paintbrush in a jar of turpentine, wiped her hands on her smock, and switched her long, fat, single braid of hair from one shoulder to the other. "He'd probably still be reciting now if *I* hadn't fallen asleep."

I laughed again. "They never said being a poet's muse was easy."

"Yeah, but they never said it would be torture, either. I'm more of a martyr than a muse! I'm starting to feel like the girl in this painting." She stomped over to the hi-fi and turned Coltrane down to a less creative level. "Want some coffee? It's still hot."

"Sure do," I said, following her into the kitchen area and sitting down at her round wooden table. "And I'm *dying* to finish telling you about what happened to me yesterday!" I paused to let the urgency in my voice take effect. "This is big, Ab, it really is. I'm really going to need your help on this one."

She shot an interested look over her shoulder as she was pouring the coffee. "Start talking, kiddo. I'm all ears. You were up to the point where some TV personality had lured you into her limousine. See? You thought I wasn't paying attention, but I was." She brought our full cups over to the table and sat down. "So who was the leading lady, anyway? Loretta Young?"

"No more guessing games!" I screeched. "It was Ginger Allen, okay? The one and only Ginger Allen. And she wants me to do some secret detective work for her."

"What?!" Abby cried, eyes bulging out of their sockets. I'd never seen her look so amazed. And I don't mind telling you I was delighted to be the cause of her amazement. Most eye-popping surprises between Abby and me took place the other way around. "I don't believe it!" she said, her voice vibrating like a just-plucked banjo string. "The biggest television star in all of New York wants you to be her private eye?!"

"Well, yes, in a manner of speaking."

"What manner? What speaking? Why you? And what the

hell does she want you to do?" The unflappable Abby Moscowitz was flapping all over the place.

I stirred some milk and sugar into my coffee and lit up a cigarette, prolonging my moment of glory as long as possible. Then, unable to stand the suspenseful tension myself, I caved in and spilled the whole story.

Abby was rapt. She listened to every word of my detailed account as if I were Moses preaching from the mountain. She didn't interrupt me once! When I told her about the four separate attempts against Ginger Allen's life, her beautiful face contorted into about fifty different expressions of astonishment and horror. And when I told her about my talk with the gigantic but gentle Woodrow, disclosing that he had agreed to help me in my investigation, her features turned as soft and mushy as sponge cake. It wasn't until I told her about Ginger's phone call that morning, and how the demanding star had summoned me to the Stork Club that very same night, that Abby sat up tall as a tree in her chair and started acting like her usual dynamic, straightforward self.

"I've got a smashing dress for you to wear!" she whooped.

I should have known she'd make the wardrobe her primary concern. If Abby could have her way, every outfit at every murder scene would be color-coordinated and artfully accessorized.

"My cousin Rachel gave it to me just last week," she said, grinning like a goat. (Okay, goats don't really grin. I'm just a fool for alliteration.) "She bought it at Saks to wear to a wedding—and that's the only time she's ever had it on. She's gained so much weight since then, she can't fit into it anymore."

A warning buzzer sounded in my skull. "When was this wedding?" I asked. "1942?"

Abby gave me an indignant look. "No, stinker. It was just a couple of months ago. My cousin Rachel's a very healthy eater." She lit a cigarette and blew the fumes in my direction. "Would I send you to the city's most fashionable nightclub in an outmoded frock?"

Considering some of the dresses Abby had loaned me in

the past, I was tempted to make a joke right then. But I wisely reconsidered and kept my lips sealed. Abby was my dearest friend, and the world's most magnanimous gift horse. I couldn't afford to look her in the mouth (whatever that means).

"Just wait till you see it," she said. "It's the most! It has a tight, black off-the-shoulder top and a full red taffeta skirt with about a thousand black lace petticoats underneath. And there's a wide, black belt that laces up like a corset. You'll look so hot they'll call the fire department."

"But I don't want to look hot!" I cried. "I want to look elegant, sophisticated, subdued. I need to fade into the woodwork, not draw any attention to myself. I'm going to be hunting for a possible murderer, don't forget, so the more invisible I can be, the better."

"Oh, don't be such a cube!" she sputtered, flipping her braid off her shoulder, sending it swaying down her back. "You're so square it's scary. How many times do I have to say it? You have to bait the beast before you can trap him, you dig?"

I knew there was something to what she said, but I also knew that some situations called for more caution than others. "I don't know, Abby," I demurred. "I feel like I've got to be really careful this time—go *way* undercover. My picture was in the paper a while ago, remember, and there were several articles about me. That's where Ginger got my name. What if the person who's trying to kill her also read those articles, and saw that picture, and recognizes me? I'll be in big trouble then."

"My point exactly!" she insisted, "You need to look like somebody else entirely. And do you remember how you looked in that newspaper photo, babydoll? Let me refresh your memory: scraggly hair, no makeup, drab, wrinkled hospital gown. Take my word for it, Paige, if you wear my cousin Rachel's dress tonight—and let me do your face and fix your hair—nobody, but nobody, will have a clue in the cosmos who you are."

I hated to admit it, but she was making a lot of sense.

"Okay, okay! I'll wear the damn dress. Where is it? I'll try it on."

"It's upstairs," she said, with a big Ava Gardner smile. "But I don't want to go up to get it right now. Jimmy might wake up and start reciting again. I'll bring it over to your place later, along with my jewelry box and makeup kit. What time do you have to go out?"

"I'm being picked up at seven."

"I'll be over at five."

"Thanks, Ab," I said, face flushing warm with gratitude. "What would I do without you?"

"Act like a shnook and look like a mouse," she replied.

Chapter 7

ANOTHER CUP OF COFFEE AND A BAGEL with cream cheese later, I returned to my own apartment. Abby was eager to get back to work on her painting, and I felt compelled to start writing Mike's story. I felt compelled to *finish* Mike's story, too, since Ginger had already planned the rest of my weekend for me.

After running upstairs and putting on a pair of lavender capris and a black turtleneck—yes, I have one, too; everybody who lives in the Village has one—I planted myself in my tiny spare bedroom (I mean *office!*) and read through all the clips Mike had given me. This didn't take long, since there were only four articles in the file—four brief newspaper accounts that gave only the barest facts of the crime in question. And from these bare facts I was supposed to compose eight full pages of titillating, bone-chilling, blood-curdling copy!

(The deities of Destiny themselves must have given me my crazy name, because hardly a day goes by that I'm not, in one way or another, by one person or another, myself included, being pressured to live up to it.)

Groaning out loud, I took a stack of typing paper out of the drawer and plopped it on top of my desk—the brand-new (to

me) secondhand desk that Abby and my office friend Lenny
had given me for Christmas. I stuck a piece of paper in the
carriage of my baby blue Royal portable and rolled it up to
typing position. Then I stared out the window for two or three
minutes, down into the weed-choked rear courtyard where the
stray cats liked to congregate, and tried to think positively
about my situation: I would have to spend the day spinning a
few stark facts into a scintillating eight-page yarn (just call me
Rumplestilskin!), but at least I had a nifty little well-stocked
office to work in. I had a dictionary, a thesaurus, a fresh typewriter ribbon, and a wildly overactive imagination. What
more could a striving crime-writer named Paige Turner need?

Intelligence would have helped, I guess, but it wasn't
really necessary. (Not for the editors and readers of *Daring
Detective* magazine!) I cranked out one paragraph, and then
another, and one page, and then another, and then finally—
two hours and fifty-six minutes later—my (I mean Mike's)
story was finished. It wasn't the best tale I'd ever written, but
I'm sure you can understand why: it's hard to focus all your
skills and attention on a murder that's over and done with
when you know another one may be just about to happen.

"THIS IS HORRIBLE!" I CRIED. "IT LOOKS
like something Rhonda Flemming or Linda Darnell would
wear in a pirate movie!" I wasn't exaggerating, either. The
dress Abby had just zipped me into was wild and wanton,
with a bodice that was begging for a ripping.

"Oh, shut up, Paige," Abby snapped. "This is the hottest
new style of the season. It's what all the big stars are wearing.
I'll bet Ginger Allen has one just like it."

"Yeah, maybe," I snarled, "if it's a costume for her show!
This would be perfect for a sultry gypsy skit, or a savage fla-
menco number. It is *not*, however, perfect for the Stork Club."
I stamped my foot and spit out my words with certainty,
though I hadn't the slightest idea what styles fashionable
Storkettes were sporting—this season or any other.

Abby was on the verge of losing her temper. I could tell by
the way her eyes were flashing and her nostrils were flaring

that she was about to perform a flamenco of her own. "You'd better cool it, Paige, you dig? I've been pampering an excitable, oversensitive poet all afternoon, and I'm not in the mood for one of your infantile outbursts. Either you pull yourself together and let me doll you up for the evening—in this gorgeous, glamorous, perfectly Storkworthy *shmatte*—or I'm packing up my makeup and jewelry and going home. Splitsville, baby. Bye-bye!"

"I give up!" I cried, flying into a slight (okay, *substantial*) panic. "You win, you win!" The only dress-up dress I owned was black, boring, and five years old. It was also at the cleaner's.

"That's the spirit," Abby said, with a triumphant grin. "Now spin around a few times and let me take a look at you."

I did as I was told. I felt like a total idiot, but in the interest of speeding things up so I would be ready to meet Woodrow on time, I twirled around my kitchen like a giddy tot in a tutu.

"Something's wrong," Abby said, knitting her brow, studying my appearance with an artist's eye. "I know! Too many petticoats! Take one off."

I gratefully yanked the bulkiest black lace petticoat down over my hips, stepped out of the starched, scratchy contraption, and tossed it on a kitchen chair. Then I stood in front of the open coat closet and took another look at myself in the full-length mirror on the back of the door. "That's better," I said, smoothing down the red taffeta skirt of the dress. "At least now I'll be able to walk by a table without knocking over all the wine glasses."

"And without turning a single head," Abby said, scrunching up her nose in further disapproval. "But I can easily fix that!" She stepped over to me and yanked both sides of the off-the-shoulder black knit top of the dress down to the midpoint of my upper arms. "This ain't no turtleneck, you dig? You're supposed to show some cleavage."

Abby thought cleavage was the answer to all the world's problems. I thought it was more likely the cause.

"Sit down," she said, before I could complain about my

near nudity. "I'll do your makeup. And then I'm going to put your hair up in a slinky French twist. You'll look so suave you'll slaughter 'em!"

I was getting a little tired of Abby's sprightly attitude. "Perhaps you've forgotten," I grumbled, sitting down in a huff at the kitchen table, "but my purpose for going to the Stork Club tonight is to *prevent* a slaughter, not provoke one."

Abby didn't say anything. She just pushed my hair off my face, tilted my head back, and started slathering liquid foundation all over my cheeks and chin.

"I'm really nervous about this whole thing, Ab," I went on, hoping to divert at least a portion of her attention from my face to my feelings. "I'm not a private eye! I'm just a person who writes about crime. And every murder investigation I've ever gotten involved in has been *after* somebody has been killed, not before!"

"What difference does that make?" Abby asked, madly rubbing powder into my nose pores with a synthetic sponge. "The investigation process is the same. You're still just looking for the bad guy."

She was missing the point entirely. "That's not the problem!" I exclaimed. "I'm not so much worried about *how* I'm going to find the bad guy. What I'm worried about is *when*! Don't you see? What if I can't figure out who's trying to kill Ginger in time? What if she actually gets murdered? Then one of America's most beautiful and adored TV stars will be dead, and it will be my fault!"

"No it won't," Abby said, stretching one of my eyelids to the limit and painting on a stripe of black eyeliner. "It'll be the killer's fault."

"Well, yeah, sure, but try telling that to Ginger Allen! She'll still be dead!"

"In which case she won't be thinking about whose fault it is." Abby stepped back for a second, took a hard look at my face, then came at me again, brandishing a cake of mascara and a very tiny brush. She spit into the mascara, scrubbed the brush through the resulting gunk, then began lacquering the lashes of my left eye. "And besides," she added, moving on to the right eye, "you don't know for sure if somebody really is trying to kill Ginger Allen, or if that's just what Ginger Allen wants you to believe."

This thought had occurred to me before. It was, after all, quite possible that Ginger had dreamed up the whole attempted murder scenario just to get some free publicity, deciding to use me as her patsy (okay, her *Patty*) to break and spread the news. But I really didn't think that was the case. Ginger's call for secrecy had seemed both urgent and sincere—and since she was already the most popular TV star in town, not to mention the second-most famous redhead in the whole darn country, I figured her need for free publicity was minimal.

And even if she does just want publicity, I reminded myself, *she wouldn't need me for that. All she'd have to do is pick up the phone and call Walter Winchell.*

"Yie domph finkso," I said. I was trying to tell Abby that I thought Ginger was telling the truth, but it's very hard to talk when somebody's pulling your lips in every which direction and smearing them with greasy lipstick.

Fortunately, the makeup ordeal was soon over. "Hot damn! You look fantastic!" Abby declared, stepping back to admire her new painting. "You should jazz yourself up like this all the time, kiddo. You look like a bigtime TV star yourself!"

I didn't tell her how uncomfortable that made me feel. I simply wasn't in the mood for another one of her dogmatic lectures on the importance of being glamorous.

"Next, a little jewelry," she said, clasping a pair of sparkly red earrings on my lobes and a string of onyx beads around my neck. "And now for the hair!" she cried, grabbing a brush and tearing into my tresses with great exuberance. The way she was going at it—tugging and pulling and twisting and jabbing—I wondered if there'd be any hair left in my scalp when she was through. I howled out in pain a couple of times, but that did nothing to curb her fury.

Finally—after what seemed like hours, but was probably just five minutes of extreme cruelty and torture—my new upswept hairdo was complete. "Voilà!" Abby whooped, pulling me to my feet and standing me square in front of the mirror on the closet door. "If you aren't the chicest-looking chick in Manhattan, I'll eat my goddamn easel."

I hated to admit it, but Abby was right. I looked really good. And classy, too. Not classy enough for a White House ball, maybe, but surely snazzy enough for dinner at the Stork. There was only one problem: I still looked like myself.

"You're a magician, Abby," I said. "I never looked so stunning in my life! But I'm still worried somebody will recognize me. That picture of me in the paper wasn't altogether horrible, you know. It had a certain hospital panache. And if the would-be killer saw that picture and has a better than average memory, then he might know who I am. And he might figure out why I'm there. And then he might decide he has to get me out of the way. Permanently, I mean."

"I already thought of that," she said, "so I brought you these!" She pulled a pair of glasses out of the pocket of her smock and thrust them into my hands. There was a look of pure delight (or was it devilment?) on her face. "Go ahead! Put them on. You'll be so incognito you won't know who you are yourself!"

I looked down at the glasses in my hand. They weren't my style, to say the least. The plastic frames were pearly and slanty, like cat eyes, and the pointy corners were studded with tiny rhinestones. They looked like something Zsa Zsa Gabor would wear if she ever deigned to be seen in a pair of glasses, which of course she wouldn't.

I wasn't keen to wear them myself, but I knew they'd be the perfect disguise. Eager to see how different I'd look, I leaned toward the mirror, flipped open the earpieces, and slipped the pearly peepers on.

Once again, Abby was right. I didn't even recognize myself . . . for the simple reason that I couldn't see.

"Holy Toledo!" I blurted, leaning closer to the mirror, trying desperately to bring my distorted features into focus. "Where the hell did you get these bleary specs? At a 3-D movie?"

"No, silly. I bought them off a pushcart on the Lower East

Side. They sell used glasses there for fifty cents a pair. Aren't they groovy? I thought they'd be a good prop for a *Ladies' Home Journal* illustration—not that I'll ever get an assignment from *that* snooty rag."

Abby's carefree babble was driving me up a tree. Didn't she understand what a serious stew I was in? I propped my hands on my hips and turned to face her. (At least I *thought* I was facing her. Everything looked so blurry, I might have been eyeball to eyeball with the refrigerator.) "Tell me, Abby, did you ever try on these glasses yourself?" My foot was tapping a scornful staccato on the floor.

"Of course I did!" she said. I couldn't make out her facial expression, but her voice had turned a trifle testy.

"And when you had them on," I continued, spewing sarcasm with every syllable, "could you actually see anything?"

"Well, no, but—"

"But?! But what?! But you thought it was groovy to be *blind?!*" By this point I was practically shrieking. "You thought I'd have more luck searching for a lurking murderer if I had no sense of sight?"

"Oh, don't be so dramatic!" Abby growled. "So it's a little hard to see through the lenses. Big deal! All you have to do is wear the glasses down low on your dainty little *shiksa* nose and look out over the top. They'll still be a great disguise. God, Paige! You're so fussy you make me want to scream."

I didn't have time for any screaming—hers *or* mine. As I tried lowering the glasses on my dainty shiksa nose, I caught a glimpse of the kitchen clock. It was five minutes to seven. I had to go meet Woodrow.

"Jeez, I'm really late!" I cried, snatching the glasses off my face and sticking them in my purse. I grabbed my gloves and my fur jacket (okay, Abby's fur jacket) off the chair in the living room and lunged for the door. As I stepped out into the hall—looking as good as I possibly could (and probably ever would)—my petty grievances dissolved altogether. "Thanks so much for everything, Ab," I said, gushing with gratitude. "Even the goofy goggles. I'm sorry I'm such a finicky witch." Then, as I turned to head down the stairs to the street, I gave her one final peace offering: "You really saved my life tonight!"

I thought if I stated it as a fait accompli, it would be more likely to come true.

Chapter 8

THE DARK BLUE LIMOUSINE WAS PARKED right where it was supposed to be, on the northeast corner of Sixth and West 3rd. I waited for a break in the traffic, then made a mad dash across Sixth Avenue, feeling—and no doubt looking—like an addled ostrich in seamed stockings and high heels. Woodrow saw me coming, and by the time I made it across the street, he was standing by the side of the car, holding the rear door open for me.

"Evening, miss," he said, giving me an ear-to-ear smile. His mustache was grinning, too.

I gave him a big smile in return. "Sorry I'm late, Woodrow! Have you been waiting long?"

"Just a few minutes, miss. Nothin' to fuss about."

I got into the car and slid toward the middle of the plushly upholstered back seat. Woodrow closed the door, hurried around to the driver's side, and then lowered his bulk behind the wheel with a deep, resounding "oof!"

"It's nice to see you again, Woodrow," I said, stretching toward the front seat. "How're you doing?"

"Just fine, miss. Just fine." He fired the engine up and pulled the limousine out into the steady stream of traffic heading north. I waited for him to say something more, but he didn't.

"You know you really don't have to call me 'miss' all the time, Woodrow," I said. "I call you by your first name, and you can call me by mine. It's Paige, remember?"

"Yes, miss, I remember," he said.

"So then you'll call me Paige, okay?"

"Oh, no, miss! I couldn't do that! Miss Allen wouldn't like it, miss. I'm not supposed to call anybody by their first name, and I'll get in a mess of trouble if I do."

"But Miss Allen doesn't have to know, does she? You can call me Paige when she's not around."

Woodrow was silent for a moment; then he heaved a hefty sigh. "It's not that I wouldn't like to, miss. You're a right nice person, and I'd be proud to use your name. But I just can't let myself get familiar with any of the white folks I meet on the job. Miss Allen wouldn't stand for it. And I can't call you by your first name when she's not around because I might get in the habit of it. And then I might forget myself and call you by your first name when she *is* around. And that just wouldn't do, miss. That just wouldn't do at all."

It sickened me that so many people in our society were still hell-bent on keeping Negroes "in their place," but there wasn't a damn thing I could do about that now. I had to worm my way *into* that society, not stand outside and form a picket line. "You're right, Woodrow," I surrendered. "We'd better not rock the boat." I didn't know what I hated more, the country's bullheaded bigotry, or my own lily-livered acquiescence.

Leaning against the soft leather backrest, I turned to look out the window. We were still heading uptown on Sixth, crossing 23rd, sailing smoothly through the choppy waves of Saturday evening traffic. It was getting dark; the cars all had their lights on.

"Has anything happened since yesterday, Woodrow?" I pulled myself forward again. "Has Miss Allen had any more close calls?"

"Not that I heard tell of, miss." He kept his eyes fastened

on the road ahead. "But if something did happen," he added, "I'd sure enough be the last to get the news."

"Maybe so," I said, with a meaningful sniff, "but that doesn't mean you'd be the last to *know*."

Woodrow let out a soft chuckle, but he didn't say anything. He'd been trained to keep his thoughts and words—as well as his knowledge—to himself, and I realized that if I was ever going to get him to reveal his impressions of Ginger's relatives and friends, I'd have to ask him pointed, specific questions. So, when he stopped for a red light at 28th Street, I started doing just that.

"Do you know if Miss Allen's sister and brother-in-law, the Burnetts, are going to be at the Stork Club tonight?" I inquired.

"Yes, miss," he said, giving me a quick glance over his shoulder. "They're there already. I dropped them off with Miss Allen and Mr. Marx on my way downtown to get you."

"What is Miss Allen's sister like?" I asked, leaning as close to the front seat as I could. "Is she smart? Funny? Pretty? Are she and Miss Allen very close?"

"I wouldn't know about that, miss. Them being close, I mean. Mrs. Burnett's the real quiet type, so it's hard to guess her feelings. I can't tell if she's smart or funny either, since she never says anything. I do know what she looks like, though, and it pains me to mention it, but she's kind of on the homely side—not very pretty at all. Leastways, not next to Miss Allen."

Nobody looks pretty next to Ginger Allen, I muttered to myself, *except maybe Liz Taylor or Marilyn Monroe or Ava Gardner . . . or Abby Moskowitz.*

The light turned green and we forged ahead. "What about Mr. Burnett?" I probed. "Can you tell me anything about him?"

"Well, now, Mr. Burnett . . . he's a whole 'nother story, miss." Woodrow lifted his chauffeur's cap for a second to give his half-bald scalp some air, then repositioned the cap squarely on his extra-large head. "He's smart like a fox, but he struts like a fool. Ever since Miss Allen got him a job on her show, he's been acting like he runs the place. He's always jawin' off about something. Either the scenery's not right, or the lights aren't bright enough, or Miss Allen's costume is ugly, or the skit's not funny, or she's singing all the wrong songs. If it's not one thing, it's something else. I never heard so much squawking in all my natural life—and I grew up on a chicken farm."

I smiled. At least Woodrow felt free to express his sense of humor with me. "What job does Mr. Burnett have?" I asked. "Producer? Set designer? Assistant director?"

"That's the strange part of it, miss. He's just a stagehand. And he's only been working there for about a year."

"Gosh!" I said, for lack of a better exclamation. "Then how does he come off acting so critical and bossy?" I gave the matter a few seconds of thought and added, "Better yet, why does Miss Allen let him get away with it?"

"I don't know, miss. I surely don't know. She never lets anybody else sass her that way."

I flopped back in my seat and lit up a cigarette. (Smoking helps me think, I think.) We were crossing 40th Street now, gliding past the iron fence and long row of trees lining the Sixth Avenue border of Bryant Park. The Stork Club, I knew, was on 53rd, near Fifth, so my destination was drawing nigh. And my time alone with Woodrow was growing short.

I took two fast puffs on my cigarette and then squished it in the ashtray. "Do you know the director, Thelonious Kidd?" I hurried on, leaning so far forward I thought I'd bust my garter belt. I would have gotten down on my knees and scooched closer to the front seat, but I couldn't afford to get any runs in my nylons. "Does he have a friendly relationship with Miss Allen? Do they socialize often?"

"Mr. Kidd goes out with Miss Allen and Mr. Marx sometimes," Woodrow said, "but not a whole lot. Leastways, not in my . . . I mean, Miss Allen's limousine. They might go out together in other cars, miss, or maybe Mr. Kidd takes a taxi and meets them in more places than I know about. I just can't say for sure."

"But you've driven them to a few places together, right?"

"Yes, miss."

"And how did they act? Were they chatting? Laughing? Arguing? Enjoying each other's company?

Woodrow gave me a solemn look in the rear-view mirror. "They weren't acting any way special. Not talking too much, just being polite. One time Mr. Kidd had a lady friend with him, and *she* was talking up a storm, but it was all just no-account gossip, and nobody paid her any mind. One other time, when it was just the three of them, Mr. Marx and Mr. Kidd were talking about business, and Miss Allen got a little uppity because they weren't talking to her. But soon as she stopped complaining, the conversation stopped, too. They rode all the rest of the way to the restaurant in a powerful shush."

Powerful shush. I loved Woodrow's odd but perfectly descriptive combination of words.

"Have you ever driven Mr. Kidd and Mr. Burnett at the same time?" I asked. "I mean, have you ever seen them together?"

"Once or twice, miss." Woodrow made a right turn and proceeded east on 52nd Street. "Miss Allen took them both to a network party at the Plaza just last week. It was just the three of them."

Ginger went to a party with her bachelor director on one arm and her stagehand brother-in-law on the other? How cozy. Was this the same party where she was given the (supposedly) poisoned cocktail? "That's interesting," I said. "Do you know if Mr. Marx and Mrs. Burnett joined them there?"

"I don't think so, miss. When I picked up Miss Allen to take her home, Mr. Burnett was the only one with her. Even Mr. Kidd was gone."

Woodrow drove through the intersection at Fifth Avenue and motored on toward Madison. Being familiar with the pattern of the city's one-way streets, I knew he would swing left on Madison, and left again on 53rd, and then head back to Fifth. Only three blocks to go, and I still had a thousand questions left to ask!

I finally narrowed it down to one: "When Mr. Kidd and

Mr. Burnett were in the car together, how did they behave toward each other?"

"They were both kind of quiet, miss. Talking some to Miss Allen, but not saying a word to each other."

"So Mr. Burnett wasn't squawking as much as usual?"

"Didn't fuss about a thing."

Woodrow slowed the limousine down, slithered past the other fancy cars lining the curb, and then pulled to a stop at the mouth of the green canopy leading to the entrance of the Stork Club. He was about to get out of the car and open the door for me, but the club's blue-uniformed doorman beat him to it.

Before sliding over to get out of the car, I gave Woodrow a secret pat on the shoulder and said—in a voice too low for the doorman to hear—"Thank you, my friend. Will I see you later?"

"No way to tell, miss," he murmured, shooting me a furtive and apologetic smile. "Miss Allen controls my whereabouts, not me."

As the Stork Club doorman helped me out onto the sidewalk and led me—nervous and self-conscious—up to the entry of the famous nightspot, I realized Woodrow and I were now in the very same boat. Miss Allen was controlling my whereabouts, too.

HAVE YOU EVER HAD THE FEELING THAT you were some kind of freak in a sideshow? A bearded woman, perhaps, or a man with no arms and legs? Well, that's the way I felt as I stepped into the chained-off entryway of the Stork Club. I didn't know why all the people on the other side of the chain—the recent arrivals who had already been admitted to the lobby—were staring at me, but I couldn't have felt more freakish if I'd been a midget with two heads.

Is one of my petticoats showing? I wondered. *Do I have spinach in my teeth? Or could it be—oh, my God!—that they all recognize me?* I was fairly certain that *that* was not the case, but just to be on the safe side, I took Abby's glasses out of my purse and put them on. Then, straining to see over the top of the frames, I made my way over to the half-blurred, tuxedo-clad man stationed, like a guard dog, at one end of the chain. (This chain, you should know, was made of real fourteen-karat gold. I read about it in Winchell's gossip column.)

As I stood there waiting to be admitted to the club, the man in the tuxedo looked me over from head to foot, wrinkled his brow in reproach, then stared at the door for a couple of seconds as if expecting someone else to enter. "Will a gentleman be joining you, madam?" he inquired, speaking in such a snotty tone of voice I wanted to smack him in the face with my clutch purse. (A dead fish would have been better, but I didn't have one on me.)

So that's it! I realized. *Everybody's looking at me because I'm alone. A woman at the Stork without an escort! How scandalous!*

"I'm meeting someone inside," I said, "assuming you'll be kind enough to unlatch your precious metal barricade and allow me to enter." Glaring at him over the top of my glasses, I pronounced each syllable with haughty precision. "My name is Patty Turner. *Mrs.* Patty Turner. I'm with the Ginger Allen party . . . Oops! Pardon me, sir! I guess you'll sleep much better tonight if I call it the *Leo Marx* party."

The Master of the Chain was unaffected by my huffy tantrum—and totally unimpressed by my name-dropping. He gave me a steely-eyed gaze and then checked the leather-bound list sitting on the small pedestal to his left. "Yes, here you are, Mrs. Turner," he said, pointing to the spot where my name was listed as if that were the only place in the universe where I actually existed. "Several members of your party have arrived and been seated." He unhooked the gold chain and—aiming his rude, contemptuous nose toward the ceiling—motioned for me to enter. "You may leave your jacket with the coatcheck girl and proceed through the lobby to the next entrance. Someone will show you to your table."

I passed through the opening in the golden gate without a word. I suppose I should have said "thank you," but I wasn't feeling very grateful. Besides, it's hard to focus your energy on being polite when your eyes can't focus on anything at all!

I kid you not. The glasses distorted my vision so much I felt downright dizzy. If I hadn't known better, I would have thought the whole lobby was under water. In order to find the coatcheck room, I took the so-called spectacles off my face and carried them in my hand.

Big relief. My equilibrium returned and I could actually see where I was walking—past a row of private telephone booths and several tall arrangements of fresh flowers, toward a small, mirrored cubbyhole set into the right-hand wall of the lobby. The coatcheck room, I presumed. Two coatless couples were milling around near the cubbyhole, smoking, whispering among themselves, and watching me approach with disdainful, downright condemning looks on their faces. You'd have thought it was *illegal* for a woman to enter a nightspot alone! (In some uptown nightclubs it probably *was*.)

Ignoring their scathing stares, I walked up to the coat counter, removed Abby's fur jacket, and handed it to the platinum blonde coatcheck girl. (Yes, I was able to do it without a man's help!) Then I straightened my naked shoulders, stuck my own nose in the air, and—petticoats swishing like palm fronds in a typhoon—strode off to make my second (and hopefully final) unescorted Stork Club entrance.

It was a pompous performance, to say the least. But if you've gotten to know me at all by now, you'll understand my lofty behavior: I was acting like the Queen of Sheba because I still felt like a sideshow freak.

Chapter 9

THE TUXEDOED GENDARME (OKAY, *MA-
jordomo*) at the next entrance didn't give me any trouble. He
merely asked for my name, looked it up on *his* list, and then
summoned a white-jacketed captain to show me the way to
the Cub Room (where, I knew from both Winchell's and
Dorothy Kilgallen's columns, the VIPs were always seated).

I followed the captain past the long, crowded, mirrored
bar, and on through the thick glass door at the end of the barroom. This led us into the L-shaped main dining room, which
was also paneled in mirrors and dripping with crystal chande-
liers. The windows were draped in golden silk and midnight-
blue velvet, and all the cushions of all the chairs at all the
hundred or more tables were covered in yellow and gray satin.

The dining room was almost filled to capacity in spite of
the early hour (it wasn't yet eight o'clock), and the band was
in full swing, playing a snappy version of Perez Prado's new
hit, "Cherry Pink and Apple Blossom White." Many eager,
well-dressed, beautiful young couples were dancing.

All of a sudden, after we'd made our way into the middle
of the main dining room, my guide stopped in his tracks and
made an abrupt about-face. "I'm very sorry, madam," he said

to me, plump cheeks reddening in embarrassment, "but I've brought you to the wrong place. It's my first day on the job and I don't know my way around yet. Please follow me back to the barroom and we'll enter the Cub Room from there."

As I turned and followed my leader back the way we'd come, I couldn't help wondering if the red-faced captain was telling the truth. Had he honestly been confused about the location of the Cub Room, or had he just taken one look at me and—temporarily forgetting the majordomo's directions—decided I didn't belong there?

(Okay, okay! So maybe I was being a little paranoid now. But paranoia's a spiraling psychosis, you know. It's like an addiction. Once you start thinking of yourself as a persecuted misfit, it's really hard to stop.)

At the door to the famous Cub Room (referred to by all the gossip columnists as the "Snub Room"), there was yet another guard dog. He was dressed in a tuxedo and had really big teeth. The better to bite me with, I figured. How many Stork Club inspections did a person have to pass before being allowed to sit down and look at a menu?

For me, it was three—but the third time was a charm. Ginger must have told the guard dog to watch for me and show me right in, because I didn't even have to give him my name. He greeted me with a toothy smile and directed me to a large table in the rear of the shoebox-shaped dining room. Luckily, I spotted Ginger's red hair from a distance, then had the presence of mind to walk the length of the room to her table before putting my glasses back on. Otherwise, I'd probably still be stumbling in circles around the tables in the front, bumping into tray-bearing waiters and upending silver ice buckets.

And I certainly wouldn't have noticed all the famous people I passed along the way. I wouldn't have seen that Walter Winchell himself was sitting at a table near the entrance, talking on a phone, taking notes, and searching the room for fresh scandals. I wouldn't have had a clue that Errol Flynn was dining (okay, *drinking*) with a very young blonde in one corner, or that Orson Welles was sitting by himself at a table for two, happily puffing on a giant cigar and simultaneously sawing into a steak the size of an area rug. I never would have known that I was in the same room with Mayor Robert F. Wagner, and actress Jean Simmons, and playwright Eugene O'Neil's daughter, Oona, and the Duke and Duchess of Windsor—and I wouldn't have seen that George Sanders and his wife, Zsa Zsa Gabor, were sitting at a table directly to my right. (Was that the very same table Sanders shared with Ann Baxter in the Stork Club scene of the 1950 movie *All About Eve*? It was possible since that scene had been filmed right here in the Cub Room.)

Being so close to the glamorous (and, I thought, gaudy) Miss Gabor, and considering that she looked right into my eyes for a moment, I was doubly glad that Abby's sparkly secondhand spectacles were hidden in my hand instead of displayed on my face. Zsa Zsa might have spied them and wanted them back. I passed by the Sanders's table without incident, however, and continued my trek toward the bright, red-haired beacon at the back of the noisy, crowded, smoke-filled dining room.

"Patty!" Ginger squealed as soon as she saw me. "I can't believe it's really you! It's so wonderful to see you again!" She jumped out of her seat, squeezed her way around the table, and grabbed me in a hug so tight I almost spit up on her shoulder. The facts were in: Ginger was as skilled an actress off the screen as she was on.

As soon as she broke away, I took a deep breath and put on the glasses. "It's good to see you, too," I said, even though I couldn't and it wasn't. "How many years has it been?" I was hoping to pin her down on the date of our purported college graduation so I could avoid any possible story or timeline mismatches.

"Who's counting, darling?" Ginger whooped, cleverly sidestepping the question and rendering it moot. "The less said about that, the better! We don't want to give away our ages, now, do we?" She linked her arm through mine and tugged me over to the head of the table where a short, thin, indistinct figure was standing next to his or her chair, presumably waiting to meet me.

"This is my husband, Leo Marx," Ginger said. "Isn't he cute? And, Leo, this is my long-lost college roommate, Patty Turner."

Tucking my chin into my chest, I lowered the bridge of my glasses to the tip of my nose and peered over the lenses at the tense, wiry little fellow standing before me. He was anything but cute. He had coarse brown hair, small brown eyes, swarthy skin, and a great hooked beak of a nose that would have put any eagle to shame. I calculated he was in his early forties.

"It's nice to meet you, Mr. Marx," I said, extending my gloved hand for a shake. After two or three seconds had passed and he still hadn't taken hold of my hand, I became rather embarrassed, dropping the neglected paw to my side and tucking it into the red taffeta folds of the skirt of my dress.

"We're glad you could join us, Mrs. Turner," Leo said, in a strikingly deep and mellifluous voice, punctuating his words with an audible snort. Considering the size and shape of his schnoz (see how Abby's vocabulary has rubbed off on me?), I was surprised the snort wasn't more of a honk. He sized me up with his cold brown eyes and, gesturing toward an empty place at the table, said, "Please sit down, Mrs. Turner. We're blocking the aisle. Ginger will sit next to you and introduce you to the rest of our guests."

Look who's giving the orders now!

I slid into my designated seat—on the cushy leather banquette positioned against the back wall of the room—and Ginger slipped in next to me. Leo resumed his seat at the head of the table.

"This is Patty Turner, everybody!" Ginger said, still playing her part to perfection. She seemed so thrilled to see me that even I believed her. After giving a syrupy little spiel about our college roommate days, she introduced me to the other people at the table. Tex and Toni Taylor were sitting directly across from us, next to Leo but with their backs to the room, and Claire Burnett was sitting next to them. Rusty Burnett was sitting at the other end of the table. The empty seat

to my left on the banquette was, I presumed, intended for my
so-called date, Thelonius Kidd.

"I can't imagine what's keeping Theo," Ginger complained. "He swore on his mother's grave he'd be on time
tonight."

"That means he'll be two hours late," Rusty griped. "At
least that's the way it always goes at rehearsals. He tells
everybody else to be there at two, then he shows up at four.
Either he's a thoughtless bastard, or he needs a new watch."

I slipped my glasses down my nose and took a good look
at Ginger's outspoken brother-in-law. He was handsome in a
stocky, athletic, bulldog kind of way, and his close-cut hair
was the color of copper. It wasn't half as bright and bedaz-
zling as Ginger's hair, but it packed a wallop just the same.
Rusty's wide-set hazel eyes were searching and intense, and
his square, clean-shaven face was gleaming with a golden tan.
A recent cruise to Cuba? I wondered. *Or does Rusty spend his
lunch hours baking under a sun lamp?*

Ginger's sister, Claire, on the other hand, wasn't gleaming
at all. She looked so dull and lusterless I thought she might
have been spackled with adobe. Her pale skin was mottled
with freckles, and her short, tightly permed brown hair looked
as dry as dust. She was wearing a frayed and faded olive-
green blouse, which was adorned with just one frill—a large
olive-green bow that began just beneath her chin and drooped
all the way down her chest like an overgrown baby's bib. *This
plain, pitiful creature is the younger sister of the wildly talented, staggeringly gorgeous Ginger Allen? What a shadow
to grow up in! How can the poor girl bear to get out of bed in
the morning?* I felt so sorry for Claire I could hardly breathe.

Tex and Toni Taylor inspired a quite different reaction.
Their twin hairdos (teased and sprayed blonde pompadours),
their matching manicures (clear frost), and their artfully
made-up faces (a bit too heavy on the rouge) made me want
to laugh out loud. They must have spent the whole day in the
beauty parlor. Together. And Liberace must have been over-
seeing the operation.

I wasn't shocked by the couple's extraordinary appearance—I had seen pictures of the darling duo in one of the many fan magazines published by Orchid Publications (the same company, believe it or not, that published *Daring Detective*)—but I did find it surprising that they would make such an effort to create and maintain an eye-popping image. They were, after all, *radio* personalities, not TV stars. They were meant to be *heard,* not seen. Why all the emphasis on their looks?

"I'm hungry," Rusty grumbled. "Do we have to wait for Theo to get here before we can eat?"

"I'm sure Mr. Kidd will be joining us soon," Leo said, giving Rusty a menacing sneer. "I spoke to him this afternoon, and he was looking forward to meeting us here tonight. He was especially eager to meet Mrs. Turner." Leo nodded in my direction, but never made eye contact. His tone was chilly and sharp. Knife sharp.

"Oh, who cares when Theo shows up?" Ginger blurted. "We're perfectly capable of having a good time without him!" Her green eyes were beaming like traffic signals, giving us permission to GO. She nudged Leo with her elbow and told him to order a bottle of champagne. He frowned in annoyance, but quickly complied.

"I have an announcement!" Toni Taylor suddenly spoke up, in that girlish, breathy voice so familiar to radio listeners all across the nation. Her extra-long false eyelashes were batting so hard and so fast I thought they'd swat the radishes right off the relish plate. "*Breakfast with Tex and Toni* may be moving to TV! Isn't that absolutely thrilling?! We got a call from CBS just this morning! They want to put us in the seven-thirty-to-eight time slot on Tuesday evening. We'll replace Jo Stafford, lead into Red Skelton, and they'll change the name of the show to *Dinner with Tex and Toni.* Isn't that just too, too fabulous? Tex and I are so excited we could just pop!" To prove it, Toni inflated her chest to the bursting point. It was a miracle her large pink breasts didn't pop all the way out of her strapless pink dress.

Tex was visibly taken aback by his wife's abrupt announcement. He shot Toni a look of sheer panic, then stared down at the tablecloth for a few anxious seconds, growing more nervous with every breath.

"Is that true, Tex?" Leo inquired. "Has CBS made you an offer?"

Finally pulling himself together (sort of), Tex raised his head, bared his capped teeth in a perfect white smile, and stroked one side of his stiff pompadour. "Uh . . . yes, it's true, Leo, and . . . uh . . . I wasn't going to bring it up tonight, but . . . uh . . . I have to admit . . . it's a real honor." Tex stammered his words in the low, resonant baritone that—thanks to the sponsor of his morning radio show—I'd come to associate with Aunt Jemima syrup and pancake mix commercials. "And it's a once-in-a-lifetime opportunity, Leo. Don't you agree?" As Tex aimed his pleading eyes in Leo's direction and lifted his highball glass to his lips, I saw that his hand was shaking.

"Don't be stupid," Leo said, words blasting from his mouth like buckshot. "You can't just pull up camp and move over to CBS. Don't you ever talk to your lawyer? You're under contract to me—and to NBC—for three more years."

"Yes, I'm aware of that, Leo," Tex stuttered, sweat beading on his crinkled forehead, "but you know how hard we've been trying to break into television. And NBC won't let us in the door. They think we're only fit for radio. But radio's dying—you know that, Leo! This is our first real chance to cross over, and if we don't act on it, it could be our last." Tex paused for a moment and took another shaky sip of his drink.

Leo sat rigidly in his chair, drinking nothing and saying even less.

"Three years is a very long time in an artist's career," Tex stumbled on, "but a very short time in the life of a network. This deal would mean the world to us, but next to nothing to you. So we thought maybe we could all get together and come to some kind of agreement. You, us, CBS, and NBC. You've been such a good friend for so many years, Leo, we thought you might be willing to let CBS buy out our contract."

"Think again," Leo said. Those were his only two words, but you could tell from the set of his jaw they were final.

"Hey, that's enough!" Ginger broke in. "No more talk about business! This is supposed to be a party for my friend Patty, and I don't think she's interested in all this boring shoptalk."

Ginger couldn't have been more wrong. I was very interested, indeed. Especially since the emotional business discussion had revealed one glaring, unmistakable motive for murder. (Okay, okay! So it was a motive for murdering Leo more than Ginger, but a good detective examines all the angles, even when they're obtuse.)

The wine steward appeared with our champagne and ceremoniously popped the cork. As he was maneuvering his way around us, filling our stemmed crystal glasses, a tall, sandy-haired man in a white dinner jacket strolled up to our table. Both his black bow tie and his wide, silly grin were notably askew. He stood at one corner of the table, between Rusty and Claire, swaying back and forth like a willow in the wind. When the wine steward moved closer and filled Claire's glass to the brim, the swaying man snatched it right out of her hand, threw his head back, and began guzzling the contents.

"Put that glass down this instant, Theo!" Ginger shrieked. "You're stinking drunk already!"

It seemed my date had arrived.

Chapter 10

EVEN WHILE SLOBBERING, BELCHING, AND
weaving around in an alcoholic daze, Thelonius Kidd was a
good-looking man. His light brown hair was thick and wavy,
his eyes were azure blue, and his mouth kept curling up in the
most engaging smile. His cleft chin and dimpled cheeks made
him look strong and soft at the same time.

"Where the hell have you been?" Ginger asked, as he
lurched around the back of Rusty's chair and lowered his
lanky frame onto the banquette next to me. "We thought you
weren't coming."

"Almost didn't," he mumbled, smiling.

"And why the hell not?!" Ginger was getting mad now.
Her face was turning as red as her hair.

"Couldn't remember where I was supposed to go." Theo
sank lower in his seat, dropped his head on the leather backrest, and grinned up at the ceiling. I wasn't sure if he was truly
plastered or just putting on a performance of his own.

"Well, now that you *are* here," Ginger went on, "the least
you could do is sit up straight and say hello to your date." She
had softened her strident tone, but she was still fuming.

Theo groaned and pulled himself into a more upright position. Then, belching again, he peered out through his half-closed lids and fastened his bleary gaze on me. "Hi, I'm Theo—the black sheep of this distinky . . . distinguished social gathering. And who, may I ask, are you?"

Ginger made no move to introduce me, so I did it myself. "I'm Patty," I said, pushing the glasses back up to my eyes. "Patty Turner. I went to school with Ginger." I thought of offering my hand for a shake, but in my sightless condition, I was afraid I'd sock him in the stomach by mistake.

"Hey, can we order dinner now?" Rusty whined. "I haven't had anything to eat since lunch!" Unaware of how dopey he sounded (everybody in the whole damn restaurant probably hadn't eaten since lunch!), he stood up and leaned over the length of the table, seized a rib of celery off the relish plate, and took a ferocious bite. Then he settled himself back in his chair, crunching loudly. (I didn't actually see this whole scene, but I heard it clearly.)

Lowering the glasses on my nose again, I watched as Leo motioned to our waiter for menus. He (Leo, not the waiter) was obviously upset about something. Was it Tex and Toni's desire to terminate their contract, or Theo's drunken tardiness? Was it Rusty's brash, demanding attitude, or the fact that Ginger was treating him (Leo, not Rusty) with something somewhat short of respect? He couldn't possibly be mad at Claire for anything, I figured, since she hadn't said a word all evening. But what about me? Had I offended him in some unknown, unforeseeable way? Did he know who I really was and why I was there? (My paranoia was rearing its ugly head again.)

The waiter handed out the menus and I hastily memorized my selection: a crabmeat cocktail to start; and for my entrée, broiled royal squab Casanova (I had no idea what that was, but the goofy name appealed to me). Then, while the others were still studying their menus, I raised my eyes and surreptitiously scanned their faces, looking for character clues (i.e., signs of murderous intent).

Theo was nodding off, so I quickly skipped over him. I also skipped Ginger—whom I certainly didn't suspect of trying to kill herself!—and Leo, whose anger I found intriguing, but inscrutable. Rusty was in a rapturous trance, pouring over the menu so fervently I felt sure he had nothing but food on his mind.

Claire was staring at the menu, too, but I could tell she wasn't reading it. Her eyes weren't moving at all. She looked as if she were sitting in mourning at a funeral instead of dining in the Cub Room at the Stork. Her head was bowed, her shoulders were sagging, and the corners of her thin, colorless mouth were turned so far downward I half expected them to crawl over the edge of her chin and creep all the way down her neck. What a piteous sight! The wretched woman was paralyzed. But what was the cause of her paralysis? I wondered. Indecision? Fear? Pain? Repulsion? And if it was the last, who repelled her the most? Her sister, her husband, the others at the table, or herself?

Number of questions: oodles. Number of answers: none.

Tex and Toni looked almost as miserable as Claire. Leo's refusal to let them out of their contract had clearly hit them pretty hard. Tex's makeup had begun to melt, oozing down the sides of his face in thin rivulets of sweat, and one of Toni's eyelashes had come partially unglued. Toni kept dabbing at her damp eyes with her napkin and heaving one dire, woeful sigh after another, while Tex kept clearing his throat and drumming his manicured fingers on the tabletop. Sitting *very* close together—like two enormous parrots in a tiny canary cage—they seemed stricken, defeated, unable to speak.

After the waiter reappeared and took down our orders, including Theo's (he woke up just long enough to request the chicken hamburger à la Winchell), I asked Ginger to show me the way to the ladies' room. "I'm afraid I'll get lost," I said, but what I meant was, *I need to talk to you right now!*

Ginger flashed me a look of indignation, which she quickly turned into a dazzling smile. "Of course, Patty!" she purred, getting up from the table and waiting for me to do the same. "Just follow me, pussycat!"

•   •   •

I TRAILED GINGER THROUGH THE DIN-
ing room and one flight up to the women's lounge. As soon as
we stepped inside, Ginger twirled around to face me and sputtered, "What's your goddamn problem, Paige? Can't you piss
by yourself?" She flounced over to the long, mirrored makeup
counter and plopped herself down on one of the black-and-
white striped silk-covered chairs.

Gee! Are all famous TV stars this warm and friendly?

"I just thought we should have a talk," I said, glad to see
that we were in the powder room alone, but keeping my voice
down to a whisper just in case. "I need to know if you've
picked up any new clues or formed any suspicions about who
your attacker may be."

She turned her back to me and admired her peachy complexion in the mirror. "I appreciate your concern, pussycat,
but couldn't this inquisition have waited till later? I didn't
want to leave the table! I thought something was going to happen, and I didn't want to miss it."

"What do you mean?" I said, sitting down in the chair next
to hers. "What did you think might happen?" I was so eager
for information—*any* information—that I was practically
drooling.

"Oh, nothing that would interest you," Ginger simpered,
patting her hair and smoothing the scoop neckline of her
green crêpe de Chine dress. "I just wanted to see if Tex or
Toni would say anything more to Leo about getting their stupid show on TV. They've been pestering him for ages. But
they just don't get it! They're not good enough for television!
Leo's given them several screen tests, and they make fools of
themselves every time. They're as entertaining as a pair of
dead newts."

"CBS seems to have a different opinion," I said, needling
her on purpose. One nasty disposition deserves another, I always say. Mainly, though, I was just hoping to ruffle her
feathers and incite a hasty reaction—i.e., goad her into spewing out some candid data. *Any* data—about *anything*.

Big boo-boo. Ginger tore her gaze away from the mirror
and aimed it—like a spear—at me. "You're a snotty little

shit, aren't you? I knew it the minute I met you. I'm glad you're working for me, but I'm not at all pleased with your attitude. You think I'm an arrogant bitch, and it shows."

She had me there. I did think she was an arrogant bitch. I was surprised, though, that she had detected my feelings so accurately. I hadn't realized that she was such an *observant* arrogant bitch.

"Does it matter to you what I think?" I asked.

"Not in the least," she insisted. "I just didn't want you to imagine that you had me fooled."

"I can assure you that such a notion never entered my head."

"Good. At least we understand each other." Returning her attention to her mirror image, Ginger took a tube of lipstick out of her purse and applied another coat of coral muck to her mouth. "I'm going back to the table now," she said, swiveling around in her chair toward the door. "I'm sure you can find your way back by yourself."

"Wait!" I yelped, in shock. Why was she being so nasty and evasive? Had she forgotten that she had *asked* me to help her, that I was trying to save her life? "If I'm ever going to get anywhere in this investigation," I urged, "there's a lot I need to know. For instance, are you in love with Leo? How long have you been married? Is he a good husband?" Once I got started, I couldn't stop. "Do you have a will or any life insurance? What's your relationship with your sister like? When did she marry Rusty Burnett, and what kind of man is he?" So many questions, so little time.

No time, as it turned out. The door to the lounge swung open and three coifed, perfumed, and tipsy young women walked in. They recognized Ginger immediately and began giggling and whispering among themselves. I could tell they wanted to stop and talk to her, but—to my great relief—they kept right on walking and passed through the door to the lavatory.

"I can't answer those questions now," Ginger said. "I've got to get out of here quick. If I'm still around when those bid-dies come out of the john, I'll be signing autographs for a god-damn week."

"So, when *can* you answer them?" I pressed. "I'm work-ing in the total dark here!"

"Tomorrow at brunch," she promised, adding that Woodrow would pick me up at eleven, on the same street where we'd met this evening.

"Okay," I conceded. What else could I do? (For a moment I considered flogging the facts out of her, but soon realized my muscles were no match for hers.)

Ginger checked her reflection in the mirror again and gave her hair another pat. Then she stood up from her chair, picked up her purse, looked me straight in the eye, and said, "There *is* one thing I should tell you, though"

"What's that?" I begged, hoping she had something to say about the potential murder I still felt obliged (and determined) to prevent.

"You look awful in those glasses," she declared. "They're ridiculous. Why the hell are you wearing them?"

Big sigh of frustration. "I didn't want anybody to recog-nize me."

"*You?*" she hooted. "Why would anybody recognize *you?*" Her green eyes were glinting with gleeful contempt.

"As you know, my picture was in the paper a couple of months ago. I was afraid somebody might remember it."

"I wouldn't worry about that if I were you."

"Why?"

"Because your face is so forgettable it's funny."

My search for clues came screeching to a stop. Now I knew the true identity of the person who wanted to kill Gin-ger Allen. It was me.

YOU'RE PROBABLY WONDERING WHY I didn't walk out right then and there. How could I sit there and take such taunting and relentless verbal abuse? Well, for one thing, I was used to that kind of mistreatment. Pomeroy, Mike, and Mario had been dishing it out to me on a daily basis at the office. And besides that, I was hooked—no, not on the abuse, silly, but on the investigation itself. I was raring to solve the *Who's-Trying-to-Kill-Ginger-Allen?* puzzle before it was too late, and I was avid to uncover all the facts that would bring the would-be assassin to justice. Both my curiosity and my conscience had, as usual, gotten the best of me.

Oh, there was one other reason, too. I was really hungry, and I wanted to see what the broiled royal squab Casanova tasted like.

Another big boo-boo. The squab (which I learned, to my horror, was *pigeon!*) was dry, and the gloppy stuff they poured on top of it looked and tasted like papier-mâché paste. (I ate my share of that stuff as a kid, so I know what I'm talking about.) The flaming crêpes suzette I had for dessert weren't all that great, either. And they almost set my bangs on fire.

Still, I wouldn't have given a damn about the dinner if the conversation had been at all edifying. But it wasn't, of course. (Why should my luck at turning up any good leads change now?) Ginger was doing all the talking, prattling on and on and on about how wonderful her college years had been, how many great plays she'd starred in, how many handsome athletes had fallen head over heels for her irresistible charms, how many wild parties she'd gone to, and blah, blah, blah.

I tried to change the subject a couple of times, to get some of the *other* people at the table to talk about themselves, but my efforts were a total bust. When I asked Leo what his work was like—how many TV shows he produced, and so forth—he just gave me a suspicious look and asked me why I wanted to know. I muttered some inane comment about being a big fan of the television arts, and took another sip of my café diable. I tried to bring Claire into the conversation by asking her where she and Rusty lived, but she just stared down at the white tablecloth and gave me a one-word answer: "Levittown." And when I inquired how she liked living in that enormous, fairly new Long Island housing development, she expanded her reply to two words: "It's okay."

I tried to get Rusty and Theo to talk about their jobs on Ginger's show, but neither one was in a communicative mood. Rusty seemed too uncomfortable to say anything in front of Theo, and Theo seemed too drunk to say anything in front of anybody. Tex and Toni were still distraught about what had happened earlier, so I left them alone.

Finally, I'd had enough. (More than enough, if the truth be known.) The second I finished my after-dinner cigarette and stubbed it out in the Stork Club's signature ashtray (a big black bowl of a thing that took up half the table), I thanked my hosts and announced that I was leaving.

"Don't be ridiculous," Ginger said. "We're going on to Toots Shor's for a nightcap. You'll come with us and Woodrow will drive you to your hotel later."

No way, Doris Day! I felt if I had to spend one more minute in the company of these fragile, angry, hurt, rapacious, controlled, and controlling people, I'd go insane. I told Ginger I had a migraine headache and would catch my own cab home.

I was lying, of course—about the headache *and* the cab. After giving the coatcheck girl a dollar (a whole dollar!) to retrieve Abby's fur jacket for me, I just had enough left for the subway. That was fine with me, though. The subway was fast, and the faster I could get away from there, the better.

Chapter 11

I GOT HOME A LITTLE AFTER MIDNIGHT.
Hoping Abby would still be up and in the mood for a pow-wow, I stood with my ear to her door for a few seconds, listening for sounds of activity. But all was quiet within. No jazz on the hi-fi, no poetry recital by Jimmy, no barks of excitement from Otto. I heard the phone ringing in my own apartment, though, and hurriedly let myself in to answer it.

"Where have you been?" Dan said, sounding upset. "This is the third time I've called. I thought you'd be home all night, slaving away on Mike's story."

"I *was* slaving away," I said, "but at the office, not here." (Don't look at me that way! At least *most* of my testimony was true! Just change the word "office" to "Stork Club" and you've got a statement I could swear to.)

"Why did you go into the office?" Dan wanted to know. "Did you have to use the clip files?"

Wasn't it sweet of him to provide me with the perfect excuse? "Yep!" I said, trying to sound breezy and casual, choosing not to elaborate (it didn't seem like such a whopping fib that way).

Dan let out a reproachful groan. "I'm not happy about that,

Paige. You know I don't like you walking the streets and riding the subway by yourself so late at night. It's not safe—or suitable—for a woman."

Jeez! Haven't I had to defend my solitary female status enough for one night? I took off my gloves and Abby's jacket and slapped everything down on the couch. "Suitable?" I croaked, temperature rising. (The way Dan was talking, you'd think being a widowed working girl was a disgrace!) "You believe my conduct wasn't *suitable?*" I was teetering on the verge of outrage.

"Well, I, uh—"

"Listen!" I cut in. "I'm unmarried and I have to work for a living. And sometimes I have to work in the office at night. And since I don't own a car, or make enough money to take cabs, I have to walk a few blocks and take the subway to get to the office. And then, when I've finished doing the work for which I will, because I'm a woman, be very poorly paid, I have to walk a few more blocks and catch another subway train to get back home. So it seems to me that my behavior tonight was entirely *suited* to my circumstances. Can you give me one good reason why it wasn't?"

"All right! Enough!" Dan said, laughing. "I get your point. My word choice was totally *un*suitable. I'm sorry."

"Apology accepted," I said, hating myself for using my honest indignation to cover up my big fat fabrication, but loving Dan to pieces for being such an open-hearted, open-minded man (about some things, at any rate).

"So did you finish the story?" he asked. "Can we get together tomorrow as planned?"

"Sorry, babe, no can do. I've completed the research, but I haven't written a word yet. I'll be chained to my desk all day and night." (It's amazing how, once you've produced the initial lie, the sequels just keep on coming.)

"Too bad. I really miss you, kid. And I'm going to be involved in a big case next week, so I don't know when I'll be able to stop by."

"What case is that?" I asked, jumping at the opportunity to change the subject.

"You really think I'm going to tell you?" Dan said, laughing again. "The last thing I need is for you to be sniffing around at my heels, trying to dig up details for a new story."

"I agreed not to do that anymore, remember?"

"Yes, and since I want you to live up to that agreement, I think it's best if I don't tempt you with any tidbits."

"Spoilsport."

Dan was silent for a second, then muttered, "How many times do I have to tell you, Paige? Homicide is *not* a sport." I could almost see the stern but adorable look on his face. (Dan looks so cute when he's serious.)

"No, but *you* are," I teased, "and a darn good sport, too. And I miss you so much I can taste it. Can you come over for a while tonight, after you get off work?" I was exhausted and preoccupied, but I still wanted to see him. (Okay, I wanted to *feel* him too, but that's really none of your beeswax.)

"Now I'm the one who has to say no," Dan replied. "I've got at least two hours of paperwork to go before I knock off. You'll be sound asleep by then."

"I guess you're right. I'm so tired I'm almost sound asleep right now."

"I'll say goodnight then, Paige. Go to bed. Sweet dreams."

I gave Dan a grateful phone smooch, dropped the receiver in the cradle, and wearily climbed the stairs to my bedroom. Sweet dreams would be nice, I mused, but after the dreadful evening I'd just been through, even a nightmare would be welcome.

TURNING OVER IN BED AND OPENING MY eyes (a rather difficult task since my lids were glued shut with mascara), I caught sight of the clock on my night table. It was 9:45! *In the morning!* (I deduced this fact from the streaks of bright sunlight shooting through the sides of my bedroom window shade. Am I a slick detective, or what?)

"Oh, lordy!" I squealed aloud, leaping out of bed in a bugeyed panic. (Whenever I'm really upset about something, I tend to act like Hattie McDaniel.) I had a mere hour and fifteen minutes to get dressed for brunch at Ginger's and race

over to 6th Avenue to meet Woodrow! And what the hell was
I supposed to wear? My one good dress was at the cleaners.
And Ginger had said we'd be going on to the Copa later! *Oh,
lordy, lordy, lordy!*

I didn't even put on my bathrobe. I just ran barefoot down
the stairs in Bob's old Army T-shirt, lunged like a lunatic out
into the hall, and began pounding on Abby's door with the
side of my fist. "Abby! Abby! Are you up yet?" I bellowed,
knowing darn well she wouldn't be. As far as Abby was concerned, Sunday mornings had been invented just for sleeping
(or other supine bedroom activities).

"Please, Abby!" I cried. "Please open up and let me in. I
need help!" When she didn't answer, I started kicking the
door with my heel.

Finally, after more than a few minutes of my hollering and
pounding and kicking, she unlocked the door and yanked it
open. "Oh my God, Paige! What's the matter?" she shrieked.
"Are you all right?" Her loose black hair was flying in all directions and her red chiffon nightie was swirling around her
voluptuous torso like a tornado.

"I'm in big trouble, Abby! You've got to help me!"

She pulled me inside and slammed the door. "What's happening?" she sputtered, grasping my shoulders with both
hands. "Is somebody stalking you? Did somebody break into
your apartment? Has somebody tried to kill you?"

"No, no! It's nothing like that!" I cried. "I didn't mean to
scare you. I just wanted to wake you up."

Abby dropped her hands from my shoulders and gave me
a dirty look—a *very* dirty look. "Are you out of your idiotic
mind?! How could you do that to me? I almost had a heart attack! It was just a few months ago that I saw you shot and
bleeding on your kitchen floor, you know! It took me four
solid hours to clean your splattered cabinet doors and mop the
sea of blood up off your goddamn linoleum! How dare you
come banging on my door and screaming your stupid head off
like this? I thought you got shot again. I thought you might be
dying!"

"Sorry, Ab," I said, ashamed of being so thoughtless. "I

never meant to alarm you. Please believe me! I just didn't think. I got up very late, and I was so wigged out about what I was going to wear to Ginger Allen's brunch this morning, that I just lost my head altogether. I've got to meet Ginger's chauffeur in less than an hour, and I've got to look chic. And I've got to wear something that will be good for the evening, too, since Ginger said we were going to the Copa for dinner. Oh, God, what am I going to do? My black dress is at the cleaners! Do you think I could get by with my navy sheath?"

"Oh, no!" she protested, mood changing on a dime. "You look like a *shmegegge* in that *focockta shmatte!* Stay right here. I'll go upstairs and find you something." She twirled around and scrambled up the stairs in a red chiffon whirlwind. Hell hath no fury like Abby Moskowitz contending with a fashion emergency.

While she was gone, I snatched a cigarette from the pack of Chesterfields sitting on the kitchen table and smoked it in one puff (okay, so maybe it was three or four puffs, but the point is, I was fuming fiercely). I'd have smoked another one, too, if Otto hadn't worked his way down the steps—kind of sliding on his belly since his legs were so short—and come scuttling over to me. I snatched him up in my arms, sat down at the table, and settled the little pooch on my lap, stroking him from head to tail in a warm, languid, steady rhythm that did us both a world of good.

"Here!" Abby cried, tearing down the stairs with two hangers of clothes held high in one hand. "This should do the trick. It's a silver-gray suit with a hot-pink silk shell. You can wear the jacket buttoned for the brunch, then later, when you get to the Copa, you can take it off and be a hot-pink knock-out. I did a painting of this getup for a B. Altman catalog and the model was just your size."

"Gee, thanks, Abby," I gushed, putting Otto down on the floor and standing up to take the hangers from her hand. "You're a lifesaver. I don't know what I'd—"

"Yeah, yeah, yeah," she interrupted. "You don't know what you'd do without me. It seems I've heard that song before." She bent over and scooped Otto up in her arms. "I, on the other hand, know exactly what I'd do without *you*." She winked at me and walked over to the foot of the steps. "I'd go right back upstairs and crawl back into bed with Jimmy, you dig?"

I dug. I blew her a kiss and hurtled home to get dressed.

I WAS TEN MINUTES LATE, BUT WOOD-row didn't seem to mind. As he opened the car door for me, a wide, white smile split his broad, brown face in two. "Mornin', miss," he said. "Mighty fine day."

Frankly, I hadn't noticed. I'd been so focused on my feet (running down city sidewalks in stiletto heels isn't easy) that the crispness of the bright spring air and the splendor of the clear blue sky had escaped my attention. "Yes, it is, Woodrow," I said, taking note of the budding dogwoods lining the avenue and filling my lungs with their fragrance. "A very fine day, indeed." I hoped the rest of the day would be fine too, but I had a sneaking suspicion it wouldn't.

Woodrow helped me into the car, hustled himself into the driver's seat, and pulled out into the northbound traffic. As I prepared to lean forward to ask him a few questions, I saw that two peculiar stool-sized objects were protruding from the back of the front seat.

"What are these things sticking out back here, Woodrow? Are they chairs? Can you sit on them?"

"Uh, yes, miss. That's what they're made for. They're extra seats for when you've got more people in the car. I pulled them out for Mr. and Mrs. Burnett last night. I musta forgot to close 'em up afterward."

Well, that was all I needed to hear. In the bat of an eye, I was sitting sideways on the stool protruding from the passenger's side, with my right arm folded over the backrest and my chin propped on my wrist. "This is great!" I said. "Now I can see you and talk to you without straining my spine or breaking my neck!"

Woodrow wasn't as thrilled about the new seating arrangement as I was. He turned and gave me a nervous look, let out a troubled sigh, then quickly returned his eyes to the road. I was sitting too close for comfort (his, not mine), but for the sake of my investigation (and the shape of my backbone) I chose to stay put.

"So Mr. and Mrs. Burnett were in the car with Miss Allen and Mr. Marx last night," I said. "Was anybody else with them?" I felt pressured to get the questioning underway. The Sunday morning traffic was light and we had reached 38th Street already.

"No, miss," Woodrow said. "It was just the four of them. They went from the Stork Club to Toots Shor's. And then, about three o'clock in the morning, they came out and I drove them home right quick. Miss Allen wasn't feeling good."

My sneaking suspicion snuck all the way up to my scalp, making my hair stand on end. "Oh, no!" I said. "What was wrong with her? Was she sick?" Now I was the one getting sick. *Why, oh, why didn't I stay with her last night?*

"I don't know if she was sick or just inebriated, miss. She couldn't hardly walk by herself. Mr. Marx and Mr. Burnett had to brace her up between them, strap their arms around her back, and lug her out to the car. Then they laid her down on the back seat." He shot me an anxious glance. "I asked did they want me to drive her to the hospital, miss, but Mr. Marx, he said no. He said she just needed to get home and get to bed."

"That's all he said?" Seemed kind of cold-hearted to me.

"Well, no, miss," Woodrow went on. "He said something about bad publicity, too. He told Mr. Burnett that if any of the newspapers got wind of what happened, Miss Allen would lose a lot of fans."

"And how did Mr. Burnett respond to that? Was he concerned about Miss Allen's physical condition?"

"No, miss, can't say as he was. He laughed out loud and said Mr. Marx had the right idea—that home in bed was where Miss Allen belonged."

"He *laughed?*"

"That's right, miss."

"Was Miss Allen's sister upset?"

"Can't rightly say, miss. She didn't let on."

I sat quietly for a few minutes, spinning the new information around in my skull. Had Ginger simply had too much to drink, or had somebody poisoned her nightcap? Why did Leo want to take her home instead of to the hospital? Did he believe she just needed to sleep it off, or was he hoping she would sleep forever? And why had Rusty laughed? Because he found humor in Ginger's drunkenness, or because he found joy in the thought that she might soon be dead?

Number of questions: eight. Number of answers: zilch.

At that particular moment, though, there was only one question that really mattered, and it was burning like a bonfire in my brain: *Is Ginger still alive?*

"Did you speak to Miss Allen this morning, Woodrow?" I asked, keeping my voice soft and steady so as not to frighten him. I was surprised he seemed so unsuspecting, but I was glad he was being calm. One crazy person was enough for one car. "I hope she's feeling better."

"I don't know how she's feeling, miss, on account of I didn't hear from her today."

"No?" Abject terror time. "Then how did you know when and where to pick me up?"

"She told me last night, miss, when I was dropping them off at Toots Shor's. As soon as the other folks got out of the car, she leaned over and whispered the time and place to me, said I had to keep it secret. Said if anybody asked, I should pretend I was picking you up at the Waldorf instead of downtown in the Village."

"I see," I said, still working to keep my panic under wraps. I was aching to ask Woodrow to turn on the radio so I could listen for breaking news bulletins (okay, death bulletins), but—in the interest of preserving his present, and possibly short-lived, peace of mind—I kept my raging curiosity contained. "How much farther do we have to go, Woodrow? Where does Miss Allen live?" I peered out the window and saw that we were on Madison Avenue now, crossing 74th.

"Just three blocks ahead, Miss, and one block over. Fifth Avenue and Seventy-seventh. Corner building. We'll be there in a jiffy."

It may have been a jiffy, but it felt like a decade to me. (Time crawls when you're having a nervous breakdown.) As soon as we turned the corner onto Fifth, however, my breathing slowed down and my blood pressure dropped below bursting. There was no ambulance in sight. There were no police cars parked in front of Ginger's building; no hordes of photographers and reporters swarming the street and sidewalk; no wailing, grieving fans.

So far, so good.

Woodrow pulled up next to the maroon awning stretching from the entrance of Ginger's building to the curb, got out of the car, and—jumping in front of the approaching doorman—opened the back door for me. I was out of that limo in a flash. "Where do I go, Woodrow? What's the apartment number?"

"No number, miss. Just take the elevator all the way up to the top. Miss Allen and Mr. Marx live on the whole fourteenth floor—the penthouse."

I patted Woodrow's sleeve, thanked him for the ride, and—springing ahead of the uniformed doorman—pushed my way into the building.

Chapter 12

I WHISKED THROUGH THE LUXURIOUS lobby barely noticing the marble floors, vases of fresh flowers, and Tiffany fixtures. Even the man sitting behind the desk near the elevator made little to no impression. I remember telling him I was there to see Ginger Allen, and I think he asked for my name, but I don't recall if I said it was Paige—or Patty—Turner. And if he made a call on the house phone after that, I have no memory of what he said. My mind was doing the mambo (i.e., writhing and bumping with so many feverish fears and fantasies I felt dizzy).

What if Ginger was in the process of dying, that very minute, in her bed upstairs? I knew from various *Daring Detective* stories I'd written or edited that some poisons took a long time to work. Or maybe she was dead already! Maybe Leo had poisoned Ginger's drink at Toots Shor's, waited a couple of hours until she collapsed, and then hauled her home to die, figuring her autopsy would prove when the poison had been administered, and that his name would become just one in a *very* long list of suspects (i.e., everybody who'd been in the nightclub that night). And maybe Leo was now keeping Ginger's demise a secret from the household help (and, by ex-

tension, the police and the press) for as long as possible—a
relatively easy task since it wasn't yet noon and Ginger could,
in all believability, still be sleeping.

Or maybe Rusty was the murderer. Or even Claire! They
had been at the nightclub, too. Either one of them could have
slipped the cyanide or arsenic or strychnine into Ginger's
nightcap. And, considering that Woodrow hadn't brought
them all back to the penthouse until sometime after three this
morning, and that a heck of a lot of alcohol had probably been
consumed by that time, it was entirely possible that the innocent but inebriated Leo was now sleeping it off on the couch,
unaware that his wife was lying dead in her bed in the other
room.

And what about Theolonius Kidd and Tex and Toni Taylor? Any one or all three of them could have reconnected with
Ginger and her party at Toots Shor's. So it was conceivable
that one of them had dispensed the toxic dose and then shuffled his or her merry way home, looking forward to reading
the grim reports of Ginger's sudden death in the next day's
newspapers. I had no idea what Theo's motive might have
been, but I had a pretty clear notion how certain intense professional ambitions might have driven Tex or Toni to commit
the dirty deed.

So can you dig the crazy state I was in? Do you understand
the way my mind was reeling with possible murder schemes?
And churning with glaring suspicions? And jumping to wild
conclusions? Can you imagine the tension (okay, trepidation)
with which I entered the wood-paneled elevator and allowed
the uniformed operator to propel me skyward to the penthouse?

Because if you can, then you'll also understand why I almost fainted when a strange, tall, ghastly looking man in a
black mourning suit—a glowering mortician, for God's
sake!—opened the door to Ginger's apartment and motioned
for me to enter. Okay, okay! So it turned out he wasn't really
a mortician but rather a butler who just *looked* like a mortician. Still, you can't blame a girl in my overheated condition
for making rash presumptions.

Or for acting like a damn fool, either. "Where is she?" I spluttered, staggering into the marble entryway and bracing my back against the wall for balance. "I want to see her right now! If you know what's good for you, you'll take me to her this minute!" In an effort to look strong and masterful, I stepped away from the wall and stamped my foot on the floor. If Ginger was by some miracle still alive, I was determined with all my *Daring Detective* heart to see that she remained that way.

"To whom are you referring?" the butler intoned, looking down his long skinny nose at me. "Who is it you wish to see?"

"Don't play games with me!" I roared, stamping my foot again. "I want to see Ginger Allen, and I want to see her *now!*"

"What's the trouble, Boynton?" came a deep, mellifluous voice from around the corner, accompanied by quickly advancing footsteps. "Is there some kind of problem?" I recognized the pleasing voice immediately, so I wasn't surprised when the decidedly *un*pleasing face and body of Leo Marx marched into view.

Leo, on the other hand, seemed more than a little surprised to see me. "What are you doing here, Mrs. Turner?" he said, scowling, walking over to me but not offering his hand. "Didn't Ginger call to tell you the brunch was canceled?"

Uh oh!

"No, she didn't," I said, thrown for a loop, madly searching my addled brain for a way to deal with this new development. "I was home all morning and the phone didn't ring once!"

"That's odd," Leo said, looking perplexed. (For real or by design? I couldn't tell.) "She told me that she spoke to you." His great beak of a nose was wrinkled in contempt. (For me or for Ginger? I couldn't say.)

"Well, she *didn't!*" I insisted, telling the god's honest truth for once, but feeling like a faker just the same. "The last time I spoke to her was last night, when I was leaving the Stork Club. And she reminded me of the brunch right before we said good night. Why would she cancel it all of a sudden?"

Leo's swarthy scowl turned even swarthier. "That will be

all, Boynton," he said to the butler, indicating with a sharp jerk of his head that the ghoulish man should go away and leave us alone. And be damn quick about it.

"Yes, sir," Boynton said, giving Leo a stiff little bow. Then he spun around on his heels and strode out of the foyer, disappearing down a corridor to the right.

I wasn't sorry to see him go.

Leo listened to Boynton's retreating footsteps for a few seconds, not saying a word until the butler was out of earshot. Then he pierced me with an icy stare and declared, "Ginger canceled the brunch because she's not feeling well, Mrs. Turner. I apologize for any inconvenience this may have caused you, but now I really must ask you to leave. My wife needs her rest."

Yeah, right! I muttered to myself. *If I leave now, she may be resting for all eternity!*

"I'd like to see her before I go," I said, standing firm and tall. (Thanks to my skyscraper high heels, I had Leo beat by a good three inches.)

"That's impossible," he said. "She's sleeping. She doesn't want to be disturbed."

"I promise I won't disturb her," I explained. "I'll just stick my head in, say hello, and see if there's anything I can do for her. She'll feel better just knowing I'm here." I had no intention of leaving that apartment until I had determined the true status of Ginger's health.

Leo was getting mad. He clearly wasn't used to having his dictates disputed. Especially by pushy, loud-mouthed, four-eyed females like me.

The instant *that* thought crossed my mind, I almost had a stroke. The glasses! They were still in my purse! In all my craziness and confusion I had forgotten to put them on. Had Leo recognized me and figured out my real name? Did he know the real reason I was there? I yanked the spectacles out of my bag and slapped them on my face, praying to all my lucky stars that I hadn't blown my cover.

As far as I could see (which, thanks to the glasses, was less than an inch in front of my nose), Leo had no reaction to my sudden change in appearance. He was too busy reacting to my dogged demands to see Ginger. "I must insist that you leave now, Mrs. Turner. This may come as a great shock to you," he said, voice slimy with sarcasm, "but there's nothing whatsoever you can do for my wife. Your help is not required. We have servants to attend to all her needs." His derogatory tone was, I decided, intended to offend me, to make me fly out of there in an angry huff.

Ha! Leo didn't know who he was up against. I wasn't about to fly anywhere—except to Ginger's rescue. "Will you show me the way to your wife's bedroom, or do I have to find it myself?" I croaked, sweeping past Leo's shadowy form, and heading like an idiot for the entryway I knew was there, but couldn't quite perceive. I almost made it, too. A mere fourteen inches to the left, and I would have been breezing into the living room, instead of barreling, like a defective robot, smack into the foyer wall.

"Mrs. Turner!" Leo cried, as I stumbled back from the marble partition, whimpering, cradling my cracked noggin with one hand. "Have you hurt yourself? Are you okay?"

I was shocked by the unexpected collision, but even more shocked by Leo's concern. He sounded, for one brief inexplicable moment, as though he actually cared! "I, uh, I'm okay, Mr. Marx . . . at least I think I am." I felt like a total dodo, but I didn't say anything about that.

"Let me take a look," Leo murmured, walking up close to me and removing my hand from my still-throbbing forehead. His touch was cool, but kindly. "You're not bleeding," he said, "but you'll probably have a big lump on your head by this evening. I'd better have Boynton make you an ice pack."

"Oh," I said, not knowing how to respond. I was struck speechless by Leo's sympathetic behavior. And I was even more astonished when—out of the amazing, everloving blue—he took me by the hand and led me, like a child, out of the foyer and into the living room.

"Come with me, Mrs. Turner," he said. "I'll take you in to see Ginger now."

*   *   *

HER BEDROOM WAS AS DARK AS A TOMB.
She was lying flat on her back in an enormous bed with a pink
satin sheet pulled up under her chin. A ruffled pink satin sleep
mask covered her eyes. (At least I thought the sheet and mask
were pink. The lack of light in the room made the colors hard
to pin down.) She was lying so perfectly still that she looked
more dead than alive. Actually, she didn't look alive at all.

"Are you awake, dear?" Leo whispered, tiptoeing closer to
the bed, gingerly touching Ginger's shoulder. "Mrs. Turner is
here to see you. She wants to know how you're feeling."

When Ginger didn't move or groan or respond in any way,
a chill shot down my spine. I snatched my glasses off my face
and took a fuller, totally unimpeded look. *She really is dead!*
I screamed to myself. *And Leo is either putting on a great act,
or he doesn't even know she's gone!* I was so upset I thought
I was going to fall over dead myself.

Leo leaned down until his mouth was nearly touching her
ear. "Can you hear me, dear?" he murmured. "Are you awake?"

That did it. "Well, I am *now!*" she screeched, sitting bolt
upright in the bed, tearing the sleep mask off her face in a
fury. "How could I sleep in all this racket? I thought I told you
to leave me alone!"

Not only was Ginger still alive, she was *kicking.* (And her
foot was nowhere near the bucket.)

"Don't blame your husband," I quickly broke in, stepping
closer to the bed. "The fault is all mine. When he told me that
you weren't feeling well, I insisted on seeing you. I practically
forced him to bring me in here." I didn't want Ginger to blame
Leo for my mistake, and I wanted to make sure she realized
how desperately worried I had been—how utterly seriously I
was taking her claim that someone was trying to kill her.

"Patty!" she snorted, ignoring the import of my confession. "What the hell are you doing here? I told you the brunch
was canceled."

"No you didn't," I said, annoyed by her accusatory tone.

"I did too!" she snapped. "I called you this morning and
told you not to come."

"No, you didn't," I repeated, seething inside. "And you

didn't tell Woodrow, either, because he came to pick me up at the very time you said he would." First I'd been frantic that Ginger might be dead—now I was sorry she wasn't.

"Well, I *meant* to tell you," she said, shaking her hair out with her fingers, looking totally unconcerned (not to mention unapologetic). "I guess I fell asleep instead." Leaning back against the plush pink satin pillows and padded pink satin headboard of her vast, magnificent bed, she breathed a discontented sigh. "Open the drapes, Leo, and light me a cigarette. Then go tell Boynton to bring me some coffee."

As Leo whisked over to the window to obey the first of Ginger's orders, I marveled to myself how self-assured (okay, self-*centered*) the country's second-most famous redhead was. "Bring *me* some coffee," she had said. The word *us* probably didn't exist in her whole narcissistic vocabulary! (Which really teed me off since I hadn't had a thing to eat or drink all morning, and I was in dire need of caffeine. And maybe a sandwich. Deviled ham or chicken salad would've been nice. I had, after all, been expecting a whole brunch!)

Leo pulled the heavy brocade drapes open and sunlight poured into the room, revealing that all the satin trappings of Ginger's enormous bed were, indeed, pink, and that Ginger's normally peachy complexion was as white as a sheet (a plain cotton one, I mean). She was either sick, or she had a humongous hangover. Or maybe she really *had* been poisoned, I mused, remembering from my research that some wealthy society ladies of the Victorian era had taken small but regular amounts of arsenic to make—and keep—their skin fashionably pale.

Leo put a heavy cut-glass ashtray down on the night table, gave Ginger a cigarette, then lit it for her with a large silver table lighter. "I'll go see about the coffee," he said, making a hasty retreat across the soft gray cloud of a carpet and letting himself out of the bedroom, clicking the door closed behind him.

"Are you okay, Ginger?" I asked as soon as he was gone. "You look a little under the weather. What happened after I left last night?" I pulled the chair away from the pink satin-skirted dressing table, shoved it over to the bed, and sat down.

Ginger gave me a nasty sneer and exhaled a stream of smoke in my direction. "I feel like shit, if you must know. And I don't have any idea what happened. One minute I was laughing and drinking and telling Tex and Toni why they should be satisfied to stay in radio, and the next thing I knew my head was spinning like a goddamn top. I almost fell off my goddamn chair! And I don't remember a thing after that."

"Did you have too much to drink, or do you think you were poisoned?"

"How dare you ask me that question?! I'm no lousy drunk! Of course I was poisoned!" Her green eyes were glowing in outrage. "It's a goddamn miracle I didn't die."

A miracle or a pity? I wasn't so sure.

"Who do you think did it?" I asked, hoping she had finally noticed *something* suspicious, that she would have at least one teensy-weensy little clue to offer.

But that would have been a *true* miracle. "How the hell am I supposed to know?" she shrieked. "That's *your* job! And if you had come with us to Toots Shor's like I told you to, then you could have seen what was happening. You could have prevented me from drinking the poison and nailed the person who's trying to kill me in one goddamn swoop!"

To say that Ginger was mad would be like calling a hurricane drafty. Now *she* wanted to kill *me*. And I had to admit I understood her position. I should have stayed with her last night. I was wrong to abandon her the way I did. I was a rotten detective. I was a slothful sleuth!

"Did you tell Leo that you were poisoned?" I probed. "Did you ask him to call a doctor?"

"Are you crazy? If Leo knew somebody was trying to kill me, he'd call the police and the FBI and the CIA as well as the doctor. He'd call President Eisenhower, for Christ's sake! He'd cause such a scene, my ass would be fried. I'd be in even more danger than I am now." Ginger took another drag on her cigarette and exhaled the fumes in my face. "So I haven't had any medical attention. And now, thanks to you, pussycat, I'm

so sick I can't move. I think I've suffered some nerve damage.
I tried to get up and go to the bathroom before, but I can't
even stand up by myself, let alone walk. I may be crippled for
life, and it's all your fault."

I was about to mumble something in my own defense, but
when Leo opened the door and helped Boynton wheel a
breakfast cart into the bedroom, my words got stuck in my
mouth. I couldn't speak freely in front of Ginger's husband,
or her spooky butler, either. And besides, once I saw that there
were two cups next to the coffee pot, and two glasses of or-
ange juice, and two plates of bacon, scrambled eggs, and toast
sitting on the cart, my need to defend myself evaporated completely.

My stomach, it seemed, was much hungrier than my ego.

Chapter 13

"GET THAT GODDAMN FOOD OUT OF here!" Ginger bellowed. "It's disgusting! The smell is making me nauseous!"

Was she testing me, trying to determine how much torture I could take? I gave Leo a look of sheer desperation, which he quickly comprehended and—joy to the world!—responded to. "Sorry, darling," he said to his irate wife. "I thought you and Mrs. Turner might be hungry. But since you're not, and Mrs. Turner surely is, Boynton will wheel the table out to the terrace, where your friend can sit and enjoy her meal without disturbing you." Without waiting for a reply, Leo opened the French doors leading to the terrace and Boynton pushed the cart outside.

I was so grateful for Leo's courtesy I could have kissed his scrawny neck. But I still didn't trust him. What had brought about this sudden change in his personality? Why was he being so nice to me? And which Leo was the real Leo—the polite and considerate man standing before me now, or the cold, ruthless (and possibly murderous) TV producer I'd met last night?

"Thank you, Mr. Marx," I said, stepping out onto the balcony before Ginger could kick up a fuss. "It was kind of you to bring this lovely breakfast."

"There's an ice bag on the cart, too," he said. "You should apply it to your forehead as soon as you've finished eating." He nodded and gave me a tight little smile. "I'll close the doors now, so the food odors won't drift inside." He dismissed Boynton and they both disappeared.

I sat down at the cart in the warm spring sunshine and devoured my breakfast. Then I devoured Ginger's, too. (Well, it could have been poisoned, you know! And after the way I'd failed her last night, I felt I owed her my utmost protection now.) After finishing off the feast, I took a few moments to guzzle a second cup of coffee and survey my surroundings.

The long, straight, narrow terrace stretched like a runway along the entire 77th Street side of the penthouse, from the master bedroom, past the dining room, to the living room. Each room opened onto the terrace through a series of glass-paned French doors. The waist-high stone walls of the balcony were crawling with English ivy, and the polished flagstone floor was bordered with large hand-painted pots containing numerous different species of plants and trees. It was a lush and beautiful setting.

Picking up the ice bag and holding it to my head, I rose to my feet, walked over to the edge of the balcony, leaned over the wall, and gazed down at the tops of the trees and the roofs of the cars lining the street below. Surprised at how high the fourteenth floor was, I watched with childlike delight the doll-sized people strolling down the sidewalk. And when I raised my head and shifted my gaze to the left, I was treated to an airy, dreamy, bird's-eye view of Central Park.

Then Ginger threw open the balcony doors and brought me back down to earth. "Where's my goddamn coffee?!" she howled, standing legs apart in the doorway. With her sheer black negligee clinging to her ultra-white skin and her flame-red hair shooting sparks in the sunlight, she looked like a demon, a hellcat, a comic strip Brenda Starr gone wrong. "I was waiting for you to bring me some coffee," she said, "but you never did!"

"Sorry," I said, even though I wasn't. "I didn't realize . . ." I broke off my words and paused for a moment, staring at her sturdy limbs, taking in the full effect of her strong, surefooted posture. "Hey! You're walking!" I said. "That's great! I guess you're not crippled for life after all."

Ginger looked down at her bare feet and then sheepishly back up at me. "Well, I can't walk *far*," she whined, "and my legs are in terrible pain. I've got to lie down this minute! Come inside and bring me some coffee. Heavy on the cream and sugar." With that, she whipped herself around and leapt like a gazelle back to her bed.

I FIXED GINGER'S COFFEE AND, LEAV-ing the ice pack and my glasses outside on the cart, carried the china cup and saucer in to her night table. I was so used to serving coffee to the guys at work, the demeaning chore was barely bothersome. (Okay, okay! So it bothered me a lot! I didn't like being treated like a maidservant—by Ginger Allen or anybody. But you might as well know this about me right now: I'd serve a cup of my own blood to Count Dracula if I thought it would help me prevent or solve a murder and write a good story.)

"So who was with you at Toots Shor's last night?" I asked, sitting down on the chair near her bed. "I take it Tex and Toni were there. Did Thelonious Kidd go, too?"

"Yes," she said. "Everybody who was at dinner with us went. Everybody but you." She took a few gulps of her coffee, giving me a dirty look over the rim of the cup.

"Did you run into anybody else you know?"

"Of course! Toots always gets a good crowd. That's the whole point of going there—to see people."

"So who did you see?" I asked, hoping the list wouldn't be long. I had too many likely suspects to investigate already.

"Umm, well, Frank was there—Mr. Sinatra, to you—and Lana, and Rita, and Bogie and Bacall, and that hot new model, Suzy Parker, and Art Linkletter, Mamie Van Doren, Betsy Palmer, Red Buttons, Milton Berle, and—"

"Enough already!" I said, holding both hands up to stop

her recital. "I get the picture." I was relieved that all the names were famous. I couldn't imagine any one of the people she mentioned being a murderer (except maybe Uncle Milty).

"Tell me more about Leo," I said, deciding to drop the line of questioning about last night and get down to business. "How long have you two been married?"

"Oh, I don't know. Five years or so."

"Is he a good man? Does he love you?"

Ginger put her empty cup down on the night table and, sighing loudly, fell back against the mound of pink satin pillows. "Of course Leo loves me. I'm beautiful and talented and I make a lot of money. I'm the perfect wife."

Somehow I doubted that. "And is Leo the perfect husband?"

"Yes," she said, staring up at the ceiling, adding nothing.

"And are you in love with him?"

"Sure."

"So your marriage is a happy one."

"You could say that."

Aaargh! Getting Ginger to talk about her personal life was like pulling teeth. (And I don't mean itty-bitty baby teeth, either. I'm talking great big whopping, severely impacted molars.) Was she ever going to open up to me? How could I be expected to save a life I knew nothing about?

"What kind of person is Claire?" I asked, hoping Ginger would find it easier to talk about her sister than her spouse. "She's younger than you are, right?"

"Right. I'm three years older. Nobody can ever believe it." Ginger's pale, lipstickless lips curled into a self-satisfied smirk.

"Did you and Claire get along well as children?"

"Who the hell knows? She was so ugly and dull and mopey I didn't pay much attention to her."

"But you pay a lot of attention to her now," I said.

Ginger gave me a quizzical look. "Huh? Why do you say that? What do you mean?"

"I mean you take her out to the Stork Club, and to Toots Shor's, and probably lots of other fancy places, too. Places she'd never even get to set foot in without you. So you obviously feel very close to her now. I heard you even gave her husband a job on your show."

"Who told you that?" Ginger was still lying back on the pile of pillows, but she didn't look relaxed.

"Oh, I don't know," I said, lighting myself a cigarette, trying to act nonchalant. "Somebody mentioned it last night. Maybe it was Theo. Or it might have been Rusty himself . . ." (It had really been Woodrow, of course, but, like any responsible journalist, I wasn't about to reveal my anonymous source. Or get my helpful new friend in trouble with his boss.)

Ginger heaved another loud sigh and closed her eyes. "I have a hideous headache. Hand me my sleep mask. It's on the floor by the night table."

I picked the ruffled pink satin visor up from the carpet and handed it over. "You're not going back to sleep, are you?" I asked, getting nervous. "There's so much I need to know. You promised you would answer all my questions today!"

"I said that before I was poisoned, pussycat." From the tone of her voice, I half expected her to stick her tongue out at me. "And it just so happens I'm not feeling too good right now. My legs are throbbing, and my stomach is churning, and my head is so woozy I think I'm going to faint." She shot me a condemning glance and yanked the sleep mask down over her eyes. "If you had stayed with me last night, this wouldn't have happened." She burrowed her head deeper into the pillows and heaved another heavy sigh. "But now I'm sick, and hovering at death's door, and I need to rest. I'm so weak . . . I'm losing consciousness . . . I'm fading fast . . ." As if to prove her words, she lay perfectly still on her pink satin sheets and pillows—like a corpse in an expensive casket. (An uncommonly beautiful and sexy corpse, that is, wearing a black negligee and a pink blindfold. *If Abby did a painting of this scene,* I couldn't help thinking, *it would make a great* Daring Detective *cover.*)

There was a sudden loud knock on the door. Ginger's body stiffened, while mine jumped out of the chair and stood like a watchtower next to her bed.

"Who's there?" Ginger screeched. Her voice was so shrill and piercing I wished I had on my earmuffs. "What the hell do you want? I'm trying to get some sleep in here!"

Leo opened the bedroom door and stuck his head in through the crack. "I'm sorry," he said, "I didn't know you were sleeping."

"I'm sick, Leo," she scolded, "and I need my rest. I have a horrible headache. Just tell me what you want and go away."

He opened the door wider and stepped all the way into the room. "Mark Goodson's on the phone," he said. "He wants you to be the Mystery Guest on *What's My Line?* tonight."

Ginger let out a shriek that could have waked the dead. She shot up to a sitting position and ripped the sleep mask off her face. "Aha! The bastard finally called me! He took his sweet time about it, but I knew it would happen someday!" The color rushed back to her cheeks and her eyes turned bright as beacons. "So what did you tell him, Leo? Did you say I would do it?"

"I said you weren't feeling well, but that I'd talk to you about it."

"Good. Then I don't have to decide right now. I can keep the bastard waiting, like he did me."

"No you can't," Leo stressed. "He's hanging on the phone for your answer, and he wants it right away. If you can't do it, he's going to call Rosemary Clooney. She's in town to do *The Ed Sullivan Show.*"

"Jesus Christ! Haven't the viewers seen enough of that bitch already? She's on *Your Hit Parade* every goddamn Saturday night, and Perry Como had her on his show last week! Every time you turn on the set she's on the screen. If I have to listen to her sing 'This Ole House' one more time I'm going to puke!"

Neither Leo nor I reminded Ginger that *she* was on television every week, too.

"And why did that bastard Goodson call me so late in the day?" she sputtered on. "Am I just a goddamn fill-in? Somebody must have canceled on him at the last minute."

Leo nodded. "Judy Garland was scheduled for tonight, but

she got her dates mixed up and missed her flight to New York."

"That figures!" Ginger said, grinning. "Judy's so drunk and drugged-up all the time, she never knows what day it is."

"So what should I tell Mark?" Leo asked, growing impatient. "Do you want to be the Mystery Guest tonight or not?"

"Oh, all right!" she said, with an exaggerated groan. Ginger was trying to look teed off, but I knew she was secretly delighted. (One faker can always spot another.) "Tell Goodson I'm sick as a dog, but I'll do the show anyway. I owe it to my fans. And I owe it to the whole damn country to keep Rosemary Clooney off the air whenever I can."

Leo gave his wife a dubious look. "Are you sure you feel strong enough to—"

"Oh, shut up, Leo! I've been trying to get on *What's My Line?* for two goddamn years. It's the most popular game show ever! They haven't taken me because we're two different networks and they'd rather promote their own people. But my image needs a shot in the arm, and you know it. And this is the best way to get it."

Her image needs a shot in the arm? That's the first I've heard about that!

"Tell the bastard I'll be there," she said. "And find out what time he wants me."

Chapter 14

HAVE YOU EVER BEEN STUCK IN AN AIR-
plane during a thunderstorm? There you are, strapped in a seat
you can't get out of, while the cabin bounces back and forth,
and dips up and down, like Dorothy's little shack on its whirlwind trip to Oz. A total stranger is piloting the plane, and the
forces of nature are pounding the plane, and there isn't a darn
thing in the world you can do to control your tumultuous present, or your dangling future, or the curdling contents of your
stomach.

Well, that was the way I felt that Sunday afternoon. I was
trapped in my seat on the plush sofa in Ginger Allen's luxurious living room, praying for the storm to be over, longing to
take back the controls of my own life, and cursing the day I'd
ever signed on for this rocky flight to nowhere.

I had wanted to go home, but Ginger wouldn't hear of it. I
simply *had* to accompany her to the *What's My Line?* studio
that night. So what if the show was broadcast live and didn't
go on the air until 10:30 P.M.? What was more important, my
life or hers? (She actually used those very words.) If I didn't
go with her, she insisted, something horrible could happen—
like it did last night.

Though I had begun to believe that nothing more horrible than too much drinking had taken place the night before, I was too skittish to chance it. What if I was wrong? What if Ginger *had* been poisoned? And what if the poisoner, upon learning that his latest attempt had failed, had devised a more foolproof plan (or concocted a more lethal dose) for tonight?

Since the identity of the Mystery Guest was always kept a deep, dark secret, I knew Ginger's would-be murderer might not find out about her *What's My Line?* appearance until it was too late for him to make the scene (i.e., try to kill her at the studio). But I couldn't take *that* chance, either. Secrets, like scandal, traveled fast in the TV industry.

So there I sat, hour after hour, all by myself in Ginger's ritzy living room, flipping through magazine after magazine (old issues of *Coronet, The Saturday Evening Post, Collier's, Photoplay, Vogue,* and *TV Guide,* each of which featured Ginger Allen on the cover), while a succession of hastily summoned "ists"—a facialist, a manicurist, a makeup artist, and two hairstylists—traipsed in and out of Ginger's bedroom, making her look beautiful and perfect for her dazzling and (hopefully) *live* TV appearance to come.

I was so bored I wanted to kill myself. And I filled the time wallowing in rampant self-pity. *I could be necking my brains out in the movie theater balcony with Dan right now,* I whined to myself, *sneaking glimpses at* Blackboard Jungle *on the screen and looking forward to a juicy steak dinner at Schrafft's, instead of plodding through outdated periodicals, waiting for a world-class prima donna to tell me what to do next, and wondering when, if ever, I'll be free (okay,* smart) *enough to pursue more important personal goals than solving homicides and writing crime stories.*

Can you understand my angst? I was so ticked-off at Ginger—and annoyed at myself for getting involved with her—that I was beginning to question the validity of my whole darn career. I was considering quitting my job at *Daring Detective* and giving up my paperback novel-writing pursuits and walking out on the Ginger Allen case for good.

I might have done it, too (well, the last part, anyway), if

Ginger hadn't finally burst out of her bedroom and waltzed into the living room, yelling for Leo to come see how gorgeous she looked, and, most importantly, calling for Boynton to bring us some dinner. (Yes, she actually used the word *us* this time!) She was starving, she said, and she was in the mood for roast capon and lyonnaise potatoes and string beans almondine. And a lovely bottle of wine—the Sancerre would be fine. And would Boynton please serve our dinner in the formal dining room on the double? She hadn't eaten a goddamn thing all day!

In her smashing red dress and matching state of mind, Ginger was really getting on my nerves. But at least I wasn't bored anymore. And I loved the lyonnaise potatoes.

The wine was good, too, and by the time Ginger, Leo and I got in the elevator to go downstairs, we'd all had quite a bit of it. But after we'd sashayed through the lobby, exited the building, and allowed Woodrow to help us into the dark blue limousine waiting at the curb, I came to a sober realization: in my agitated and somewhat inebriated mental condition, I had accidentally left my glasses on the terrace.

I wanted to zip back upstairs to retrieve them, but Ginger wouldn't allow it. "Not on your life, pussycat," she barked. "Why should I be delayed by your brainless negligence? This show is much more important than your stupid glasses are, and I'm going to get there on time if it kills me."

Lord forgive me for wishing that it would.

WOODROW DROVE US STRAIGHT TO CBS-TV's Studio #52, which was located in the old Mansfield Theater on West 47th Street, and delivered us to a designated point around the corner from the main entrance. There we were met by a short, bouncy young sweater girl named Candy, who escorted us into the building through an unmarked door, and then led us upstairs via a dingy, deserted, circuitous route that was chosen, she said, to make sure the Mystery Guest didn't accidentally run into any members of the panel. "Otherwise, you wouldn't be a mystery anymore!" she chirped, leading us on to the makeup room.

Candy, Leo, and I waited in the hall while Ginger went in, sat down, and submitted to having her nose repowdered and her lipstick reapplied. "If you get one fucking smudge of powder on my new dress," she warned the gentle, middle-aged makeup lady, "you'll wish you were never born."

And after that polite exchange, Candy led us on to wardrobe, where Ginger reluctantly allowed another motherly matron to study the drape of her dress, brush the lint off her shoulders and skirt, straighten her hemline, and check her nylons for runs. "You look perfect!" the wardrobe lady finally pronounced, beaming her approval.

"I didn't need *you* to tell me that," Ginger snapped.

A lovely time was being had by all.

Candy then escorted us down a dark, narrow hallway to the crowded, noisy control room. She introduced Ginger to the director of the show, and—while he was giving Ginger instructions on how to make her onscreen entrance and sign in—Leo and I were offered seats in the row of folding chairs set up behind the control desk. I sat down, but Leo didn't. He walked over to the far side of the room and stood talking with two men that he obviously knew.

This was the first time I'd ever been in a TV studio, and, to me, the control room seemed out of control. The show was already on the air—a fact I deduced from the twelve black-and-white images displayed on the twelve monitors affixed to the opposite wall (and also from my watch, which read 10:45). Six men were sitting at the control desk in front of me. They all wore headsets and microphones and were madly turning dials and pushing buttons on their control boards. And they were all talking at once. Not to each other, but to other men—producers, directors, cameramen, technicians, engineers, electricians, etc.—who were stationed down on the floor, or onstage, or backstage, or God knew where else in the theater.

Several other people were standing around the control desk—chatting, laughing, telling jokes, glancing at the monitors, and making offhand comments about the show in progress—and some of the people sitting in the row of folding chairs next to me were yakking, too. The wife of one of the producers was there with two friends from her bridge club, and they were so excited about being in the same room with Ginger Allen that they kept chattering to each other and letting out shrill little squeaks of joy.

Meanwhile, Ginger had started complaining about something or other to the director, and Leo was still prattling with his pals, and one of the show's sponsors was yelling at one of the men at the control desk for cutting his commercial short. And through it all, the audio portion of the show was booming at top volume. It was bedlam, pure bedlam. I was the only silent person in the room. And the only one actually watching the show.

John Daly, the host, was controlling the game with his usual wit and ease, and the four members of the panel— Dorothy Kilgallen, Steve Allen, Arlene Francis, and Bennett Cerf—were trying to guess the occupation of the current contestant—a short, balding man who manufactured brassieres.

"Can your product be used to carry things?" Dorothy Kilgallen asked. (Big laugh from the studio audience, who knew what the man did for a living.)

"Uh, yes," the embarrassed contestant answered.

"Would I have one in my house?"

"Yes, I think so."

"Would I use it when I go shopping for food?"

Coming to the aid of the contestant, who didn't know how to answer, John Daly said, with a smile, "Yes, Dorothy, I'm almost certain you would." (Laugh.)

"Could the product be used to carry meat?" Dorothy continued. (Huge laugh from the audience.)

"Well, yes," Daly said, still answering for the confused contestant. "I suppose you could phrase it that way."

"And would I also use the product to carry bananas?" (More hilarity.)

"No, Dorothy, I'm quite sure you wouldn't. That's eight down and two to go. We'll continue the questioning with Steve Allen."

When I turned around to check on Ginger, she was gone.

Knowing it was almost time for her to go onscreen, I figured Candy had led her down the "secret passage" to the special Mystery Guest stage entrance. But I still felt anxious and antsy. What if somebody killed her on the way?

No such luck. After Arlene Francis determined the brassiere manufacturer's occupation, and after a curvy blonde in a bathrobe urged the female viewers to use Stopette deodorant, John Daly reappeared on the screen, instructed the panelists to put on their blindfolds, and said, "Will you come in, Mystery Guest, and sign in please?" And then suddenly there she was—in living black-and-white, on all twelve monitors, signing the name Ginger Allen on the blackboard, and greeting the studio audience with a smile as bright as Broadway on her shining silver face.

The applause was thunderous. And judging from the audience's wild and joyful reaction, I concluded it was Ginger's ego, not her image, that had needed the shot in the arm.

Daly began the questioning with Bennett Cerf, who grinned and asked the obvious: "Can I assume from the deafening cheers and applause that you are in the entertainment business?"

"Yes," Ginger said, disguising her voice in such a high-pitched yet sexy tone she sounded like Shirley Temple in heat. The audience loved it.

"And am I right in surmising that you are of the female persuasion?" Cerf wanted to know.

"Yes you are, sir," Ginger warbled.

"Are you an actress?"

"Yes I am, sir."

"And are you in the movies?"

"Oh, no, sir," she cooed.

"That's one down and nine to go," John Daly said, "and the questioning continues with Dorothy Kilgallen."

Looking like a peacock in her elaborately feathered eye mask, Dorothy tilted her chinless head and said, "The audience's response to your entrance was really quite astonishing. Therefore, you must be very well-known and very popular. And since you're not in the movies, am I correct in assuming that you are in the exciting, brilliant, booming world of television?"

"You betcha," Ginger said, looking very pleased with herself.

"And are you the star of a weekly Monday night television show that is adored by viewers coast to coast?"

Ginger batted her false eyelashes and peeped, "I'm very happy to say I am!"

"I see!" Dorothy continued, with a knowing smile. "And are you the beautiful redhead who just happens to be the most talented actress and comedienne ever to grace the TV screen?"

"Why, yes!" Ginger squealed, panting with pleasure, so thrilled with Dorothy's assessment of her charms and skills she could barely contain herself.

"Then I know who you are!" Dorothy proclaimed. "You're my very good friend and very favorite TV star in all the world—Lucille Ball!"

You could have heard a pin drop—in the studio *and* in the control room. The most horrible of all things had happened. A widely celebrated, immensely respected, enormously popular and powerful *What's My Line?* Mystery Guest had just been humiliated on national TV.

The camera didn't know which way to turn. Ginger's stricken expression and crumbling composure were painful to behold, and Dorothy Kilgallen's feathered face was flaming red with shock and embarrassment (okay, *gray* with shock and embarrassment, but even behind the mask and on the black-and-white screen, you could tell she was blushing profusely). Dorothy knew from the audience's silence she had made a huge mistake, but she didn't yet know which famous actress had now become her enemy for life. And John Daly was so flustered he didn't know what to do or say next.

Arlene Francis saved the day. "That's two down and one to go," she jumped in, smiling, "and *that* one has to be *my* very favorite TV star in all the world—the stunning, the supremely talented, the unsurpassable . . . Ginger Allen!"

A communal whoosh of relief swept over the stage and the

studio audience and the control room and, I was sure, the viewing audience at home. And then the cheering began. The applause was so loud, and so charged with emotion, you'd have thought the Virgin Mary had just entered and signed in. It was a leaping, shouting, standing ovation. Even the four panelists ripped off their blindfolds, vaulted to their feet, and started clapping like there was no tomorrow (a finale Dorothy Kilgallen was no doubt praying for).

Ginger smiled demurely, kissed John Daly on the cheek, curtsied to the studio audience, and then glided across the stage to shake hands with each of the panelists in turn. When she got to Dorothy, she smirked and stuck her nose in the clouds. She was acting like the Queen of England, but I knew she felt more like the Prince of Fools. And no amount of flattery or applause or fawning adoration would ever make up for the shame she had suffered on live TV tonight.

Leo couldn't soothe her damaged psyche, either. No, she definitely did *not* want to go to the Copa or the Stork or El Morocco. How could he even suggest such a thing?! Couldn't he see how devastated she was? She wouldn't set foot in any of those nightclubs ever again! She couldn't face anybody! Her goddamn life was over! How could she even go to work in the morning? It was too, too humiliating. Woodrow should drive them home immediately, and then take Patty back to her hotel. She didn't want to see or speak to anybody. She wanted to be left alone. She just wanted to die.

Chapter 15

WOODROW AND I DIDN'T TALK MUCH ON the way downtown. I was too preoccupied—and too exhausted—to come up with any good questions or engage in any meaningful conversation. And Woodrow was too inhibited—and too indoctrinated—to speak unless he was spoken to. Finally, though, as we came to a stop at the light at the Sheridan Square intersection, he turned his head to the right and aimed his wide eyes at me.

"Is Miss Allen going to be okay, miss?" he asked. "She looks kinda sickly to me."

From my vantage point (i.e., sitting sideways on the extra perch that protruded from the rear of the passenger's seat with my chin propped on the backrest) I could see the tiny beads of perspiration on his forehead. They glistened like rubies in the red glare of the stoplight. "I don't know, Woodrow," I admitted. "Things aren't going too well for her right now. She swears somebody poisoned her drink last night, but I don't know if that's true. She may have just consumed too much alcohol."

"Oh, I can't hardly believe that, miss. Why would Miss Allen have to lie to you?" The beads of sweat on Woodrow's brow turned green and he turned his attention back to his driving.

I gave him the only answer I could think of. "It's possible she's just using me in some kind of scheme to get some free publicity."

"I can't hardly believe that either, miss. Seems like Miss Allen's always trying to dodge publicity 'stead of looking for ways to get more."

"Then why was she so hot to go on *What's My Line?* tonight?"

"That's different," he said. "Being on that show is like winning a special award. It's a mighty big honor." (I doubted that Ginger felt honored by the experience now.)

"You could be right, Woodrow," I said, "but I really don't know what to think. Miss Allen's very hard to read. She's a complicated person."

Woodrow let out a soft whistle. "Ain't that the truth, miss? She's harder to read than the fine print on a loan shark's contract."

I giggled. It was the first laugh I'd had all day. And for a moment I felt relieved and happy—relieved that I was nearly eighty blocks away from Ginger Allen, and happy as a clam that I was just two blocks away from home.

But my relief and happiness didn't last long. As Woodrow turned the corner onto Bleecker and steered the long, wide limousine down the short, narrow street to my apartment, I saw a familiar figure leaning against the wall of my building. The man was tall and broad shouldered, wearing a tan trench coat and a grey fedora. He was languidly smoking a cigarette and staring at me through the window of the limo with a stern, distrustful look on his hard but handsome face.

It was Dan, of course, and he wasn't very glad to see me.

Oh, lordy, lordy, lordy!!! I shrieked to myself. *What the hell am I going to do now? How on earth am I ever going to explain this one?* As Woodrow opened the door and helped me out of the car, Dan just stood there, one shoulder propped against the brick wall, blowing smoke into the damp night air and silently watching my every move.

"Are you going to be okay, miss?" Woodrow asked, low-ering his voice to a whisper and casting nervous sidelong glances at Dan. "Who's that man standing over there? Do you want me to take you someplace else, or stay with you awhile?"

"No, Woodrow," I said, voice loud enough for Dan to hear. "That won't be necessary. Thanks for your concern, but I'll be fine. I know it doesn't look like it, but this man's a friend of mine."

"Well, if you're sure, miss . . ."

"I am, Woodrow. Don't worry."

Giving Dan another nervous glance, Woodrow sat back down behind the wheel and slammed the driver's door closed. Then he rolled down the window and anxiously motioned for me to come closer. "That fellah looks mighty suspicious to me, miss," he whispered. "Are you plum sure you're gonna be safe? Or should I drive on over to Whelan's all-night drug-store and call the police? They'll be here in a jiffy."

Just what I need—more cops!

"Please don't worry about me, Woodrow, I'm going to be fine," I said, even though I knew I wasn't. "You go on home and enjoy the rest of your night. There isn't much of it left."

He finally took me at my word, pulled away from the curb, and drove slowly toward Sixth Avenue. I had the feeling he was watching me in his rearview mirror all the way.

Dan was still watching me, too, looking me over from head to foot—taking in my fancy silver-gray suit, hot-pink silk blouse, and mile-high black patent leather stilettos—and wondering how and why I happened to be arriving home after midnight in a chauffeured limosine, and who I'd chosen to spend the day and evening with instead of him.

"Well, aren't you going to say anything?" I asked him. I was so nervous my voice was shaking.

Dan glared at me for a couple more seconds, then dropped his cigarette to the sidewalk and ground it out with his heel. "I think I'd rather hear what *you* have to say."

"Then you'd better come upstairs for a drink," I said, wobbling over to unlock the door to my building. "It's a long story."

NO WORDS CAN DESCRIBE THE MENTAL panic I was in. If I couldn't come up with a totally believable and acceptable explanation for my fancy clothes and questionable behavior, my relationship with Dan would be over. For good. I was plum sure of it. Dan had divorced his wife when he lost his trust in her, and I knew if he lost his trust in me tonight, he'd walk out the door and I'd never see him again. And I didn't want that to happen. Oh, god, how I didn't want that to happen. I was praying with every cell in my convulsing, pounding heart that that wouldn't happen.

And so I hung around the kitchen counter for as long as I could, slowly pouring us each a glass of Chianti and straining every cell in my brain to make up a good story to tell him. But what in the world could I possibly say? That I'd been working on Mike's story in the public library, and that the rich lady sitting next to me had spilled ink on my dress when she was trying to refill her fountain pen, and that she'd insisted on taking me to her place, and giving me a change of clothes, and then taking me out for a late dinner, after which she had her chauffeur take me home? *Aaargh!* Consummate liar that I had become in recent months, I couldn't do any better than that.

Which was why I finally decided that my only reasonable course of action was to tell Dan the truth.

I carried the two glasses of wine over to the kitchen table, sat down across from him, took a deep breath, and began at the beginning . . . Five cigarettes and two more glasses of wine later, I had divulged every detail of the entire Ginger Allen saga—from the first moment Woodrow had entered the *Daring Detective* office and asked me to accompany him downstairs to meet his famous boss, to the final hour after the *What's My Line?* fiasco, when Woodrow took Ginger and Leo back to their apartment and then brought me home.

To say that Dan was displeased would be like calling Hamlet a little mixed up. He wasn't screaming or yelling at me or anything like that, but he was smoking one cigarette after another and pacing the floor in circles like a caged panther.

"I'm an idiot," he growled. "I should have known you were lying from the start, when you told me that fairy tale about having to write Mike's story over the weekend."

"That wasn't a lie!" I protested. "I *did* have to write Mike's story. It has to go to the typesetter tomorrow morning!" I crossed my arms over my chest and gave Dan a self-righteous pout. "I just finished it a little sooner than I thought I would."

"Did you have to work on the story today?"

"Well, no, I—"

"Then you lied about that."

"Yes, but—"

"I don't like being lied to."

"I know, but—"

"But? But what? But you thought you could get away with it since I'm such a simpleminded jerk?"

"No, I never—"

"You never what? Never even considered telling me the truth? Never wanted me to know that you had broken your promise to me and were now working on another unsolved murder story?" Dan smashed his cigarette in the ashtray, sat back down at the table, and skewered me with his angry stare. His jet-black eyes were burning like coals.

"But I *haven't* broken my promise!" I said. "This isn't an unsolved murder story—in fact it isn't a murder story at all. Nobody has been killed!"

I scored a major point with that one. Dan's fierce expression softened a bit as he realized the truth of my assertion. He didn't look like a caged panther anymore. Now he just looked like a wolf. A wolf with rabies. "That doesn't change anything," he snarled. "There's still a killer on the loose. You're in just as much danger as you would be if somebody *had* been murdered. Maybe even more."

Was Dan a good guy, or what? Even after learning that I'd lied to him, he was still primarily concerned about my safety. You gotta love a guy like that. And I did, more than ever.

"But what if Ginger's so-called killer doesn't even exist?"

I pointed out. " Then I wouldn't be in any danger at all! And you want to know something, Dan? More and more I'm leaning toward that conclusion. I'm beginning to believe that Ginger is either imagining things, or that she is lying—that she made up the story about somebody trying to kill her just to get more attention and sympathy from the public."

"Then why didn't she go straight to the newspapers?" he snapped, still seething. "Why would she just tell you—and only you—about the murder attempts and then swear you to secrecy? Nice try, Sherlock, but it doesn't add up. Sounds like your precious client is avoiding attention instead of seeking it." His tone was sarcastic and bitter, but I could see that his interest was piqued. (In the race for the curiosity crown, Dan and I always ran neck and neck.)

"She is *not* my 'precious client'!" I sputtered. "I don't even like her. And I'm not in her employment, either. She's not paying me one red cent! All I'm getting out of this is an exclusive story."

Dan gave me a harsh, incriminating look. "And if your precious client gets murdered, that'll be worth one hell of a lot."

My heart sank like a brick to the pit of my stomach. How could Dan say such a horrible thing to me? He knew I didn't care about the money and that I was more focused on preventing Ginger's murder than writing about it. How could he be so condemning? Was he so mad that he just wanted to hurt me—get even with me for telling one itsy-bitsy fib (okay, *big fat lie*) to him? Or did he feel so utterly duped and deceived that he had lost all faith in me, doubting my motives as well as my promises?

I was about to throw myself at Dan's feet and beg for his understanding when he suddenly stood up from the table, stuffed his cigarettes and lighter in his shirt pocket, and strode over to the living room chair where he'd tossed his hat and coat. (No gun and shoulder holster; it was his day off, remember?) He shoved his arms into the sleeves of his trench coat, set his fedora at an irate angle on his head, and made for the door.

"Are you leaving?" I asked, heart pounding against the inside of my ribcage like a mallet. I wanted to dive across the floor and pull his legs out from under him—anything to delay his departure!—but my muscles refused to move. I sat immobile as a rag doll in my chair.

"I have to go," Dan fumed. "Might say something I'd be sorry for."

"Will you be back?" I whimpered. The tears were pushing against the backs of my eyeballs, squeezing their way into my tear ducts, threatening to spew out in a violent gusher. "Will you call me tomorrow?"

"I don't know," he said, shooting me a murderous glance. Then he yanked open the door, stormed out into the hall, and disappeared down the stairs.

.

Chapter 16

I THOUGHT I'D NEVER STOP CRYING. I was blubbering like an idiot when I lurched across the hall and held my ear to Abby's door, hoping to hear music or laughter or poetry or barking inside. And when I realized from the dead quiet (and from the time on my watch—2:15 A.M.) that Abby and Jimmy and Otto were probably already in bed, I started bawling even harder. And as I staggered back to my own apartment, and slugged down another glass of wine, and then climbed the stairs to my miserably lonely bedroom, I was wailing like a banshee (whatever that is).

You may think I'm exaggerating, but I'm not. I was crying harder than I'd ever cried in my life (if you don't count the month of gut-wrenching sobbing I'd undergone after learning that Bob would never be coming home from Korea). I wept as I took off Abby's fancy clothes and put on one of Bob's old Army T-shirts. I sniveled like a baby the whole time I was washing my face, brushing my teeth, closing the bedroom window shade, crawling between the covers, setting the alarm, and turning out the bedside light.

And then—just like all the weak, drippy, pathetically dependent women who populated all of Orchid Publications' leading romance and confession magazines—I cried myself to sleep. Well, it was more like a drunken stupor than sleep, I guess, but whatever it was, I lost consciousness. Totally. And when my alarm clock started screaming in the morning, I wasn't crying anymore.

I slapped off the alarm, amputated my body from the bed, and dragged my spiritless self into the shower. As the water splashed down on my aching head and shoulders, I shoved all thoughts of Dan into the darkest closet of my mind and closed the door. I couldn't deal with my emotions right now. If I let them out into the light they'd grow bigger and multiply and eat me for breakfast.

I had to focus on more functional things, like getting out of the shower, drying myself off, getting dressed, rushing to the subway, taking two trains to get to work, riding the elevator up to the office, making the coffee, opening the mail, preparing my desk for the busy Monday to come, and busting my brain to figure out a way to nail the illusive—perhaps imaginary—villain who was trying to kill Ginger Allen.

"DID YA FINISH MY STORY?" MIKE WANTed to know. He and Mario had just arrived and hung their hats and coats on the tree. Harvey Crockett was in his private office, reading the morning papers and downing his first cup of coffee, and Lenny was hunched over his desk in the rear, working on the cover pasteup. Brandon Pomeroy hadn't come in yet (he rarely made an appearance before noon). As for me, I was wading through a sea of page proofs.

"Yes, I finished your story," I grumbled, trying to keep the resentment out of my tone. "It's on your desk."

"And how was your weekend, cupcake?" Mario taunted, strutting over to my desk with a mile-wide sneer plastered on his chubby face. "You look awful. So tired and bedraggled! I bet you were up all night writing. What a shame!" His bulging brown eyes were dancing with glee.

"I was up all night, but I sure wasn't writing," I said, forcing my lips into a suggestive smirk. I knew from past experience that the best way to aggravate Mario Caruso was to hint that your love life was better than his.

His face fell. "So when did you write Mike's story?"

"Oh, I finished it Friday evening, before I ever left the office," I chirped. "As you said yourself, I wasn't named Paige Turner for nothin'!"

"I don't believe you," he said, scowling. "Even you can't write that fast. You had to do *some* work over the weekend."

"Not on your life," I insisted. "Not this girl! All I did was romp and play. I went to a wild beatnik poetry reading at Chumley's on Friday night, and Saturday night I had dinner at the Stork Club. Everybody who's anybody was there—Errol Flynn, Orson Welles, Zsa Zsa Gabor, Ginger Allen—"

"Now I know you're lying," Mario said with a sniff.

"Yeah!" Mike chimed in. "They'd never let somebody like you into such a famous, snobby nightspot."

"He's right!" Mario hooted, leering at me and scraping his fingers through his slicked-back hair. "I'm surprised at you, cupcake. With a name like Paige Turner, you shoulda been able to make up a better story than *that!*"

Mike and Mario laughed their fool heads off for a couple of minutes, snorting and crowing like morons, slapping each other on the back like victorious teammates after a big ball game. (Their all-time favorite sport was to make fun of my unfortunate name.) They were making such a racket that Harvey Crockett stuck his head out of his office and yelled at them to pipe down.

Then he yelled at me to get him another cup of coffee.

"Ditto," Mario jeered, giving me a nasty wink before heading down the aisle toward his desk in the back of the workroom.

"Double ditto," Mike mocked, sitting down at his desk next to mine. He picked up my (I mean *his*) story, propped his feet up on the desk, and began to read. (Actually, he may have been just pretending. Mike's reading skills were as poorly developed as his writing techniques.)

I rolled my eyes at the ceiling, groaned silently to myself, and got up to fetch the coffee. There was no point in protesting (unless I wanted to get fired). So what if I was the best (some would say *only*) writer on the *Daring Detective* staff? So what if I did all the proofreading, editing, and rewriting? So what if my last exclusive story had been featured on the cover—at double the usual print run—and had been a total sell-out? I was a *woman,* don't you know, and the only female employee, which meant my primary professional role was to make the coffee and serve it to my male "superiors" with a sugary, submissive smile.

My second-most-important yet mindless mission was to clip all the major crime reports out of the city's daily newspapers (both the morning and afternoon editions) and put them in a file for our illustrious (make that *odious*) editorial director, Brandon Pomeroy, who would then read them (if he wasn't too drunk to see) and decide which stories were bloody and sexy enough to deserve *DD* coverage. So, when Mr. Crockett was finished reading (and making a crumpled mess of) the morning papers, he always gave them to me for clipping.

And this Monday morning was no different.

"Here!" Mr. Crockett said, when I brought him his second cup of coffee. "I'm done with these. You can clip 'em now." He hoisted the large, disheveled mound of newsprint up off his desk and plopped it in my arms. Since there were four big city newspapers in the pile—the *New York Times*, the *Herald Tribune,* the *Daily Mirror,* and the *Daily News*—it was a hefty, unwieldy load. But if Mr. Crockett noticed my difficulty and discomfort in balancing the batch of papers, he didn't let on.

"Did you do what I said?" he asked, leaning back in his squeaky chair and relighting his stinky cigar stub. "Did you get me tickets to the Dodgers' opening game?"

"Yes, sir, it's all taken care of."

"And what about the lunch reservations?"

"I made them, sir. For four at twelve thirty at the Quill."

"Yeah, okay. And I have an appointment at the barbershop, right? What time is that for?"

"Eleven forty-five, sir."

"Good. I can go straight to lunch from there."

"Yes, sir," I said, arms aching to put down the newspapers (and lips longing to stop mouthing the word *sir*). "Will that be all, sir?"

"Uh, yeah . . . that's all . . . for now. You better get to work on the clipping."

"Yes, sir," I mumbled, thinking how much I was sounding and acting like Woodrow. (Chauffeurs and secretaries—slaves under the skin.)

As I left Mr. Crockett's office and headed up the aisle toward my desk in the front of the workroom, I passed by Mario's desk. And when he saw me struggling under the cumbersome load of newspapers, he pounced on the opportunity to make fun of me again. "Would you look at this, boys?" he called out to Mike and Lenny. "Paige Turner's in hog heaven now. She's got a whole lot of pages to turn!" Lenny didn't react to the remark, but Mario and Mike began snickering like little boys who had just tied a tin can to a cat's tail.

I ignored them and staggered onward. Finally reaching my desk and dropping the heavy stack of newspapers down on top of it, I sat down, scrawled CRIME CLIPS: APRIL 4, 1955 across the face of a manila file folder, and took my scissors out of the drawer. Then I lifted the *New York Times* off the top of the stack and began skimming the contents: Nine Puerto Ricans had been sentenced to six years for seditious conspiracy (i.e., fighting to free Puerto Rico from U.S. control by force, violence, and opposition), and a mob of Afghans had attacked the Pakistani embassy in Kabul. Australia was sending troops to Malaya to resist Communist aggression, the Reds were working to construct an atomic-powered combat plane, and the French government was preparing to "crack down" on Algerian rebels.

Blessed are the peacemakers.

Even Macy's had turned militant. The store had taken out several full-page ads to announce that they were "launching" an "aggressive" storewide sales "campaign" and "slashing" prices "to the bone" on many of their most popular items. Bouffant Nylon Can-Can Petticoats were now just $2.99

each! And stockings were just 79 cents a pair! You could get an all-wool spring suit for just $25.88, a washable Dacron dress for $5.99, and a cultured pearl necklace for the unheard-of low price of $19.98! But you'd better hurry, hurry, hurry! Better "march" right over to Macy's and do your spring shopping while the "war" on prices lasted!

There were very few sexy or bloody crime reports in the *Times* (which focused on straight news rather than sensationalism), so when I folded it up and put it aside, there were just two clips in the folder. I found plenty of juicy crime stories in the other three papers, however (whose Monday morning editions were always jam-packed with wicked weekend wrong-doings), and it took me over an hour to cut them all out.

When I finished the clipping, I tossed the mangled and shredded newspapers in the art department's large wastepaper can and put the folder full of crime clips on Pomeroy's desk. He might never get around to reading them, but at least they would be there upon his arrival, thereby saving me from one of his demeaning alcoholic outbursts. (A woman-hater to the core, Pomeroy jumped at every chance, however insignificant, to find fault with my job performance.)

I lit up a cigarette and dove with a vengeance back into the proofreading. I had to stay busy, keep my mind engaged. I couldn't let myself think about Dan. I didn't *dare* think about Dan. (If Mike and Mario ever caught me crying, I'd have to kill myself.) But the proofreading didn't do the trick. I couldn't stay focused for more than two seconds at a time. Dan's gruff but gorgeous face kept materializing on every page, hovering like a cloud over wavy columns of illegible words. The only surefire way to lock Sergeant Street out of my head, I soon realized, was to keep my head filled with more crucial and immediate concerns.

Like who, if anybody, was trying to kill Ginger.

I continued to stare down at the page proofs, correcting an occasional typo or error in punctuation, but my mind was off and running. Was hubby Leo the one? Did he have some kind of financial motivation, or some deep emotional purpose, or was he just sick to death of living with a shrew? Could it be

Ginger's younger sister, Claire? Could Claire's jealousy and hatred of Ginger have finally overcome her passivity, and turned her into a poisonous viper? And what about Claire's husband, Rusty Burnett? Or Theo Kidd? Or Tex and Toni Taylor? Did any one (or all) of them have a driving desire to see Ginger dead? (From what I'd witnessed and experienced, just about anybody who'd ever met the abusive TV star could have reason to feel that way!)

And what the heck's going to happen next? I wondered. Would Ginger call me and demand that I meet her at the studio, or her apartment, or some other fancy nightclub after work? Would she expect me to play bodyguard every night? Or would she hide out in solitary for a while, nursing her *What's My Line?* wounds, refusing to go out in public—or see anybody, including me—until her boredom outweighed her shame? Most importantly, would there be any further attempts (real or imagined) against her life?

Questions, questions—nothing but questions as far as the eye could see.

And yet I was responsible for finding the answers . . . Well, not *really,* of course. I mean, I hadn't signed a contract or anything; there was no written law that said I had to keep working on this crazy case. There was just my own personal unwritten law—the one that compelled me to live up to all of my commitments, and to continue my undying quest for truth and justice. (Okay, okay! So maybe I read too many Wonder Woman comic books when I was a kid. But there was nothing I could do about that now. The brain damage was already done.)

I kept staring down at the page proofs and torturing myself with unanswerable questions for a good twenty minutes or more, getting nowhere fast, making myself more confused and upset than ever. I felt desperate, incompetent, and utterly helpless. (And for a person who prides herself on being strong and self-reliant, those are pretty hard feelings to take!) I was floundering . . . sinking . . . drowning . . .

And then a funny thing happened. PING! A light bulb lit up over my head (just like in the aforementioned comic

books). POW! I thought of something I could actually *do*.
Something that might lead me to an answer or two, or at least
prompt me to ask the right questions. WHAM! I didn't have
to sit here like a moron waiting for Ginger to call and tell me
where to go and what to do next. I had investigative plans of
my own! I had an exact destination and mission in mind. And
you know what else? BANG! I wouldn't have to put myself
in any danger whatsoever. BOOM! I wouldn't even have to
leave the building.

Chapter 17

I COULDN'T WAIT FOR MY LUNCH HOUR
to start. I was so eager to kick my new clue-hunting expedition into action that all I could do was stare at the office wall clock, mentally pleading with the hands to hit noon, and praying to all the gods and godesses that ever did, or didn't, exist that Brandon Pomeroy wouldn't saunter into the office until after I had scooted out.

Eventually, but none too soon, my prayers were answered. The clock struck twelve and Pomeroy's chair was still empty. Mr. Crockett had already left to go to the barber, but Mike, Mario, and Lenny were still sitting at their desks, looking down at their work and simultaneously sneaking snoopy glances at me. Putting on a big show, I jumped up from my desk and bellowed something about how starving I was. Then I grabbed my purse, gloves, jacket, and beret (I wanted my nosy coworkers to think that I was going *out*), and made a hasty exit.

Afraid that Pomeroy might be arriving just as I was leaving, I ran down the hall like a thief, nearly twisting my ankle in the process. (As I may have mentioned before, it's really hard to run in high heels.) When I reached the heavy glass doors to the largest, most elaborate office on our floor, I pushed them open and ducked inside. The entire reception area was walled in glass and, therefore, visible from the hall, so I darted over to the receptionist's desk and tried to convince her to buzz me in right away. If Pomeroy happened to step off the elevator and look through the glass and see me standing there—in the pale lavender and deep purple entryway of Orchid Publications—there'd be hell to pay.

(Sorry, but I have to break into the action right now and do some serious explaining. Please bear with me, because you'll need to know a few things about Orchid Publications in order to understand why I was in that particular establishment, and why Pomeroy would have been ticked off to find me there.

I'll make this as short as I can: Orchid Publications was the largest publisher of grade-B women's periodicals—romance, confession, movie, television, beauty, gossip, and horoscope magazines—in the country. The company also published *Daring Detective* magazine, but this fact was kept secret from the public in order to preserve Orchid's prissy feminine image—which was why the *DD* operation was situated in a totally separate office about sixty yards down the hall.

Orchid Publications was owned by the super wealthy and powerful publishing magnate, Oliver Rice Harrington, who, in addition to over a hundred magazine titles, owned sixty-two newspapers and four major book companies and God knew how many mansions, yachts, airplanes, automobiles, mistresses and politicians. Mr. Harrington also had the dubious distinction of being an elder relative of Brandon Pomeroy—which should give you a pretty good idea why a lazy, shiftless, martini-swilling Harvard man like Pomeroy had been hired as the editorial director of *Daring Detective*, and why he was allowed to float into work whenever he damn well pleased.

It should also explain why either Pomeroy *or* Harrington would have been somewhat less than happy to see a *DD* employee like me hanging around the off-limits lavender reception area, sullying Orchid's prissy feminine image with *DD*'s sleazy blend of murder, sex, and gore. And if you take into

account the fact that Orchid published lots of fan magazines—and, therefore, lots of stories about Ginger Allen—
then you should also be able to figure out why I *was* there.)

"I'm a staff writer for *Daring Detective,*" I told the skinny
blonde receptionist, whose pale lavender suit was a perfect
match for the pale lavender wall behind her. "I'm doing a special retrospective on celebrity murders, and some of our files
have been lost or misplaced. So I spoke to my boss about this,
and he then spoke to your boss, and Mr. Harrington said I
could come here and use Orchid's files for my research. And
I sure hope that's okay with you, because I'm up against a
really, really tight deadline, and I need to dig up as much information as fast as I possibly can." Hoping to add an even
stronger sense of urgency to my words—and thereby gain a
quick, unquestioned admittance—I tried to look extremely
desperate and nervous (which was a snap since that was exactly how I felt).

"Hold on a sec," the skinny blonde said. "I'll call the file
room, see if anybody's there to help you." She gave me a
sympathetic wink, picked up the phone, and dialed three numbers. I didn't know the young woman's name, but I had seen
her before—in the elevator and downstairs in the lobby coffee shop—and I assumed from her swift and cordial reception
that she also remembered seeing me.

"Hi, Bessie," she said to the person who answered the intercom. "A writer from *Daring Detective* is here. She needs to
use our files for a special article she's working on. She says
Mr. Harrington sent her. So, can I let her in to see you?"

Bessie must have said okay, because the receptionist
glanced up at me, gave me another wink, and then warbled
into the mouthpiece, "Thanks, Bessie. She's on her way."
Hanging up the phone, she gestured toward the office entrance and buzzed the door open. "Go to the end of the hall,
take a left, and then go all the way to the end of that hall. The
file room's on the right. The two file clerks have gone out to
lunch, but Bessie, the supervisor, is there, and she's expecting
you."

I uttered a heartfelt thank you and hurried through the door.

This was the first time I'd ever set foot in the Orchid office, and I was dying to take my time, snoop around a little bit, see how the other half (i.e., the prissy feminine half) lived. But I couldn't afford to waste another second of my dwindling lunch hour. I rushed down the long, quiet, well-lit halls as fast as I could, paying little attention to the framed enlargements of magazine covers that lined the cream-colored (not lavender!) walls. Most of the offices I passed were empty (it was everybody else's lunch hour, too), but I did hear a few typewriters clacking and catch an occasional glimpse of a prissy but hungry female eating a sandwich at her desk. Some of the office doors were closed, and behind one of them I heard a medley of high-pitched chit-chat, shrieks, and giggles.

As I neared my destination, a short, scrawny older woman wearing red plaid bedroom slippers and a mint-green smock over her dress came out into the hall to meet me. A burning cigarette dangled from one corner of her mouth. "Are you the writer from *Daring Detective*?" she asked, in a scratchy voice with a Midwestern twang. "The one who wants to use the files?"

"The one and only," I said, smiling my dopey face off. I had a feeling it would be wise to stay on Bessie's good side.

"Okay, come on in," she said, turning around and leading me into the file room. I didn't really need her to show me the way. I could have followed the trail of ashes on the floor. "You caught me just in time, you know. Five more minutes and I'd'a been down in the automat puttin' on the feedbag." She took the cigarette out of her mouth and squished it in a nearby ashtray that was already filled to the brim with butts. "I'll give you a quick tour of the place and explain the filing system, but that's all you'll get from me, sister. I'm not gonna stay here to help you. I'm hungry as a moose, and I don't skip lunch for nothin' or nobody."

So much for prissy and feminine.

"That's fine, Bessie," I said, glad that she'd be leaving me to my own devices. The last thing I needed was to have her looking over my shoulder, policing my endeavors, dropping ashes down my neck.

"Okay, this here's the photo section," she said, pointing one arm out straight and sweeping it in a wide arc around the right half of the room, "and the clip files are over here on the other side." The room was enormous, but so crammed full of tall, deep, bulging metal-and-wood file cabinets that it felt small and claustrophobic. The overhead fluorescent fixtures cast a creepy, bluish glow. "You lookin' for articles or pictures?"

"Articles," I said, knowing they would have pictures, too.

"Good. That simplifies things," she said, leading me into the area where the clip files were located. "Now, what kind of information you lookin' for? We got medical and science, fashion and beauty, historical events and some astrology stuff, but mostly what we got is articles about celebrities and popular movies and TV and radio shows."

"That's what I need," I told her. "The celebrity files."

Bessie whipped an open pack of Luckies out of her smock pocket, tapped one cigarette halfway out, removed it from the pack with her teeth, and then sucked it between her lips like a soda straw. "You want the stars themselves or the press kits about the shows?" she asked, flicking open a Zippo and lighting up.

"The stars," I said, keeping my responses short, hoping Bessie would just show me the files and leave. I was dying to start digging for info, and the remaining minutes of my lunch hour were ticking away fast.

"Okay, sister, they're around the bend," she said, cigarette bobbing with each syllable. "Follow me."

She led me down one aisle of file cabinets, around the corner, and halfway up the next aisle over. I felt as though I were walking through an ancient maze—the kind with narrow parallel paths and tall thick hedges on either side. "The celebrities start right here," she said, indicating a row of cabinets on the left, "and they go all the way up, and around, and down, and up, and around, and down again. They're alphabetical, of course, and the really big stars have more than one folder. I try to keep the clips chronological inside, but so many people mess with these files every doggone day, it's practically impossible."

"Well, thank you so much, Bessie," I quickly jumped in. "I think I can figure everything out from here. I appreciate your help, but I don't want to take up any more of your time. The automat must be getting crowded already."

"You're right about that, sister. I gotta get going." She gave me a squinty, suspicious look and brushed some ashes off her bosom.

"You can't take anything out of this room, you know. Only Orchid employees are allowed. You can use the work table over there if you want, but don't leave a mess. You better put everything back exactly the way you found it."

"Don't worry," I assured her. "You'll never even know I was here."

"Good. That's the way I like it."

Cigarette dangling, Bessie turned and began walking up the aisle toward the entrance to the file room, red plaid slippers scuffing softly against the floor. When she reached the end of the aisle, she unbuttoned and removed her mint-green smock, revealing a brown-and-white striped shirtwaist underneath. Tossing the smock over the back of a chair, she made a quick right turn toward the door and, without another word, disappeared behind the tall bank of file cabinets. I wondered if she would remember to change her shoes.

GINGER WAS IN THE A'S, OF COURSE— third cabinet over, second drawer down. Four huge, overstuffed file folders bore her name. I pulled two of the folders out of the tightly packed file drawer and lugged them, along with my hat, jacket, gloves, and purse, over to the work table. Then I went back and got the other two.

Sitting down at the long wooden table and tucking my hair behind my ears, I took a deep breath and opened the heftiest, most recent, file. There were far too many clips for me to even think of reading them all, so I just flipped them over—one by one, like pages in a book—skimming for articles that seemed likely to offer the most pertinent data. Some of the clips were from newspapers, and some were from major magazines like *Life, Collier's,* and *Mademoiselle.* Most, however, were from the fan magazines, Orchid's titles included.

There were hundreds of articles about *The Ginger Allen Show* itself, of course, and some of them gave the location of the studio where the live show was broadcast (studio 8H in the RCA building at 30 Rockefeller Plaza). I memorized the address. Then I glanced over the many photos and skimmed through the glowing write-ups about the "brilliant and gifted" Ginger Allen and her "fabulous" cast and crew. Leo and Rusty were largely ignored, but there were several pics of Theo Kidd, whom *Photoplay* identified as "the wildly handsome playboy director who has the privilege of spending every working hour of his oh-so-lucky life with television's most talented and tantalizing temptress."

Oh, brother! I snorted to myself, thinking how absurd fan magazine copy could be.

There were scads of articles about Ginger's "idyllic" home life, including numerous photos of the same "elegantly appointed penthouse rooms" in which I had spent an interminable afternoon and evening the day before. I laughed when I saw the pictures of Ginger's bedroom and read it described as "the plush pink retreat where the busy star unwinds, soothes her senses, and replenishes her soul." Whoever wrote those words had obviously never witnessed one of the busy star's cursing, screaming, plush pink boudoir tantrums.

Even more absurd were the florid (and, I thought, totally fraudulent) stories about Ginger's "nurturing domestic nature" and her "highly developed" homemaking skills. Some of the clips revealed the happy housewife's "cherished" cleaning and cooking tips and offered a few of her favorite "down home" recipes. And that wasn't all! One of the "better" magazines (*Good Housekeeping,* if you haven't already guessed) ran a six-page, full-color, at-home photo spread of Ginger "working" in the kitchen, putting something in the oven, stirring something on the stove, wearing a ruffled white organdy apron over a green organza cocktail dress. Boynton was nowhere in sight.

Judging by the number of fashion clips in the file, Ginger's clothes were of never-ending interest to her fans. More than a third of the articles focused on her "effortlessly stylish" wardrobe, picturing Ginger in the gorgeous gowns, furs, dresses, and expensive jewels she was known to prefer, but also showing her in suits, hats, slacks, sweaters, shorts, swimsuits, lingerie, and even costumes from her show. And Ginger's beauty routine was a sizzling-hot topic as well. Scores of features outlined her "easy and natural" face cleansing and moisturizing techniques and revealed her "simple" makeup and hairstyling "secrets." None of these fashion and beauty articles mentioned the legion of dress designers, wardrobe assistants, skin care experts, cosmetologists, and hairdressers at Ginger's beck and call.

And none of the articles in the whole damn folder told me anything I didn't already know!

Letting out a thunderous groan, I closed the file, pushed it aside, and began flipping through the clips in folder number two. Just more of the same. More senseless, witless, gushy articles written, it would seem, for the sole intention of praising Ginger Allen to the hilt. The only interesting thing I learned was how few of the stories showed pictures of Leo or discussed Ginger's marriage to him. In most of the pieces, in fact, he wasn't referred to at all.

And I couldn't help wondering why. Was this some kind of devious publicity plot? Did Ginger keep her husband in the shadows because of his small stature and less-than-handsome features? Did she think his physical imperfections might have a negative effect on her own glorious image? Or did Leo hide in the dark for his own personal purposes? Did he have ulterior business or political concerns that caused him to seek and maintain a low profile?

Oh, great. Just what I need. More questions . . .

Despairing of ever finding any answers, and seeing from my watch that my lunch hour was practically over, I flipped through the clips in the third folder as fast as I could, detecting nothing. Zilch. Naught. Zero. Slapping the file closed and shoving it to the side, I pulled the fourth and final folder under my nose and opened it with a heavy heart (not to mention sagging shoulders). My expectations had sunk so low I was inclined to ditch the last phase of my expedition altogether.

Which would have been a great big fat mistake, since a third of the way through the final folder I found the gem I had been looking for. It was a clue! A genuine, bona fide nugget of information! It appeared in one of the earlier articles—a short piece from the February 28, 1950 issue of *Look* magazine titled "Ginger Allen Swings from Radio to TV." It came in the form of a photo—a small black-and-white snapshot of Ginger kissing the cheek of a handsome young soldier in uniform.

I recognized the young soldier immediately, and I wasn't unduly surprised to see Ginger kissing his face. I was, however, shocked to the bone when I read the caption under the photo: *Though joyous about beginning her new career in television, Ginger was brokenhearted the day she had to bid farewell to her dearly beloved Korea-bound fiancé, Private First Class Rusty Burnett.*

Chapter 18

I WAS SITTING AT MY DESK, PRETEND-ing to edit a story (but actually twisting my brain in a knot over the new—or, rather, *old*—information I'd dug up about Ginger and her sister's husband, Rusty) when Brandon Pomeroy finally appeared at the office. It was 2:30 in the afternoon and, as usual, the skunk was drunk.

"Good afternoon, Mrs. Turner," he said, in his typical lofty and arrogant tone. Removing his hat and hooking it on the rack, he then straightened his tie, smoothed the lapels of his custom-made suit, and breezed past me to his own desk across the aisle from mine. (No matter how inebriated Pomeroy happened to be, he never let it show. He never staggered or stumbled or hiccuped or slurred his words. His hair and clothes were never the least bit disheveled, and he never, ever, ever told dirty jokes or broke into song. Only a slight shakiness gave him away.) "I assume all the proofs are ready for the afternoon pickup," he said, sitting straight and tall in his chair, stuffing his pipe with a special blend of Cuban tobacco. "The messenger will be here in fifteen minutes."

"Yes, sir," I said. "Everything's ready to go."

"New copy, too?"

"Yes, sir."

"Did you write all the necessary captions?"

"Yes, sir, I did. They're typed, specced, and ready for the typesetter."

Pomeroy paused, lit his pipe, then exhaled a stream of fruity fumes in my direction. His brow was wrinkled and his mustache was twitching. I knew he was trying to think of some other task to grill me about—some project I might not have accomplished—hoping to find some reason to belittle me and criticize my job skills (two of his favorite hobbies). But his liquid lunch had clouded his cognitive powers and, though he spent a full minute in deep concentration, all he could come up with was a wan question about the newspaper clips.

"I see you've done the morning crime clips," he said, "but where, pray tell, is the afternoon folder? It's late! It should be on my desk by now."

"Yes, sir, I know. But Mr. Crockett scooped up the afternoon papers the minute they came in, and he's still reading them. He hasn't given them to me to clip yet." *Yahoo!* I crowed to myself. Pomeroy couldn't find fault with me about *that*. Mr. Crockett was his boss as well as mine, so he had to keep his carping, critical mouth shut.

Finally, still desperate to uncover some failing of mine—*any* failing—Pomeroy snarled, "Is the coffee fresh?"

"Absolutely, sir," I lied. "Made a new pot just a few minutes ago." I wasn't worried that he would discover my fib. Pomeroy never drank coffee in the afternoon because it might put a dent in that three-martini glow.

"Then bring me a cup," he demanded. "Black. No sugar."

"Yes, sir," I said, groaning inwardly, knowing he didn't even want the stuff. He just wanted to make me serve him. I got up from my desk, poured him a cup of coffee, and delivered it to him with a dazzling smile. "Here you go, sir," I chirped, mentally throwing a custard pie in his face. (Take it from me—a well-timed, clearly imagined fantasy can alleviate even the most humiliating indignity.)

Unaware that his face was dripping with curdled custard

and whipped cream, Pomeroy took the cup from me and set it down on his desk. Then, without taking a single sip or uttering a word of thanks, he swiveled around in his chair and turned his back to me, aiming his soppy mug toward the wall. Stretching his long legs out in front of him, he crossed his ankles, folded his arms, and allowed his chin to fall to his chest. It was time for his afternoon nap. And if I had any luck at all, he'd snooze till the cows came home—or at least until closing time.

I was about to return to my desk when Mr. Crockett stuck his head out of his office. "Hey, bring me some more coffee will ya, Paige?" he barked. "And come get the papers to clip. I'm done reading 'em now."

IF I HAD KNOWN WHAT WAS GOING TO transpire after I gave Mr. Crockett his coffee and hauled the afternoon papers back to my desk, I might have torn my hair out by the roots and run screaming from the building, searching for sanctuary, looking for a small, dark, solitary place where I could hide from the future. Forever.

But I didn't know.

So I didn't have the sense to run away. I just dropped the jumbled pile of papers down on top of my desk, sat down, and took out my scissors—so bored with the thought of leafing through even more newsprint, and cutting out even more articles, that I wanted to strangle myself. There was only one news clip I was interested in—the 1950 *Look* article with the picture of Ginger and Rusty. The *engaged-to-be-married* Ginger and Rusty! How had it come about that Rusty married Claire instead? I was longing to take the clip out of my purse (I cannot tell a lie—I nipped it!) and look at it again—see if I could glean some further insight from the frayed and yellowing scrap of paper.

But my probe into the past would have to be postponed. Right now I had to delve into the present—i.e., search for heinous crime reports in today's afternoon editions. The *Journal American* and the *World Telegram and Sun* and the *New York Post* were waiting. Heaving a hurricane-force sigh, I lifted a thick, upside-down section of newsprint off the top of the messy pile of papers, flipped it over, and slapped it down, face up, in front of me.

And that's when I stopped breathing.

And when my blood stopped pumping through my veins.

And when the earth stopped spinning on its axis.

That's when the top headline on the front page of the *New York Post* shot up off the paper and struck me, like a torpedo, right between the eyes: TV STAR GINGER ALLEN PLUNGES TO HER DEATH FROM PENTHOUSE BAL-CONY!

God, no! I shrieked to myself, fighting off an intense wave of nausea, forcing my stricken lungs to draw in some air, straining to keep myself from passing out. *No, no, no, no! This can't be true! Please, please, please, God, don't let this be true!*

I jumped to my feet and lunged for the other newspapers, madly shuffling through the stack to find the front pages of the *World Telegram* and the *Journal American.* Their head-lines would be different, I told myself. The *Post* had made a ghastly mistake. Ginger Allen was alive and well—either hard at work in her Rockefeller Center studio, preparing for tonight's broadcast of her show, or reclining in her pink satin bed, nursing her wounded ego (or another hangover) and yelling at Leo to call in the emergency crew of hairdressers and cosmeticians.

But it wasn't the *Post* who was mistaken. It was me. The *Telegram*'s major headline cried out, TV'S GINGER ALLEN DIES IN TRAGIC FALL!, and the *Journal*'s boldface banner screamed, GINGER ALLEN CRUSHED IN FATAL PLUM-MET FROM 14TH FLOOR!

I stood staring at the headlines for an eternity, until the words disintegrated and began swirling away from me in an ever-descending spiral. Feeling dizzy and sick to my stomach and afraid that I might lose consciousness, I tore my eyes away from the newspapers and lowered myself to my chair. I needed to sit. I needed to breathe. I needed to think.

(I also needed to cry, but I didn't dare. If either of my

bosses or any of my nosy coworkers discovered my associa-
tion with Ginger—if they caught even the slightest hint that I
had been involved with her in any way—then all hell would
break loose. They would figure out that I was working on a
story—or at least *had* been—and they wouldn't stop badger-
ing me until I gave them the whole lowdown. And then, after
that, they'd probably alert the newspapers and the police,
which would bring *DD* a lot of free publicity, don't you know.
Then my cover would be blown to smithereens, and my life
would become a three-ring circus—and God only knew who
the ringmaster would be, because it sure as hell wouldn't be
me.)

I snatched a cigarette from the pack in my purse and
brought it to my lips, but my hands were shaking so badly I
couldn't strike the match to light it. After the third try, I gave
up and tossed the unlit weed and the whole book of matches
in the wastebasket. Then I sucked up my courage and forced
myself to read the articles that accompanied the appalling
headlines.

All three accounts gave out the same sickening details: At
approximately 2:30 this morning, Ginger had fallen from the
terrace of her penthouse apartment, landing on the roof of a
car that was parked at the curb. Her beautiful face had been
demolished and many bones had been shattered, including her
neck, which had snapped in two. She died on impact. Police
do not suspect foul play. They are, however, considering the
the possibility of suicide. They report that the actress was
alone in her apartment when the dreadful incident took place,
and they quote her husband as saying she had been severely
depressed in recent weeks and under a psychiatrist's care. No
suicide note was left behind, but all other signs indicate that
Ginger, in a state of inebriation and despair, had climbed onto
the waist-high stone ledge of her 14th-floor balcony and taken
a deliberate nosedive to her death.

Severely depressed? Under a psychiatrist's care? Ginger
had never said anything to me about *that*. The only concern
I'd ever heard her express was that somebody was trying to
murder her. She had been extremely upset after the *What's My*

Line? episode, but could such a frivolous, essentially mean-ingless occurrence have actually caused her to want to kill herself? I didn't think so. From what I knew of Ginger's aggressive, self-centered nature, she'd have been more likely to kill Dorothy Kilgallen than herself.

"Paige? Are you okay?" Lenny said, suddenly appearing at my desk and leaning down to look into my eyes. "What's the matter with you? You look like you've seen a ghost."

(Ever since he saved my life—which is a whole other story and too long to repeat here—Lenny has believed he can see into my soul. And you want to know something weird? He really can.)

"Did you hear about this?" I asked him, shoving the *Post* under his nose and pointing at the headline. "It's so horrible . . . and so sad."

Lenny looked down at the newspaper and his eyeballs nearly popped out of his skull. "Oh, my god!" he cried at the top of his voice. "Ginger Allen's dead?! I don't believe it!" He snatched the paper off my desk and pulled it up close to his face, lifting his bottle-thick glasses above his pitifully myopic eyes so he could read the article's small print.

Aroused by the commotion, Mike and Mario jumped out of their seats and scrambled up to my desk. "What's going on?" Mike sputtered. "Did you say Ginger Allen's dead? What happened?"

"She fell off a balcony," I mumbled, hating to utter the harrowing words.

Mario's face was gleaming in morbid delight. "You mean she fell off a balcony in a theater? That's really funny! What a way for an actress to die!"

"It wasn't that kind of balcony," I growled, feeling sick to my stomach again. "It was the terrace of her penthouse . . . Here!" I said, thrusting the front section of the *Journal* into his pudgy, nail-bitten hands. "You can read all the gory details for yourself."

"Yeah," Mike said, "and read it out loud so I can listen."

"Please don't!" I begged. I couldn't bear to hear the gruesome particulars recounted—especially not by a goon like

Mario. "We have to be quiet," I urged. "We might wake up Mr. Pomeroy."

"If you think I'm sleeping, Mrs. Turner," Pomeroy snapped from across the aisle, back still turned, "then you're even stupider than I thought. I'm aware of everything that's going on." Slowly rotating in his swivel chair to face us, he stuck his noble nose in the air and said, "And that's how I know you've all been hanging around like half-wits, gawking at newspapers and salivating over the death of a fatuous TV star, instead of doing the work you're paid for. Very *well* paid for, I might add. But if any of you are as eager to lose your salaries as you seem to be, then please don't mind me. Just go on with your gab fest. We can easily find some other idiots to fill your jobs."

Without a word (or even a grunt) of protest, the guys flapped the newspapers down and scurried, in single file, back down the aisle to their own desks. Lenny gave me a searching, mournful look as he passed by.

Pomeroy was looking at me, too, so I had to get back to work—fast. Heart heavy with anguish and shame, I smoothed the *New York Post* out in front of me, picked up my scissors, and steeled myself to begin the loathsome clipping.

"Cut out all the Ginger Allen articles first," Pomeroy demanded, "and give them to me at once."

I didn't want to do that. "But they're calling her death a suicide, sir."

"So what?"

"So I thought I wasn't supposed to clip any suicide reports. You said *DD* doesn't cover stories like that. You said there's nothing thrilling or sexy about people killing themselves." (I knew that rule didn't apply to celebrity suicides, of course, but I was stalling as hard as I could. I couldn't bear the thought of turning Ginger's tragic demise into just another pile of news clips—either for our files, or for Pomeroy's private reading enjoyment, or for Mike's reference while writing *DD*'s sure-to-be-next cover story.)

Pomeroy gave me a self-satisfied sneer. "When a big star like Ginger Allen kills herself, it's not only sexy and thrilling, it's profitable. *Very* profitable. I should think you would know that by now, Mrs. Turner. Ginger Allen's suicide will be our next cover story, and I'll be putting Mike to work on it right away. So cut out the damn articles and give them to me. Now."

"Yes, sir," I said, turning back to the *Post* and sadly putting my scissors to work.

Every snip was painful to me. Not just because Ginger was dead, or because I felt partly responsible for her death, but also because I believed that most of the so-called facts printed in the newspaper clips were wrong. I felt certain, deep in my bones, that Ginger's death was a homicide, not a suicide. And I had no doubt that unless I could find a way to prove that my singularly held beliefs were true, somebody was going to get away with murder.

Chapter 19

WHEN THE HANDS OF THE OFFICE CLOCK
hit 4:15, I began clearing the decks for a speedy escape. I
sealed, stamped, and addressed all the outgoing mail,
recorded and filed all the paid invoices, filed a small stack of
used stock photos, and prepared a package of proofs for the
next pickup. I drained, cleaned, and refilled the Coffeemaster
for the morning, then emptied and washed all the coffee
cups—a routine that required three separate trips to the
ladies' room.

Though I was almost always the last to leave at the end of
the workday, today I was the first. I told Mr. Crockett I was
having bad "female trouble" and needed to go home right
away. His face turned flame red (as I knew it would) and, staring down at the floor like a mortified schoolboy, he granted
his immediate permission. "Run along, then," he said, but
what he meant was, "please get out of here before I die of embarrassment." I smiled and gave myself a mental pat on the
back. It worked every time. (At least being a woman was
good for *something*.)

I hurried up to the coat rack, put on my beige jacket, red
beret, and white cotton gloves, bid a gloating goodbye to

Mike and Mario (Pomeroy had gone back to sleep), blew a quick kiss to Lenny, then grabbed my purse and dashed for the elevator. When I landed in the lobby, the burnt hamburger smell wafting from the adjoining coffee shop made my knees buckle. I was so hungry I almost staggered inside, took a seat at the counter, and ordered the blue-plate special (well, I never had any lunch, you know!). But I couldn't do it. The thought of sitting down and eating a meal when I knew Ginger would never enjoy another mouthful in her life (or, rather, death) was intolerable to me. I'd probably throw up.

I pushed my way through a revolving glass door to the street and inhaled deeply, hoping the fresh air would curb my hunger. But even breathing made me feel guilty. The only thing I could do to clear my conscience was sprint one block over to Lexington Avenue, take the uptown IRT to 77th Street, and then run three blocks over toward Fifth, to the street where Ginger had lived—and died. I didn't know what to expect or what I hoped to accomplish. I just knew I had to be there.

It was a zoo. Both sides of 77th Street, from Madison to Fifth, were so packed with people I could barely make my way forward. I felt like I was trying to navigate the 42nd Street subway station at rush hour. Knees and elbows were coming at me from all directions. Men were stepping on my feet. Reporters were shouting, flashbulbs were popping, fans were screaming and crying. Had the world gone totally insane? Had all of humanity been transformed into a swarm of vultures?

Hugging my purse to my side and holding my beret in place with one hand, I muscled my way toward Ginger's building, toward the section of the sidewalk and street I knew to be under her penthouse terrace. Don't ask me why I did that. I knew the area would be cordoned off, that nobody would be allowed to get too close to the spot where Ginger had landed. But I really had no choice in the matter. I was being pulled like a magnet to metal, like a criminal to the scene of the crime.

The closer I got to Fifth Avenue, the more agitated I became. I kept looking up toward the stone parapet of Ginger's balcony, praying that she would suddenly appear and start waving to her fans—that she would lean out over the ivy-covered wall and cry, "Look! I'm still alive! It was all a trick. I did it to get your attention. I'm sorry if I frightened you, but I just wanted to find out if you still loved me!"

It was a foolish fantasy, I knew—but still, I wouldn't have put it past her.

Eventually, when I finally accepted the fact that Ginger wasn't going to materialize, I stopped looking up at her terrace and started looking for her limousine instead. Maybe Woodrow would know something about what had happened before the fall, if Ginger had gone anywhere, and who, if anybody, had been with her. I wondered if he'd been questioned by the police and, if so, what he had, or hadn't, told them. I also just wanted to see his big brown face—his very wise and friendly face—and make sure that he was all right.

I pushed my way out to the curb and craned my neck in both directions, searching the street for the navy blue limo. I knew it was a long shot, of course. And even if I did find the car, I realized, the chance that Woodrow would be inside, seated in his usual position behind the wheel, was next to nonexistent. He certainly wouldn't be there waiting for Ginger. Who knew if he even had his job anymore?

The entire block was lined with police cars and the limousine was nowhere in sight. My heart sank to my trampled toes. If I couldn't locate the limo, I speculated, I might never locate Woodrow. And what the hell would I do if Leo had let Woodrow go? How would I ever find him again? I couldn't look him up in the phone book because I didn't know his last name.

Maybe Leo would give me Woodrow's number, I thought. But how could I even ask him for it? The man was in mourning, for God's sake. I couldn't exactly call him up and say, "Hey, since Ginger doesn't need him anymore, do you think Woodrow could do some work for me?" Ugh! That would disgust me even more than it would Leo. I could, I supposed, go upstairs and pay Leo a condolence call and try to worm the number out of him then. But that would be too icky for words. Even for me.(Do all detectives have to sink so low?)

But, hey! Wait a second! I cautioned myself. *What if Leo was the murderer? Then it would be really dangerous for me to show any interest in talking to Woodrow. Leo would find that* very *suspicious, for sure, and then Woodrow and I could both be in for some serious trouble.* (See what a clever sleuth I am? You can't outwit Paige Turner!)

The best thing for me to do, I figured, would be to go right up to the front door of the building and tell the doorman, or the policeman, or whoever was standing guard, that I was an old friend of Ginger's, and that I had left my glasses upstairs in the penthouse, and that I couldn't see a thing without them, so would they please get Leo on the intercom and tell him I was there, because I was sure he'd want to see me in his hour of need—just as much as I wanted to *see* him, which I couldn't do without my glasses.

It was an outrageous premise, I knew, but one that I thought Leo would find wholly believable—except maybe for the seeing part, since he had watched me walk into a wall while wearing the specified specs. But if Leo bought my story and let me come upstairs, maybe I'd get the chance to snoop around a little bit, check out the scene. Perhaps I could locate Ginger's address book and either find and memorize Woodrow's number, or—better yet—swipe the darn book altogether. (Had stealing the clip about Ginger and Rusty from Orchid's files made my fingers permanently sticky?)

I was about to charge into action—try to work my way up to Fifth Avenue and around the corner to the building's entrance—when reality reared its ugly head again. Who the hell was I trying to kid? Even if Leo was willing to let me enter the penthouse, that didn't mean the police would allow it. Until Ginger's death was officially ruled a suicide, they would protect the scene as diligently as they would a homicide scene. They'd never let some "screwball female" go traipsing around the apartment and outside on the terrace, messing up the evidence, poking her nose into police matters, and scrambling through Ginger's drawers looking for an address book to snatch.

I'd be a fool, I knew, to even try.

Okay, so call me a fool, because I *did* try. I tried as hard as I could. I felt I owed it to Ginger. Hugging my purse to my chest like a football, I folded my arms, pulled my elbows in tight against my ribs, and began shouldering (okay, *shoving)* my way through the riotous crowd toward the goal line. I was determined to fight to the finish, to work my way up to the door of the building and then weasel (by whatever means necessary) my way up to the penthouse.

But I didn't get very far. As I neared the cordoned-off section of the curb—the area beneath Ginger's terrace where she had landed—I encountered yet another obstruction. It was a tremendous, formidable, and utterly impassable obstruction. It was an obstacle so significant and important that it even had a name: Detective Sergeant Dan Street.

TO SAY THAT I WAS UNHINGED WOULD be like calling the Three Stooges slightly uninhibited. I was so freaked out, and so desperate to keep Dan from seeing me, that I dropped down into a squat on the spot, hopelessly trying to shield my face from the jutting fists, knees, and elbows of the mob. If Dan saw me here, he'd never forgive me. And he'd banish me from the premises to boot.

But what was *he* doing here? I wondered, struggling to waddle in the opposite direction, guarding my face with my purse. This wasn't Dan's precinct! He didn't belong here! Why was he leaning against that squad car, chatting with a uniformed officer, smoking a cigarette, and drinking coffee from a paper cup? Was he just observing, or conducting an unauthorized personal investigation, or had he managed to turn the department on its ear and get himself assigned to this case?

Puzzled and panicked, I duck-walked a few feet away, then had to stop. My knees were breaking and my spine was bent like a pretzel. I was getting socked in the skull with leather brief cases and swinging camera bags. I couldn't take it for another second. Keeping my back turned squarely toward Dan, I rose to full height (which is five foot seven, in case you've been wondering) and continued to squeeze my way through the grieving, shouting, picture-taking throng, retracing my steps toward Madison.

Oh, lordy, lordy, lordy! Just let me get out of this mess in one piece, and unseen by Dan, and I'll never, ever, ever play detective again. No kidding! I really mean it! I'm not lying! Honest. (If you're taking me at my word now, just let me say one word about that: don't.)

The crowd had grown even larger, stretching around the corner onto Madison and halfway down the block toward 76th Street. It was the height of rush hour and it seemed that everybody in the city was rushing *here* straight from work—either to cry and shout and beat their breasts, or to pay their last respects, or to get a ghoulish glimpse (and maybe a good snapshot) of the very spot where Manhattan's most famous and popular redhead (Lucille Ball, it should be noted, lived in California) had plummeted to her hideous, face-crushing, neck-splitting, bone-shattering death.

I dashed across Madison and kept on running all the way to the subway stop at Lexington. I never once looked back. There was no point. I couldn't see anything through the tears.

Chapter 20

I GOT TO ABBY'S APARTMENT JUST IN time for happy hour. The door was wide open, the cocktails were being poured (Abby had declared it Tom Collins night), Jimmy was pacing around the kitchen, bragging about his new poem (a short piece he'd composed in his sleep), and Otto was so glad to see me I thought his skinny little string bean tail would twirl right off his skinny little streamlined butt.

It was good to be home.

"Holy moley!" Abby cried when she turned away from the kitchen counter and saw me standing in the doorway. "What the hell happened to you? You're a mess! Where have you been? To a one-hour girdle sale at Gimbel's?"

"It was worse than that," I said, tearing off my hat, gloves, and jacket and tossing the whole conglomeration on a kitchen chair. "I was at the scene of a murder."

"What?!" Abby and Jimmy croaked in unison. They stood frozen in the middle of the kitchen, staring at me with their mouths hanging open. Abby was busting for further details; Jimmy was just wondering what in the world I was talking about.

"I was outside Ginger Allen's penthouse," I said, "on the street where she died. It's pure pandemonium up there. Disgusting." I sat down, took a Chesterfield from the open pack on the table, and lit up.

"What do you mean, *murder?*" Abby probed, stepping over to the table and handing me my much-needed drink. "The papers said it was suicide."

"Yeah, because that's what the stupid police are saying." I started gulping the Tom Collins as if it were ice water.

"Well, the police should know," Abby said, giving me a stern, motherly, don't-go-asking-for-trouble look. "They're the ones gathering the evidence, you dig?"

"Yeah, but they haven't gathered nearly enough of it," I growled. "And if they officially declare Ginger's death's a suicide, they won't even look for any more. This is really drastic, Abby. Don't you see? Ginger was murdered, and I'm the only one who knows it! Except for the murderer, I mean."

"Whoa!" Jimmy bellowed, finally finding his tongue. "What's going on here? What are you talking about? Ginger Allen was murdered? How do *you* know?"

I tried to explain, starting at the top, but quickly found that I couldn't. It was too painful for words. Literally.

Abby stepped into the silence. "Let's not bother Paige with too many questions right now, okay, baby? She's too tired and upset. And hungry, too, I'll bet." Abby put her hand on the back of Jimmy's neck and snaked her fingers through his hair. "I'm guessing you're pretty hungry, too, sweetie," she murmured into his ear, "so why don't you run across the street to John's and get us a pizza? I'll tell you all about everything later, when we're alone . . . if we have time," she added, with an ultra-sexy smirk. Moving her mouth closer to his ear, she gave his lobe a little lick.

"Umm, okay," Jimmy mumbled, blushing with masculine pride. If he had been a peacock, his tail fan would've spanned the width of Wyoming. "I'll take Otto with me," he said, picking the little dog up in his arms. "It's time for his walk."

A single stroke down Otto's back, a sultry smooch on Abby's lips, and he was gone.

"Thanks, Ab," I said, relieved. "I couldn't bear to relive the whole story right now . . . And I'm so hungry I could eat a whale."

"I see you're thirsty, too," she said, eyeing my empty glass. "Want another one?"

"Yes, please."

Abby poured me another Tom Collins and brought it to the table with her own. Then she sat down across from me and, leaning forward on both elbows, gave me a troubled look. "Are you okay, kiddo? This must've hit you pretty hard."

"It's awful, Abby. If I had been a halfway decent detective, Ginger might still be alive. I feel so guilty I can hardly breathe."

"Oh, shut up, Paige! That's crazy talk! It's not your fault." She angrily flipped her long black braid from one shoulder to the other. "Do you hear what I'm saying? Listen to me, and listen good: It's not your fault!"

"Not directly, but—"

"Not even *in*directly!" she squawked. "All you were doing was trying to *help* the woman. You had nothing, I repeat, *nothing* to do with her death."

"But you don't know what I was thinking," I cried, madly puffing on my cigarette. "Ginger was such a disagreeable person, and so hard to work with, I wished she *would* die a couple of times. God forgive me, I even wanted to kill her myself!" I threw my head back and slugged down most of my second drink.

Abby reared back in her chair and let out a raucous laugh. "Now you're talking," she crowed. "Now you're sounding like a real human being, instead of some mealy-mouthed martyr with a tinfoil halo and a pair of plastic wings. You've got to get off this *meshuga* 'I'm to blame' bandwagon right now, Paige! Stop feeling sorry for yourself, and start focusing your energies on finding the person who's really to blame. And by that I mean the murderer. Or have you forgotten all about him?"

Abby's words were like a splash of cold water—a quick, sharp slap in the face. In spite of the fact that I had suffered a

horrible shock, and that I hadn't eaten a thing all day, and that
my head was spinning with the two extra-strong highballs I'd
almost completely consumed, I could actually feel myself
coming to my senses. I crushed the Chesterfield in the ashtray
and sat up tall as a tower in my chair. "You're right, Abby. *I*
didn't kill Ginger Allen. It was some *other* deranged and demented lunatic."

We both had a good laugh over that one.

And then we buckled our belts (okay, belted down the rest
of our drinks) and set our minds to figuring out who the other
lunatic might be.

FIRST, I TOLD ABBY ABOUT EVERYTHING
that had happened since the last time we'd talked about the
case (which had been Saturday evening—just two days
ago!—when she was dolling me up for the Stork Club). I gave
her a thorough rundown of the most important details—from
my torturous and only somewhat informative night at the
Stork, to the endless afternoon at Ginger's penthouse, to the
horrific and embarrassing (for Ginger) night at the *What's My
Line?* studio.

Abby was intrigued. Especially by Ginger's disastrous
Mystery Guest appearance. "How humiliating!" she cried.
"And it happened on national TV! On the most popular Sunday night show ever! I'll bet Ginger really *did* kill herself,"
she declared. "Lots of people would commit suicide if their
egos were destroyed in a coast-to-coast public spectacle like
that!"

"Not Ginger," I said, with conviction. "I think she'd kill
everybody who saw the show before she'd kill herself."

Abby giggled. "Was she really such a bitch?"

"The bitchiest," I said, feeling guilty again. (Speaking ill
of the dead is not one of my favorite pastimes.)

"Then there may have been more than one person who
wanted to kill her."

"Yeah, probably thousands."

"So, how are you going to narrow the field?"

"I really don't know," I said, shrugging and shaking my

head. "All I can think to do is start with the people I know—the group I met at the Stork Club. That would be Ginger's husband, Leo Marx; her sister and brother-in-law, Claire and Rusty Burnett; her director, Thelonious Kidd; and the famous radio couple, Tex and Toni Taylor. Although Ginger would never talk to me about any of these people, or give me any real clues to go on, I can't help thinking that she invited me to the Stork that night for a reason—that it was her way of introducing me to the prime suspects, the people she believed most likely to want her dead."

"Or maybe she just needed you to round out the table—make it an even eight." Leave it to Abby to focus on the social angle.

"No, I had the distinct impression that she had coerced Theo Kidd to come as *my* date, instead of the other way around."

"Then that lets *him* out," Abby proclaimed, slapping her hand on the table, jumping to conclusions as usual. "That's one down and five to go," she said, sounding just like the moderator of *What's My Line?*

I gave her statement some thought, but came to my own conclusion. "That is not a logical assumption," I said, in a teacherly tone of voice.

"Oh, who cares about Theo anyway?!" she sputtered. "Or the rest of those jokers, either! You should be focusing all your attention on Leo. He's the one who did it! It's always the husband."

I smiled at her swift, predictable deduction. "Correction," I said. "It's *usually* the husband. Not always, just usually."

"Well, that's good enough for me! Why waste your time investigating those other schmucks when all the odds point to Leo?"

My head was starting to feel a little fuzzy, so I stood up and walked around the room for a few seconds—from the kitchen area into the studio and back again. "It's just that all those other schmucks, except maybe Theo, seem to have such plausible motives for murder," I said. "Tex and Toni have been trying to get into television for years—ever since it started, I bet!—and Ginger may have been responsible for keeping them off the screen. They're under contract to Leo and NBC, but it's possible that Ginger was the one who was really pulling the strings." I sat down and lit up another cigarette.

"And Ginger's sister, Claire, may have had a more powerful motive than anybody," I went on. "Claire is shy, mousy, unhappy, and *very* unattractive. She's had to live in the shadow of her dazzling older sister her whole life. That alone could make a girl jealous and hateful. But when you add the fact that Claire is dirt poor while her famous sister was filthy rich . . . well, that's enough to turn a hateful girl homicidal."

"Claire's really that poor?" Abby said. "Like, totally penniless?"

"Well, no, not *that* poor," I said, "but she's not well-off at all. She and her husband Rusty live in one of those low-priced little development houses out in Levittown. They probably got it on the GI Bill, and I'd bet my last breadstick they had to borrow the one-hundred-dollar deposit from Ginger. I'm guessing all of Claire's clothes are her sister's cast-offs, and that she and Rusty never went out unless Ginger was footing the bill. And I'm pretty sure their only income has been from Rusty's salary as a stagehand on Ginger's show. Actually, I'd bet everything Claire has was a hand-me-down from Ginger—even her husband."

"Huh?" Abby honked. "What do you mean by that?"

"I mean Rusty Burnett was engaged to Ginger before he married Claire."

Abby's right eyebrow arched all the way up to her hairline. "Well, *that's* pretty damn interesting," she said, shooting me a wicked smile. "Sounds like something out of *True Confessions.*"

"Nope, I got it out of *Look* . . . Here," I said, taking the filched news clip out of my purse and handing it over the table to her, "read this and you'll see why I believe Rusty may have had a motive for murder, too."

Abby read the article, then stared at the photo and caption for a good thirty or forty seconds. From the length and inten-

sity of her examination, I expected her to come up with a
wise—or at least witty—observation. But what she said was,
"Hey, this Rusty guy is pretty cute. He looks great in a uniform, but I bet he looks even better without it. Do you think
he'd do some modeling for me?"

"Jesus, Abby!" I shrieked. "Here I am wondering if the
man's a murderer, for crying out loud, and you're just wondering how he'd look without his shirt!"

She gave me a hurt look. "Well, that's not *all* I was wondering about!"

"Oh, really? Were you imagining him without his pants as
well?"

"No!" she said, looking indignant (instead of ashamed, as
I thought she should). "I was wondering about a lot of
things—like why Ginger married Leo instead of Rusty, and
why Rusty married Claire, and if Ginger was still in love with
Rusty, or vice versa, and if either Claire or Leo knew. But
since I couldn't answer any of those questions, I figured I
should stop wasting my time wondering, and try to think of
some *tangible* way I could help you find out the truth.

"And that's when I thought," she continued, "that since
Rusty probably doesn't have his stagehand job anymore, he
might need to make a little extra cash—in which case I could
hire him as a model, and work my secret investigative black
magic on him while he's posing, and maybe dig up a few important clues in the process. I was only trying to assist you,
you know! But if you don't want my help . . ." She punctuated
her final words with a dramatic sigh and a pitiful pout.

It was all I could do not to laugh in her face. I knew a
phony performance when I saw one. (Abby was sounding and
acting just like I do when I'm trying to make up some outrageous excuse or explanation for Dan.) I didn't laugh, though.
I didn't even chuckle. I didn't want to embarrass her anymore
than I already had. And besides, I really did want her help.

"Your idea's a good one, Ab," I said, "but far too risky. I
wouldn't let you be alone with a potential murderer even for
a minute, and certainly not long enough to paint his picture.
And I wouldn't want Rusty coming here to your studio either,

finding out where we both live." I paused for a few moments, fleshing out a new scheme. "There's another way you might be able to help me, though, if you really want to."

Abby perked up immediately. She liked to play detective almost as much as I did. "Just say the word, Miss Marple. I'm ready to roll! What've you got on your sneaky little mind?"

"Remember a couple of weeks ago when Jimmy borrowed a friend's car and the two of you drove out to Coney Island?"

"Sure do. We ate Nathan's hot dogs and rode the Cyclone three times. It was a blast."

"So, do you think you could get Jimmy to borrow his friend's car again?"

"I guess so. Why?"

"I really want to talk to Claire," I told her. "In person and alone. And I think the best way to accomplish that would be to just show up on her doorstep—out of the blue and bearing a basket of fruit—to pay her a condolence call. Under those circumstances, it would be pretty hard for her to turn me away."

Abby gave me a knowing look. "I get it. You want Jimmy to drive you out to Levittown."

"Well, I could take the train out, I guess, but I'm not familiar with the Long Island Railroad, and even if there's a close and convenient stop, I'd still have to take a taxi to Claire's house. And that would look kind of suspicious, don't you think? I mean, why would her sister's long-lost college roommate, a woman she's met only once in her life, suddenly take a train and a taxi all the way out to Levittown to offer her sympathy? Wouldn't it seem more reasonable if I was out on Long Island visiting friends, who just happened to live nearby, and who were happy to drive me over to her house for a short visit?"

"Much more reasonable," Abby agreed, "and a hell of a lot more fun. We could all go out together, you dig? You, me, Jimmy, and Otto. Jimmy's pal's crate is soooo cherry. It's a halftime Henry rag-top with snowballs, a leather jacket, and four on the floor. A real asphalt eater."

My eyes rolled back in my head. "Forgive my ignorance, but what did you just say?"

"I said Jimmy's friend's car is really cool. It's a 1950 Ford convertible with whitewalls, leather upholstery, and a four-speed floor shift transmission. A very fast automobile." She winked and gave me a goofy grin.

"I didn't know you could speak Hot Rod," I teased.

"Oh, it's just a little something I picked up from Jimmy. He's a poet, you know—very good with words."

"Damn straight," Jimmy said, suddenly striding into the kitchen, carrying Otto in one arm and a large, warm, fragrant pizza box in the other. "I'm a lean, mean, eloquent machine. But right now I've got just one thing to say—let's eat!"

More poetic words were never spoken.

Chapter 21

WHILE WE WERE DEVOURING THE PIZZA, Abby asked Jimmy if he could borrow his friend's car again sometime soon.

"Yeah, no problem, babe. Biggie won't mind. That's how he got his nickname—he's got a big heart. Or is it because he's a big fool? I can't remember. Anyways, I can get his car anytime I want it, as long as somebody else isn't using it."

"Do you think you could get it tomorrow?" I asked. "From about five o'clock in the evening till, say, around eleven o'clock at night?"

"Probably could," Jimmy said with a shrug. "Biggie and I have been friends since third grade. I always protected him on the playground. He'll do anything for me."

"That's great!" I said, stuffing a big hunk of crust in my mouth, chomping it to a pulp, and swallowing it with a re-sounding gulp. "Then maybe you and Abby and Otto could pick me up right after work tomorrow, and we could motor out to Levittown for a drive-in cheeseburger, a chocolate malt, and a side order of murder and mayhem."

"Huh?" Jimmy said, looking at me as if I were an alien from another planet.

"Never mind about all that right now," Abby jumped in, putting her head on Jimmy's shoulder and nuzzling her nose to his neck. "I'll explain everything later, baby. Then you'll call up Biggie and seal the deal. But in the meantime, sweet daddy-o, Paige and I are in deep need of spiritual enlightenment. We need lyrical language to soothe our frazzled nerves. Could you recite your new poem for us, and take us to cloud nine?"

Oh, yuck! Was I going to have to listen to another Jimmy Birmingham "opus" just to get a ride out to Long Island? Why did my every female endeavor have to extract a masculine price?

Needing no further persuasion, Jimmy wiped the tomato sauce off his mustache and beard and scooched his chair back from the table. He picked Otto up off his lap, cradled him in the crook of his elbow, and stood up from the table, looking as tall and proud as Gary Cooper in *High Noon*. "I wrote this last night in my sleep," he said, speaking to Abby and me as if we were worshipers in his own personal parish, "and I think it has meaning for all crazy cats—all dads and dolls who want the word from the bird." He took a piece of notebook paper out of his pocket, unfolded it, and in his deep (dare I say sleepy?) baritone, read:

> Poky moments of spastic love abound
> Symbols of other times surround
> The neon igloo inside that resides
> Lingering pieces of discarded dreams
> Reveal to all as to what it means
> Deranged souls needing to be fed
> More spirit kisses for the head
> Allow it all in the spinning sperm
> Of foggy miasma.

"Wow!" I said, for lack of a better word. "That's really something, Jimmy!" In the interest of getting out to Levittown in one piece, I didn't tell him what kind of something I had in mind.

"Ohhhhh, baby!" Abby cooed. "You're amazing. Your style is unique and utterly atomic!" I could tell from her choice of words she was being diplomatic, too. "Nobody else can write like you," she insisted.

And who would want to? I wondered.

"Yeah, I think it's pretty good myself," Jimmy said, beaming, setting Otto down on the floor. "I'm glad I remembered it when I woke up. I think I'll go read it at the Vanguard tonight." (For reasons beyond my comprehension, Jimmy had a standing invitation to recite his new poems onstage at the Village Vanguard—a popular jazz joint on Seventh Avenue— whenever he felt like it.)

"Great!" Abby said. "I'll come with you. A hot new trio is playing here this week. You want to join us, Paige?"

"Thanks, but no thanks," I said, cringing at the thought. "I'm beat. This has been a really tough day. And I have to write up some notes for my new story. You kids go ahead without me. It's almost nine thirty—the first set's probably in full swing already."

I rose from the table and hurriedly gathered up all my stuff from the kitchen chair. Otto got excited and began scuffling around at my feet, his hard little toenails tapping a wild staccato on the linoleum. I bent down and fondled his warm floppy ears. Then I straightened up, thanked Abby and Jimmy for the pizza, and—courtesy of Tom Collins and my painful high heels—wobbled home.

THE MINUTE I GOT INSIDE, I PUT MY stuff down on the kitchen table, kicked off my shoes, and padded into the living room to turn on the TV (a floor model Sylvania that was still costing me six bucks a month). *The Ginger Allen Show* was supposed to go on—live—at nine thirty, and I wanted to see what would happen. Would some network executive come onscreen and make an announcement about Ginger's death? Would Thelonious Kidd emerge to talk about what a wonderful person and talented performer she had been? Would Ginger herself come forth to admit that her suicide had been staged, that her tragic demise had been nothing but a terrible hoax? (Yes, I really *am* that dopey. I really *was* still hoping for the impossible.)

But none of my imagined scenarios took place. Not only did Ginger not make a miraculous appearance, but her name was never mentioned at all. There was a public service announcement for the Red Cross, and a commercial for Lustre-Creme shampoo, and another one for Jantzen's new line of "shape-insurance" swimsuits, and then—at the very moment when you expected to hear the opening bars of her familiar theme music and see *The Ginger Allen Show* logo pop up on the screen—on came an old Roy Rogers movie! Can you believe that? A 1939 western titled *Saga of Death Valley*, of all things. (Oh, well. You've got to be grateful for small favors, I guess. At least it wasn't one of Lucille Ball's early flicks.)

I turned off the TV and headed upstairs, intending to change my clothes, plant myself in my little office, and begin typing up the notes for the Ginger Allen story I was now more determined than ever to write. I needed to get everything down on paper—every occurrence, every conversation, every facial expression, tone of voice, and possible clue I could recall—before the revealing details began to dissolve and disperse in (to borrow a couple of loopy but appropriate words from Jimmy "The Bard" Birmingham) the *foggy miasma* of my memory.

And I had other good intentions as well, you should know. I meant to remain steady, poised, safe, and close to the phone—in case Dan called. Or, better yet, came by.

But you know what they say about intentions, don't you? Even the best ones often go astray. And that was exactly what mine did, the very second I reached the halfway mark on the stairs. They fell apart, went crazily astray, and led me all the way back down the steps instead of up. I darted over to the kitchen table, put on my jacket, beret, and gloves, squeezed my aching feet back into my black patent leather pumps, and struck out for the NBC-TV studio where—but for fortune (or, rather, the lack of it)—Ginger Allen would have been singing, dancing, acting, and laughing right about now.

No, I didn't expect to find her there—the old Roy Rogers

movie had finally convinced me that she was really dead. I
just wanted to see if anybody else connected with the show
was there—Theo, or Rusty, or maybe even Leo. Maybe one
or all three had shown up on the set out of habit, so accustomed to spending their Monday nights in the studio that they
didn't know where else to go, what else to do. Or perhaps they
had gone there hoping to draw some comfort from each other
and the customary surroundings. Or maybe they had been
called to the studio for an emergency meeting or some other
professional purpose.

And if Leo *was* there, maybe Woodrow would be there,
too, I thought, waiting outside in the limo to take Leo home—
or to El Morocco, or the Stork, or wherever else he wanted to
go to drown his sorrows (or celebrate his homicidal success).

Then again, maybe nobody would be there, and I would
wind up wasting the night in a wild goose chase. But that was
a risk I was willing to take. Nothing wagered, nothing won.
And wild geese didn't bother me at all. What bothered me was
the idea of sitting around with my head in the sand, taking the
safe and easy way out, not even trying to identify Ginger's
killer so he could be brought to justice.

I dashed over to Sixth Avenue, scrambled down the steps
to the subway, and caught an uptown express. And less than
twenty frantic minutes later, I jumped off the train at the 50th
Street station, hurried up the stairs to the street, and walked
(okay, *ran*) around the corner toward the entrance of the RCA
building. I kept searching the streets for Woodrow, but the
navy blue limousine was nowhere to be seen.

When I reached the entrance at 30 Rockefeller Plaza—
known to people in radio and television (and to readers of the
gossip columns) as 30 Rock—I took a deep breath and
ducked inside. Except for the small band of reporters and photographers milling around near the door (hoping, no doubt, to
ambush some lingering members of Ginger's cast and crew
on their way out), the place was almost deserted.

It was the first time I'd ever been in the elegant 70-story
RCA building, and I was tempted to just stand there for a
while, gazing at the famous and impressive "American

Progress" mural that covered the walls and ceiling of the enormous entryway. But I couldn't take the time. It was after ten o'clock. The building would surely be closing soon. Barely glancing at the Art Deco fixtures and the gleaming wooden railings of the wraparound mezzanine overhead, I hurried onward, toward the numerous banks of elevators stretching down the middle of the beige-and-black marble lobby.

When I located the row of elevators designated for floors one through ten and saw that one elevator was open, and that the operator was still on duty, I slowed my pace and walked right up to him. "Eighth floor, please," I said, remembering that Ginger's show had been broadcast from Studio 8H, and hoping that the studio numbers correlated to the floor numbers. Shoulders back and head held high, I quickly stepped into the wood-paneled enclosure, moved to the center, then turned around to face the front. I was doing my best to look serious and official—as though I knew where I was going and had an unquestionable right to be there.

"You headin' up to 8H?" the skinny blond operator wanted to know. His maroon and gold uniform was too big for him. He looked like a kid in his daddy's suit. "'Cause I'm not s'posed to take anybody up there, you know. They're not doin' *The Ginger Allen Show* tonight, on account of the star just killed herself. Most of the people who had tickets to the show heard about it before and didn't bother comin' in. But there's been a few folks who didn't hear anything, so they showed up to see the show, and I had to tell 'em all to go home."

"I didn't come to see the show," I told him, doing a swell imitation of Katherine Hepburn (upper-crusty accent and all). "I'm Mr. Leo Marx's private secretary. He called and asked me to come here tonight to take notes during an urgent meeting. They're waiting for me now. Take me up, please."

Either I was a really good actress, or the elevator boy was really gullible, because the next thing I knew he slapped the elevator doors closed, gave his shiny brass lever a wicked crank, and sent us shooting upward so suddenly and so fast I left my stomach on the ground floor. And when we came to an abrupt halt on eight, and he yanked the doors open to let me out, I realized I'd left my nerve at ground level too.

Oh, lordy, lordy, lordy! I whimpered to myself, stepping out into the long, dark, deserted hallway, elevator doors screaking closed behind me. *Whatever possessed me to come here? What if somebody (namely, the murderer) sees me? And what in the world am I supposed to do now that I* am *here? I don't even know which way to turn!* I was in a frightful state, whipping my head back and forth, straining my eyes from one end of the dimly lit hall to the other, wondering if it was too late for me to begin a new career in bull fighting, or tightrope walking, or something nice and relaxing like that.

(As you may have noticed, I have these slight mental breakdowns every once in a while—okay, fairly often. They don't mean anything, though. They're just my way of letting off steam, facing my inner fears, and reminding myself what a stupid idiot I am.)

Anyway, I was in such a panic that I almost didn't see the big sign on the wall right in front of my face. (Well, it was pretty darn dark in there!) Written in bold red letters on a pure white background, the sign said: STUDIO 8H, and there was a big red arrow pointing to the right. Once I pulled myself together and began breathing evenly again, the sign came into focus. So I sucked up my courage and went where the big red arrow told me to go.

The door to Studio 8H was halfway down the hall. I couldn't have missed it if I'd tried. Not only was the closed door itself clearly marked, but there were several signs around the entrance indicating which show would be broadcast when, and whether or not a show was currently in rehearsal or on the air. And if that wasn't enough to grab your attention, both sides of the hall leading up to the studio entrance were lined with life-size cardboard cutouts of NBC's most popular stars. Sid Caesar, Imogene Coca, Dinah Shore, Milton Berle, Groucho Marx, Red Buttons, George Gobel, Wally Cox, Loretta Young, Gayle Storm, Tony Martin, Donald O'Connor, Jack Webb—they were all standing there, big as life, welcoming you to the wonderful world of television.

Ginger was there too, of course—wearing an emerald-green evening gown and a big coral smile—standing like a queen at the very head of the line, closest to the studio door. Her red hair was gleaming, her green eyes were glowing (even in the semi-darkness!), and her graceful arms beckoned you to enter her studio of dreams.

I gave her a wink, made her a solemn promise (about you-know-what), and said a silent prayer for the safe passage of her soul. Then I slowly, carefully, soundlessly opened the door to 8H and slipped—like a thief—inside.

Chapter 22

HUGGING THE WALL NEAR THE STUDIO entrance, I stood listening to my ragged breath and walloping heartbeats for a few seconds, waiting for my shadowy surroundings to come into focus. But when they finally did—when I actually perceived the scene stretched out before me—I couldn't believe my eyes. This was no mere studio. This was a huge theater with a big stage and a balcony and everything! It was a building within a building. The windowless arena was at least ten stories high, and judging from the sea of theater seats fanned out across the balcony and the floor in front of me, I figured it could accommodate anywhere from a thousand to fifteen hundred people.

At the moment, though, there were only two in the audience. They were sitting right next to each other, in the very center of the very first row, and they were so intensely involved in their private (and seemingly overheated) conversation they had no idea that I had just entered the studio. To make sure they would remain unaware of my presence, I snuck deeper into the shadows at the rear of the theater and crouched halfway down behind the last row of seats.

This new vantage point made it impossible for me to see

the two faces in the front row, but that didn't matter. I didn't need even one glimpse of their features to know who they were. Their twin hairdos—those preposterous, stiffly sprayed, mile-high blonde pompadours!—gave me all the identification I needed. It was Tex and Toni Taylor, America's favorite radio couple. And though I couldn't hear a word they were saying (or, rather, *whispering*) to each other, I could see from the way they were gesturing with their hands and fidgeting in their seats that they were in a twitch about something.

I was trying to get up the nerve to creep a few rows ahead—hoping to get close enough to hear some of the darling duo's hushed dialogue—when Rusty Burnett suddenly strode out from the wings, weaved through a cluster of TV cameras, and walked up to the front of the well-lit stage. "Okay, that's it," he said to the Taylors, leaning down, talking over the edge of the stage in a normal and perfectly audible speaking voice. "We got the test on film, so you two can go home now. Leo's got everything he needs. He said he'll call you in a few days."

"A few days?" Tex squawked. "Why do we have to wait so long? Why can't we talk to him now? We've been waiting for years already!"

"That's right!" Toni chimed in. "He should give us his answer now. I can't take this anymore. The suspense is killing me!"

Rusty stood up straight, crossed his brawny arms over his barrel chest, and gave them a scornful look. "You got a hell of a lotta nerve, you know that?" he said. "Ginger killed herself last night, in case you forgot. Leo's in bad shape. He's got the press to deal with, funeral arrangements to make, lots of business to take care of. The last thing he needs is to have you two breathing all over him, begging for a shot at the big time. He came in tonight, didn't he? Just so's you could make your pitch and do your little screen test? So you better back off now, and leave him alone. Leo will decide about your friggin' show in his own sweet time."

"Is that the way you talk to a lady?" Toni sputtered, aghast.

"No, that's the way I talk to a pain in the ass," Rusty said.

"No problem, Rusty!" Tex jumped in, erupting in nervous laughter, trying to make light of the situation. "Toni's just tired, that's all. And when she's tired she gets a little impatient. Isn't that right, sweetheart?" Tex turned and shot his wife a pleading look. "Please don't worry about us," he said, facing Rusty again. "We're just fine. And we don't mind waiting at all. You tell Leo to take all the time he needs."

"I'll do that," Rusty said, smiling smugly.

"Thank you," Tex muttered. Toni didn't say anything.

"Good night, then," Rusty said, turning and stomping off the stage, disappearing behind the wings.

A split second later all the stage lights were turned off, and the theater was plunged into darkness. (The darkness wasn't *total*, you should know. It was just dreadfully dim and murky—the kind of darkness you hated as a kid, when, even though your bedroom door was left open a crack and the hall light was still on, you were too scared to go to sleep.)

Tex and Toni sat in silence for a few seconds, no doubt stunned by their rude lights-out dismissal. Then they stood up and—whispering frantically to each other—began making their way toward the bright red letters of the electrified exit sign over the nearest studio door. I stayed where I was—crouched low behind the last row of seats, holding my breath and straining my ears—as they slowly stumbled and sputtered up the aisle toward the exit. The closer they got, the clearer their words became.

"That man's a beast!" Toni said. "And who does he think he is to speak to us that way? The last I heard, Rusty Burnett was nothing but a lousy stagehand!"

"Yeah, there's something fishy going on here," Tex replied. "All of a sudden Rusty's acting like the star of the show. Did you see the way he was swaggering and ordering the cameraman around? I don't get it!"

"Do you think he has any influence over Leo?" Toni's high-pitched voice was crackling with concern. "Because if he does, then we might have made a horrible mistake. What we did could wind up hurting us instead of helping us."

"Well, we can't worry about that now," Tex insisted.

"What's done is done. There's no turning back. Ginger is dead, and Leo has total control, and that's what we have to focus on."

"But Rusty is related to Leo, you know. What if Leo decides to—"

"Don't even think about it," Tex interrupted. "Leo's smart, and he's the boss, and he'll do right by us. If it wasn't for Ginger, he'd have put us on TV a long time ago. I'm sure of it."

"You better be right," Toni said, reaching the door first but stepping aside, waiting for Tex to open it for her. "I'll go out of my mind if—"

I couldn't hear the rest of her sentence. Toni's words were cut off as Tex ushered her out of the studio theater and into the hall, pushing the door closed behind them.

Rising out of my crouch at last (my knees were killing me!), I stood trembling in the darkness, wondering what to make of the scene I'd just witnessed, and madly striving to plan my next move. Should I wait till Tex and Toni were gone, then make a dash for the elevator, hoping to get down to the lobby before anybody saw me, and before the building was locked up for the night? Or should I run up onto the stage and sneak behind the curtain—through the same side opening where Rusty had disappeared—to see if Rusty or Leo or Theo or any other people were still there? Maybe they were having some kind of secret backstage powwow. And if they were, shouldn't I at least try to find a good hiding spot and listen in?

Yes, you should! I told myself, remembering the postmortem promise I had made to Ginger (or, rather, her life-size cardboard image) just minutes ago. So what if all I wanted to do was curl up in the fetal position on the floor of NBC-TV's Studio 8H, fall into a deep, dreamless sleep, and forget that I had ever met the country's second-most beloved redhead? What I *wanted* to do didn't count. What I was *driven* to do was all that mattered—even to me (okay, *only* to me).

I straightened my shoulders, sucked in a chestful of oxygen, and marched down the aisle to the foot of the stage. Heart pounding like a berserk beatnik's bongos, I tiptoed up the steps to the darkened platform. Then—holding my hands out in front of me so I wouldn't accidentally crash into one of the huge TV cameras stationed around the sides of the stage—I began inching my way forward, praying to God (and Allah, and Buddha, and even Ginger) that I wouldn't trip over any of the treacherous wires or cables coiled like snakes across the lightless floor.

Luckily, I made it to the proper passageway without incident. Then I came to a halt, took off my high heels, tucked them under my arm, and—hoping against hope that my luck would hold (and that I wouldn't get any runs in my nylons)—crept backstage in my stocking feet.

IT WAS EVEN DARKER BEHIND THE CUR-tain. If it hadn't been for the thin shaft of light streaming in through the slightly open door ahead, I never would have seen that the entire backstage area was piled up with scenery. Painted backdrops, false fronts, tarps, draperies, artificial trees, fake animals, furniture—you name it, it was back there. I held my breath and stood still for a moment, listening for sounds in the shadows. Hearing nothing but the gurgling of my own stomach (pizza takes a long time to digest!), I finally slithered down the narrow path toward the light and stuck my nose through the open door.

There was another hallway on this side of the theater, and the overhead lights were beaming. I could see, and easily read, the words stenciled on some of the doors lining the opposite side of the corridor: WOMEN'S DRESSING ROOM, MEN'S DRESSING ROOM, MAKEUP, WARDROBE, PROPS. Not all of the doors were labeled, but one of them—the one directly across the hall from where I was standing—boasted a shiny gold star and the name GINGER ALLEN.

Seeing that the hallway was totally deserted, I decided to sneak across the floor and let myself into Ginger's dressing room. I figured I could hide out in her private quarters for a few minutes, catch my breath, and snoop around for clues at the same time. Pretty nifty plan, right?

Wrong.

The door was locked.

And so there I was, standing as big as you please out in the middle of the brightly lit hall, quivering like the coward I truly am, in plain sight of God and everybody. (Okay, okay! So it wasn't exactly everybody, since nobody at all was there. But somebody *could* have been there, you know, and it could have been the murderer, for pity's sake—and then my goose would have been pretty much cooked. Burnt to a crisp, more like it.)

I was so nervous I was about to run for the elevator, get out of the building as fast as I could, and make a mad dash for home. But then I noticed that a door halfway down the corridor was standing agape, and that some garbled noises—sounded like voices to me!—were emanating from the open room. Baited like a trout (well, I *was* looking for a worm, you know), I hugged my shoes and purse tight to my chest and began slinking across the cool gray linoleum tiles toward the alluring sounds.

I snuck right up to the side of the door, but I didn't dare look in. If I had been able to see the people inside, then they would have been able to see *me*, and that was a risk I couldn't take. I wished I had my (I mean, Abby's) glasses with me. At least that way, if I happened to get caught lurking around in the hall like a loon, I could assume my Patty Turner identity and pretend that Ginger had given me a ticket for tonight's show. I could assert that I was so upset by my dear college roommate's suicide, that—even though I knew her show had been canceled forever—I had come to the theater anyway, searching for her closest coworkers, longing to share my overwhelming grief and express my condolences.

Without the glasses, though, the Patty Turner trick would be dangerous. Leo was the only one of the Stork Club group who'd ever seen me sans spectacles. And just because he hadn't recognized me (or hadn't seemed to, at any rate), that didn't mean nobody else would. Any one of them might have seen my picture in the papers. And any one of them might be the murderer. And if the murderer recognized me as Paige Turner, dame detective (*that,* believe it or not, was what the newspapers had called me!), then he would know the real reason I was here, and who I was really searching for (i.e., *him*).

A sticky situation, to say the least.

So, as I stood there flat against the wall on one side of the open door, straining my ears to catch every single word coming out of the room, I was also straining every single cell in my body to stay silent. If I couldn't remain un*heard,* then I surely wouldn't remain un*seen.*

"You know what I think?" a strong male voice said. "I think we're rushing into things too fast. Where's the friggin' fire? Ginger died less than twenty-four hours ago. Why do we have to pick her replacement right now?" I could tell from his vocabulary and powerful projection that the speaker was Rusty Burnett.

"We don't," Leo said (I recognized his smooth baritone immediately). "We could sit on our hands and wait for some ignorant NBC execs to fill the time slot with one of their own awful programs. Believe me, they've got plenty of them lined up. But then we'd lose our lucrative Monday night niche, and we'd lose Ginger's loyal following—an audience I've spent five years studying and coddling and building up to the biggest NBC-TV viewership ever. Is that really what you want to do, Rusty? Kiss all the hard work and profits goodbye?"

"Well, no, I—"

"Leo's right," another male voice broke in. "We've got to move fast. I don't know about you, Burnett, but I want to keep my job." Was that Thelonius Kidd, the director, talking? I couldn't tell. Whoever it was sounded sober, and the only time I'd ever heard Theo utter a word, he'd been drunker than Dean Martin ever thought possible.

"Okay," Rusty said, "so we gotta move fast. But does that mean we gotta go with the first thing that comes along? Are you tellin' me that Tex and Toni Taylor are the friggin' best we can do?"

Somebody giggled, and it sounded like a woman. Was it Claire? (I honestly couldn't say, since I'd hardly heard Ginger's sister speak, and I'd *never* heard her laugh.) *If Theo's in there, it could be one of his girlfriends,* I thought, remembering that the *Photoplay* article I'd read in Orchid's file room had referred to Theo as the "wildly handsome playboy director." Or maybe it was just a wardrobe girl, or a makeup girl, or an actress wangling for an audition. Surely Leo wouldn't have a new lady friend already! I moved my ear a little closer to the door, hoping the woman would say something to distinguish herself.

But Leo's voice was the next to come through. "The Taylors are definitely our best bet," he insisted. "They've got name value, a big radio following, and—now that they've jazzed up their appearance—strong visual appeal. They're good talkers and interviewers, and they can sing and dance a little, too. Ginger's fans will love them. Believe me, I know this audience, and I think Tex and Toni can keep them for us. You have to keep the audience if you want to keep the sponsors."

"But how will the NBC brass feel about the switch?" the unidentified male speaker wanted to know. "If they put *The Tex and Toni Show* on TV, they'll lose the *Breakfast with Tex and Toni* radio show. Won't that put a crimp in the deal?"

"Yeah, Leo," Rusty barked, "what do you say about that?"

"I say you both need to take a course in broadcasting." Leo was beginning to lose his patience. "How can you be so short-sighted? NBC doesn't have to lose a goddamn thing. Tex and Toni can do both shows, and each will publicize the other. It's a sweetheart situation. NBC will eat it up. Especially after they see the test we made tonight. But we'll lose the time slot if we don't act fast. And by that I mean *right now.*"

The room fell into silence while those inside mulled over what Leo had said. I held my breath and froze like a statue, terrified of making a sound and alerting them to my presence. But when the three men all started talking at once—yakking about how time was of the essence and how Leo needed to pitch *The Tex and Toni Show* to the network first thing tomorrow—I relaxed a little bit and leaned closer to the door, trying to separate one sentence, and one speaker, from another.

That's when I picked up on the woman's voice again. At

first she was just laughing, but after a couple of seconds she started talking as well. "This is so funny!" she said, between giggles. "I can't help thinking how mad Ginger would be if she knew what you were doing."

It was at that very moment—as I was craning forward, focusing all my energy and concentration on trying to identify (or at least memorize) the female speaker's voice—that the dreaded disaster occurred. My black patent pumps dropped out of my arms and tumbled, in the most sickening and cinematic slow motion imaginable, toward the floor. And then they landed—in a loud, thumping clatter of shoe leather and metal-tipped stiletto heels—right in front of the open door.

"What the hell was that?!" Rusty croaked.

"Hey, somebody's out there!" the unidentified man cried, clomping to his feet, scraping his chair aside, and barging for the door in an audible, fire-breathing fury.

I was really dying to know who the onrushing anonymous man was, not to mention the giggling woman, but for some curious (okay, *cowardly*) reason, I didn't stick around to find out.

Chapter 23

LEAVING MY PRACTICALLY BRAND-NEW pair of five-dollar pumps in a sad jumble on the floor, I charged down the hall like a racehorse and ducked through the door leading to the backstage storage area. Two people were running down the hall after me. I could tell from the cadence (and rapidity!) of their encroaching footsteps. Feeling certain that I was on the verge of being caught—or at least *seen*—I veered off the pathway leading out to the stage and forged my way deep into the recesses of the big piles of scenery stored closest to the door.

This sudden detour slowed me down quite a bit (running over great big clumps of canvas and squeezing your way through huge, unstable stacks of props and stage furniture isn't easy, you know), but at least I was hidden from view. And the backstage area was quite dark. If I stopped lumbering ahead, and stood very still, and kept perfectly quiet, maybe my pursuers would never even realize I was here. Maybe I could just hole up here for the rest of my life—living behind the false front of that little picket-fenced cottage over there, sleeping in a cardboard bed, dining on rubber chicken, watering my wooden flowers . . .

A loud wham brought me to my senses. My pursuers had burst into the backstage area, crashing the door against the wall in their haste. (At least that's what it sounded like. From my frozen position behind a tarp-covered stack of chairs and an upended wooden desk, I couldn't see what was happening.) "She's in here somewhere," the anonymous man sputtered. "I saw her go through this door!"

"Here, girlie, girlie, girlie!" Rusty Burnett called out, mimicking a kid calling his cat. "Come out, come out, wherever you are!" He sounded excited, like he was having a good time.

"Maybe she went out on the stage," the other man said, voice receding as he stumbled in that direction. "Hey, turn on the lights, will ya? I can't see a thing."

Uh oh! I had forgotten about the lights. Why did there have to be lights? I wasn't in the mood for lights!

But on they came, blinding me with their brightness, stealing away my cover, exposing me, like a runaway prisoner, to their searching beams. I couldn't continue to stand there, so naked and afraid, and so close to the men who were chasing me that my capture was sure to be mere seconds away. I had to make a break for it, and I had to do it *now*.

Throwing all caution, and every shred of my ladylike composure (stop laughing!) to the winds, I dropped down to all fours and started crawling like a demented lizard around and through the piles of props and scenery, toward the opposite side of the backstage area—the other side of the theater.

"Hey!" Rusty shouted. "I heard something! She's over here! She's trying to get away! Come quick!" I could hear him plowing his way through the cramped storage area, as hot on my heels as a bloodhound with a fresh, strong scent.

"I'm right behind you!" the other man cried. "Jump her if you have to. Don't let her escape!"

Well, this little exchange not only scared the living daylights out of me, but it also ticked me off. Nobody, but *nobody,* was going to jump me! I vaulted to my feet, wheeled around in a half circle, and started pushing and pulling and turning over all the furniture and props and false fronts and backdrops in my wake. A china cabinet, a chest of drawers, a plaster of Paris cow, a tall plywood replica of the Eiffel Tower—I sent everything crashing to the floor behind me, building a high, jagged wall between myself and the enemy. Then I spun around, ran a few feet ahead, and did it again. Folding chairs were flying, lampposts were toppling, fake palm trees were falling, and two angry, roadblocked men were yelling and cursing their heads off.

You never heard such a racket in your life.

When I reached the other side of the storage area, I threw open the side door and blasted out into the dimly lit hall, clutching my purse to my chest, holding my beret to my head, and running faster than I ever had in all my born days. I'm not kidding. If you had been there watching me race for the elevators, you would have seen nothing but a streak. A dazzling, whizzing streak of motion with no face and no shoes—just a red beret stuck, like a flattened cherry, on top.

But in spite of my incredible speed, I never made it all the way to the elevators. As I was running down the hall I caught sight of a door marked FIRE ESCAPE, and—without a breath of hesitation—I jerked it open and ducked inside. And then I kept on running like a madwoman down, down, down the steep, rough, cold cement stairs. It was almost pitch-dark in that winding, fireproof stairwell, and I kept my left hand linked to the metal handrail as if it were a coal miner's lifeline. Though I was sick about losing my new high-heeled pumps, I was grateful as all get-out that I didn't have them on.

Three or four flights down I heard the heavy fire escape door clank open above. Stifling all my huffs and puffs and grunts of exertion, I came to an abrupt standstill on the stairs, trying, but failing, to silence my banging heart. Did they know I was down here? Were they going to come barreling down the steps after me? And why were they chasing me anyway? Who did they think I was? Were they afraid that I'd overheard something incriminating? Was one of them the murderer? Were they in on it together? If they caught me, what would they do? Would I be shoved over the handrail and

down the stairwell the same way Ginger was pushed off her
balcony?

"She ain't here!" Rusty yelled to his accomplice. "It's
pitch dark and dead quiet. She musta grabbed the elevator. We
gotta get down to the lobby quick!" There were some scraping and rustling sounds and then the heavy door clanged shut.
Except for my hammering heartbeats, all was still.

Whew!

Legs wobbly with relief, I released all my pent-up huffs,
puffs, and grunts, clasped my white-cotton-gloved fingers
more securely around the handrail, then continued my shoe-
less scramble down the stairs.

There were two doors at the bottom of the staircase. One
of them, I figured, would lead to the lobby, the other to the
street. Trouble was, I didn't know which was which. My frantic hustle down the twisting steps had left me dizzy and confused. Not wanting to open the lobby door even a fraction of
an inch (my reasons for this should be abundantly obvious), I
stuck my face up close to the outer edge of each exit, trying
to peer through the miniscule splits between the doors and the
jambs.

I couldn't see a thing, of course. I did, however, *smell*
something. There was a faint stench seeping in through one of
the doors, and after a brief analysis (i.e., another whiff), I figured out what the odor was. Automobile exhaust fumes. This
had to be the door to the street! I had finally sniffed out a clue!

I cracked the door open and peeped outside. Yep. I was
right. The door opened directly onto a side street, and once I
saw that the coast was clear, I lunged out onto the sidewalk
and started running for the subway as fast as I possibly could.
The cement was hard, cold, and gritty under my feet, and my
stockings were getting ripped to ribbons, but I kept on running like a bat out of hell (a perfectly apt description in this
case, since I had—by this point in my nerve-wracking expedition—gone totally batty, and now believed the RCA Building to be the headquarters of Hades).

I never looked back. I was running so hard, and panting so
loud, and focusing so intently on my urgent race to the sub-

way, that I was blind to everything that was going on around me. I didn't know if there was any traffic in the street or any other people on the sidewalk. I didn't notice if any reporters or photographers were still hanging around the area, and I had no idea whether Rusty Burnett and his covert cohort had tracked me out of the RCA building into the night.

I also didn't know that a car was following me.

I WAS JUST A FEW YARDS AWAY FROM Sixth Avenue when it finally registered in my addled brain that the pavement ahead of me was aglow—that both the street to my left and the sidewalk in front of me were glaring with light, and that the twin beams of illumination were coming from behind and advancing in sync with my running feet. *Headlights!* I screamed to myself. *I'm being chased by headlights!*

To say that I was startled by this sudden discovery would be like calling an earthquake unsettling. I was shocked out of my skin, and terrified to the core, and if there had been a sewer manhole in the near vicinity, I would have yanked off the cover, jumped down into the hole, and pulled the heavy lid closed over my head. Dense darkness, smelly sewage, and scuttling rats were far less frightening to me at that moment than the thought of being run over by a car.

But there was no manhole to dive into. My best hope of escape was the subway, so I propelled myself around the corner at Sixth Avenue and continued my dash for the IND entrance. I tried to run faster, but I couldn't. My legs and lungs were already being taxed to the limit.

When the headlights followed me around the corner, I went into a panic so deep it was deadly. I couldn't breathe, and my heart felt like it was going to burst. Realizing I had to slow down enough to inhale at least as much oxygen as I was expelling, I slackened my pace to a sprint instead of a gallop. And then—finally taking the risk of letting my face be seen—I snapped my head around to grab a glimpse of the car that was following me, praying with all my might that it would be a police car. And that the driver would be Dan.

(Well, it was possible, you know! Dan *could* have been casing the area around the RCA Building and seen me sneak out the side door and go running down the street. He could have come to the conclusion that I was in trouble and decided to follow me for my own protection. And if that was the case, then I had been busting my lungs and bloodying the soles of my pitiful feet for nothing!)

No such luck.

It definitely wasn't a police car. It was a long, sleek, champagne-colored Cadillac, and I had never seen the damn thing before in my life.

Because of the darkness and the glare of the headlights, I couldn't make out who was driving the car, but I saw in an instant that the oncoming automobile was about to overtake me. Putting on another burst of speed (abject fear can produce some pretty potent adrenaline), I shot my eyes back to the sidewalk and took off like a rocket for the subway. (Okay, so it wasn't really like a rocket. It was more like an overloaded bus with four flat tires, but what do you want? It was as fast as I could go.)

Suddenly the Caddy screeched to a stop behind me, and I heard the car door open and slam shut. Then a rush of heavy footsteps charged after me—getting louder and louder, coming closer and closer—until a large hand grabbed hold of my shoulder and stopped me dead in my tracks. Panicked beyond words, but determined to stand up to my assailant and fight for my life, I dropped my purse to the ground, squeezed my eyes into tight, protective slits, spun around on my heels, and began pummeling my attacker's chest with both fists.

"Miss! Miss!" a deep male voice cried out. "Please don't do that, miss! I didn't mean to scare you! I'm not going to hurt you!" The man didn't grab my arms or push me away. He just stood there, like a giant tree, letting me hit him repeatedly in the trunk.

My eyes popped open in sudden awareness and surprise. "Woodrow!" I cried, so relieved I thought I might faint. "Is it really you?"

"Yes, miss," he answered. "It's me."

"Oh, my god! I'm so sorry I hit you. I thought you were the murderer."

"No, miss," he said, eyes widening in alarm. "I swear I never killed a soul!" Sweat was beading on his dark brown brow and beginning to dribble down his fleshy cheeks. He took a white handkerchief out of his breast pocket and mopped his face and mustache dry.

"I'm so glad to see you!" I sputtered. "I've been looking all over for you! I wanted to talk to you so much. I'm so distressed about what happened."

"Yes, miss. I thought you would be. So when I saw you running out of Miss Allen's, I mean the RCA Building, I thought I better catch up to you right quick. You looked like you were in trouble, and I wanted to help you if I could. I didn't mean to scare you. I was hoping you'd see it was me and stop running and get in the car. I was afraid to shout out. And I knew it wouldn't look right if I got out and chased you down the street. Folks don't like it when a Negro man runs after a white woman. Finally, though, I had to catch you 'fore you ducked down in the subway."

Woodrow was right, of course, and I understood immediately why he had motored along behind me the way he had. What I didn't understand was why he was driving a champagne-colored Cadillac instead of the navy blue limo. "I couldn't tell it was you," I said. "Whose car are you driving? Where's Miss Allen's limousine?"

"That's Miss Allen's husband's car, miss. I'm working for Mr. Marx now. Miss Allen's limousine got taken away by the police, and when they're finished with it, it's goin' straight to the body shop. Mr. Marx says he wants to sell it soon as it's fixed. Says he never wants to see it again as long as he lives and breathes."

"Because it stirs up too many memories?" I asked.

Woodrow jerked his head from side to side, shooting nervous glances up and down the street. "Can we go talk in the car, miss? It's a awful sad story. And I feel mighty uncomfortable standing out here on the sidewalk. Somebody might see us and call out a lynching party. "

"Of course," I said, snatching my purse up off the sidewalk and quickly heading for the car. I suddenly felt as anxious for Woodrow as for myself. There hadn't been a lynching in New York in over fifty years, but there had been many other incidents of racial discrimination. Plenty of people were still violently opposed to the *Brown v. Board of Education* ruling delivered just under a year ago, and angry segregationists were lurking everywhere. Likewise, members of the Ku Klux Klan had strongholds in upstate areas like Buffalo and Peekskill, but were known to make furtive forays into Manhattan just to stir up trouble.

There was no doubt about it. When speaking to a white woman in the dead of night in the middle of a near-deserted street, a Negro man had to be careful. Very careful. Almost as careful as a woman with a killer on her tail.

Chapter 24

WOODROW OPENED THE BACK DOOR OF the Caddy for me and I ducked inside. Then he hurried around the car and folded his massive frame into the driver's seat. "I'll just drive around a little bit, if that's okay with you, miss," he said, turning the key in the ignition. "We won't attract any attention that way."

"Good idea," I said, as eager as he was to leave the area. "But what about Mr. Marx? Isn't he expecting you to pick him up?" I slid to the middle of the plush leather interior, leaned forward, and stuck my chin over the back of the seat in front. It was much easier to talk to Woodrow in the Caddy than it had been in the limo.

"Yes, miss, but he told me to be here at twelve thirty and it's only midnight now. I didn't have anything else to do so I got here early. Thought I'd listen to the radio and take a little nap." Woodrow pulled the car away from the curb and headed uptown on Sixth.

"That's swell!" I said, heart doing a happy flip-flop in my chest. "Then would you have time to take me home, Woodrow? I lost my shoes tonight, and my feet are feeling a little the worse for wear."

"Be glad to, miss," he said, turning the corner on 50th and heading toward Fifth. "I saw you were barefoot before, but I didn't want to say anything. Thought you'd think I was being nosy."

"Oh, no, Woodrow. I would never think that. You can ask me anything, anytime." I propped my forearm on the back of the front seat and then my chin on top of my forearm. I started to explain how I had lost my pumps, but suddenly didn't want to take the time. "I'll tell you about the shoes later," I said, "but right now I want to know about Miss Allen's limousine. Why did the police take it away? Why does it have to be fixed? And why is Leo in such a hurry to get rid of it?"

Woodrow turned right onto Fifth and aimed the Caddy downtown. He mopped his brow with his handkerchief again and let out a deep, dog-like moan. "It was plum awful, miss. The whole roof of the car is dented in so bad it looks like a asteroid hit it."

"What happened?" I asked, although I had a sudden sickening feeling that I already knew.

"That's where Miss Allen fell, miss . . . when she went off the balcony. It was horrible. She landed right on top of her own car. You wouldn't think a little body like Miss Allen's could make such a huge, deep dent in a car roof like that, but I guess the force of the fall . . ." Woodrow's gravelly voice trailed off into a soft, inaudible whisper.

I couldn't speak at all. The image of Ginger's small bones, pale flesh, and beautiful face colliding with the hard metal dome of her navy blue limousine made the words clog in my throat. And the contents of my stomach turn. And the heat of my body blaze far above normal. I slid over to the car window, rolled it down, and, laying my head against the backrest, let the night air swoosh over me like a wave of cool water.

When my stomach settled and my temperature sank below boiling, I slipped back over to the middle of the back seat and asked, "Were you there when it happened, Woodrow? Did you see her fall?" I hated having to phrase my question so bluntly, but it seemed the best way to get a blunt answer.

"No, miss. I was around the corner on Madison, getting a

200 Amanda Matetsky

cup of coffee in a all-night drugstore. I left the car parked on Seventy-seventh Street, like I always do, and walked around to the drugstore for my break, just passin' the time till I was supposed to be back at the car to take somebody somewhere."

"Somebody? You mean you didn't know who you would be driving, or where you would be taking them?"

"No, miss. All's I knew was I had to be waiting on Seventy-seventh Street at two thirty in the mornin' to drive somebody home. That's what Miss Allen whispered to me—right after she told me to take you home. It was after the *What's My Line?* show. Remember? That suspicious-looking man was standing outside your apartment, and I was worried about leaving you alone?"

"Yes, I remember," I said, heart bumping at the recollection of my last encounter with Dan, and my final meeting with Ginger, and at the shocking realization that it had all taken place *last night.* Less than twenty-four short hours ago. It seemed more like a century.

I sat back against the car seat and lit up a cigarette. Then I quickly leaned forward again. "The papers said that Miss Allen fell off the terrace at two thirty—the very same time you were supposed to be picking somebody up. Are you sure you didn't see anything?"

"Oh, I saw something all right," Woodrow moaned. "Something that's gonna haunt me for the rest of my natural born days. I saw Miss Allen's poor twisted body lyin' up on top of that limousine like a heap of broken twigs. You could see her neck was busted. She musta landed right before I got there."

"You mean you were the one who discovered the body?"

"Yes, miss," he said, voice catching in his throat. Woodrow's eyes were planted on the road ahead, but I could tell that they were focused on a different vision.

"How horrible for you," I said, feeling so sorry for the gentle chauffeur my eyes welled up with tears. I wouldn't let myself cry, though, for fear of causing Woodrow further pain. "What did you do then?" I asked, trying to nudge the conversation in a less horrifying direction. "Did you notify the police?"

"I didn't do it myself, miss. I ran around to the entrance of Miss Allen's building and rang the buzzer and banged on the glass till Mr. Pyle—the man who sits at the lobby desk all night—woke up and came to the door. Then I told him what happened, and he ran out to the car to see for himself. And then I stayed with the body while he ran back inside and called the police."

"Did Mr. Pyle also call the penthouse and inform Leo?"

"I don't know if he spoke to Mr. Marx, miss, but he surely did call up to the penthouse, 'cause it was no time at all before Miss Allen's butler came running out to the street in his robe and slippers."

I took a deep drag on my cigarette. "You mean Boynton?"

"Yes, miss. Mr. Boynton was in a powerful state of upset. He was walking around in circles and shaking like a leaf. He stayed outside till the police came."

"Did Mr. Marx come downstairs, too?"

"No, miss, he didn't." Stopping the car at a red light on 13th Street, Woodrow turned and gave me an anxious glance. "I don't know why Mr. Marx never came down, miss. Maybe he collapsed, or went into shock, or just couldn't bear to see his poor wife crumpled up that way. Or maybe he wasn't home."

When the light turned green, Woodrow hooked a right and headed west on 13th. There was so little traffic that our trip downtown had been quite fast. Much *too* fast for me, since I had tons of questions left to ask, and just a few minutes left to ask them in.

"What about the person you were supposed to meet at two thirty and drive home?" I hurried on, snuffing my cigarette out in the ashtray. "Did he or she ever show up?"

"No, miss. Leastways nobody ever came over to me and said anything. But since I didn't know who I was supposed to be meeting, I guess the person coulda been there without me knowing it. After the police rushed in with their sirens and flashing lights, a small crowd gathered round right quick.

People in the buildings close by were getting out of their beds and coming down to the street to see what was going on."

"How long were you there, Woodrow? The police must have questioned you at length."

"They sure did, miss. They asked me a whole lot of questions and then they told me to stay there in case they needed to ask me some more. They didn't let me leave till after Miss Allen's body and the limousine were taken away. I got home about six o'clock in the mornin'."

"Did the police question Mr. Pyle and Mr. Boyton, too?"

"Yes, miss."

"Did you overhear anything that was said?"

"No, miss. They both talked to the detectives inside. I was the only one questioned out on the street."

"They didn't let you go in and sit down in the lobby?"

"No, miss. Mr. Pyle would never allow it. I stood outside the whole time."

I was disgusted that Woodrow had been treated that way, but I didn't say anything to him about it. Such a verbalization would, I knew, only embarrass him further.

"So you never saw or spoke to Mr. Marx at all?" I barreled on, growing anxious over the diminishing time. We had already turned onto Seventh Avenue and were now whooshing toward Bleecker at an all-too-steady speed.

"No, miss, not until he called me up this afternoon and said he wanted me to work for *him* now. He told me the garage attendant where he parks his Cadillac would give me the keys and the car, and I should pick him up at eight."

"That's all he said? He didn't mention his wife or how she died?"

"Not even once, miss. Not when he called me this afternoon or when I picked him up this evening."

"That's cold!" I cried, surprised by Leo's seeming lack of emotion. (He had, after all, been so nice to me when I walked into the wall at the penthouse.)

"Yes, miss," Woodrow agreed. "Powerful cold."

I intended to explore this point further, but when Woodrow turned the corner at Bleecker Street, I totally lost my train of thought. Suddenly my brain was consumed with an entirely different question: Would Dan be waiting for me outside my apartment as he had been last night?

At this point I was hoping he would. I really wanted to tell him about everything that had happened to me in the last twenty-two hours. I was dying to find out why he had been at Ginger's penthouse this evening, and—in the hope that he might now have some influence over the case—I wanted to share with him every single clue I'd picked up about Ginger's murder so far. (I was also longing to see his gorgeous face, and wrap my arms around his trusty neck, and plant my lips on his luscious mouth—but you knew that already, right?)

Sometimes my wishes come true, but ordinarily they don't. And my arrival at home tonight was as ordinary as could be (except for the chauffeur-driven Caddy, of course). Dan was nowhere in sight, and my dashed hopes fell to the floor of my heart with a splat.

"HERE WE ARE, MISS," WOODROW SAID, pulling to a stop in front of my apartment. Then he surprised me by shifting sideways, turning his face squarely toward mine, and giving me an intense, beseeching look. "You know what you said before, miss, about me asking you questions whenever I felt like it? Did you really mean it? Is it okay if I ask you something now, before you go inside?"

"Of course, Woodrow. Ask me anything you want."

He lifted his chauffeur's cap, ran his gloved hand over his partially bald cranium, then set the cap back in place. "I don't mean to be nosy, miss. And the good Lord knows I don't want to cause any trouble. It's just that after everything that's happened, and after all the things we been talking about, I got this one awful question in my mind, and it's eating me up inside."

"I think I know what your question is," I said, deciding to spare Woodrow the anguish of asking it. "You want to know if Miss Allen jumped off the balcony or if she was pushed."

"That's right, miss," he said with a heavy sigh. "That's it exactly."

"It's what I want to know, too, Woodrow. I'm thoroughly

convinced she was pushed, but I don't have any proof yet. I'm not giving up, though. I'm going to keep on looking for the truth, no matter how long as it takes. So, please, if you see or hear anything that seems important, will you call me up and let me know?"

"Yes, miss," he said, looking so sad I wanted to comfort him in some way—pat his cheek or give him a hug of reassurance (gestures I knew I couldn't make without causing him *dis*comfort instead).

Woodrow and I exchanged phone numbers, then sat in silence for a few moments, reluctant to leave each other's company. I felt as though we were sitting together in church, holding our own private memorial service. But the ceremony didn't last long. The seconds kept ticking away, and in no time our time was up. Woodrow got out of the car, opened the rear passenger door, and helped me rise to my ragged feet on the sidewalk. Then he drove uptown to meet Leo and I hobbled upstairs alone.

Chapter 25

I LISTENED AT ABBY'S DOOR FOR A FEW
seconds but heard no signs of life inside. Figuring Abby and
Jimmy were still digging the jazz at the Vanguard, I unlocked
my own door and staggered in.

I was so tired I couldn't see straight. Tossing my hat,
jacket, gloves, and purse on a kitchen chair, I walked straight
over to the counter and poured myself a glass of Chianti. I carried the glass of wine upstairs to the bathroom, set it down on
the edge of the sink, plugged the rubber stopper in the bathtub
drain, and turned the hot water on full blast. Then I went into
the bedroom and removed my clothes, carefully peeling off
my shredded stockings.

Seconds later I was immersed in scalding water up to my
armpits, alternately massaging the soles of my abraded feet
and sipping wine from a steamy jellyglass. *If Dan's going to
call at all,* I thought, *it'll probably be right now* . . . But, no,
the phone didn't ring, so—rather than dashing downstairs for
a wet and naked conversation with the man I loved—I
chugged the rest of my wine, reclined against the back of the
bathtub, sank down until the water lapped against my chin,

and submitted my weary flesh and bones to some serious soaking.

I don't remember too much after that. I must have gotten out of the tub, dried myself off, put on one of Bob's old Army T-shirts, and crawled into bed, because that's where I found myself in the morning—tangled up in my flowered bed-sheets, with my face pressed into my pillow and one fully extended thumb poised close to my gaping, drooling mouth.

I rubbed the sleep out of my eyes and shot a worried look at the clock. It was just seven fifteen. By some miracle I'd be able to make it to the office on time! I'd have to move fast, though. Very fast.

Leaping out of bed like a demented frog, I splashed some cold water on my face, brushed my teeth and hair, slapped on some makeup, and got dressed in my dark red sweater set and tight black pencil skirt. I squeezed my sore feet into an old pair of black leather slingbacks, grabbed a fresh pair of white gloves from the top dresser drawer, darted downstairs for my purse, jacket, and beret, and then scrambled—fully dressed but by no means fully conscious—down the stairway to the street.

It was, as Woodrow would say, a "mighty fine" day, but I scarcely noticed. I was too busy just trying to walk. (Well, my feet were really hurting, you know! And the sidewalks were so packed with other racing-against-the-clock commuters that if you didn't stay on your toes, they were bound to get stepped on.)

The subway was so crowded I never got a seat. Hanging onto a leather strap for dear life, I stood weaving, lurching, and bumping into other dangling passengers through the entire (make that *entirely awful*) underground trip uptown. By the time I climbed into the light at 42nd and Third and walked the block to the office, I felt as though I'd worked a whole day already—that it was time to knock off, go home, and get back into bed.

And if I had known what the rest of the day was going to bring, that's exactly what I would have done.

•　•　•

"WHO AM I HAVING LUNCH WITH TO-day?" Mr. Crockett asked, plunking the messy mound of morning papers down on my desk and walking over to the coat tree. "I can't remember. Is it Dominick Luster, the photo agent, or Lou Panchetta from the printer's office?"

"It's Dominick Luster, sir," I said. "You're supposed to meet him at the Quill at twelve thirty."

"Oh," he said, plucking his hat off the tree and planting it squarely on his white-haired head. "Then I've got plenty of time to check out the newsstand, get a shave, and have my shoes shined before I go. But what about later? Do I have any appointments this afternoon?"

"Just one, sir—with your chiropodist. He'll be here at three thirty to trim your corns and toenails." (Yes, Mr. Crockett's chiropodist made office calls! He appeared once a month—his little black bag of tootsy tools in tow—to cut, file, scrape, and smooth the boss's feet into shape. Luckily, the building's nighttime cleaning service was responsible for emptying and scouring Mr. Crockett's wastebasket, not me.)

"*Humpff,*" Mr. Crockett replied, which I knew was his way of saying, "Bye-bye. See you later." He pulled the office door wide, maneuvered his considerable weight through the opening, and disappeared into the hall.

The minute the door swept all the way closed, I dove for the morning newspapers, burning to read the new articles about Ginger. I knew there would be lots of them, but I hadn't yet seen a single one. Mr. Crockett had grabbed all the papers and whisked them off to his private den as soon as he'd arrived, which had been just seconds after I'd opened up the office, turned on the lights, and plugged in the Coffeemaster.

Ginger's death was still front page news in all four morning editions, even the *New York Times*. There wasn't much new information, though. The articles merely reiterated the ghastly details of Ginger's fatal plunge from her penthouse terrace, giving slightly more graphic descriptions of her "mangled" corpse, and revealing that the body had been clad in a "see-through" black negligee (sex sells, don't you know). All four papers were still calling Ginger's death a suicide, but

only one of them—the *Herald Tribune*—released the news
that her funeral would be held at Saint Patrick's Cathedral, at
ten o'clock in the morning this coming Saturday, the ninth of
April. I engraved the date and time in my memory.

As I was cutting out these front page articles and putting
them in a manila folder for Pomeroy (who hadn't come in to
work yet), I took a closer look at the photo the *Daily Mirror*
had run with its story. It was a large picture of the crowd of
journalists, police, spectators, and mourners that had, according to the caption, been gathered outside Ginger's penthouse
the day before. Wondering if I might spot Dan's face in the
crowd, I lowered my nose to the newsprint and studied the
photo more carefully, searching for a handsome, noble, dark-
haired head in a cocked fedora.

But if Dan was in the picture, I couldn't find him. The only
face I recognized was my own.

Oh, lordy, lordy, lordy! I gasped to myself, not wanting to
believe my horrified eyes. I squeezed my lids tight shut for a
second, then slowly opened them again, praying to God that
by the time that photo came back into focus, my image would
be gone.

God wasn't listening. There I was—in living black-and-
white, for all the world to see—on the front page of one of the
city's major newspapers! I had a sad and startled grimace on
my grainy gray mug, and I was facing the camera head-on.
Would Dan see this picture and become even madder at me
than he already was? Would the murderer examine the shot
and recognize me? Would Pomeroy single me out and then
come to the angry realization that I was working on my own
Ginger Allen story?

To avoid the possibility of the last occurrence, I quickly
folded the *Daily Mirror* clip into a tiny square and stuck it
deep in the bottom of my purse. Harvey Crockett hadn't spied
me in the picture, and it was more than likely that Pomeroy
would be too drunk to pick me out of the crowd, but I wasn't
taking any chances. I might not be able to hide my identity
from the murderer, and I probably wouldn't manage to escape

Dan's wrath, but I was *not*—if I could help it—going to risk getting fired.

Quickly returning to my clipping chores, I madly flipped through the rest of the papers and cut out all the other crime reports. I also read and clipped the additional "special, in-depth" articles about Ginger—the glowing career retrospectives, the wistful biographical pieces, the "fond" looks back at her "enchanted" youth. (I doubted that sister Claire's youth had been even half so full of enchantment. And I couldn't help noticing that Ginger's 1950 engagement to Private First Class Rusty Burnett wasn't mentioned at all.)

"Hey, get a load of *her*," Mario said to Mike as they were walking past my desk on their way out to lunch. "Paige Turner's turning pages again."

"Yeah, man!" Mike said, playing along. "Doesn't she ever stop?"

"Not till her page-turner's finished," Mario said. "Not till she reaches her *climax*." Mario leered at me over his shoulder, making sure I had grasped the sexual thrust of his asinine punch line (as if I could have missed it!). Then he and Mike burst out of the office and scuffled down the hall, laughing so loud you could hear them all the way to the elevators. (It never ceases to amaze me how little true wit it takes to amuse the adolescent mind.)

I folded up all the newspapers and put the file of clips on Pomeroy's desk. Then, in a desperate hustle to make my lunch hour escape (i.e., get *out* of the office before Pomeroy came *in*), I grabbed my purse and gloves and darted up to the coat rack for my jacket and beret.

"Hey, where are you going?" Lenny called out from his desk in the rear of the workroom. "What's your hurry? There's nobody here but us. I want to talk to you!" He jumped out of his chair and strode up to the front of the office in a flash.

"I'm sorry, Lenny," I said. "I've got to run. I'm meeting Abby for lunch and I'm already late." It wasn't that I didn't want to tell him the truth, it was just that I didn't have the time.

"I don't believe you," Lenny said, skewering me with his knowing gaze. "You look funny, like you're up to something. Something dangerous." His narrow face was flushed, and his bottle-thick glasses were even more crooked than usual.

"That's just crazy!" I cried, lifting my brows, widening my eyes, putting on the most innocent expression I could muster. I was trying to imitate Snow White, but I probably looked more like Dagwood Bumstead. "All I'm up to is having lunch with Abby," I insisted. "And I want to get out of here before Pomeroy shows up and finds some reason to keep me from going."

I hated having to lie to Lenny this way, but I was in a hurry. And I didn't want him to worry about me. And I really didn't believe the pressing "something" I was about to get "up to" would be all that dangerous.

Shows you what a numskull I could be.

THE LOBBY OF THE RCA BUILDING looked different in the middle of the day than it had in the middle of the night. Naturally, it was a whole lot brighter. The dazzling sun pouring in through the glass-walled entrance and the higher wattage beaming from the Art Deco fixtures had banished the scary shadows for good (or at least until later). It was a lot more crowded, too. So many people were moving in and out of the heavy glass doors, streaming across the marble floor, getting in and off the elevators, standing around in circles and talking, that I felt I was in a train station rather than an office building.

Heartened by the horde and the light and the noise, I made a beeline for the elevators, glad to be caught up (okay, *concealed*) in the confusion. All of the elevators were manned and working, so there was no wait at all. I stepped into a crowded car and huddled with the other passengers as we were lifted and jounced, floor by bumpy floor, to 8.

Several people got off the elevator with me and began walking in various directions. I followed along behind a man in a gray flannel suit who was heading toward Studio 8H. There were other people walking up and down the hall as well, so I didn't feel conspicuous. I did, however, cast a stealthy glance at every face I passed, just to make sure I didn't recognize it—or vice versa.

Studio 8H was in use (a dress rehearsal for *The Colgate Comedy Hour*), so it was impossible for me to sneak inside and pass through the theater to the hall on the other side—to the place where I had stood eavesdropping the night before. Thinking I might reach the far hall by forging straight ahead, I walked past the line of life-size cardboard cutouts of the network's top TV stars and continued my trek to the end of the corridor. Then I headed up the hall to the right, hoping it would take me where I wanted to go.

It did. When I saw three scantily clad chorus girls wearing tall red feather headdresses enter the hall from a door on the right and then disappear behind another door marked WOMEN'S DRESSING ROOM, I knew I was in the right place. Several people were milling around near the backstage entrance, popping in and out of wardrobe and makeup, transporting costumes to and from the dressing room. I took a deep breath and charged into their midst, praying I wouldn't be stopped, questioned, and turned away.

I wasn't even noticed. I walked right through the busy area without so much as a frown or a lifted eyebrow. Then, emboldened and relieved by the presence of so many people, I hurried on toward the office where last night's powwow had taken place. Stopping at the doorway where I had dropped my shoes, I gave a little knock on the closed, unmarked door, thinking I had arrived at Leo Marx's office and that—due to his plan to meet with NBC execs today—the scheming producer would be inside.

I wasn't the least bit nervous, believe it or not. I felt strong and secure and eager to pursue my investigation into Ginger's death. I had two credible reasons for coming to see Leo—to pay my condolences and to ask for the return of my glasses—and I had a string of sneaky questions I was itching to spring. Where was he, for instance, when Ginger fell? How long had Ginger been depressed and seeing a psychiatrist? Did he really believe she had killed herself?

I wasn't expecting Leo to answer my questions honestly, you should know. I just wanted to observe his reaction and hear what his responses would be. Sometimes you can learn more from the way people behave and speak than from the actual things they say (unless they are, like me, as good at acting as they are at lying).

There was no answer to my initial knock, so I straightened my spine and knocked again, much harder this time. Still no answer. Groaning with disappointment, I tried again. Dead silence. *Arrrgh!* Had I lied to Lenny, given up my lunch hour (not to mention my *lunch!*), and raced across town for nothing? Would my courageous, clue-hunting return to the RCA Building turn out to be a colossal waste of time? Unwilling to accept defeat so early in my expedition, I considered kicking the door down and ransacking Leo's office for evidence.

Don't worry! I wasn't stupid enough to do it. The instant that plan occurred to me, I discarded it . . . well, the kicking-down-the-door part, anyway. I wasn't in the mood to attract the attention of *The Colgate Comedy Hour* crowd. I was, on the other hand, kind of interested in sneaking into Leo's office and sniffing around a little bit. Maybe I could learn something important or find something incriminating to make my excursion worthwhile. Maybe Leo's door would be unlocked . . .

I lowered my hand to the doorknob and gave it a little tweak. To my utter surprise and delight it clicked open. Pushing a narrow split in the door, I put one eye to the breach and peeked inside. The room was dark. I couldn't see a thing. Opening the door a few inches wider, I slithered into the office and quickly closed the door behind me. And then I just stood there for a couple of seconds, hugging the wall in the darkness, waiting for my wildly beating heart to calm down, reeling with the shock that I had actually gotten this far.

Which was nothing compared to the shock I experienced when I flipped on the light and saw what was going on.

Chapter 26

"WHAT THE HELL?!" THELONIUS KIDD sputtered, his startled blue eyes blinking in the light. "Who are you? What do you think you're doing? Get out! Get out of my office right now!"

If I'd had my wits about me, I would have followed Theo's directions and fled his office in an instant, never to return. But my wits were nowhere to be found. They had packed their bags and hightailed it to Outer Mongolia. I was thunderstruck and senseless—frozen in position like the proverbial deer caught in the headlights.

Theo was frozen in position, too. The most astonishing, scandalous, embarrassing, and revealing position imaginable. He was standing crouched over the top of his big mahogany desk, with his pants pulled down around his knees and his bare haunches curved around the side of the desk like parallel parentheses. Between Theo and the desk—with her pale breasts pressed flat to the desktop and her blonde curls bobbing beneath her lopsided red feather headdress—was a young, terrified, near-naked *Colgate* chorus girl.

"You've got a lot of nerve!" Theo growled at me, pulling away from the girl and yanking up his pants. "This is my private office. Who the hell are you and what do you want?" He turned to face me, angrily zipping his fly and buckling his belt, showing no signs of self-consciousness or chagrin. The young chorus girl backed away from the desk and, cringing and whimpering like a frightened puppy, struggled to cover herself with her skimpy red costume.

"Oh, shut up, Milly!" Theo said to her. " Don't be a sap. Pull yourself together and scram. I'll catch you later."

Milly yelped and stumbled for the door, holding the bodice of her costume in place with one hand and the crest of red feathers to her head with the other. Tears were rolling down her cheeks. I gave her a sincerely apologetic look and—seeing as both of her hands were occupied—opened the office door for her. She lurched out into the hall and flew away, shedding tiny tufts of red down in the air behind her.

I was longing to follow in Milly's footsteps—to get as far away from the noxious Thelonius Kidd as possible—but I stubbornly held my ground. I had recognized Theo's voice, you see, and now that I knew him to be my unidentified pursuer from the night before, I wanted to find out everything I could about him. And since Theo seemed to have no idea who I was, I felt I could adopt my Patty Turner persona and ask him a few questions without putting myself at too much risk.

"Okay, talk!" Theo snarled, getting angrier by the second. "Tell me who you are and what you want or I'll call building security and have you thrown out."

"I'm Patty Turner," I said. "Don't you remember me? I was your date at the Stork Club last Saturday night."

"Huh?" Theo raked his fingers through his sandy brown hair and gave me a squinty look, obviously taken aback. "Stork Club?" he said, as though he'd never heard of the place before.

"That's right," I said. "I was Ginger Allen's roommate in college, you see, and when I called to tell her I was coming to New York for a few days, she invited me to a small dinner party at the Stork. And she invited you as my escort."

Theo cocked his head and gave me a slow once-over.

"Now that you mention it," he said, "I do remember going to the Stork. But I don't remember you. And that surprises me," he added, with an unmistakably lecherous gleam in his eye, "because you're pretty hot stuff. You're the kind of girl a man doesn't forget." He stretched his lips in a randy smirk and moved a few steps closer.

"Well, you were pretty drunk," I said, telling the truth, but not the whole truth. I forgot (okay, *neglected*) to explain that I had been wearing glasses when we met. (I felt the less said about my phony disguise, the better.)

"I'm *always* drunk," Theo admitted, "and that's never cramped my style before." His randy smirk grew wide with pride. So wide his dimples were blinking. "I know a hot chick when I see one," he boasted, "and I can't believe I let a doll like you slip through my fingers." He came closer and grasped my shoulders in his eager hands.

Uh oh! Shark attack! And this fish has fingers!

I quickly extricated myself from Theo's clutches and, acting as cool and nonchalant as I possibly could under the unsettling circumstances, went for a little stroll around his office. I was pretending to admire the plush carpet, expensive furniture, and framed photos of famous TV stars on the walls, but I was really looking for more clues to Theo's character. Was his beastly sexual behavior a sign of other brutish (i.e., murderous) proclivities?

I inspected the surface of the playboy director's casting couch (I mean, *desk!*), and then scrutinized the shelves of the mahogany credenza behind the desk, finding nothing incriminating, or even suspicious. Several bottles were sitting on top of the credenza, but they appeared to contain liquor, not poison. The only two things that grabbed my attention were my shoes—the pair of patent leather pumps I had dropped here the night before—which were now tucked in the far corner of the bottom shelf.

I was really dying to get those shoes back. They were almost brand-new, and they had cost me five bucks, and I truly hated the idea of leaving them as a free gift for a possible murderer (or one of his girlfriends). But what was I going to

do? Snatch them up and say they were mine? Confess to
being the snoopy Cinderella who had dropped her slippers
while fleeing the scene at the stroke of midnight? *No way,
Doris Day!* That would have been plum stupid, not to mention dangerous. Maybe he had killed Ginger, and maybe he
hadn't, but one thing was downright certain: Thelonius Kidd
was no Prince Charming.

"So what if I was your date at the Stork?" Theo said,
scowling, annoyed that I had spurned his hands-on advance.
"That doesn't explain what you're doing here now. How did
you know where my office was, and why did you come?"

"Ginger and I were supposed to have lunch together
today. She told me to meet her here on the eighth floor and
she'd show me around the studio before we went out to
Sardi's. She said your office was right down the hall from her
dressing room."

Theo gave me a look of contempt. "Ginger's dead," he
said, "so I don't think she'll be keeping that appointment."

Appalled by his sarcastic tone, I didn't know how to respond. I stood in silence for a couple of seconds, staring
down at my shoes (the ones on my feet). Then finally, after
an interval of intense discomfort, I chose to play it straight
(and, hopefully, safe). "I can't believe what happened," I
said. "It's so, so horrible. I'm stricken with grief, and you
must be, too. The whole country is mourning this terrible
tragedy."

"Yeah," Theo said. "It's awful." A look of sorrow flitted
across his handsome face. Was the sadness real? Was Theo
more upset than he was letting on?

"That's why I came here today," I continued. "I couldn't
sit alone in my hotel room anymore, crying my eyes out, listening to the radio, watching television, and reading those
hideous newspaper reports. I had to talk to somebody. Somebody who knew and loved Ginger as much as I did. Somebody who might be able to tell me why she did this terrible
thing."

"Well, you came to the wrong place, babe." Theo
shrugged his broad shoulders and fingered the deep cleft in

his chin. "I don't know why the hell she did it. She was rich as Rockefeller and as beautiful and famous as Marilyn Monroe. She had more than enough to live for."

"But the papers said she was depressed and seeing a psychiatrist. Is that true?"

Theo laughed. "Every TV star I know is depressed and seeing a psychiatrist. It's a job requirement."

"What was Ginger depressed about?" I inquired.

"How the hell should I know? She didn't confide in me." Theo was getting testy again. All of a sudden, out of nowhere, he started pacing around the room like a nervous coyote.

"Do you think she and Leo had a happy marriage?"

"How could they? There's no such thing!" In the course of his roundabout pacing, I noticed, Theo was pacing closer and closer to me.

I took several steps backward and positioned myself near the closest wall. "Was Ginger worried about her career?" I asked. "Did she think her popularity was slipping?"

"Not on your life!" Theo snorted. "She thought she was the fucking queen of the world."

"Did Leo say anything to you about Ginger's state of mind? Did he ever mention the name of her psychiatrist?"

Theo stopped pacing and stormed over to me, skewering me with his hot blue gaze (which was easy for him to do since his eyes were now just inches away from mine). "Hey, what's with the third degree, babe? Are you a goddamn detective or something?"

"Uh, no . . . of course not! I'm just curious. Ginger was a very good friend of mine and I—"

I never got to finish that sentence. I simply couldn't get the words out of my mouth. For the simple reason that Theo had grabbed me by the shoulders again, pushed me back against the wall, and—pinning me to the wall with the full force of his lean, greedy body—covered my mouth with his own.

Well, that did it. I wasn't curious about Theo Kidd anymore. I now knew more about the playboy director than I had ever wanted to know (including the twofold fact that he had a long tongue and had been drinking Scotch that morning). And rather than being determined, as before, to hold my ground, I was now busting to break away.

Literally.

First, I busted Theo in the head with my own head (which, you may recall from its recent run-in with a marble wall, happens to be very hard). Then, as Theo reared back from *that* blow, I bent my right knee into a bludgeon and busted him in the you-know-whats.

Everything went smoothly (for me) after that. Theo was doubled over in pain, so I was free to straighten my beret, pat my hair into place, sneak my patent leather pumps off the lower shelf of the credenza, and—cradling the shoes to my breast with my purse—saunter over to the door and slip through it to the hall. Minutes later, I was out on the street and headed back to work.

All's well that ends well, I always say—even if it's just another false start.

LOOK, I *KNOW* I SHOULDN'T HAVE SNITCHED my shoes. It was a really, really foolish thing for me to do. I might as well have left Theo a note telling him I was the one who had been eavesdropping on the secret *Tex and Toni Show* meeting that had taken place last night; that I was the barefoot wonder who had toppled the backstage scenery and foiled his and Rusty's attempt to catch me.

But what can I say? As dim-witted as my pump-pinching performance had undoubtedly been, I would do it all over again. I really liked those shoes. And as Abby says, sometimes a girl's just gotta do what a girl's gotta do.

When I arrived back at the office—breathless and bedraggled and carrying my pumps under my arm—Lenny went berserk. "Where the hell have you been?" he cried, rushing up to meet me at the coat tree. His cheeks were tomato red, and his glasses were perched on his prominent nose at an impossible angle. "Abby called while you were gone, so I know you weren't having lunch with her like you said! Why did you lie to me, Paige? Are you in trouble? What's with the shoes? And what's that big red bump on your forehead?"

I might have found Lenny's nosy concern annoying, but I didn't. After all I'd been through in the last forty-eight hours—all the shocks and surprises, the running and the hiding, the fight with Dan, and the fighting off of all manner of attacks—well, let me just say that it was nice to have somebody worry about *me* for a change.

"What did Abby want?" I asked, trying to deflect Lenny's anxious solicitude. (As nice as it was, I couldn't deal with it right then.)

"I don't know," he said. "She wants you to call her. Soon as you can."

"Okay, I will. But where is everybody? It's almost two o'clock. I'm really late. I thought I'd have to face an inquisition."

"This is your lucky afternoon!" Lenny croaked. "Crockett had to make an emergency trip to the printer and he took Mike and Mario with him. The printing press went crazy and ate up most of the film. They have to fix some of the layouts and shoot parts of the issue all over again, so they'll be there for the rest of the day."

"And where's Pomeroy?" I asked. "Still drinking his lunch?"

"Probably. But he'll be back any minute. So you'd better talk fast. I want to know what you're up to, and I want to know *now*." The redness had spread from Lenny's cheeks to the rest of his face.

"I'm working on another story," I admitted, "but I can't tell you about it right now. I've got to call Abby before Pomeroy gets back. If he catches me making a personal phone call, he'll fly into a rage, and then you and I both will have a ghastly afternoon."

Lenny knew what I was saying was true. "Okay," he surrendered, letting his head droop down between his shoulders, "but you'd better tell me everything soon. I can't stand being in the dark like this!"

"I know, Lenny, I know. And I'll clue you in pronto. Promise!"

Lenny moped back to his desk and I darted over to mine. I dialed Abby as fast as I could and sat down, turning my back to Lenny and my face to the door. While I was waiting for Abby to pick up, I changed my shoes.

"Howdy, Pardner!" Abby answered, guessing (obviously correctly) that the call was from me. "How's tricks?"

"I'll fill you in you later," I said. "Right now I'm in a huge hurry. Just tell me—was Jimmy able to get his friend's car?"

"Whatever Jimmy wants, Jimmy gets," she proudly announced. "We'll be waiting in front of your building at five thirty, in a hot red Ford convertible, with the top down, and the tank full, and a road map to Levittown in the glove compartment."

"That's great, Abby," I chirped. "Thanks a million!"

"A million what?" she teased. "Tiddly winks? Bobby pins? Ju Ju Bees? Just make it a double Scotch and we're even." She smacked her lips in an audible smooch and hung up.

I pushed the button to click off the line, but kept the receiver held to my ear. I wanted to make another call. I wanted to dial the Midtown South Police Precinct and ask for Dan. This was strictly against the rules, of course (it's highly improper for a woman to call a man at his office, in case you haven't heard), but I didn't care. Since Dan hadn't called or come to see me, I had no choice but to try to get in touch with him. I was desperate to convince him that Ginger's death was murder, not suicide, and that he should persuade the department to redirect the investigation. (I was also desperate to hear his voice, but that goes without saying.)

Before I could finish dialing the precinct number, the office entry bell jingled and Brandon Pomeroy marched in. I said a loud goodbye to nobody and slapped the receiver back in the cradle.

"Who was that?" Pomeroy wanted to know.

"The typesetter," I said. "I called for a pickup."

"*Humph,*" he grunted, hooking his hat on the tree and

stepping over to his desk. Then he sat down in his swivel chair, rotated his back toward me, lowered his head to his chest, and—without another word or grunt—fell into a boozy snooze.

This was, indeed, my lucky afternoon. Now, if my luck could just last through the evening . . .

Chapter 27

THE SHINY RED CONVERTIBLE WAS SIT-
ting right where Abby had said it would be—at the curb in
front of my building—with the motor running. Jimmy was in
the driver's seat and Abby was sitting so close to him that they
looked like a sideshow oddity (one body, two heads). Otto
was standing on his hind legs in the passenger seat, front legs
propped up against the car door, watching the steady flood of
people pouring out of the building through the revolving glass
doors.

The second I stepped out onto the sidewalk, Otto spotted
me and started barking to get my attention.

"Hello, baby," I said, arriving at the car and reaching over
to pat his silky head. I stroked the length of his sausage-
shaped body and then fondled his velvet ears. "Did you miss
me, sweetie?"

Otto answered by licking my palm and fingers till they
were slick with slobber. I was glad my clean white gloves
were nestled safely in my pocket.

"Hey, Faye, whaddaya say?" Abby warbled, breaking herself away from Jimmy and leaning over to unlock the door.
"Can you dig this crazy car? Get in, get in! You'd better sit up

front with us—it's not so windy up here." Tying her black chiffon scarf tighter under her chin, she scooted back across the tan leather upholstery and reattached herself to Jimmy.

I opened the door and got in, helping Otto to burrow a comfy nest in my lap. "Hi, Jimmy," I said. "Thanks so much for doing this. And please thank your friend Biggie for me, too."

"No sweat," Jimmy said, straightening his shades, smoothing his beard, looking as cool as cool could be. He turned on the radio, found a song that he liked ("Sh-Boom" by the Crew Cuts), and dialed the volume up loud. Very loud. People on the street were turning to look at us, which was probably exactly what Jimmy wanted.

"This is my favorite song!" Jimmy crowed, happily pulling the red convertible out into the heavy rush hour traffic. To prove his sworn allegiance, he began singing along with the Crew Cuts at the top of his lungs: *"Sh-boom, sh-boom, ya-da-da-da-da-da-da-da-da-da, Sh-boom, sh-boom, ya-da-da-da-da-da-da-da-da-da . . ."* Well, you get the picture. Jimmy's favorite song lyrics made just about as much sense as his own poetry.

"So, what's shakin', Sherlock?" Abby said, gazing at me through the dark lenses of her totally unnecessary sunglasses. (It was five thirty on an overcast April evening, not a sunbeam in sight.) "Do you know who the murderer is yet?" Abby was a woman of many virtues, but patience, like chastity, had never quite made the list.

"I still don't have a clue," I said, hating to admit my sleuthful shortcomings. "I've gathered a few more facts, but nothing conclusive." I anchored my beret more securely on my head and buttoned my jacket up to the collar. It was too chilly to be driving with the top down, but I didn't ask Jimmy to raise it. I didn't want to cramp his style. Or put Abby in the awkward position of taking sides. At least Otto was keeping my lap warm.

"Oh, Paige, you're such a cube!" Abby badgered. "Why bust your *kishkes* digging for more facts when you've got all the info you need? Ginger's husband did it. It's *always* the husband."

"Oh, yeah?" I said. "Try telling the police that. They don't even believe it was murder!" I was annoyed at Abby's willingness to jump to easy conclusions, but I wasn't in the mood to argue with her. "Look, we've had this conversation before, Ab, and I see no reason to have it again. I'm well aware of your views on this subject, and I know you're acquainted with mine. Can't we just leave it at that?"

"Oh, all right!" she snapped. "But when the killer turns out to be Leo, don't say I didn't tell you!"

I laughed. "Okay, it's a deal."

"Sh-boom, sh-boom, ya-da-da-da-da-da-da-da-da-da . . ." Jimmy turned left at 33rd Street and headed for the entrance to the Queens Midtown Tunnel—the white-tiled tube that would take us under the East River to Long Island. As we entered the tunnel the radio went dead and Jimmy and the Crew Cuts stopped singing.

"So, what's the scoop, Snoop?" Abby inquired. "What new facts did you dig up?" In the gloom of the tunnel she finally took her dark glasses off and put them in her purse. Jimmy left his on. I wondered if he could see well enough to get us through the dim, narrow passageway alive.

The bumper-to-bumper trip through the tunnel was so slow I was able to give Abby a quick rundown of current events before we exited in Queens and began inching our way toward the toll booth (and before the radio came back on full blast). Abby was amazed at all I'd been through since our pizza party last night, and more than a little impressed with me. I could tell by the way she was staring at me, with her mouth hanging open and her eyelashes aflutter (or were they just flapping in the breeze?).

"Oy vey, Paige!" she cried, straining her voice to be heard over the radio. (Chuck Berry was singing "Maybellene" now, and Jimmy was bellowing along.) "You've gotten yourself in such a deep pile of *dreck!* Why would Theo and Rusty chase you through the crashing backstage scenery and out of the

building that way? They must have figured out who you really are."

"I wondered if that was possible," I hollered. "But when I stumbled into Theo's office this afternoon, he didn't have any idea who I was. He didn't even remember me as *Patty,* let alone Paige."

"Well, he's sure as hell going to remember you now!" Abby shrieked, laughing. "I can't believe you kneed him in the nuts. That's so unlike you! And how's your head?" she asked, turning serious. "Does it hurt?"

"Not too much. I've got a new bump on my forehead, but it's hidden by my bangs."

"You know you never should have swiped your shoes!" she yelled.

"Yeah, I know," I muttered.

We pulled up to the booth and I gave Jimmy a quarter for the toll. *"Oh, Maybellene, why can't you be true?"* he howled, handing the coin to the grimacing toll taker. Then Jimmy pulled the red convertible into the far left lane of the Horace Harding Expressway—the expanded road some people had begun calling the Long Island Expressway—and picked up speed for the suburbs.

IT WAS A MISERABLE TRIP. THERE WAS tons of traffic, lots of new construction, and a myriad of unexpected detours. It took us an hour and a half to get there, and by the time we drove onto the grounds of the huge, sprawling Levittown housing development, I was so cold my teeth were chattering. I'd had to take off my beret to keep it from being blown away, and my hair was now matted in a wild tangle that resembled Tarzan's jungle. Even Abby looked a little shabby (which was saying a lot since she almost always looked Ava Gardner gorgeous).

Only Jimmy and Otto had survived the journey in style. Jimmy's hair was a bit mussed, and he'd removed his shades somewhere along the way, but his de rigueur black turtleneck—plus his all-out, full-tilt opera performance—had kept him toasty and energized. Otto had spent part of the trip standing—hind legs planted on my thigh, front legs perched on the door, nose pushed into the wind, soft ears billowing behind—but most of the time he took a lap nap. All he needed was a brisk walk for a pee and he'd be fine.

It took us a while to find the right house. It was totally dark now and all we had to go on was the number and street name I'd gotten from the phone book. As we drove through the dusty acres of last year's potato fields, around the winding, treeless streets bordered with identical Levitt-built ranch houses, I couldn't help remembering that Bob and I had dreamed of moving here when he got home from Korea. We'd hoped to buy one of these houses (on the G.I. Bill—a hundred dollars down with a 30-year $7,500 mortgage), where we could be happy and comfortable, and start our own family in a protected place of prosperity and peace.

It had been a beautiful dream, but not a practical one. We should have known that in every war, the tragedy always precedes the peace. Big time.

"Hey, there it is!" Abby cried. "Over on the left. The white house with the blue door! Stop!"

She was right. 79 Sugar Maple Road. The house where Claire and Rusty Burnett lived. It looked so small and uninteresting—so insignificant! Could this bare, lifeless, unadorned structure be sheltering a cold-blooded killer? I didn't know the answer to that question, of course, but I was determined to find out.

"You guys wait here," I said, combing my tangled hair with my fingers, trying to make myself look presentable. "Listen to the radio. Take Otto for a walk. I'll be back in a little while."

"But what if you're not?" Abby asked. "Should we storm the castle or call the police, or what?"

"I don't know," I said. "Use your best judgment." I realized I might be putting my life in Abby's, Jimmy's, and Otto's hands (or paws), but I felt safe in their inventive, loopy, smart, snuggly, way-out beatnik watchfulness. I slapped my beret back on my head, got out of the car, straightened my skirt, and forged up one of the two narrow cement driveway strips toward the Burnetts' front door.

There was no car in the carport, but enough light was shining through the flimsy blue curtains on the front windows of the house that I felt certain someone was home. I hoped it would be Claire, and that she would be alone. (In my experience, wives tend to be more talkative when their husbands aren't around.) I wished I had on my (I mean, Abby's) glasses, so that I would look like Patty instead of Paige, but seeing as that was impossible, I knew I'd just have to make the best of things. I took a deep breath and rang the bell. Twice.

Somebody shuffled up to the door, fiddled with the locks for a few seconds, and then cracked the door open about two inches. "Who's there?" said a nervous, cautious female voice. "What do you want?" I couldn't see the woman's face, but since I knew this to be the house in which Claire lived, I had a pretty strong suspicion it was her (I'm so clever sometimes it kills me).

"It's Patty Turner, Claire," I said, softening all my edges, trying to look sensitive and sympathetic (which wasn't easy since I felt like kicking and screaming my bumpy head off till somebody made a full confession). "I've come to pay my condolences and to talk to you about Ginger. I hope this isn't a bad time."

The door opened an inch wider. "Patty Turner? Ginger's college friend? You don't look like her." Claire was squinting at me through the crack in the door.

"I was wearing glasses when we met," I hastily explained. "I don't have them on now because I accidentally left them at Ginger's apartment last Sunday, and I haven't had the heart to go and ask for them back. I don't want to disturb Leo. It's all so horrible and sad. I just can't believe what's happened."

"You were at the penthouse on Sunday?" The door was all the way open now—and so were Claire's small brown eyes. She looked as if she'd just seen a ghost.

"Yes, I had brunch and dinner with Ginger and Leo and then went with them to the *What's My Line?* broadcast."

"Did you go back to the penthouse after the show?"

Claire's tiny brown irises were flitting around in their sockets like trapped houseflies.

"No, I didn't," I said, taking note of her anxiety then hastening to ease it. "Woodrow drove Ginger and Leo home, and then took me back to my hotel. I was asleep by twelve thirty." I was hoping Claire would accept my story and relax enough to let me inside.

Bingo. Her eyes stopped flitting and her stiff shoulders sagged with relief. "Come in," she said, standing away from the door and motioning for me to enter.

I shot a backwards glance at Abby and Jimmy and—seeing that they were parked discreetly across the street with the lights and the radio turned off—stepped into the house with a sense of relief of my own.

The front door opened into the kitchen/laundry room/dining room. The stove, refrigerator, cabinets, and counter were on the right; the dinette set was in the middle; the washing machine was straight ahead, right next to the door to the living room. Compared to Ginger's penthouse, this was a sad, paltry, pitiful excuse for a home. Compared to *my* apartment, it was paradise. For one brief, ecstatic, and hideously painful moment, I imagined myself standing at the stove, happily stirring a hearty stew, and Bob sitting at the pink and gray Formica table—looking fit, splendid, and gloriously alive—waiting for his dinner.

"How did you get here?" Claire asked. "And why do you want to talk to me?" She stood hunched in the middle of her kitchen, wearing a faded blue-flowered housedress that said one of two things: either her husband loved her so much he didn't care how she looked, or he loved her so little it made no difference how she looked. Because of the forlorn expression in Claire's housefly eyes, I had a feeling it was the latter.

"I was out on Long Island visiting some friends in Roslyn," I told her, "and since I was so close, I asked them to bring me here tonight. I wanted to tell you how devastated I am about Ginger's death, and see if there's anything I can do. Also, I felt a strong need to talk to you about what happened. I didn't know Ginger was depressed. And I had no idea on earth she was suicidal. Please believe me! If I'd known, I never would have left her that night."

"Do you want some coffee?" Claire mumbled. "I made a fresh pot about an hour ago."

"Yes, thank you," I said, truly grateful for the offer. I was as tired as an Egyptian slave, and as cold as a witch's you-know-what, but maybe, just maybe, if I fortified myself with enough caffeine, and played all my cards right, and worked my inquisitive little tail off to get Claire to talk about Ginger . . . well, maybe I'd *finally* learn something important.

Of course, I'd be giving Claire the chance to learn something important, too, but I was too wound up (okay, *wigged out*) to worry about that.

Chapter 28

"HAVE A SEAT," CLAIRE SAID. SHE GES-
tured for me to sit at the kitchen table, then walked over to the
stove to pour the coffee.

I sat down in one of the six chrome and pink vinyl dinette
chairs, and—glad to see an ashtray on the table—lit up a cigarette. "You have a very nice house," I said. "Have you lived
here long?"

"Two years," she said. Her voice was as flat and lusterless
as her dull brown hair. "We moved in right after we got married." Claire brought some cream and sugar to the table, went
back to the counter for the coffee, then returned to the table
carrying a cup and saucer in each hand. Setting one full cup
in front of me, she carried her own around to the other side of
the table and sat down—in the chair furthest from mine.

"Gee whiz!" I said. "You and Rusty are practically newly-
weds." (Okay, so I was being obnoxiously cute. But, what do
you expect? I was trying to get the woman to talk, for Pete's
sake. And if that called for a gee whiz or two, what of it?)

"Yes," Claire said, stirring sugar into her coffee with a far-
away look in her eye. "It was a whirlwind courtship. We mar-

ried just a few days after he got back from Korea. In March of 1953."

"Did you have a big wedding?"

"No, it was small. We were married by a justice of the peace on Ginger's terrace. Just a few of my sister's best friends were there."

"But what about your friends? And Rusty's friends?"

"We don't have any." Claire took a sip of her coffee and then started chewing on one of her fingernails.

I took a drag on my cigarette, searching my brain for another leading question, hoping to hit a nerve. "You and Ginger were very close, weren't you?" I asked.

"What makes you say that?" Claire gave me a wary look.

"Well, she threw you a nice wedding at her penthouse. And she gave your husband a job on her show. And she also took you and Rusty out on the town a lot, to some very ritzy places. It sounds like you were very loving sisters."

"Yes, I suppose it does," she said, offering nothing more.

"How will you ever bear this terrible loss?"

Claire shifted her gaze downward. "I don't know. It's very painful." (Call me distrustful, but from the faint, involuntary smile that stole across Claire's lips at that moment, I had the feeling she was bearing the loss just fine.)

I crushed my cigarette in the ashtray and took a few swigs of my coffee, stalling for time. I was trying to think of a way to get Claire to laugh, or giggle, so I could compare her voice to the voice of the woman I'd heard laughing in Theo's office the night before. But I soon gave up on that idea. It's really hard (and just a tad inappropriate) to crack jokes about a sister's suicide (or murder).

"Did you or Rusty see Ginger after the *What's My Line?* broadcast?" I asked. "She was so disturbed by that embarrassing experience, she probably wanted some friendly company."

"No, we didn't see her," Claire snapped. "It was late Sunday night. Rusty and I were both at home watching TV together. What were we supposed to do? Jump in the car and drive into the city to hold Ginger's hand just because she was *embarrassed?*"

"Oh, no!" I quickly exclaimed, rushing to smooth Claire's ruffled feathers. "I certainly didn't mean to suggest—"

"Besides," she interrupted, "Ginger told us she wanted to be alone."

"So, you spoke to her after the broadcast?"

"Yeah, for a few minutes. She called us when she got home."

Hmmmm, I murmured to myself, mulling over the things Claire had said, but deciding not to continue the same line of questioning. (The ruffled feathers had spoken for themselves.) "The papers said Ginger was so despondent she'd been seeing a psychiatrist," I ventured on. "Is that true?"

"Well, I don't know how *despondent* she was," Claire said, in a mocking tone, "but she *was* seeing a shrink. Every Tuesday and Thursday at four. Rain or shine."

"Did Ginger ever tell you what was bothering her—why she felt she needed a psychiatrist?"

Claire's lips curled upward in another faint smile. "No. She said she just wanted to understand herself. But I don't think 'understanding' had anything at all to do with it. Ginger wasn't the type to question her own feelings or motives or behavior. She thought everything she said and did was perfect. If you ask me, Ginger went to a shrink just because it's in vogue. Everybody who's anybody is in psychoanalysis these days, and Ginger was always frantic to stay in style."

Claire's words rang true to me. I thought of all the fashion layouts I'd seen in the Orchid Publications files—Ginger Allen modeling a new hat, or a new fur piece, or a daring new style of loungewear—and I figured that, for Ginger, seeing a shrink probably ranked right up there with sporting the season's latest shade of nail polish.

I gulped down the rest of my coffee and then posed my next question. "Well, if Ginger wasn't despondent, and if she was seeing a psychiatrist just to be chic, then why did she kill herself? Because the hemline of her new cocktail dress was too long?"

Claire giggled. Then she laughed out loud. And now I had the answers to two more of my questions: 1) no, Claire and Ginger hadn't been close and loving at all, and 2) yes, Claire *was* the woman who'd found the conspiratorial proceedings at the secret *Tex and Toni Show* meeting last night so amusing. Her nasal snickers and horsy guffaws were both memorable and unmistakable.

Suddenly cutting her laughter short, Claire rose to her feet and walked over to the kitchen counter. I thought she was going to fetch the pot and pour us some more coffee, but she didn't. She merely turned around to face me, leaned back against the counter, and crossed both arms over her faded, blue-flowered breast. "You're asking a heck of lot of questions," she said. "Are you a reporter or something?"

Yipes!

"No, of course not!" I croaked. "I'm asking a lot questions because I really cared about Ginger and want to know what happened. I shared a dorm room with her for four years, don't forget, and we became very close during that time. She was the best friend I ever had, and I'm so hurt and shocked by her suicide, I simply can't help wondering why she did it."

Claire wasn't buying my charade. She stood leaning against the kitchen counter with her arms crossed over her chest, staring at me the way a marksman stares through a gunsight. Did she know who I was? Had she recognized me from the newspaper photos? Not knowing what to say or do, I just sat there—still and speechless as a statue in that silly chrome and pink dinette chair—while Claire studied me suspiciously. Taking in every detail of my appearance, she raked her eyes over the full length of my body, from my face down to my shoes.

My shoes!

I was wearing the shoes I had dropped in the doorway of Theo's office last night!

Oh, lordy, lordy, lordy! Please don't let Claire notice the shoes!

But she did, of course. And the second she spotted them, a look of angry awareness fell over her mottled face. Pushing away from the counter, she took two menacing steps toward me. "I'll ask you to leave now, Mrs. Turner," she said. "I don't believe you went to college with my sister, and I don't appreciate your prying, underhanded questions about her death. You've invaded my home under false pretenses, and my husband's going to be furious when he finds out. So, I suggest you leave this house this minute, before he gets home"

That was the best idea I'd heard all day.

I RAN OUT OF THE HOUSE AND STRAIGHT across the street to the car. I was relieved to see that the top had been raised. The windows were closed, too, and so foggy I couldn't see through them. Desperate to make a fast getaway, I yanked the passenger door open and jumped inside.

"Oh, for god's sake!" I cried, when I sat on Abby's feet and finally grasped the reason for the steamy windows. "Have you two been making out this whole time?! What are you, anyway—a couple of sex-crazed teenagers?! I've been inside that house risking life and limb to catch a vicious killer, and you've been *making out?!* I can't believe it! I thought you were standing guard over me! I thought if anything bad happened you'd rush in to save me! Jesus! What a fool I was to count on you! I should have known you wouldn't focus on *me* if you were anywhere near each other!"

(I guess you can tell from the number of exclamation points in the above paragraph that I was having another one of those slight mental breakdowns I mentioned earlier. But do you blame me? I mean, it isn't very comforting to know that your best friend in all the world is—even under the most ominous of circumstances—more inclined to lock lips with a lousy poet than to stay on her toes for you. But that wasn't all that was bothering me, okay? The truth is, I was so jealous I couldn't see straight. I hadn't made out with Dan since last Friday—four whole days ago!—and, despite Theo Kidd's recent loathsome assault on my mouth, my lips were desperately lonely.)

"Oh, shut up, Paige!" Abby said, yanking her feet out from

under my bottom and swinging herself around to a sitting position. "Don't get your keester in a kink. We just got a little bored, that's all. And we haven't been making out the *whole* time, you dig? Just the last fifteen minutes or so." Her head scarf was now slung around her neck like a bib, and I could see from the light of the street lamp that her lipstick was smeared all over her cheeks. Jimmy's, too.

"Fifteen minutes?!" I shrieked. "Do you know what can happen in fifteen minutes? Knives can be thrown! Guns can be fired! Necks can be broken! Whole herds of people can be hurled off of balconies!"

"These are ranch houses," Jimmy said. "They don't have any balconies."

Aaargh! If I'd had a rope I might have strangled myself. Or Jimmy. "Where's Otto?" I asked, giving up on my unrepentant human colleagues and looking around for my trusty canine friend.

"In the back," Abby said. "Sleeping."

And so he was—curled up like a donut in the far corner of the back seat. Even my blustery tirade hadn't woken him up. Some watchdog he turned out to be.

"I'm starving," Abby said. "Let's go get something to eat."

Oh, what's the use?

"That's a good plan, Fran," I said, suddenly coming back to my senses (and hopping down off my high horse). "Put the pedal to the metal, Jimmy!" I was dying to get out of there before Rusty showed up. And dying of hunger, too.

Jimmy fired up the engine and wiped a clear patch on the foggy front window with his hand. Then he flipped on the radio, peeled away from the curb, and—singing "Ain't That a Shame" along with Fats Domino (thank God it wasn't the Pat Boone version!)—hauled Biggie's cherry asphalt eater out of the Levittown development and back onto the main drag.

Our (okay, *my*) current search for the murderer had come to a hasty end. Now we were just hunting for hamburgers.

Chapter 29

WE GOT BACK TO THE CITY AROUND eleven. Jimmy dropped Abby and me off in front of our building, then he and Otto zoomed away down Bleecker to return the car to Biggie. Abby and I staggered up the stairs to the landing between our apartments, both so tired we could barely move. I was exhausted from a long, grueling day of clipping, filing, proofreading, coffee making, sleuthing, and shoe swiping. Abby was worn-out from . . . what? Too much necking?

"Want to come in for a drink?" she asked. "Jimmy bought a bottle of tequila today. It's got a worm in it. Isn't that cool? Jimmy says it's an aphrodisiac."

"That's the last thing I want," I said, laughing (though I really felt like crying). "I'm oversexed as it is. And I don't know when, if ever, I'll see Dan again—so, I need to stifle my urges, not heighten them."

"What happened?" Abby inquired, unlocking the door to her apartment and pushing it wide. "Did you and your daring detective have another tiff?"

" 'Tiff' is hardly the word," I said, with a heavy sigh. "It was a battle royal—a knock-down-drag-out fight to end all fights. Dan left here in a rage and I haven't heard from him since Sunday."

"I'm sorry, kiddo," Abby said, looking sadder than Edith Piaf on a rainy day. (For Abby, man trouble is the worst kind of trouble there is.) "Come on in," she coaxed. "Jimmy won't be back for a while. We'll have some tequila and suck on some lemons and you can tell me all about it."

I was tempted by the tequila, but turned off by the worm. And the only thing I really wanted to do at that moment was go to sleep (or slip into a coma, whichever came first). "Thanks, Ab," I said, yawning, "but I'm too tired for anything but bed. I have to go to work tomorrow, and I still have a murderer to catch."

Abby giggled. "Oh, Paige, you're such a scream!"

"What do you mean?" I bleated, getting rankled again. "You think there's something funny about murder? You find it hilarious that a stone-cold killer is flitting around our city free as a dirty bird?"

"No, silly," Abby said, still giggling. "It was just funny the way you *said* it. 'I still have a murderer to catch,' as if it were just another routine, humdrum chore on your daily list of things to do."

"Well, that's the way it's beginning to feel," I said, heaving another woeful sigh. I took my keys out of my purse and unlocked my own door. "I'm not kidding, Ab. I've been working on this story for just four days, but it feels like forever. And I still don't have a clue who the murderer is. This homicide may never be solved. I could be looking for Ginger's killer for the rest of my life." I pushed my door open, stepped inside, and—turning back around to face Abby—leaned wearily against the jamb. "Of course, if the killer identifies me before I identify him, then my life may be over a bit sooner than I'd planned."

"*Oy vey!*" Abby cried. "Please don't talk that way, Paige! It takes my *kishkes* out. It makes me so *meshuga* I could *plotz!*" She flipped her long fat braid from one shoulder to the other and gave me a fierce, pleading look. "Who the hell cares who killed Ginger Allen, anyway? So what if she was a famous TV star? She was still a first-class bitch, and a sorry excuse for a person, and she wasn't worth one—I'm talking *one*—single hair on that little round dopey thing you call your head. So, why put your life in danger on her account?"

"There's such a thing as justice, you know," I said, with a haughty sniff.

"Oh, no, there isn't!" she screeched. "You could easily get killed by the same goddamn killer you're looking for! Where's the frigging justice in that?!"

I'd never seen Abby so upset (except for the time she found me shot and bleeding on my kitchen floor). And I don't mind telling you her words gave me pause—made me think twice about continuing my quest for the truth. But after I thought it over for the third time, I found that I was still as dedicated and determined (okay, *deranged*) as ever.

"I can't help myself, Ab," I said. "I have to see this thing through to the end. It's just the way I am. It's *who* I am. Once I start turning the pages, I can't stop till the story's over." I shook my head and gave her an apologetic smile. "You see the bleary shape I'm in? Now *I'm* the one making silly references to my silly name. I need to get some sleep."

"Oh, all right!" Abby huffed, backing off, even though she clearly wanted to continue the discussion. "But don't think I'm getting lazy, Daisy. You can go to bed tonight, but I expect you to listen to every damn word I have to say tomorrow."

"Okay, Ab. That's fine with me—if you're sure you won't be too busy making out." I gave her a big wink and a goofy smile, and closed my door before she could start screeching again.

I WAS WEARING A SHEER BLACK NEGLI-gee and poised to dive off the top of the RCA Building when the doorbell rang. Coming fully awake in a single second, I shot up to a sitting position in my bed and grabbed the clock off my bedside table. Slanting the face of the clock into the beam of street light sneaking through the side of my bedroom window shade, I looked at the time. It was a quarter to two.

What the hell was going on? Who could be ringing my bell so late at night? Had the murderer figured out who I was, found my address in the phone book, and come to pay a homicidal house call? I vaulted out of bed and scooted over to the window, pulling the shade further away from the window frame, peering down at the shadowy figure standing on the sidewalk below.

My heart did a perfect cartwheel. It was Dan!

Letting out a muffled whoop of joy, I bounded out of the bedroom, scrambled barefoot down the stairs in the dark, leapt like a dancer to the door, and buzzed Dan in. Then I took a deep breath and opened my door, sticking my head out into the dimly lit hall to watch him ascend.

I didn't know what to expect. I was trembling in dreadful anxiety *and* hopeful anticipation. Had Dan come to make up or break up? I watched him climb the stairs to my apartment in the same way a nervous defendant watches the jury re-enter the courtroom.

I didn't get a good look at Dan's face until he reached the landing. And even after we'd made eye contact, I didn't know what to think. His eyes seemed glad to see me, but the rest of his face looked mad.

"Hi," I said, moving to the side of the doorway, flipping on the kitchen light, and motioning for him to enter.

He didn't say anything. He took a few steps inside, then just stood there in silence, shifting his weight from one foot to the other, taking his hat off and raking his fingers through his thick dark hair, looking so gorgeous I felt weak in the knees.

"It's good to see you," I said. "I've missed you. I tried to call you this afternoon, but—"

"Cut the small talk, Paige," he broke in. "I saw your picture in the paper today. At the crime scene. What were you doing there?"

Uh oh!

"The same thing you were doing," I said, jumping to my

own defense. "I was looking for clues, trying to figure out who killed Ginger Allen."

"Some people think she killed herself."

"But you're not one of them" I observed. "Otherwise, you would have called it the *suicide* scene, not the *crime* scene."

Dan smiled in spite of himself. "Ever the clever detective, aren't you, Paige?"

Heartened by his semisarcastic tone (I figured semi- was better than entirely), I gave him a thin smile in return. "*Never* clever is more like it," I humbly confessed. "Especially this time around." I walked over to the kitchen counter and held up the bottle of Chianti. "Want some?" I was trying to act calm, cool, and collected, but my knees were still as weak as water.

"Yes," Dan said, taking off his trench coat and tossing it over the back of the living room chair. He set his hat down on top of his coat, but left his suit jacket and shoulder holster on. Loosening his tie a bit (a very *little* bit), he took his usual seat at the kitchen table.

As I walked over to the table with our wine, I realized that Dan was staring at me, with a puzzled, bug-eyed look on his face. He looked like Ricky always does when one of Lucy's outrageous shenanigans first comes to light.

"What the heck have you got on?" he wanted to know. "Is that supposed to be a nightgown—or a uniform?"

Oh, lordy, I groaned to myself. *I forgot to put on my robe before I came downstairs!*

"Uh, well, uh . . . it's a little of both," I stammered, both embarrassed by my state of near undress, and hesitant (I mean, *really* hesitant) to explain my weird emotional dependency on my late husband's old T-shirts.

"That's an Army T-shirt, isn't it?" Dan asked.

"Um, uh, yes . . ."

"Did it belong to Bob?"

"Well, er, yes . . ."

"And that's what you like to sleep in?"

"Well, yes, but—"

"Looks comfortable," he said, smiling again. Then he

cocked his head and gave me a friendly wink. "Damn sexy, too."

Hallelujah! The battle was over. In spite of my military nightie (or, more likely, *because* of it), Dan had declared a cease fire. Sheer black negligees were for sissies. From now on I'd clad myself in khaki.

I gave Dan a grateful grin and sat down, hurrying to hide my naked legs under the table. (I may be oversexed, but I'm overly modest, too.) "So, you believe Ginger was murdered, right?" I blurted, so eager to discuss the case with him I couldn't contain myself. "I saw you at the crime scene, and since I know that Ginger's neighborhood isn't in your precinct, I figure you voiced your suspicions at headquarters and got yourself assigned to Ginger's case. Is that what happened?"

"More or less," he said, taking his Luckies and his lighter out of his shirt pocket, setting them on the table, and drinking some of his wine. "I haven't actually been assigned to the case, but I've been given official permission to take part in the investigation."

"We're both in the same spot then," I said, striving to align our positions. I was hoping Dan would start relating to me as a fellow investigator, not as a nosy girlfriend.

"Nice try, Paige," he said, firing up one of his Luckies, "but we're not in the same spot at all, and its time you stopped pretending that we are. I'm a legitimate homicide detective, doing the job I've been trained to do, and I've been *officially* appointed to work on this case."

"Well, I was officially appointed, too!" I protested. "I was appointed by the murder victim herself! You can't get any more official than that!"

I expected Dan to get angry again, to start hollering at me for all the usual reasons (i.e., not keeping my promises, putting myself in danger, ya da da da da da da da da da), so, I was really surprised when he leaned back in his chair, took a couple of pensive puffs on his cigarette, and then said—in a firm, yet temperate tone—"You're right, babe. This is your case more than anybody's. I was wrong to give you such a hard time about it. If it weren't for you, nobody in the whole damn department, including me, would have questioned the suicide finding, and the Ginger Allen case would now be closed. For good."

I couldn't believe my ears. Had Dan just *apologized* to me? Had he just acknowledged that I had a right to investigate Ginger's death? Was he actually going to discuss the case with me in a fair, equitable, and impersonal manner? There was only one way to find out.

"So, have you dug up any good evidence?" I asked, panting like an overheated poodle. "Do you know who the murderer is?"

Dan gave me a solemn look and took another drag on his cigarette. "I found the smoking gun," he said, "but I don't yet know who fired it."

"The smoking gun?!" I said. "You mean you and the police have definite proof that Ginger was murdered?" I was delighted that Dan was talking to me, but even more pleased that he seemed to have uncovered a major piece of the puzzle.

"Well, the detective in charge isn't calling the new evidence *proof,* per se, but he admits it's pretty strong stuff. And he's shifted his own position on the case from suicide to murder, so I guess something has been proved to *him.*"

"Like what?!" I begged. My curiosity was eating a hole in my brain. "What did you do? What did you find out?" I threw my head back and downed my entire glassful of wine.

"Well, the first thing I did was call for a second autopsy," Dan said. "Knowing what I'd learned from you—that Ginger had believed somebody was trying to murder her—I thought the first report might be superficial. I had a hunch the medical examiner had accepted the department's swift conclusion that Ginger committed suicide, and that he had, therefore, performed a basic, routine autopsy—not the extensive, in-depth, fine-tooth-comb postmortem required in a homicide investigation."

"And were you right?" I urged. "Did the second autopsy show anything new?"

"It showed that Ginger had been heavily sedated before the

fall—*very* heavily sedated—and due to the advanced disso-
lution of the sleeping pills in her stomach, and the large
amount of narcotics in her blood, the medical examiner now
believes she was totally unconscious at the time of the plunge.
There were some finger-sized bruises under her arms, and
several scrapes on the backs of her heels, suggesting that she
was dragged out onto the terrace by her armpits. And the long,
thin scratches going down her chest, coupled with the snags
and rips on the front of her flimsy negligee, indicate that her
limp body was propped against the prickly, ivy-covered stone
wall of the terrace, and then shoved—head first—over the
top."

I felt sick to my stomach. I had been clamoring for details,
but Dan had given me more than I bargained for. At least Ginger had been unconscious when the fall took place, I told myself. At least she hadn't seen the roof of her limousine
zooming upward like a meteor toward her beautiful face, or
felt the galactic, spine-crushing impact of her final landing.

"Are you sure she was still alive when she was pushed?" I
asked. "She hadn't already died from an overdose of sleeping
pills?"

"No, the autopsy is quite conclusive on that point. Her broken neck was the cause of death."

"Okay, so now we *know* Ginger was murdered," I said,
darting over to the kitchen counter to grab the bottle of Chianti and bring it back to the table. It was all I could do not to
plug the bottle into my mouth and suck the rest of its contents
into my churning stomach. "But have you learned anything
else?" I pleaded, pouring us each a refill. "Anything that
could help identify the monster who did this horrible thing?"

"I've unearthed a few facts," Dan said, stalling, picking up
his drink and raising it to his lips.

"Well, what are they?!" I cried, begging for bones. I was
on the verge of a heart attack.

Dan gave me a playful, seductive look over the rim of his
glass. "I'm not ready to disclose that information just yet," he
teased. He took a sip of wine then set the glass down on the
table."It's *your* time to talk now, babe. Turnabout's fair play,

right?—and I'm not spilling another bean until you cough up everything you know." He sat up straighter in his chair, stubbed his cigarette out in the ashtray, and gave me an eager, expectant look.

I couldn't believe it! Manhattan's most celebrated and respected homicide detective was sitting right here in my kitchen, discussing the evidence in a major headline-making murder case with me, and asking for *my* investigative input! I was thrilled right out of my skin. I thought I died and went to heaven. This was my crowning crime-busting moment, and—as sick and tired of murder as I was—I meant to make the most of it.

Chapter 30

MY MOMENT IN THE SUN LASTED FORTY-
five minutes. I told Dan about everything that had happened
since the last time I'd seen him—from my sneaky invasion of
the Orchid file room to my hot rod trip out to Levittown—
drawing each episode out to epic proportions, relating every
single detail I could remember, relishing each and every second of my newfound (and most likely fleeting) sense of importance and power.

I downplayed the danger angle as much as I could, of
course, describing my midnight shoe-dropping, scenery-
crashing escape from the RCA Building in the most comical,
least threatening terms possible, and telling the story of my
visit to Theo's office, and of his sexual siege on the *Colgate*
chorus girl, without mentioning the fact that the lecherous director had also set siege on me. (If Dan found out about that,
he might kill Theo—and then I'd have *another* murder on my
head!)

When I came to the end of my tale, the Chianti bottle was
empty, and the ashtray was so full that the cinders were
spilling out onto the tabletop. "So what do you think?" I asked
Dan. "I don't know what any of this means. I'm more con-

fused than ever. At first I thought the killer was Leo, then I thought Tex or Toni, then I thought Rusty or Theo, and now I'm thinking Claire. Actually, they *all* seem guilty as sin to me."

"Yeah, they're a pretty rotten bunch," he said, shaking his head in disdain.

A new idea suddenly streaked into my head. "Maybe they really are all guilty!" I whooped, jumping out of my chair and pacing around the kitchen, too excited to sit still. "Maybe they planned the whole thing together!" The more I paced, the more believable (to me) my new theory became. "They held that meeting and made the Tex and Toni screen test the very night after Ginger's fall. Actually, it was the *same* night, since the fall occurred so early in the morning. And nobody at that meeting was in shock, or upset, or even the least bit sad about Ginger's death. I know! I was there! All they cared about was filling her TV time slot! It was the vilest thing I ever—"

"Simmer down, Watson," Dan said, chuckling.

I stopped pacing and propped my hands on my hips. "What the hell are you laughing at?" I spat. "It's all so hideous and disgusting! The idea that Ginger's six closest friends and relatives would band together to plot her murder is—"

"Preposterous," Dan broke in. He gave me a patronizing smile. "You've been reading too many Agatha Christie novels."

I was stung. "What's so preposterous about it?" I cried. "All six of them were at that meeting, and they seemed *glad* that Ginger was dead. I think they all despised her."

"You're probably right on that point," Dan said, "but you're forgetting one important thing: they despise each other, too. Even the ones who are married to each other. I've spoken to all of the suspects at length, and their obvious contempt for each other—not to mention their mutual distrust—is so thick you'd need a saw to slice it. They're far more competitive than they are collaborative."

"They were collaborating pretty darn well at that secret midnight meeting!" I said, throwing my hands up in the air. Detective Street was starting to tick me off.

Dan looked at me in the same way a school principal looks at a failing student. "For your information, the meeting started at nine, not midnight," he said, "and there was nothing secret about it. A couple of NBC honchos suggested that Leo meet with his staff to discuss the programming emergency. Leo is one of the network's more successful producers and they wanted to give him first crack at the coveted time slot."

"Oh," I said, suddenly feeling dumber than mud.

"They were collaborating on keeping their cherished place in the TV schedule, *not* on covering up a communal murder," Dan added, rubbing it in.

"But why were Rusty and Claire there?" I asked, trying to recoup my investigative integrity. "Since when are a show's stagehand and the star's sister considered members of the producer's staff?"

"Since it was learned that Claire will inherit half of Ginger's estate," Dan said, "plus *all* of her fifty-one percent interest in Marxallen Productions—the television production company she and Leo formed five years ago, at the launch of their marriage and the birth of Ginger's television career."

Hmmmm, I mused to myself. *I guess Claire and Rusty won't be living out in Levittown much longer.*

"All right, that explains a lot," I grudgingly admitted, sitting down at the table again. "But one thing about that night still bothers the hell out of me."

"What's that?" Dan asked, lighting another Lucky.

"Why did Theo and Rusty run after me when I dropped my shoes?" I probed. "They were truly desperate to catch me! And it doesn't make any sense. If they weren't trying to hide something, then what the heck were they so frantic about? Why did they chase me out of the building the way they did?"

"They *were* trying to hide something," Dan disclosed, "but it didn't have anything to do with murder. Or with you." He took a deep drag on his cigarette, then blew a perfect smoke ring into the motionless kitchen air.

"So, what did it have to do with?" I spluttered, sounding like Daffy Duck in the throes of a wacky conniption. One

more minute of this torture, and I'd start pulling out my hair.
Dan's, too.

"It was all about protecting their future," Dan said. "Theo
explained the whole thing to me when I questioned him this
morning in his office. He said they thought you were one of
the press people they'd seen hanging around the RCA Building that night—a striving gossip columnist, maybe, or a paid
snoop for Winchell or Kilgallen—and they were afraid you'd
overheard too much. And since they didn't want the news of
their unsigned, unprotected Tex and Toni deal splattered all
over the next day's papers, they tried to chase you down to
pay you off. They just wanted to buy your silence, babe. Too
bad you didn't let them nab you," he teased. "You could have
made yourself a nice little bundle."

Aaargh!

"Did you blow my cover?" I asked him. "Did you tell Theo
who I really was?" I wondered if Theo's seeming ignorance
of my identity this afternoon had been just an act.

Dan looked as though he'd just been punched in the stomach. "How could you ask me a question like that, Paige? It's
an insult! I'd never do anything to put you in danger, and you
know it." Now *he* was getting ticked off at *me*.

"I'm sorry, Dan," I said. "I didn't think you would do it on
purpose, you know! I just thought it might have slipped out of
your mouth by accident in the heat of the interrogation."

Dan sat up taller in his chair. "I'm a trained and experienced investigator," he said, neck turning stiff before my very
eyes. "*Nothing* slips out of my mouth by accident."

"No, of course it doesn't," I soothed, sounding as soft and
self-effacing as Melanie in *Gone With the Wind*, but feeling as
shrill and self-defensive as Scarlet. "I'm just so surprised that
you and Theo discussed the incident in the first place. How
did the subject come up? Did you ask him about it, or did he
just volunteer the information?"

"I asked him about it," Dan said.

"But how on earth did you know to ask him about it? How
did you even know it happened?" I was totally agog. Did Dan

have a crystal ball hidden away somewhere, or had he been following me like a beagle, watching my every stupid move?

"I had no prior knowledge of the incident," Dan stiffly replied. "I simply asked Theo why he had a pair of high heels on his shelf. He laughed and told me the whole story."

"I can't believe it!" I squeaked (absolute astonishment makes me cheep like a chipmunk). "How in the world did you even notice the shoes? And whatever made you question Theo about them?"

Amused by my feverish befuddlement, Dan began to relax. "Well, I knew the shoes were yours," he said, "and I was wondering how they got there."

"But how did you know they were mine?" I stammered. "I bought them just last week!" By now I was practically blithering.

"You were wearing them the last time I saw you, remember? It was the night Ginger's chauffeur drove you home."

"Yes, I remember," I said, "but I'm surprised you do. Whatever made those shoes stick in your mind?"

"I'm a professional detective," he said. "I'm trained to remember things."

If he used the word *trained* one more time, I thought I'd scream!

"But that's not the only reason," he added, flashing me one of his breathtaking, bone-melting smiles. "You looked really sexy in those shiny black stilettos. I wasn't likely to forget that."

Well, that was all I needed to hear.

"Should I go put them on?" I asked, suddenly eager to stop playing detective. Now I wanted to play doctor instead.

"Better not," Dan said, with a lusty yet solemn wink. "Those shoes have gotten you into too much trouble already."

A sobering thought, to say the least. Would my reckless black patent leather footprints lead a black-hearted killer to my door?

AFTER DRAINING THE DREGS OF MY
wine and biting one thumbnail to the quick, I took the empty

Chianti bottle and jellyglasses into the kitchen and set them
on the counter. Then I snatched two Dr. Peppers out of the
fridge, pried off the cork-lined metal caps, and brought the
bottles to the table. (The more I drink, the better I think.)

"Here," I said, handing one of the bottles to Dan. "It
doesn't have any alcohol, but it's got gobs of caffeine."

"Good. That's what I need." He stuck the bottle in his
mouth and swigged down half of the spicy soda pop.

I took a couple of gulps and sat back down at the table.
Then I quickly turned all my thoughts and energies back to
the case. "What have you learned about Leo?" I asked.
"Was he at home the night of the murder? The papers said
he wasn't. They said Ginger was alone in the penthouse at
the time of her fall. Ha! That shows you how little *they*
know. The murderer was obviously there, and so was the
butler. Woodrow, the chauffeur, saw Boynton when he came
down to the street in his robe. Woodrow said Leo never
showed up at all, but that doesn't prove anything, I guess.
So, do you know where Leo was?" I pestered. "Have you
learned anything conclusive?"

All of a sudden, Dan looked exhausted and more than a little gray around the gills. "Leo swears he wasn't there," Dan
said, "and his alibi has been corroborated. But that doesn't
prove anything, either. Nancy could just be covering up for
him."

"Nancy? Who's Nancy?"

"Leo's mistress," Dan said.

"What?!!!" I croaked. "Leo has a *mistress?!!!*" I was
shocked down to my socks (even though I wasn't wearing
any). Leo just didn't seem like the philandering type.

"Yep," Dan confirmed. "Her name is Nancy Winters and
she lives just a few blocks uptown from the penthouse, in a
snazzy apartment leased by Leo. She's a short, plump, thirty-
four-year-old stenographer with a freezer full of chocolate ice
cream and a longhaired cat named Freddy. Leo's been paying
her rent for two years now, and he says he sleeps at her—or,
rather, *their*—place almost every night. He claims he was
there the night Ginger fell, and Nancy backs him up all the

way. They could be lying through their teeth, of course, but I'm inclined to believe them."

"Oh, my god! I cried. "I'm stunned! I never thought for a moment that Leo would have a mistress! He's such an ugly little man—very serious and tense."

"Ugly little men need love as much as anybody," Dan said. "Maybe more."

"Of course they do," I replied. "It's just that Leo never seems to *need* anything. He's always self-contained and under control. And he was so devoted to Ginger it was sickening! He catered to her every whim." I paused for a moment, then posed another question."Did Ginger know where Leo was going every night, or did she just not care enough to ask?"

"According to Leo, she knew all about his other life and was quite happy with the arrangement." Dan rubbed his face with both hands, then wearily scratched his stubbled chin. "Beats the hell out of me." As a man who valued loyalty and faithfulness above all else, Dan found such fickle dispassion hard to comprehend. Showing physical signs of his mental disapproval (as well as his fast-growing fatigue), he slumped down his his chair, crossed his arms over his chest, and closed his eyes.

I lit another cigarette, took another slug of my Dr. Pepper, and went into a frenzied trance, working to integrate the new information I'd gotten from Dan with all the other facts and theories in my mind. It didn't take me very long. After a few minutes of intense yet free-flowing concentration, it all just seemed to fall into place on its own—like a dream, or a movie, or a story that was writing itself.

Snapping out of my reverie, I said to Dan, "I've got a pretty clear scenario in my head now—about Ginger and Leo's relationship, I mean. Do you want to hear it?"

"Yeah, but make it quick," he said, forcing his eyelids open. "I'm so tired I may black out."

"Okay, here's the way I see it," I said, talking as fast as I could. "Back in 1950, when Ginger was about to make the leap from radio to TV, she broke off her engagement to Private First Class Rusty Burnett and married the wealthy and

powerful TV producer, Leo Marx, for the sole purpose of fur-
thering her television career. Leo didn't grasp Ginger's true
motives at the time, of course. He thought she loved him. And
he was so enamored with his astonishingly beautiful and talented new wife that he gave her fifty-one percent—*the controlling interest*—of Marxallen Productions, the company
they were in the process of forming to handle all their TV
deals and finances.

"Then, as soon as the ink on their marriage and business
contracts had dried, *The Ginger Allen Show* went on the air. It
was an immediate smash hit, second only to *I Love Lucy,* and
during the next three years Ginger's popularity grew to such
outstanding proportions that, by the end of 1953, she had become one of the most famous and adored stars in TV's short
history . . . and one of the most self-centered prima donnas of
all time.

"It was at that point in the saga that ex-fiancé Rusty Burnett came marching home from Korea. And within mere
weeks of his arrival he had married Ginger's sister, accepted
a stagehand job on Ginger's show, and moved his brand-new
bride out to Levittown. And it was around that very same time
that Leo set Nancy Winters up in a luxury apartment near the
penthouse and began spending all his nights there, eating
chocolate ice cream and sleeping in the plump, attentive arms
of a woman not his wife.

"And that curious sequence of events smells pretty darn
fishy to me," I said to Dan. "I mean, isn't it all just *too* coincidental for words? I don't know about you, but I'd say Leo's
abrupt leave-taking had a whole heck of a lot to do with
Rusty's sudden homecoming! And though I don't yet know
what the true cause of these strange schemes and maneuvers
happened to be, I'd bet my bongos it was—in one wicked
way or another—the true cause of Ginger's murder."

I stopped yakking and gave Dan a probing look. "What do
you think?" I asked. I was hoping he'd jump out of his chair,
and whisk me into his arms, and tell me I was the most brilliant sleuth he'd ever worked with.

"I think I'm not thinking very clearly right now," he said,

yawning. "Your summary seems to make a lot of sense, Paige, but I'm too tired to give it the attention it deserves. I'll have to mull it over tomorrow, after I've had some sleep."

I was disappointed in Dan's feeble response, but I didn't complain. The man had, after all, been working around the clock on this case—and even *trained* homicide detectives need their rest.

Chapter 31

IT WAS 4:35 IN THE MORNING. WE WERE
all out of Chianti, Dr. Pepper, and energy. I had to be at work
in less than four hours, and Dan was due in at 9:00. Dan still
looked scrumptious to me, and I could tell from the tiny
gleam in his tired black eyes that my clingy khaki T-shirt was
still having an uplifting effect, but we didn't have the time (or
the strength) to pursue such personal passions. (When you're
hot on the tail of a cold-blooded murderer, even Eros has to
take a back seat.)

"Are we getting anywhere, Dan?" I asked, standing by the
door as he put on his trench coat and hat. "Are we any closer
to catching the killer than we were two days ago?"

"Of course we are," he said, setting his fedora at a sexy
slant and giving me a bleary yet confident smile. "We've narrowed the field to six suspects, and it's just a matter of time
before one of them shows his hand." Dan hesitated for a moment, then said, "Actually, you're the one who narrowed the
field, Paige, to the six people you met at the Stork Club. And
you were right. They're the only ones with real motives—the
only ones with true axes to grind, or something to gain from
Ginger's death."

"Are you sure?" I said. "Practically everybody who ever came in touch with Ginger wound up hating her. What if some wounded cameraman or tortured makeup artist decided to rid the planet of her poisonous presence and make the world a better place?"

"It hardly ever happens that way," Dan assured me. "As an experienced homicide investigator, I know for a fact that most murders are committed by somebody really close to the victim—somebody so tormented by love, hate, or greed that homicide seems like the only answer. And in this case, our six suspects are the only ones who fit that bill. Ginger didn't have any other relatives, close colleagues, intimate enemies, or friends."

"Well, if you're certain . . ."

"I am. Believe me, I've done a thorough search. And besides, right now the question I'm working the hardest to answer is *how,* not *who.*"

I thought he'd lost his marbles. "Jeez, Dan! What's the big dilemma? She was pushed off the balcony—that's how."

"That's not the *how* I'm talking about," he groaned, looking more exhausted by the minute. "I'm talking about how the murderer got up to the penthouse before the murder, and then out of the building afterwards, without being seen. Julius Pyle, the night manager, says Leo left about midnight and never came back. And he swears Ginger didn't have a single visitor the rest of the night."

"I wouldn't set too much store on what the night manager says," I said, with a sniff. "When Woodrow discovered the body and ran around to the building's entrance for help, the worthless watchman was sound asleep."

"Yes, I know," Dan said. "Woodrow gave me the same information. But it doesn't mean anything. Even if Pyle *was* asleep—and I have no doubt that he was—it still would have been practically impossible for anyone to get through the triple-locked front door and then pilot the elevator upstairs to the penthouse. There's no operator on duty after eleven on Sunday, so Pyle has to work the elevator himself. And as an extra security measure, he keeps the elevator's cage door locked and the key in his pocket." Dan shrugged his sagging shoulders and added, "And even if the murderer was familiar with this whole routine, and knew how to work the elevator himself, he still couldn't have been sure that the night manager would be asleep—and he certainly couldn't have counted on getting the elevator key out of Pyle's pocket without waking him up."

"What about the fire escape? There must be an interior fireproof staircase." I thought of my own flight down the cement and metal fire escape at the RCA Building.

"Yes, they have one, of course, and there are no locks on *those* doors. They are, by law, open at all times. Except for the door to the street. That one's always open as an exit, but never open as an entrance. It's permanently locked from the outside, and there are only two keys. The building's owner has one, and the other one is kept in the office wall safe."

"Sounds foolproof," I said.

"Right," Dan agreed.

"So, I guess the murderer's no fool."

"Right, again."

"Well, that narrows the field considerably!" I said, getting excited again. "Both Tex and Toni seem *very* foolish to me."

Dan gave me a weary smile. "Yeah, they're so foolish they're about to step into one of the most lucrative, career-making time slots in television."

He had a point there. "So, what's next on the agenda?" I asked him. "How do we narrow the field from six to one?" *We!* I loved the sound of that word!

Dan put his hands on my shoulders and pressed down, as if to steady me. "I'm going to say something important now, Paige, and I want you to listen very carefully." His eyes were serious, drilling me clean through with their tough but tender gaze. "The closer we get to catching the killer, the more dangerous things will become. So dangerous they could be deadly. And if anything happened to you, I wouldn't be able to stand it. I'd take a long walk off a short pier. So, please, Paige, if you care about me at all, you've got to call off your private investigation right now."

"But, I—"

"No. No buts. You've done an excellent job so far, babe, and if it weren't for you, we wouldn't even know a murder had been committed, much less who the most likely suspects are. But now we *do* know, and it's time for you to back out of the case. The NYPD can take it from here, and—you've got my word on it—we're going to nail this killer to the wall."

I hated to admit it, but I knew Dan was right. It was time for me to back out of the investigation. Now that the police knew Ginger was murdered—and especially now that Dan was on the case—there was no good reason for me to continue my own search for the killer. I should quit while I was ahead (i.e., *alive*) and focus all my efforts on compiling my notes and writing the story.

"Okay," I said, without hesitation. "You win. My private detective days are over." (I was shocked at how easy it was for me to give up. But Dan's praise of my investigative work, plus the obvious wisdom of his argument, plus the way he had looked when he said he wouldn't be able to stand it if anything happened to me—well, let's just say that Dan made giving up feel good.) "I'm off the Ginger Allen case as of this minute," I said. "I promise."

Holding me at arm's length, Dan gave me a searching look. "The last time you gave me that promise, you broke it."

"Well, I'm not going to break it now," I said, really meaning it. "On my honor." To emphasize the integrity of my intentions, I held one hand over my heart and the other in the Girl Scout's pledge position.

Dan smiled and pulled me in for a hug. "If you really mean that," he said, "I may actually be able to sleep when I get home." He let me go and moved toward the door. "For a couple of hours, at least."

"Don't worry about me, Dan," I said, opening the door and watching him step out onto the landing. "I'm sick to death of this investigation. And I'm really tired of being scared. I'm going to be a good little girl from now on, and stay far away from trouble."

Too bad trouble wouldn't stay away from me.

•   •   •

I NEVER WENT BACK TO BED. WHAT WAS
the point? It was almost 5:00 A.M., and I had to leave for work
by 7:45 at the latest. It would take at least a half hour for me
to shower and get dressed. And if I went to sleep now, I'd
never get up on time. And besides, I was so happy I felt more
like dancing than napping.

Dan wasn't mad at me anymore! He was proud of me! He
still loved me! And that wasn't all. A huge burden had now
been lifted from my shoulders. I no longer had to find Ginger's murderer. Dan was going to do it for me. I felt free. I felt
safe. Now I could get back to doing what I did best, which
was writing about the search for a vicious killer, not conducting the search myself.

Filled with pride over my recent accomplishments, and
bristling with new purpose and drive, I went straight upstairs
to my little office, turned on my gooseneck desk lamp, and
planted myself at the typewriter. I hadn't written a word since
the Ginger Allen case began, and now I needed to start typing
my notes. I had to get all my facts and thoughts and impressions down on paper before they gave my mind the slip.
Every name, address, event, detail, clue, description, conversation, and expression I could remember had to be recorded.

I rolled a piece of paper into the carriage of my baby-blue
Royal portable and let my fingers out of the starting gate.
They galloped over the keys like thoroughbreds, doing their
best to keep up with my racing reflections. This was the fast
and easy part. No grammar or punctuation necessary. Just
brisk typing skills and a good memory.

Two hours and twenty-eight sloppy pages later, I'd gotten
a good third of my Ginger Allen data down. Standing up and
giving my limbs and spine a healthy stretch, I turned off the
lamp and tapped my notes into a neat pile on the desk. Then I
left my little office and got ready to go to the bigger one.

IT WAS BUSINESS AS USUAL AT *DARING*
Detective headquarters. After consuming about six cups of
coffee and reading (and crumpling up) all the morning papers,

Harvey Crockett left for an early lunch with one of his old newsroom cronies. Mario was madly laying out a new cover for the next issue, and Mike was busy writing (no doubt *mangling*) a new cover story. Lenny's nose was buried in a mile-high pile of paste-ups, and Pomeroy hadn't come in yet.

I had finished the day's filing, invoicing, and proofreading, and—thanks to my own six cups of coffee—was now clipping the morning newspapers, paying special attention to all the articles about Ginger. The papers were still calling her death a suicide and voicing the sentiments of millions by asking, over and over again, "Why did she do it?" Psychiatrists were crawling out of the woodwork like cockroaches, coming forth to give their "expert" opinions on this subject, most of them blaming the ego-exploding effects of great wealth and fame. I wondered if Ginger's own shrink was among those interviewed.

I also wondered when the police would reveal their murder findings to the press. Were they keeping the truth secret for public or for private reasons?

"Here's the new cover," Mario said, slapping his sketchy layout down on my desk. "You've got to send the new photo out for a stat and get the new headline over to the typesetter immediately. Right this minute. This is a super-rush job."

I rolled my eyes at the ceiling. Everything Mario ever gave me to do was a super-rush job.

"Don't look at me!" Mario whined. "This is all Pomeroy's fault. He made me pull the illustrated DIARY OF A SEX-MAD STRANGLER cover I had already finished and replace it with this."

I looked down at the layout, and there she was again. Ginger Allen. In a voluptuous, full-color photo showing cleavage down to here. Planted just to the left of her cleavage, in letters so bold they were brazen, was the lurid, only slightly modified headline: SUICIDE OF A SEX-MAD TV STAR.

Sex-mad? Oh, Brother! I groaned to myself, knowing Pomeroy's only possible basis for using that inflammatory term was the see-through black negligee Ginger had been wearing when she fell. I smiled at the thought that this offensive cover would have to be pulled when the truth about Ginger's death came out, but then I shuddered with the sad realization that all they'd have to do was change the word SUICIDE to MURDER.

Mike's new story would have to be scrapped, though, and a totally *new* new one would have to be written, and—due to my soon-to-be-revealed connection to the case—I was certain Mr. Crockett would assign the story to me. Maybe, just maybe, if I stuck to my guns and pointed out what a beloved national figure Ginger had been (and still was!), I could get them to change the odious (and, I thought, untrue) cover line.

There was just one problem. Because of my precarious position (i.e., my too-close acquaintance with all six of the murder suspects), my connection to the case couldn't be revealed until *after* the murderer was caught. And who knew how long that would be? I sincerely hoped, for both personal and professional reasons, it would be before this issue of *Daring Detective* went to press.

I put the sized photo and the tissue layout in one envelope, the type-specced cover line in another, addressed them both, and called for a messenger. Mario went back to his desk and I went back to the clipping. A few minutes later, Mike and Mario went out to lunch, and Lenny and I were left alone.

"If you give me half of your salami sandwich," I said to him, "I'll tell you about the new story I'm working on." (Lenny always brought his own lunch to work, and it was always a salami sandwich.)

"Really?" he said, spinning around to face me, looking as flushed and excited as a contestant on *Beat the Clock.*

"Yes, really," I said, laughing. "But you have to promise not to tell anybody else. Not a soul. Not even your mother."

(Now that I was off the case and, I thought, out of immediate danger, I felt I could confide in Lenny. He had already proved to me, once before, in the most dramatic and significant way possible—by risking his own life to save mine!— that I could trust him to the hilt.)

"I won't tell anybody anything! I swear to God!" Lenny vowed. He smacked the top down on his rubber cement jar, grabbed his black metal lunch pail (the one I'd given him last Christmas), and scrambled up the aisle of the workroom to my desk. "I've got some potato kugel, too," he proudly revealed. "My mother made it yesterday."

"Great!" I whooped, madly clearing the morning papers off my desk and making room for our midday feast. (I'd tasted Lenny's mother's kugel before and it was fabulous.)

Lenny sat down in the guest chair next to my desk and divvied up the food. "So, what's been going on?" he probed, gaping at me the way a kid gapes at a squished cat on the pavement. "Has anybody tried to kill you yet?"

"Nob thati nohoph," I said. What I meant was, "Not that I know of," but it's hard to talk when your mouth is full.

Chapter 32

I MANAGED TO TELL LENNY THE WHOLE story—my whole strange, ugly, brutal, fascinating Ginger Allen tale—before Pomeroy showed up. But then Pomeroy *did* show up—much earlier than usual!—and storytime was over. Lenny didn't even have a chance to freak out over all the trouble I had gotten myself into, or demand a written and no-tarized statement that I had truly, totally, and unconditionally abandoned my search for Ginger's killer.

"A picnic for two," Pomeroy sneered, looping his hat on the coat tree. "How sweet." He walked over to my desk and looked down at the few remaining kugel crumbs and the mustard-streaked sheets of waxed paper. "I hate to call a halt to this el-egant banquet, but it's now one seventeen, and your lunch hour was officially over at one. I will, therefore, expect you both to work until five seventeen this evening." He gave us a nasty smile, walked over to his own desk, and sat down. "And we've got a lot of important work to do this afternoon, so get back to your cage, Zimmerman. *Now.*"

Lenny bolted to his feet, balled up all the waxed paper, and stuffed it in his lunch box. Then, shooting me a look of pure disgust, he strode to the back of the workroom, plunked his lunch pail down on his desk, and got back to work on the paste-ups. Lenny was just one step above me in the office hierarchy, so he didn't dare talk back to anybody. (Anybody but me, that is.)

Swivelling to face me, Pomeroy demanded, "Did Mario finish the layout for the Ginger Allen cover? Has it been sent out for stats and type?"

So that was why he came in so early! "Yes to the first question," I said, "but no to the second. I called for a messenger, but he hasn't picked up yet.

"Then call him again!" Pomeroy growled. "We're not playing games here. This is big news! This is urgent!"

I'd never seen Pomeroy so worked up about work before. The way he was carrying on, you'd have thought *Daring Detective* was the blooming *New York Times*. Still, I shouldn't have been so surprised by his sudden clamor. The shocking death of a major celebrity always stirs the press—top newspaper and sleazy magazine editors alike—into a feeding frenzy.

"Yes, sir," I said, picking up the phone and re-dialing the messenger service.

But before anybody could answer, Pomeroy cried, "Never mind! Hang up! The stupid sap is probably on his way. And I've got something more important for you to do right now!"

I hung up the phone and waited for my orders. Something *important* for *me* to do? I doubted it seriously.

"I want you to go down the hall to the Orchid Publications file room and grab all the sexy Ginger Allen photos you can find. The sexier the better. We need at least eight good shots. Legs! Breasts! Skin! And if there are any suggestive candids of her with men—kissing or in a clinch—then grab those, too . . . What are you waiting for? Go on, go on!"

"Shouldn't you call up Orchid first and see if it's okay?" I asked.

"My cousin owns the place," he snapped. "I don't have to ask Orchid's permission for a goddamn thing."

"But they don't know who I am," I lied. "They might not let me in. Shouldn't you at least tell them to expect me?"

"Get up!" he commanded. "Get going! I'll call them while you're walking down there."

"Yes, sir," I said, resisting the urge to give him the 'Heil, Hitler!' salute. Then I rose from my chair and marched, robot-like, into the hall.

THE ORCHID FILE ROOM WAS THE HOT-test place in town, and Bessie was in all her glory. Cigarette dangling from her lips and mint-green smock buttoned over her clothes, she stood behind the long table that was now blocking the entrance to the file room, barking out orders to her assistants, writing things down on a clipboard, and looking every bit as self-important as the majordomo at the Stork Club.

The hall outside the file room was lined with laughing, chattering Orchid employees—all of whom were there clamoring for Ginger Allen photos and/or clips. The crowd was mostly female—noisy young women dressed in ruffled blouses and pastel colored skirts or suits—but some men were standing there as well, loosened neckties slightly askew, pen and pencil sets clipped in the breast pockets of their crisp white shirts.

I knew without asking that the men were the artists. That's just the way it was in the magazine business—even the *women's* magazine business. Women could be editors or copywriters or proofreaders, but the artists were all men. Even the freelance illustrators were all men (except for Abby Moskowitz, of course, who signed all of her paintings Art Montana, so everybody would *think* she was a man).

Braving the belligerent stares of the people not-so-patiently waiting their turn, I walked up to the front of the line. "Hi, Bessie," I said. "Remember me? I'm from *Daring Detective*. Brandon Pomeroy sent me to get some Ginger Allen photos. Did he call you?"

"Yeah, yeah, yeah," she said, dribbling ashes down her chest. "He called all right. Said if we didn't give you some good pictures, he'd rat us out to his cousin—old man Harrington himself!—and have us all fired. Nice guy, your boss. Must be stinko working for him."

"It sure is," I said, laughing, relieved that Bessie wasn't blaming me for the tyrannical intrusion.

"Come on in, then," she said, pulling one side of the table away from the wall, making room for me to enter the file room. "You can snitch some shots from the files before we toss them out to the mob. Better be quick, though. The walruses are hungry, and Ginger Allen is the catch of the day."

I squeezed through the narrow opening and veered to the right, where the photo files were situated. "Thanks, Bessie!" I called, passing behind her and heading toward the tall, dimly lit maze of filing cabinets. "I owe you a lunch at the automat!"

"You're on, sister," she hollered, returning her attention to the walruses barking at her door.

As Bessie's assistants were ferrying the Ginger Allen photo files up to the front check-out desk, they stopped at my side and gave me first pick of the contents. Purposely passing over the sexiest shots, I chose a few of the more flattering pix and stuck them in the manila envelope I had brought along for the occasion. I hadn't liked Ginger Allen in the least, but I had no intention of helping to further the false notion that she was some kind of sex maniac! If Pomeroy wanted those kind of photos, he'd have to find them for himself.

Aside from the mountains of publicity shots showing Ginger with numerous guest stars and other celebrities, there were very few pictures of Ginger with men. And there were no suggestive kissing or clinch shots at all. (The photo of Ginger kissing Rusty goodbye before he left for Korea had probably been taken by a *Look* magazine photographer, and would, therefore, be tucked away in *Look*'s photo files, not Orchid's.) There were some shots of Ginger and Leo together at various Emmy Awards banquets, and several candids taken at the top nightspots around town, but that was about it.

Just two of the candids caught my eye (for my own reasons, not Pomeroy's). One was a picture of Ginger, Leo, Rusty, and Claire grouped together—all looking very sullen and miserable—in a booth at El Morocco. (I could see it was

El Morocco because they were all sitting on one of the club's famous zebra-striped banquettes.) The other was a photo of Ginger and Theo Kidd, sitting together at a table for two in a different nightclub. There was no caption or date on the photo, so I couldn't tell when or where it was taken. All I could tell was that Ginger and Theo both looked lusty, rowdy, and disheveled—and very, very drunk.

Could Pomeroy possibly be right about Ginger? I suddenly found myself wondering. Had she been a little sex-mad, after all? I really didn't think so, but this photo made me think twice. I knew from personal experience that Thelonius Kidd *was* sex-mad. And I knew that he and Ginger had had a very fiery working relationship. Could they have had a fiery sexual relationship as well? An attraction so fierce it was fatal?

I took both of these candids out of the file and slipped them into my manila envelope. I wanted the photos for myself, not Pomeroy. I felt sure I would soon be writing the *true* Ginger Allen story—i.e., the murder story—and I knew pictures of the prime suspects would come in handy. Then, since I had enough pictures of Ginger but was still missing pix of two of the suspects, I thanked Bessie's assistants and left the A section of the file room, walking all the way down and around to the T's.

There was just one thin folder of Tex and Toni Taylor pictures, and I went through it in a snap. Most of the photos were network publicity shots for the *Breakfast with Tex and Toni* radio show, but there were a few at-home sets of the platinum-haired duo lounging on their white velvet sofa with their two white toy poodles, Timmy and Tammy. It amused me to see how Tex and Toni, both brunettes at the beginning of their career, had grown blonde, blonder, and blondest over the past year. I took one of the more recent photos out of the folder and stuck it in my envelope.

On my way out, I gave Bessie a list of the photos I was borrowing and promised to return them soon. Then I tucked the manila envelope under my arm and hurried past the line of

Orchid employees still bellowing for their Ginger Allen hand-outs.

As a fellow magazine staffer, I felt sorry for them. I wanted to stop and tell them they were wasting their time—that the stories they were working so hard to finish now would soon have to be yanked, trashed, and rewritten when the truth about Ginger's death came out. But I didn't dare say a word. The news would spread through the publishing industry (and into print) like wildfire, and Dan, and the police—and maybe even the murderer himself—would have no trouble tracking down the source of the blaze.

I LEFT THE OFFICE AT 5:17 ON THE DOT, setting out for my intended destination. But as I crossed under the Third Avenue El and began walking toward the subway at 42nd and Lex, it started raining. Hard. So hard that by the time I dashed down the block to the subway entrance and ducked underground, I was soaked through to the skin. This was a good thing, you should know, because up until that point (the saturation point, I mean) I had been planning to go straight uptown to Ginger's penthouse to get my glasses back.

Okay! Okay! I confess! That wasn't the *real* reason I wanted to go back to Ginger's building. I didn't care if I ever laid eyes on those stupid glasses again. The truth was I wanted to talk to the night manager, Julius Pyle, or to Boynton the butler, to see if I could find out anything more about the night of the murder, and about the building's security system—i.e., the locks, keys, buzzers, alarms, elevator, fire escape, etc. Like Dan, I had become very interested in the *how.* I thought it might lead us to the *who.*

I know! I know! I had given Dan my solemn promise that I would stay off the case. I wasn't supposed to be even *thinking* about continuing my personal homicide investigation. But that wasn't what I was doing! I swear! I was just thinking about pursuing my *journalistic* investigation. Don't you see? It was my job to write the true story, and I couldn't do that until I had uncovered the truth. And I couldn't uncover the truth just by digging around in Orchid's files. I needed to dig around in the real world, too.

Okay! Okay! So, all that stuff I just said about my journalistic investigation—about having to uncover the truth in order to write the truth—was a big fat rationalization. We both know I was just looking for an excuse to keep on looking for the killer. (I couldn't help it! I was addicted to the search!) But the real truth was that now that Dan and New York's finest were on the case, I didn't have to uncover a thing. All I had to do was sit back and wait for them to catch Ginger's killer, and *then* I could write the truth—the whole truth and nothing but.

Which was another good thing, since after I got soaked to the skin in the rain, I didn't feel like going uptown to Ginger's building anymore. I was sopping wet, shivering cold, and so tired I was virtually sleepwalking. All I wanted to do was go home and take a hot shower. And *that* was a *very* good thing, since it kept me from breaking my promise to Dan.

So, anyway, instead of taking the Lexington Avenue line up to 77th Street as planned, I took the shuttle to Times Square and then changed to the downtown IRT. And fifteen minutes after that (I was lucky; I caught an express), I got off the train at the Sheridan Square station and dragged my cold, soggy self up the stairs to Seventh Avenue.

It was still pouring, and I could tell from the heavy darkness and the thick black clouds overhead that it wasn't going to let up anytime soon. There were no umbrella stores, and not an inch of space left under any of the nearby awnings, so I tucked my chin down into the collar of my jacket and started running (okay, *swimming*) toward Bleecker.

I didn't have too far to go, but by the time I got home I was snorting like an overworked racehorse. And I felt, as well as looked, like a drowned dog. I climbed the steps as fast as I could (i.e., at top tortoise speed) and knocked on Abby's door. I wanted a dry towel, a stiff drink, and somebody to talk to—in that order. The hot shower could wait till later.

As luck (or, rather, dire misfortune) would have it, Abby

wasn't home. I let myself into my own apartment, plopped my sodden jacket, beret, and gloves on the kitchen table, and plodded upstairs to the bathroom for another, hopefully more soothing, barrage of water.

Chapter 33

AFTER MY SHOWER, I PUT ON MY BLACK
capris, a white scoop-neck sweater, my black ballerina flats,
and a new face (i.e., fresh makeup). I was hoping Dan would
drop in again and I wanted to look my best. (I had considered
donning a clean khaki T-shirt and my black patent leather
stilettos, but decided that would be too tacky—okay, *trampy*.)

The first thing I did when I went back downstairs was
check to see if Abby was home. She wasn't. My hopes for
some amusing conversation and a couple of shots of tequila
(worm or no worm) fell to the floor with a thud. Shoulders
sagging, I slumped into my kitchen, made myself a bowl of
Campbell's chicken noodle soup, and quickly consumed it,
along with a thousand or so saltines. Then, too tired to even
think of working on my story notes, I went into the living
room and turned on the TV, setting the dial on channel 4—
NBC. The news was on and I sat down to watch. *Maybe
they'll break the story that Ginger was murdered,* I mumbled
to myself. *Maybe they'll have some new evidence to . . .*

The next thing I knew, Ralph Edwards was shouting, "Jack
Benny! . . . This is your life!" I couldn't believe my ears. And
when I finally opened my eyes, I couldn't believe them, ei-

ther. *This is Your Life!* was, indeed, on the screen—and I knew for a fact that show didn't come on until 10:00 P.M.! I had been sleeping in my living room chair for over two hours! I had slept through the news, *I Married Joan, My Little Margie,* and the whole of *Kraft Television Theater.* And I was still so tired I couldn't move. So, instead of staggering next door to see if Abby was home, or stumbling upstairs to work on my story notes, or dragging my weary body up to bed, I stayed right where I was—curled up like a cat in my comfy old armchair—and went back to sleep.

So, you can guess what happened next, right? Bingo. The telephone rang.

Coming to in a flash, and thinking it must be Dan on the phone, I sprang out of the chair and flew across the room to pick up the receiver. "Hello, Dan?" I blurted. "Is that you? I've been dying to hear from you! Did you learn anything . . .?" Suddenly (okay, *finally*) coming to the realization that I might be talking to somebody other than Dan, I let my words trail off to nothing.

"Hello?" said the female voice on the other end of the line.

"Hello," I mumbled, offering nothing more. *Better keep my mouth shut. Better wait till I know who's there.*

"Is this Paige Turner?" the female voice inquired.

I wasn't falling for that old ploy. (Never reveal your own identity unless you know the identity of the person you're revealing it to, I always say.) "Who is this?" I asked. The voice sounded familiar, but I wasn't sure . . .

"This is Claire Burnett. I'm calling to speak to Paige Turner. It's very important."

Claire? Claire's calling me? She knows my real name? I didn't know what to do. Should I own up to the truth or try to continue my Patty Turner charade? "Um, er, uh, ah . . ." When in doubt, stall (okay, *stammer*).

"Paige, I know it's you," Claire said. "So you might as well stop pretending. I came into the city tonight to sort through and clean out Ginger's dressing room, and I found an article about you, picture and all, in her makeup drawer. I have it in my hand right now. It says you're a reporter for

Daring Detective magazine; that you solved a sensational double murder a few months back; that you're as smart as Perry Mason."

I giggled in spite of myself. (I'm a sucker for flattery, even when it's really dumb.) "Well, I wouldn't go *that* far . . ." I demurred.

Claire paused for a moment, let out a distinct (okay, *derisive*) sigh, then went on with *her* investigation. "Look, I'm pretty smart, too," she said. "And I've been giving this situation a lot of thought tonight—ever since I found this article about you. And now I think I've got it figured out. I think I know why Ginger kept the article, and why she invited you to the Stork Club last Saturday night."

"Oh, really?" I said. "What *do* you think?"

"I think my sister wanted you to save her life."

My soul sank like a rock in a river.

"Am I right?" Claire asked.

"Yes," I said, suddenly feeling so ashamed of my failure to prevent Ginger's death I could barely breathe.

"So, my sister knew somebody was trying to kill her?" The tone of Claire's voice had turned mournful (or was it fearful?).

"She was certain of it," I said. In the face of Claire's obvious concern, my guilt was overwhelming. I felt as if *I* were the murderer. I needed one of Abby's pep talks, and I needed it bad.

"Did she know who was trying to kill her?" Claire urged, pressing for more information. "Did she have any proof?"

"If she did, she didn't tell me."

"Do *you* know who it was?"

"Not yet," I admitted, feeling sad and suspicious at the same time.

Claire was silent for a few moments, probably thinking over the things I'd just said. Then, all of a sudden, she started breathing very heavily—sucking air in and spewing it out in a series of hard, fast, explosive gasps. And then, when she started talking again, her normal speaking voice had changed to a harsh, rough whisper.

"Can you come here tonight?" she rasped. "I've got to talk to you about something, and I can't do it over the phone."

"I don't know," I hesitated, "it's awfully late. Where are you?"

"I'm still in Ginger's dressing room, on the eighth floor of the RCA Building, 30 Rockefeller Plaza. You know where it is."

"Yes, I do, but—"

"Please come! You've *got* to. Please come right now! I have some information that—"

She let out another dramatic gasp and hung up.

I GUESS I DON'T HAVE TO TELL YOU what a turmoil I was in. What in the whole wide wicked world was I supposed to do now? Should I keep my promise to Dan and stay safe and secure at home, or should I rush uptown to hear what secrets Claire had to tell? She obviously knew that her sister's death had been murder instead of suicide. Maybe she knew who the murderer was, too.

Or maybe it was all just a trick. What if Claire herself was the killer? What if she thought I knew too much and was luring me to Ginger's dressing room just because it seemed like a good place to kill *me?*

Head spinning like a Kansas cyclone, I snatched up the phone, dialed the Midtown South Precinct, and asked to speak to Detective Street. Dan wasn't there, of course, so I wasn't able to tell him what happened and find out what he wanted me to do (as if I didn't already know). I was, however, able to leave him a message telling him where I was going and why, and asking him to meet me there as soon as possible. (That was a pretty cool solution, don't you think?)

I darted across the living room and peered out the window. It was still raining cats and dogs (actually, it was more like cows and horses). Hurrying back to the kitchen area, I snatched my short yellow raincoat out of the closet, my red plaid umbrella off the closet floor, my purse and damp red beret off the table, and headed out (as Mike would write) into the dark and stormy night.

BY THE TIME I GOT TO THE RCA BUILD-
ing, I was soaked to the skin again, but just from the mid-
thighs down. (Let's hear it for raincoats and umbrellas!) If
only I'd thought to put on my galoshes. Splashing through
ankle-deep puddles in thin ballerina flats was a sport fit only
for four-year-olds.

The lobby was practically deserted. A few late-night office
workers were exiting the elevators, forging their way home or
to the nearest bar, and one skinny, gray-haired Negro
shoeshine "boy" was sleeping in a chair in the corner. The
lobby newsstand was closed, and the second-floor mezzanine—the overhead wood-railed walkway that wrapped
around the entire lobby and served as an observation deck on
all ground-floor proceedings—was as vacant as an empty lot.

There were no newspaper photographers or reporters
hanging around the entrance as there had been two days ago.
In the dailies, suicide was a short-lived story. (I know that
sounds like a pun, but it's not! It's just the way things are.)
When the news finally breaks that Ginger was murdered, I
grumbled to myself, *she'll be front page fodder again, and
this lobby will be crawling with rabid journalists and fans.*

Closing my umbrella and shaking off the water, I scurried
(okay, squished) down the steps from the heavy glass entrance
doors, frantically searching the lobby shadows for Dan, wondering if he'd gotten my message. When I realized he wasn't
there, I thought of lingering by the entrance for a few minutes,
waiting for him to come, but I quickly ditched that idea. He
might not show up. And Claire's voice had sounded so urgent!
I felt I didn't have a minute to spare.

Sucking up a chestful of air (and every little scrap of
courage I could muster), I headed straight across the marble
floor to the first bank of elevators—the ones that serviced
floors one through ten. There was one operator in attendance
in that area, just as there had been on Monday night. It wasn't
the same fellow, though. This one was tall, dark, and portly,
and his maroon and gold uniform was too small instead of too
big. He wasn't the least bit talkative, either. He took me
straight up to the eighth floor, no questions asked.

The hallway was dim, forsaken, and quiet—so quiet I could hear the adrenaline surging through my veins. I stole down the hall to the right, walking on tiptoes and holding my breath, doing my best not to make a sound. I was glad I didn't have to take off my shoes. (Ballerina slippers are great for sneaking, I must say. Even when they're wet.)

Slithering down the long hall leading to the far hall that would eventually lead me to Ginger's dressing room, I held my closed umbrella out in front of me like a sword. As I crept past the crowd of life-size cardboard TV stars standing near the entrance to Studio 8H, I accidentally poked Milton Berle in the ribs. He didn't seem to mind. He didn't fall over or even make any noise, which was very considerate of him.

Studio 8H was not in use. It was, in fact, locked up as tight as a bank vault. I found this out when I tried to open the door and peek inside the theater (just to see if any murderers—or handsome homicide detectives—were hanging around in there).

Continuing my tiptoe trek to the very end of the long corridor, I turned right and began slinking down the next hall, past the men's and women's dressing rooms and the doors marked WARDROBE, MAKEUP, and PROPS. Knowing that Ginger's private dressing room was just a couple of rooms down from PROPS, I flattened myself against the wall like a pancake and slid sideways—and very, very slowly—toward the firmly closed gold-starred door.

When I finally reached the door, I stuck my ear to the jamb and listened for sounds inside. I couldn't hear a thing, except the deafening echoes of my hammering heartbeats and the reverberating whooshes of my own ragged breath. (You'd think, after all this time—this being my third murder investigation, and all—that I'd have developed a stronger backbone by now. You'd think I'd be able to face a potentially dangerous situation with a deeper sense of self-confidence and calm assurance. Well, all I can say about that is, think again.)

I stood in silence for a few seconds, shaking like a leaf and desperately trying to decide what to do next. Should I knock on the door and call Claire's name? No way, Doris Day. What could I possibly gain by announcing my arrival? Should I make a loud noise to try to frighten Claire and flush her out into the hall? Nope. That might just alert her to my presence, give her time to get ready to shoot me, or stab me, or strangle me . . . or whatever.

No, the only thing I had going for me at that moment—the only thing that might afford me some measure of self-protection—was the element of surprise. The power to astonish! The ability to amaze! So, the best move I could make, I figured, was to shove the door open and burst into Ginger's dressing room like Attila the Hun (or Yosemite Sam, take your pick).

But what if the door was locked? It had been the last time I'd tried to open it. Deciding I should give the knob a stealthy twist test before assuming the awesome (and possibly awkward) identity of Wonder Woman, I stretched out my hand and gave it a tiny tweak.

There was a quick, almost imperceptible click. The door was unlocked! A razor-sharp strip of light became visible in the crack. Without a whiff of hesitation, I wrenched the knob full circle, threw the door open, and lunged into Ginger's dressing room with my red plaid umbrella held en garde. I felt just like Errol Flynn at that moment, ready to fence with the evil Duke of Wherever, but I probably looked more like Lucy Ricardo preparing to carve a turkey.

What I saw when I entered that room, however, made my heart screech to a standstill and my blood turn to ice in my veins. Claire was sitting in a chair facing the door. Her arms and legs were practically pulled out of their sockets and tied behind her back (and behind the chair) with several lengths of thick, rough, industrial-strength rope. A man's necktie was pulled tight between her upper jaw and lower jaw, twisted behind her head in a double knot. Her poor lips were stretched to the widest imaginable limit, and there were numerous swellings and bloody cuts on her contorted, freckled face. Her eyes were closed and her head was tilted to one side at a very odd angle. *Oh, my God!* Was her neck broken?

I ran to Claire's side and—frantically dropping my umbrella and purse to the floor—tried to undo the knot in the necktie lashed through her mouth and around her head. *Oh, lordy, lordy, lordy!* She was totally unconscious. Her face was turning blue! Was she still alive? The way the ropes were strapped around her chest and neck, and the way the necktie was clogging her mouth, I couldn't see if she was breathing.

And when the door slammed shut and the lights went out I couldn't see anything at all.

Chapter 34

HAVE YOU EVER BEEN STRANDED IN THE depths of a coal mine, in the middle of the night, without so much as a burnt-out birthday candle? (Well, neither have I, but I'm sure it's pretty dark.) Anyway, that's how utterly black it was in Ginger's windowless dressing room at that terrifying moment in time. It was the blackest black I'd ever experienced (while fully conscious, I mean).

Knowing somebody else besides Claire was in the room with me, and feeling pretty sure it wasn't Dan, I instantly sank to a squat on the floor and felt around for my umbrella. And once I had the umbrella securely in hand, I continued to crouch there, frozen like a statue behind Claire's chair, holding my breath and straining my ears for indicative sounds.

Where was the other person standing? Was he still over by the door near the light switch, or had he silently moved to a different position in the room? (At this point I didn't know if the person was male or female, of course. I just assumed he was a "he," so that was the pronoun I used in my mind.)

After a couple of seconds of intense concentration, I detected breathing sounds from two different sources. A stream of husky respirations came flowing from a spot across the room—about halfway between the door and the far corner, it seemed—and a few faint, almost inaudible sighs were drifting toward me from a much closer proximity; from the vicinity of Claire's chair. A jolt of awareness shot through me. Claire was breathing! She was still alive! But just barely, I sensed—and for how long?

Still squatting on the floor like a frog, I held myself as still and quiet as possible, gripping my umbrella with both hands and listening for any sounds of motion or advance. Certain that the other person in the room was the murderer, and that I was in line to be his next victim (am I a great detective, or what?), I knew time was of the essence. I needed a plan, and I needed it *now*.

If I attacked first, I thought, maybe I could catch the killer off guard. If I leapt to my feet and started screaming my head off and thrashing and stabbing my umbrella around in the darkness, I might be able to crack him in the head or poke out his eye or something like that. Maybe I could disable him before he disabled me. It was a real shot in the dark, I knew, since I couldn't see a goddamn thing, but it still seemed like a viable strategy. Maybe even a 50/50 proposition. I mean, the murderer couldn't see anything either, right?

Wrong.

As I was gathering my strength and preparing to spring into action, the killer turned on his flashlight and aimed the beam straight into my eyes, blinding me and illuminating me at the same time.

"Well, what do you know!" the invisible man said. "It's Patty Turner—the phony college roommate with the phony glasses and the phony name." I couldn't see the man's face, but I recognized his voice immediately.

It was Rusty Burnett, and he sounded as jumpy and excited as a dope addict in need of a fix.

"You just couldn't leave well enough alone, could you, sweetheart?" he jeered, keeping the flashlight beam aimed at my face. "You had to keep sticking your nose where it doesn't belong. How'd you get to be so foolish? Didn't anybody ever tell you curiosity killed the cat?"

I didn't say anything. I was afraid I might start stuttering (or, worse, *crying*), and I didn't want to give him the satisfaction of knowing how scared I was.

"What's the matter, sweetheart?" he said, laughing. "Cat got your tongue?" I still couldn't see Rusty's face, but his tone of voice told me everything I needed to know. He was exhilarated. He was having a really good time. He was looking forward to killing me.

Hoping to postpone his assault indefinitely (or at least until Dan showed up), I decided I'd better start talking. It seemed the best, if not the only, way to divert the eager assassin from his ultimate goal.

"Mind if I stand up?" I asked, using every ounce of my self-control to keep my voice from shaking. "My knees are feeling a little creaky." (I also felt like a demented monkey, squatting on my haunches in the spotlight the way I was, but I kept that little gem of information to myself.)

"Okay, dollface, but you'd better take it nice and slow," he warned. "One false move, and I'll put your lights out for good."

I stood up as slowly and deliberately as I possibly could, using my umbrella as a cane, pretending I needed it for balance. "You know you might as well ditch the flash and turn on the light, Rusty," I said when I reached full height. "I already know who you are."

"Huh?" (I kid you not. Those were his exact words—I mean, *word*. And, though I couldn't see what Rusty was doing at that moment, I'd have bet my week's paycheck he was scratching his head and wondering how the heck I had figured out who he was.)

There's hope for me yet, I said to myself. *I may be dealing with a sadistic killer, but at least he's a stupid one.*

"And you know what, Rusty?" I added. "It doesn't even matter if I know who you are, since you're going to kill me anyway."

Rusty was quiet for a couple of seconds, obviously giving my statements some thought. And he must have come to the conclusion that the things I'd said were true, because a few seconds later he threw the flashlight on the floor and flipped on the overhead lights.

I was finally able to see!

But what I saw made me want to hide in the dark forever.

Rusty had a rifle, and he was aiming at me.

I know it sounds absurd, but you heard me right! It was a *rifle!* A really long, ugly, military-style rifle, and Rusty was holding it up to his shoulder and peering at me through the gunsight—finger crooked on the trigger—looking every bit as poised and proficient as the practiced soldier he used to be.

I almost passed out. Literally. The mere sight of that rifle turned my legs to Jell-O and sent my brain into a tailspin.

(Look, before you start calling me a sissy or something like that, just answer me this: Have you ever been blasted by a bullet? Because, I have. Twice. Once in the leg and once in the shoulder. And those were just tiny little .22-caliber bullets. And they hurt like hell! More than you could ever imagine! They burned though my skin, ripped up my flesh, shattered my bones, and caused me to lose so much blood that I was white as a ghost for weeks. So, I think you should understand why I wasn't anxious to find out—or even *think* about—how much damage a great big walloping rifle bullet could do!)

"I'd rather you didn't shoot me," I said, trying to sound flip instead of frantic. "I don't approve of guns. Couldn't you just strangle me or poison me instead?"

Rusty snickered. "Funny girl." I was hoping he'd lower the rifle a bit, but he didn't.

"What did you do to Claire?" I asked, stealing a quick look at her tortured form. Was she still breathing? I couldn't tell.

"I slapped her around a little bit," Rusty boasted. "Then I tied her up and poured a few arsenic and bourbon highballs down her throat."

"But, why?"

"She was thirsty."

Shaking that sickening image out of my head, I took a deep breath and staggered on. "I don't understand," I exclaimed. "Why did you kill Claire? What did she have to do with any-

thing?" I used the past tense on purpose. I didn't want Rusty
to know Claire was still alive (*if* she was still alive).

Rusty let the barrel of the rifle drop a few inches and gave
me a disbelieving look. "Are you really that dumb, or are you
just pretending?"

Now, how was I supposed to answer *that* question?

Luckily, I didn't have to. "I *had* to kill the nosy bitch,"
Rusty continued, spitting the words out of his mouth in a rage.
"When she found that newspaper article about you in Ginger's
makeup drawer tonight, she put two and two together and got
suspicious. And then, after she spoke to you on the phone, she
was convinced that I killed Ginger. So, what the hell was I
supposed to do? Just sit back and let her tell the world I murdered her sister? What kind of a man's gonna let his own wife
turn him in?"

I couldn't answer that question, either. All I could think to
do was ask another one. (Well, I had to keep him talking, you
know! Otherwise, he might start shooting. And as desperate as
I was to help Claire, I knew I had to save myself first. Dead
women aren't much help to anybody.)

"But how did you know that Claire had found you out?" I
probed. "Surely she didn't tell you herself!"

Rusty lowered the rifle another few inches and gave me an
ugly grin. "Not voluntarily," he said. "I had to beat it out of
her." He paused and smiled again, obviously enjoying the
memory. "I was standing outside this door when she was talking to you on the phone, and I heard everything she said, so I
had a pretty good idea she was onto me. And when I heard her
begging you to come meet her here, saying she had something
to tell you, I rushed in and grabbed her in a stranglehold.
Couldn't let her finger me over the phone."

"But that doesn't explain the beating," I persisted, working
to keep the revolting conversation rolling. "Was there something else you were trying to find out, or do you just get a kick
out of smacking women around?"

"The answer to both of your questions is yes," he said,
eyes gleaming.

I shivered in disgust (and *fear*—let's not forget fear!). "So, what else did you need to know?" I asked, staunchly pushing ahead.

"You mean you haven't figured that out yet, dollface?" he scoffed. "Then you're even stupider than I thought!"

And here I'd been thinking *he* was the stupid one.

"I had to find out how much you knew," he snorted. "I needed to know if I had to kill you, too."

"Oh," I said, steadily pulling the loose ends together. Well, some of them, anyway. "So, up until tonight you really didn't know who I was?"

"Right." He lowered the rifle to his side, but still clutched it with both hands.

"And you didn't know I was the one who dropped the shoes outside Theo's office—the one you chased backstage and out of the building?"

"Nope! Not until Claire spilled the beans," he said, a venomous smile smeared wide across his well-tanned face.

His ugly smirk was getting on my nerves. "But what about my sudden appearance at your house out in Levittown? That was a sure tip-off," I needled. "Didn't Claire tell you about it? And didn't my out-of-the-blue visit seem just a little bit strange to you?"

"Why should it?" he snapped, turning defensive. "Claire said you came to pay a condolence call. I didn't see anything wrong with that! I thought it was *nice!*" He took his left hand off the rifle and angrily propped it on his hip.

And that's when I started laughing. For real. No lie. No pretense involved at all. I was laughing (okay, *howling*) at the rank absurdity of it all. I had come face to face with the devil—and he was a vicious, brutal, cold-blooded killer with a sentimental attachment to condolence calls.

"What's so goddamn funny?" Rusty wanted to know.

"Oh, nothing, really," I said, stifling my manic hilarity. I tightened my grip on my umbrella and madly changed the subject. "Were you in love with Ginger?" I asked, hoping to lure Rusty into another impassioned (and, therefore, *lengthy*) discourse. "Did it break your heart when she broke your engagement and married Leo?"

Rusty cocked his head (thank God it wasn't the rifle!) and gave me a squinty look. "How did you know we were engaged? That was the world's best-kept secret. Ginger never told anybody."

"Well, she told me," I lied. "She said she broke it off while you were in Korea so she could marry Leo and become a big TV star. She said you never forgave her for it."

"That's the goddamn truth!" Rusty bellowed, jabbing the snout of the rifle down to the floor and jutting his bulldog jaw. "That was a rotten thing she did to me. I got her lousy Dear John letter right before my outfit launched a major action. I went nuts. I was so furious, I killed about forty gooks that day." His eyes started gleaming again. "It was fucking great!"

Uh-oh! "Well, uh, if you were so mad," I stumbled on, "why did you get in touch with Ginger as soon as you got back home? Why did you go to work for her? Why did you marry her sister?" *And where in the world is Dan? Isn't he ever going to come?*

To my great surprise, Rusty calmed down and began to explain himself. (It really slays me how many cold-hearted murderers feel the need to clarify their motives and convey their heartfelt emotions.) "I wanted my self-respect back," he commenced, angrily scraping his fingers through his copper-colored hair. "I wanted Ginger to divorce Leo and marry me. But the bitch wouldn't do it. She said the press would destroy her if she got a divorce—that she'd lose all her fans and her precious career. But she swore she still loved me, and she talked me into taking the stagehand job on her show so we could be together every day. And she convinced me to marry her sister so we could be together every night."

"What?!" I croaked, incredulous. "How was marrying Claire supposed to expedite your nights with Ginger?"

"Ginger had it all worked out," Rusty replied, with a facial expression that was somewhere between a gloat and a grimace. "She said if I was her brother-in-law, we'd get to go out on the town together without raising any eyebrows. We'd take Claire along every once in a while, just to make things look proper, but mostly we'd get to be alone. And if I stuck Claire in a house out in the suburbs, Ginger said, then I'd be free to spend more time in the city with her. And since I would be a *relative,* I could come and go at the penthouse without causing too much suspicion."

What tangled webs some weddings weave!

"And what about Leo?" I asked. "Was he privy to these plans?"

"I don't know when or what Ginger told him, but he got the picture pretty quick. He found himself a girlfriend, set her up in an apartment a few blocks away, and started sleeping over there every night. Which was fine with Ginger and me, since that meant we got to sleep together, too."

"And how did Claire feel about all of this?" I inquired, sneaking another glance at her roped and gagged corpus. (Or was it a corpse?! I was about to lose my mind at this point, wondering if Claire was still alive and if Dan would show up in time to save her—okay, *us.*)

"I don't know," Rusty said, "I didn't care, so I never asked. And she never complained, so I guess she didn't care, either."

"Still, it was a *very* risky arrangement," I said. "Wasn't Ginger scared the press would find out about it? If her infidelity had been exposed, her beloved career would have exploded like a bomb. A divorce scandal would have been nothing in comparison."

"Yeah," Rusty said, tensing up and hoisting the rifle to his hip. "She was scared, all right. Not so much at first, when we started out, but later, after she had me under her thumb and started getting bored. *Then* she got scared. So scared it was disgusting. We stopped going out to nightclubs unless we had Claire, or Theo, or even Leo with us, and she wouldn't let me use the front door of her building anymore. She was so damn worried the butler or the night manager would figure out what was going on, and tip off Winchell or one of the other gossip columnists, that she finagled a key to the fire escape exit from the building's owner and made me use the stairs. Do you believe that? I had to climb up fourteen fucking flights just to get laid!"

And another loose end fell into place. "So, that's how you

got up to the penthouse the night of the murder without being seen."

"Right," Rusty snorted. "I finally—for once—put those goddamn fire escape steps to good use."

I felt I had all the answers now—except for the most important one. "There's just one thing I don't understand," I said.

"What's that?" Rusty asked, still eager to rehash the details of his bizarre assignations and brutal accomplishments.

"*Why* did you want to kill Ginger?" I probed. "Wasn't that a bit like killing the goose that laid the golden egg? Or did you do it *because* of the eggs? Did you know Claire was going to inherit everything, including the controlling interest of Marxallen Productions?"

"Sure, I knew," he said. "Ginger told me about it. She said it was the only reasonable way she could write *me* into her will. Ha! What a crock that was! Ginger knew I was getting sick of her, and of our whole creepy arrangement, and she just wanted to keep her hooks in me—make sure I'd remain her spineless stagehand lover and stay married to her stupid ugly sister."

"So, you killed Ginger to get your hands on Claire's inheritance?"

"No, I killed Ginger because I hated her fucking guts. She controlled my whole life and treated me like a slave. And she wasn't even sexy anymore! She drank too much, took too many pills, and sometimes she looked so sloppy she made me want to puke. And the only person she ever cared about was herself. Herself and her goddamn career. Day and night, night and day—that's all she ever talked about. It got so I couldn't wait for her to fill herself full of sleeping pills and pass out, just so she'd finally shut up."

"Was she full of sleeping pills when you pushed her off the terrace?"

"To the brim," he said, grinning. "She was totally unconscious and limp as a wet noodle. I whisked her out to the balcony, draped her over the wall, gave her a little shove, and—oops!—she was gone."

The sadistic look on Rusty's face, plus the way he was holding (and *stroking*) the rifle at his hip, sent me into a stone-cold panic. My time was up. The game was over. Dan wasn't coming. Claire and I were both going to die . . .

But not if I could help it.

Quick as lightning, I flipped the tip of my umbrella upward, grasped it firmly in both hands, yanked the heavy wooden handle up to my shoulder like a baseball bat, and took an all-out, full-force, Mickey Mantle–style swing at Rusty's head.

The ball was high and outside, but I made a solid connection and slammed it out of the park.

Chapter 35

OKAY, OKAY! SO, IT WASN'T EXACTLY A
home run. It was more like a grounder to the shortstop. But
my lucky hit was still crucial to the game. Rusty was so
stunned by the unexpected blow that he staggered sideways a
couple of steps and raised both hands to his face, dropping the
rifle to the floor. Then I tossed down my umbrella and
snatched the rifle up in *my* hands. And before you could say
Jackie Robinson, I was gripping that rifle by the nose, resum-
ing my stance at the plate, and taking another turn at bat.

All right, here comes the part I'd rather not describe. It's
too beastly and gruesome, if you want to know the truth. I
wish I didn't even remember it. I discovered things about myself that night that will haunt me till the day I die (an event
which, thanks to my indescribably beastly behavior, was delayed for a little while). But since my name is Paige Turner,
and I'm compelled to tell you what happened, just let me give
you a quick synopsis and get it over with, okay?

Okay, here goes: I smashed Rusty in the head again, but
this time it was with the extra hard and heavy wooden stock
of the rifle. And it was an extra hard and heavy swing. (No exaggeration. I was the strongest hitter on my high school soft-

ball team, bar none.) Rusty keeled over and fell to the floor, cracking his head on the corner of the dressing table as he went down. And when he landed, his face crashed on the floor. And then I raised the butt of the rifle in the air and brought it down, like an ax, on the back of his skull—two, maybe three times—until Rusty was totally (maybe even terminally) unconscious.

It makes me sick to think about it. It was a hideous and monstrous thing for me to do. But I felt it was my only chance of survival. It was either that or get shot to smithereens, right?

Wrong.

As I was backing away from Rusty's senseless body, I pulled the rifle up to a level position in my hands and took a closer look at it, trying to make sure I didn't touch any working mechanisms or set off any accidental explosions (i.e., shoot myself in the foot). And that's when the realization hit me. Right between the eyes. There *were* no working mechanisms on this rifle. None of the parts *moved!* The carriage, the firing pin, the trigger—everything was molded from a single piece of metal and as stationary as stone.

The rifle wasn't real. It was a prop. A PROP! Rusty must have gotten it from the prop room two doors down. Jesus H. Christ! What did he do *that* for? Why on earth would he want to threaten me with a fake gun? Was he totally off his rocker? Had he been playing soldier just for fun, or had his little war game turned real in his vengeful, unstable mind?

Throwing the dummy rifle in the corner, I bounded to Claire's side and stuck my ear down close to her mouth. I detected a strong smell of bourbon. By some miracle she was still breathing. Terrified that Rusty would suddenly come to and try to kill us both again, I felt we had to get out of Ginger's dressing room immediately. Luckily, the chair Claire was tied to was on castors. I rolled her around Rusty's outspread legs in a flash, and then pushed her—like a paraplegic in a wheelchair—out into the hall. And then I whisked her down to MAKEUP, kicked open the door, turned on the light, and rolled her inside.

Slamming the door closed behind us, I madly removed the

necktie strapped through Claire's mouth and around her head, hoping to ease her breathing. Then, without even attempting to untie the impossibly tight military knots in the thick ropes binding Claire's body to the chair, I shot my eyes around the room, searching for the phone. Finally spotting it on a small taboret table, surrounded by several containers of hairspray and cold cream, I leapt across the room, snatched up the receiver, and called for an ambulance.

"Please hurry!" I cried, after giving the emergency operator the address, the floor, and directions to the makeup room. "And please send the police! There's been an attempted murder. A woman's been badly beaten and she's totally unconscious! I think she's dying! She may have been poisoned with arsenic, too, so if there's a known antidote, please tell the medics to bring some. And tell them to bring a stretcher! No, tell them to bring *two* stretchers," I said, suddenly remembering that Rusty might need one, too.

The operator wanted me to stay on the line until the medics and police arrived, but I didn't think that was the best thing to do. I felt I should go down to the lobby and look for Dan, so I could tell him where Rusty was. And then I thought I should wait outside by the entrance for the emergency crew, so I could save precious time and lead them directly to Claire.

Leaving the receiver off the hook (just in case the operator lost the address and needed to trace the call), I darted over to the door, turned out the light, stepped into the hall, and pulled the door tightly closed. Then, praying that I was leaving Claire in a safe place (i.e., well-hidden from insane military assassins), I ran back to Ginger's dressing room to take a quick peek at Rusty—make sure he was still unconscious.

But he wasn't. He wasn't even there! The fake rifle was gone, too.

Oh, lordy, lordy, lordy! I shrieked to myself, nearly prostrate with panic. *What's happening? Where did he go? Is he waiting in ambush down the hall? God help me! What the hell do I do now?*

For lack of a better plan, I took off running for the elevators. And, you can take it from me, I never ran so hard and so fast in my life. I was more powerful than a locomotive! Much faster than a speeding bullet! I was Superman in tights and ballerina slippers! And in the brief puff of time that elapsed between one of my coursing heartbeats and the next, I reached the end of one hall and started running down the other.

Rusty was nowhere in sight. I thought for a moment that he might be lurking in the cardboard cluster of famous TV stars hanging around the entrance to Studio 8H, but he wasn't. I ran through the gauntlet of life-size cutouts without a single jab, or grab, or trip, or even one spurt of make-believe rifle fire.

The closer I got to the elevators, however, the more frantic I became. Rusty was tracking me. I couldn't hear him or see him, but I could *feel* him. He was somewhere behind me—in the studio theater or one of the offices on the side—and he was about to break out into the hall and overtake me in a hostile siege of militant force and a hail of imaginary bullets.

Knowing it would be incredibly stupid of me to punch the DOWN button and just stand there waiting for an elevator to arrive (or, rather, for a psycho killer soldier to jump me in a surprise attack), I chose to make a snappy detour into—you guessed it!—the fire escape stairway. And then I scrambled down the steps in a frenzy, feet racing as fast as my heart.

I was about four flights down when one of the heavy metal doors above clanked open and bashed into the cement staircase wall. Rusty had entered the stairway! He was right behind me! He was chasing me down the fire escape steps in a fire-breathing fury! If I couldn't get down to the ground floor and out into the lobby before he caught up with me . . . well, I didn't even want to *think* about what could happen.

And so I ran much faster than I was capable of running. And I exhaled far more air than I was capable of inhaling. And I prayed more sincerely (okay, more *urgently*) than I'd ever prayed before. Which was why I became so lightheaded and confused, and twisted one of my ankles, and lost count of the number of flights I'd descended.

Which was why I thought I'd reached the ground floor when I hadn't. And why I burst like an idiot through the fire escape door, believing it would lead me to the safe haven of the building's lobby. And why I went into a total state of shock when I found myself stranded on the second-floor mezzanine instead.

BEFORE I COULD BREAK OUT OF MY mental paralysis—before I could even *think* of lunging across the second-floor walkway to the railing and looking (okay, *screaming*) down into the lobby for Dan (or *anybody!*)—Rusty crashed through the door to the mezzanine and pounced into combat position. Legs apart and slightly bent, fake rifle held tight to his shoulder, he gave out a vile snort and aimed his lunatic gaze through the phony gunsight at me.

"Hands in the air!" he ordered, voice pitched between a shout and a growl. "Don't move, or I'll blow your head off!"

I raised my hands and stood as still as my shaking legs would allow. I knew Rusty couldn't fire the rifle, but I also knew that he was *non compos mentis*—i.e., out of his everloving mind!—and this fact frightened me almost as much as the thought of getting shot. Whether he had lost his marbles when he was in Korea, or when he killed Ginger, or when he tried to kill Claire, or when I beat his brains out with the rifle butt, one thing was clear: Rusty's sense of reality was now thoroughly deranged. He was totally out of control. He was capable of committing all kinds (and any number!) of hideous warlike atrocities.

"Please don't shoot me," I begged, whimpering like a baby, deciding to pretend (okay, *reveal*) that I was terrified. I was hoping my humble submissiveness would soothe the savage beast. I was also hoping that Rusty would be so distracted by my desperate blubbering that he wouldn't notice my silent and very slow backward progress toward the mezzanine railing. I was inching my way back like a furtive slug, praying to get close enough to the outer edge of the exposed walkway for Dan, or the shoeshine man, or one of the elevator operators, or anyone else who happened to be down in the lobby, to look up and see the trouble I was in.

But what a big fat waste of hope and prayer *that* was!

Rusty caught on to my scheme immediately. He gave out a loud, angry shout, pulled the rifle tighter to his cheek, and squeezed the trigger. The trigger didn't budge, of course, and the gun refused to fire. Rusty was so furious that he went even crazier and started cursing his head off. And then he lifted the rifle up over his head in both hands and threw it—with all his masculine, militaristic might—at me.

I ducked just in time. The rifle whizzed over my head and sailed like a javelin over the mezzanine railing. And then, after three or four seconds of taut, suspenseful silence, the mock weapon hit the floor of the lobby in a metal-to-marble clatter that echoed throughout the vast and seemingly empty entrance hall. (I say *empty* because I didn't hear any sounds of reaction from below. No running footfalls. No shrieks or exclamations of alarm. No deep, delicious Dan-like baritone yelling, "Paige, are you up there? Hold on! I'm coming!")

I didn't know what to do. There was no point in running since there was no place to run *to*. (And anyway, my ankle hurt like hell—and Rusty was so much stronger than I was, I knew it would take him all of half a second to chase me down.) There was no point in screaming since there was nobody to scream *to*. (And also, the last thing I wanted to do was enrage Rusty further and make him decide to shut me up for good.)

No, the best thing I could do, I figured, was talk to Rusty—try to calm him down somehow, try to engage him in another lengthy discussion about his motives and emotions. If I could get him to *start* talking, maybe I could *keep* him talking—just long enough for me to work my way back around to the fire escape door, dart through it, and flee down the final flight of stairs to the street.

Good plan, right?

Okay, so it was a pretty crummy plan. But it was all I could come up with at the moment. (I was under a lot of pressure, you know!) So, the very instant the echoes of the clattering rifle stopped bouncing off the walls of the cavernous lobby, I took a deep breath and put my crummy plan into action.

"Hey, Rusty, how many times did you try to kill Ginger before you succeeded?" I asked, giving him an innocent smile, acting as nonchalant as I possibly could, trying to pick up our previous conversation right where we'd left off (i.e., right before I'd bonked him with my umbrella). "Did you push her in front of a bus?" I politely inquired. "Did you poison her drink last Saturday night after you all left the Stork Club and went to—"

I guess Rusty wasn't in the mood for any more talk, because he didn't even let me finish my sentence. He released a loud, spine-chilling battle cry and charged forward, grabbing me in his arms and shoving me backward across the walkway until my buttocks were pinned against the waist-high mezzanine railing. Then he reared back and slapped me across the face a few times. Hard. Then, grabbing me by the shoulders and wrenching me around until my stomach was smashed against the railing, he dealt me several hard punches in the back, and pushed down on the back of my neck and head until I was bent in two over the banister.

My beret fell off my head and tumbled downward in dreamlike slow motion. Folded headfirst over the railing the way I was (and eyes bulging *down* the way they were), I watched my little red hat fall through the air like a wounded bird, then plop down dead on the beige and black marble floor, as if shot by the fake rifle lying a few feet away. Terrified that I would soon be lying between the rifle and my beret on the lobby floor, I grabbed hold of the banister with both hands and used every ounce of strength in my body to straighten my skinny arms and force my way back to an upright position.

But my strength was no match for Rusty's. He shoved my torso down even lower, then grabbed me around the hips and started heaving the rest of my body up and over the balustrade. (Need I point out that this was the very same way Rusty had propelled Ginger over the stone wall of the penthouse terrace? Need I mention that I was so scared that the entire contents of my stomach were sure to hit the floor of the RCA lobby before I did?)

I tried to hang on to the top of the railing, but Rusty

pitched me so far forward my hold was broken. I had no grip,
no purchase, no power. I was dangling upside down like a bat
in a very high belfry. If Rusty loosened his grasp and let me
go, I would plummet to the depths of Hell—or, if I was lucky,
the bowels of oblivion. (Heaven, I knew, was in the opposite
direction.)

I squeezed my eyes shut, hugged my arms in a tight embrace across my chest, and bid a silent but fervent farewell to
my parents and Abby and Dan and Lenny and all the other
wonderful people I knew and loved. (I said goodbye to the
icky ones, too, but my heart wasn't really in it.) Then I held
my breath, said my prayers, and waited for the final page to
turn.

I CAN'T DESCRIBE WHAT HAPPENED
next—for the simple reason that my eyes were jammed
closed, and my heart was pounding in my ears, and so much
blood had rushed to my brain that my powers of perception
had flown away to avoid the flood. All I can tell you is that,
all of a sudden, without any explanation or advance notice, I
was yanked from the jaws of death—i.e., yanked back up
over the thick wooden railing—and then dropped in a near
senseless heap on the mezzanine floor.

And a few seconds later—as I lay there breathless and be-
wildered, wondering if Rusty had delayed my execution just
so he could torture me a while longer—my sense of hearing
returned. And then I picked up the shocking sounds of human
combat. Groaning, grunting, punching, smacking, whacking!

Two men were fighting, and I knew one of them was Rusty
(I was well acquainted with his ugly oofs and grunts by now).
But who was the other man? Was it Dan? I wasn't sure. The
grumbling voice was deep, but different. Could it be a police
officer or one of the guys from the emergency ambulance
crew?

With my face flat to the floor and turned in the opposite direction, I couldn't see what was going on. And when I tried to
sit up and turn around, I almost blacked out (still too much

blood in the brain, I guess). All I could do was lie back down on the floor and wait for my head to clear.

And that's when I heard the scream.

Actually, it was more like a howl. It began deep in the belly of the beast and soared up to the moon like a demonic prayer—like the anguished cry of a werewolf at midnight. Then it faltered and faded and came to an end.

With a thud.

Oh, my God! Somebody went over the mezzanine railing! Somebody fell down to the lobby floor! I knew it. I was certain of it. There was no mistaking those horrible sounds. The only question was, who had taken the dive? I was hoping with all my pounding, panic-stricken heart that it was Rusty. *Please, God, don't let it be Dan. Whatever you do, don't let it be Dan!*

I was frantically pushing myself up to a sitting position and trying to turn around when someone grabbed me by the shoulders from behind. I was so scared I couldn't speak. I couldn't breathe. I whipped my head from side to side, trying desperately to see who was there, but I couldn't get a look at the man's face. All I could glimpse were his hands (which defied identification since he was wearing *gloves!*).

I was on the verge of a total breakdown—a complete mental and physical collapse!—when the man suddenly stopped panting for air and sputtered out a string of anxious words.

"Are you okay, miss?" he gasped. "I sure do hope that awful Mr. Burnett didn't hurt you none."

And then I finally *did* collapse—in a breathtaking, bone-melting swoon of relief—right into Woodrow's great big, liberating, lifesaving arms.

Epilogue

THE REST OF THAT NIGHTMARISH NIGHT
was like a dream. I don't mean the nifty kind of dream where
you eat chocolate and get kissed and smell roses and hear vi-
olins. I mean the anxious, unsettling kind of dream that swirls
around in your head like a summer storm, with alternating
patches of clouds, rain, wind, and sun.

Which is more than a little perturbing to me right now, if
you want to know the truth, since I'm sitting here typing my
fingers to the bone, straining to complete this true crime dime
store "novel" I'm writing about the Ginger Allen case, and—
hard as I try—I can't keep all the final details in focus. Some
of my memories of that horrible night (or, rather, the *after-
math* of that horrible night) are crystal clear—sharp and
bright as the sun—but others, I admit, are kind of cloudy.

So, what's a girl (I mean, a struggling crime writer!) supposed to do? Pack up her pencil and go home? No way, Doris
Day! She's supposed to give a full, clear, and concise report
of everything she *does* remember, and just forget about all the
other stuff (i.e., the stuff she's *already* forgotten). So, that's
what I'm going to do now, if it's okay with you—just relate

my most lucid recollections as quickly as I can. I promise I'll take better notes in the future.

My most vivid memory is of limping over to the mezzanine railing with Woodrow and looking down on the crumpled, motionless, and obviously very dead body of Rusty Burnett. (I'd rather not describe the way he looked, if you don't mind. Let's just say his crazy mixed-up head had been busted for the final time.) And I remember how distraught Woodrow became when he saw the corpse. He was almost inconsolable. He started sweating and crying and moaning and begging "sweet baby Jesus" to forgive him for killing a man. A white man, no less! But after I told him that Rusty had killed Ginger and then tried to kill Claire as well as me, he felt a little better. He didn't accept my declaration that he was a hero, but at least he calmed down and stopped crying.

I remember some other things, too, like the way the emergency medics and the police and several detectives (no, Dan wasn't one of them!) suddenly swarmed into the building and started taking care of business—checking out the body on the lobby floor, hurrying upstairs to look for Claire, etc. One of the detectives spotted Woodrow and me standing stunned at the railing and ran up to the mezzanine to question us. When he realized we had all the answers, he escorted us down to the lobby, sat us down in the row of attached shoeshine seats (which, thankfully, were stationed miles away from Rusty's unsightly remains), and conducted a thorough investigation.

That's when I learned how Woodrow had miraculously materialized on the mezzanine floor in time to save my life—or, as Abby would say, my *kishkes*. In an uncharacteristically talkative turmoil, Woodrow told the detective the whole story. And, due to my extreme personal interest in the described events, I remember every word of his extraordinary testimony:

"I came to pick up Mr. Marx," he began, sweat beading on his forehead, "and it was raining real hard. So, soon as I parked the car, I took the umbrella out the trunk and came on in the lobby to wait for Mr. Marx to come down. That's what I always did for Miss Allen when it rained—met her in the lobby with the umbrella so she wouldn't get wet walking to the car . . .

"Anyway, I wasn't standing here more than three, maybe four minutes, when out of the crazy blue this big old rifle comes flyin' over the balcony and crashes on the floor. I look up to see where it come from, and that's when I see Mr. Burnett and Miss Paige." (I was honored. Woodrow actually used my first name!) "I see Mr. Burnett grab Miss Paige and push her up close to the balcony railing and start hitting her in the face! Well, I couldn't stand still for that! I know a Negro man's got no business striking a white man, but when the white man's beating up on a woman—specially a woman as nice as Miss Paige—seems like the Negro's just *got* to do something about it!

"So, I ran up the fire escape steps to the second floor, and I got there just in time to grab Miss Paige around the legs and knock Mr. Burnett out of the way 'fore he could drop her off the balcony. But when Mr. Burnett realized what was happening—when he saw me pulling Miss Paige up and then laying her down on the floor—he went right off his rocker. He come after me—punching and jabbing and kicking like a wild man—forcing me to fight back. I never meant to hurt him. I sure enough didn't. I just wanted to keep him from hurting Miss Paige.

"But I'm a big man, sir. And sometimes I don't know my own strength. And when Mr. Burnett started kicking me in the knees and trying to shove me over the railing, I musta lost my self control. I spun that man around like a top and then hit him with two powerful hard punches, one right after the other. Next thing I know he's falling backwards over the balcony and screaming like a stuck pig till he hits the floor. It was plum awful."

When Woodrow finished his account, he started crying again. But just for a second or two. He quickly pulled himself together and put on a brave face for the detective, who was so busy taking notes (and strutting around like a big-shot homicide investigator), he barely noticed Woodrow's intense emotional struggle.

Meanwhile, I was struggling with my own emotions—going nuts wondering if Claire was still alive. So, when I saw the medics rushing her out of the elevator on a stretcher and making a beeline across the lobby toward the closest exit, I chased after them to see what I could find out.

She had a concussion, one of the medics told me, and she was totally unconscious (a fact I had already discerned from one glance at her bruised, immobile, slack-jawed face). But she was still alive, he said, and they believed she was going to pull through. They didn't think she had been poisoned with arsenic, but they knew she had swallowed at least half a bottle of bourbon, and that alone could kill her, or put her on the critical list for a while. They were taking her to Lennox Hill Hospital to get her stomach pumped, he said. I could call there later to check up on her condition.

Feeling my second great surge of relief for the night, I turned and headed back across the lobby to give Woodrow the good news. And it was right then—as I was advancing past the main entrance to the building—that Dan finally appeared. He came charging through the heavy glass doors like some wild and angry beast—like King Kong in a trench coat and a gray fedora. And when he saw me passing by right in front of him, alive and walking (with just the slightest hint of a limp), he did something I'll never, ever, ever—in all my born days—forget. He let out a loud, animal cry (it was like the cry of a giant ape in the jungle, I swear!), and then he ran down the steps and swept me up in a passionate, urgent, bone-crushing embrace that lifted me off my feet and left me weak, wobbly, and weightless. I was ecstatic. I was delirious. I was Faye Wray in the palm of his hand.

I was also curious why it had taken him so darn long to get there!

"I never got your message, babe," he explained, after I'd told him about my call to headquarters. "I was sitting in a squad car outside Whelan's drugstore, taking a quick coffee break, when the word came over the radio that a woman had been beaten and possibly poisoned to death on the eighth floor of the RCA Building. I thought they were talking about you!

I figured you had come here looking for Ginger's murderer, but that the murderer had found you first. I nearly went out of my mind. I threw my coffee out the window, flipped on the siren, and drove here as fast as I could."

So happy to find me in one piece, Dan forgot to berate me for breaking my promise to stay out of the case. He just stroked my face, peered intently into my eyes, and made a series of little growling noises way down deep in his throat. I didn't need him to tell me he loved me. His eyes were saying it all.

Feeling my third big gush of relief for the night, I took Dan by the hand and led him over to the shoeshine station. I reintroduced him to Woodrow and then I gave him a quick rundown of everything that had happened in the last two or three hours, from the time I'd gotten the fateful phone call from Claire. (Actually, I had no idea how much time had elapsed. Each second seemed like a century.)

I don't remember too much after that. Dan ran off to see what the other detectives were up to, and I sat back down in one of the shoeshine seats, next to Woodrow. I propped both of my feet on the metal foot-shaped contraptions in front of my chair and let my brain and body relax (okay, *dissolve*) for the first time that night. I rested my head against the back of the cracked leather seat cushion, closed my eyes, and devoted my wholehearted attention to the pungent smell of shoe polish.

I know that Leo came down to the lobby at some point and talked to Dan and one of the other detectives for a while. Then, without a word to me or even a glance at Rusty's body, he buttoned his raincoat up tight and marched toward the exit, motioning for Woodrow to follow. Woodrow gave me a sad smile, patted my hand, and said good night. Then he stood up and hurried after Leo, umbrella in hand. As I watched my gentle giant savior barge away, I rained a heartful of grateful blessings all over his heroic head and shoulders.

I didn't learn until later (until after Dan had retrieved my purse, umbrella, and beret and helped me out to the car to drive me home) why Leo had been in the building so late—

and *where* he had been while Rusty was assaulting Claire and terrorizing me. Dan said Leo had been in the Marxallen Productions office on the 68th floor, waiting for Claire and Rusty to pack up all of Ginger's belongings and bring them upstairs. He had wanted her dressing room cleared out for Tex and Toni, who were due to begin rehearsals for their new TV show the following day.

Oh, brother! I recall remarking to myself at the time. *Come danger, death or disaster, the television show must go on.*

YOU CAN IMAGINE, I'M SURE, HOW THE news of Ginger's murder rocked the city—actually, the whole country. The explosion equaled that of the H-bomb. Every newspaper and magazine office, every radio, TV, and movie studio, every skyscraper, apartment building, house, factory, school, library, church, and synagogue in the nation was trembling (okay, *rattling*) in the shock and horror of it all. The dreadful details of Ginger's murder, coupled with the scandalous revelations about her private life, plus the thrilling accounts of the hideous but eerily appropriate death of her killer—well, like I said, you can imagine!

The press was in a frenzy, and so was I. Once the word of my involvement in the case spread throughout the industry, every reporter wanted to interview me, every photographer wanted to take my picture, and every newspaper and magazine editor alive wanted to buy the rights to my exclusive story. Even Brandon Pomeroy! (Well, he didn't actually want to *buy* the story, but he did want to *publish* it, and that was a freaky first!)

The telephone at the office was ringing off the hook, and every call was for me. Since I was the one answering the phone, however, very few of those calls were put through. I told most of the people I spoke to that Paige Turner was vacationing in Hawaii. (If you're going to tell a lie, might as well make it a good one.) I accepted the calls from the editors of the *Daily News* and the *Journal American,* though, and listened to both of their offers, eventually agreeing to write a series of exclusive articles for the latter.

These same articles, it was soon decided, would then be collected and rerun in *Daring Detective*—as a long, unbroken story, in a special magazine exclusive, at double the usual print run, with my very own byline! Harvey Crockett was the one who arrived at this happy (for me) arrangement, and Brandon Pomeroy was really annoyed about it. Pomeroy hated the fact that I was getting so much attention and making a name for myself in the mainstream press, and he vented his jealous rage at every opportunity. He made no attempt to fire me, though. I think he knew his boss (Mr. Crockett, I mean) and his elder second cousin (Mr. Oliver Rice Harrington, the wealthy publishing baron who owned *Daring Detective*) would never allow it. Not while I was the toast of the town, at any rate (not to mention *DD*'s own personal hookup to the Ginger Allen hotline).

I loved getting the *Journal American* assignment, and all the respectability and remuneration that came with it. And I exalted in the fact that I would be the featured—and accredited!—author of the next *Daring Detective* cover story. But I hated being hounded by the press and stalked by their photographers. I did *not* want my picture to appear in the papers ever again! As a motivated (okay, *maniacal*) crime writer whose success depended on total anonymity, I knew such exposure could be deadly.

Which is why I wore a disguise to Ginger's funeral. I knew the sidewalks and streets outside Saint Patrick's Cathedral would be crawling with cameras (maybe even a TV camera or two), and I didn't want any of those lenses to be aimed at me. So, I borrowed Abby's sunglasses, and her platinum-blonde wig, and a big, wide-brimmed black hat with a veil. I figured I'd blend right in with the star-studded crowd—and even if somebody *did* take a picture of me, I'd be unrecognizable.

And I was right. Even Woodrow didn't know who I was (and he had driven down to the Village specifically to pick me up!). I breezed out of my building, walked right over to him and said hello, and then slipped into the back of Leo's champagne-colored Caddy with my anonymity intact. Woodrow just stood there—eyes bulging big as quarters—still holding

the car door open and staring at me in shock. You could practically see the big cartoon question mark floating over his
head.

"It's me, Woodrow," I had to tell him. "It's Paige. I decided
I'd better go to the church incognito."

"Yes, Miss Paige," he said, chuckling, finally getting the
picture. "You sure enough had me fooled." Then he closed my
door, got back behind the wheel, and drove the Caddy uptown. I was glad for the company as well as the ride (which
Leo had okayed since he was being chauffeured to the service
in a ritzy black limousine supplied by the ritzy funeral parlor).
And I know Woodrow was glad to be in my company, too. Fu-
nerals are even sadder when you have to go alone.

Not that there was anything sad about *this* funeral. It was
more like a circus. Or a big movie premiere. The sidewalks up
and down Fifth Avenue were packed with emotional fans,
who couldn't help screaming every time a famous star
stepped out of a limo and headed up the stone steps to Saint
Pat's majestic entrance. And the atmosphere inside the cathedral was festive as well. Everybody was there—every well-
known movie and television star you can name—and they
were all aflutter, madly twisting around in their pews, waving
to each other and whispering loud hellos, craning their necks
to see what each other was wearing.

As far as I could tell from my seat in the back row with
Woodrow, nobody was truly mourning Ginger's death. The
priest delivered a standard sermon and an efficient eulogy,
and the robed choir sang a few stirring hymns, but the overall
mood was one of apathy, not grief. Leo went up to the pulpit
and said a few perfunctory words, and then Patti Page sang a
popularized rendition of "Amazing Grace," and then the
priest intoned the final benediction and invocation.

When it was over, there wasn't a wet eye in the house . . .
except for Woodrow's.

MY DISGUISE WORKED WONDERS. AS
far as I know, not a single picture was taken of me that day.
Nobody took Woodrow's picture then either. (Negro chauf-

feurs are invisible even without a disguise.) Which was too
bad, I decided, since a barrage of positive publicity could only
help him. Therefore, confident that the glare of public attention would somehow lead to the improvement of Woodrow's
social and financial position, I slyly redirected the still-blaz-
ing spotlight from myself to my shy but bravehearted friend.
I told every reporter and photographer who approached me
how Ginger Allen's chauffeur, a wonderful, strong, courageous man named Woodrow Washington (Yep! He finally told
me his last name!)—proud husband of Sarah, and loving father of Peach and Jethro (he introduced me to his family,
too)—had saved me from certain death and brought Ginger
Allen's killer to perfect justice.

And, oh, how the media loved *that* story! They pounced on
Woodrow like tigers on a slab of fresh meat. Woodrow was interviewed for every New York City newspaper, and—you
won't believe this!—his large, dark, expansive face was actually featured on the cover of *Life* magazine! (It was just a
small photo insert, but—aside from Jackie Robinson and
Dorothy Dandridge—Woodrow was the only American
Negro ever pictured on the cover of that lofty periodical. I
mean, *ever!*) And he appeared on TV, too—first on one of
NBC's nightly newscasts, then on Edward R. Murrow's *See It
Now.*

But, here's the good part: In Woodrow's case, the reporters, interviewers, and photographers were functioning as
promoters as well as predators. And it wasn't long before
some very powerful people took notice of the humble chauffeur's rare and special qualities—i.e., his unwavering loyalty,
unshakable discretion, unusual size, uncommon physical
strength, and unfaltering valor. And it wasn't long after that
that Woodrow landed a more important, more interesting, less
stressful, and more lucrative new job—as the respected and
celebrated chauffeur/bodyguard for New York City Mayor
Robert F. Wagner.

Pretty cool, right?

Right! Woodrow is so happy and proud in his new position
that he calls me at least once a week to tell me about the peo-

ple he's met and the places he's been. And his wife, Sarah,
calls me once in a while, too, to tell me how much they love
their new apartment, and how glad she and the kids are that
Woodrow doesn't have to work all hours of the night anymore.

Ain't life grand?

Speaking of which, I'm very glad to report that Claire survived and made a swift recovery. I went to see her in the hospital, and another time after she got out, bearing fruit and
good wishes and bursting with questions about Rusty's mental condition. (See what a compulsive fact-finder I am?)

Claire didn't have any definite answers, but she had some
very strong convictions, and she didn't mind sharing them.
She believed Rusty became unhinged in Korea, but didn't totally lose his mind until the night he pushed Ginger off the terrace. But after that, she concluded, he snapped completely. He
could seem quite lucid at times, but then, all of a sudden, he'd
break apart and lose all touch with reality. (Which would
explain how he could mistake a fake rifle for a real one, and
conceive that he was pouring a mixture of arsenic and bourbon down Claire's throat when it was really just pure Jack
Daniel's.)

Claire, by the way, is now blossoming like a hothouse
flower and making big news as the head of Marxallen Productions. She's gone back to using her maiden name (which
is Allen, in case you've forgotten), so her old moniker now
matches her new enterprise. And, since the first TV show her
company produced—*The Tex and Toni Show,* as you very
well know—has become such a huge, knockout, prime-time
hit (it's the only show the gossip columnists are talking about
these days!), Claire is probably on her way to becoming one
of the most powerful women in television. After Lucille Ball,
of course.

And you want to know something funny? Claire's survival
and success have made me feel a whole lot better about *myself,* now. I'm not so ashamed about my poor performance in
the early days of the Ginger Allen case. I mean, maybe I

wasn't such a defective detective after all. I couldn't save Ginger's life, but at least I saved her sister's.

AS FOR MY LIFE, IT'S PRETTY MUCH back to normal (well, as normal as an obsessive *Daring Detective* staff writer's life can be). I'm at work every Monday through Friday—making the coffee, clipping the newspapers, correcting the proofs, editing the copy, filing the photos, rewriting Mike's stories, dodging Mario's stupid jokes, enduring Pomeroy's sexist abuse, making Mr. Crockett's barber appointments, sharing Lenny's lunch, etc., etc., etc.—all the while searching for new stories to write. Pomeroy hasn't coughed up any good *DD* assignments yet—and it's possible he never will!—but I'm sure I'll eventually turn up (okay, trip over) a new tale that needs telling. I always do.

And I can't help wondering how Dan will react when that happens. Will he revert to his old fretful and irascible ways—i.e., forbid me to investigate or write about any unsolved murders ever again? Or will he be more tolerant and respectful of my intense curiosity and unwavering career goals? Maybe he'll accept me as a fellow truth-seeker, and treat me as his clue-sniffing equal, the way he did near the end of the Ginger Allen case.

Or maybe not.

Oh, what's the point of me asking these questions now, anyway? I'll have my answers soon enough. Maybe too soon. Meanwhile, I'm going to enjoy Dan's new appreciation of me while it lasts. And it looks like I'll have plenty of opportunities to do just that, seeing as he's been dropping in to see me almost every night since the big showdown at the RCA Building. Of course, it's possible that Dan's coming by so often just to check up on me—to make sure I'm not out getting myself into any more trouble—but that's okay with me. I'll take him any way I can get him.

Abby says I'm too easy. (Look who's calling who *easy!*) She's always trying to get me to go out at night—to the Vanguard or the San Remo or Cafe Figaro with her and Jimmy and Otto—instead of sitting around my apartment like a chump (that's her word, not mine!) waiting for Dan to show. "You need to jingle his bells," she says. "Spin him around the block a few times. Otherwise, he'll take you for granted, kiddo, and nothing good will come from that. You've got to get out and have some *fun,* you dig? He'll respect you more in the morning."

I understand what Abby is saying, but there's just one problem: I have a lot more fun lolling around my apartment, sipping Chianti, listening to my new Peggy Lee album, and waiting for Dan, than I do hanging out in the crowded clubs, chugging beer, blowing smoke rings, and watching Abby and Jimmy lick each other's faces. It's always nice to see Otto, and he's a doggedly attentive date, but he's no substitute for my man Dan.

And that's why I'm staying home this evening instead of going to the Minetta Tavern with my friends. (Well, it's not the only reason. The fact that Jimmy's going to be reading his new poem there tonight probably had something to do with my decision.) I'm going to have a bowl of Campbell's soup (chicken rice, I think), and a big stack of saltines, and then I'm going to relax with a glass of wine and a cigarette (okay, *several* glasses of wine and a *batch* of cigarettes), and watch TV until Dan arrives.

It's Monday night, and some good shows are on. I'm going to watch *Burns & Allen* at 8:00, *Talent Scouts* at 8:30, and *I Love Lucy* at 9:00. And then, if I'm still awake at 9:30, I'll switch the channel to NBC and take a look at *The Tex and Toni Show.* Might as well see what all the fuss is about.

ABOUT THE AUTHOR

Amanda Matetsky has been an editor of many magazines in the entertainment field and a volunteer tutor and fundraiser for Literacy Volunteers of America. Her first novel, *The Perfect Body*, won the NJRW Golden Leaf Award for Best First Book. Amanda lives in Middletown, New Jersey, with her husband, Harry, and their two cats, Homer and Phoebe, in a house full of old movie posters, original comic strip art, and books—lots of books.

Meet New York reporter Paige Turner in
Murderers Prefer Blondes
by **Amanda Matetsky**
0-425-19105-2

A feisty young widow with Brenda Starr
bravado and a fixation with following in
Agatha Christie's footsteps, Paige Turner
wants to pen a memorable mystery.
But first she must solve the murder of a
beautiful young model.

"A WONDERFULLY SASSY CHARACTER...IRRESISTIBLE."
—SARAH STROHMEYER

**"PAIGE TURNER IS THE LIVELIEST, MOST
CHARMING DETECTIVE TO EMERGE IN
CRIME FICTION IN A LONG TIME."**
—ANN WALDRON

Don't miss Paige Turner in
Murder is a Girl's Best Friend
0-425-19716-6

Available wherever books are sold or at
www.penguin.com